Oystercatcher

Greg Billington has been a teacher, fisherman and business manager, and continues to work as a marketing consultant. He is passionate about the need to preserve wildlife and to celebrate cultural differences. He much prefers air-cooled twins and the blues. He believes Gary Larson should be knighted. *Oystercatcher* is his second novel and follows *Spindrift* (2000).

Oystercatcher

Greg Billington

REED

For Chris, Nick
and Alex

Reed Publishing
Te Karuhi tā tāpui o Reed (Aotearoa) (NZ) Ltd

Established in 1907, Reed is New Zealand's largest
book publisher, with over 300 titles in print.

For details on all these books visit our website:
www.reed.co.nz

Published by Reed Books, a division of Reed Publishing (NZ) Ltd,
39 Rawene Road, Birkenhead, Auckland.
Associated companies, branches and representatives throughout the world.

ISBN 0 7900 0901 3

Cover designed by Giselle Dawson
Cover image courtesy of Mark Pickering
Text designed by Graeme Leather

Printed in New Zealand

1

ON FIRE THE thing — zigzagging up the hill through the trees and almost into him. Blind but running uphill with its eerie vapour trail and frantic rasping. And the heat: a billowing wall of crackling and exploding and coming on and coming on. The blind incendiary nearly hit him, nearly caught his legs with its smouldering arse running.

Must run too. Like the possum with seared lungs and throat burned raw. Cavorting weirdly in the undergrowth with the fear on him and ears overflowing with cries in the bush, in the leaves: a cat's eyes staring, yellow snarling, black slits, sprinting in front. Everything running and no answer anywhere.

* * *

ON A HIGH outcrop to the south of the burning valley, a large man with a black crescent moon tattooed below his right eye watched the plumes of smoke drift from the coast. In his hands he worked a short piece of green plaited flax. Over and over the thin cord was wound and unwound and pulled tight until the brown skin blanched, and all the while his stone-blank eyes slid from the glassy sea to the beach and up the broad valley to the highest ridge. Lingering on the violent tangle of charred and shimmering remains and hearing the voices — hearing the crying, and his lips began to move soundlessly in the warm summer afternoon. Seated with his long legs hanging over the edge above a great height. Dangling above wind-bent manuka and rustling flax and the voices murmuring all the while inside his head. *What use are you, Ringatu? What use are you?*

Below him but still high above the beach on a natural shelf stood a tiny corrugated iron cottage. Painted red, it glowed orange in the smoky light and the poles of the shelter next to it looked like bleached bones. Sitting on the grass alongside, the newly constructed boat — a Newfoundland dory, Mahler called it, of the open kind, without decks or cabin. Long and narrow with a high pointed bow and narrow tombstone transom. Though it was too far away to see he knew that on its unpainted, pale timber there was a name. It said 'Luke', and from each crudely formed letter the paint dribbled like blood.

A magpie rose shrill and stark as a figure staggered from the trees, arms loose and head lolling like a soft toy. A slight man with curly black hair and a pale, delicate face, clambering wearily over the verandah then emerging with a small, pale blue garment that fell unregarded as he stared out to sea. Stepping onto the grass he tumbled as though he had never seen the space.

A light came into Ringatu's eyes. Like watching a kid it was. Running his hand along the thin gunwale now, feeling the timber, then taking the transom in both hands he appeared to give the boat an experimental heft. He is too small, Ringatu thought. Such a small man. Yet, here he is.

Turning to wrestle with something in the ceiling of the shelter: a pair of oars that he tied along the thwarts of the dory with pieces of red twine. Now taking hold of the transom, and with crab-like movements dragging the stern until the dory was parallel to the edge. Pausing to lean on the gunwale with his head lowered to his forearm.

Ringatu thought about the moving of big canoes in the old times. Sometimes dragged over hills or through dense bush for many miles. Cut from the giant totara. Ghosts of another time both, but he would have dragged that waka.

Mahler pushed until the dory pointed at the water far below. Then he collapsed haphazardly and did not move, one hand draped across his chest and the other stretched, palm upwards, his right leg crooked over his straightened left.

Ringatu snorted. He understood so little, this Tom, though he was learning perhaps, like his uncle before him.

A fresh explosion in some last residue of the distant underbrush and a towering plume uncoiled above the flames.

'Yes, I see you now.' Anger sparked as he pulled on a long brown coat. 'I truly see you now.' Facing this minion of Whiro with its many eyes rolling, he raised his arms high, his fists clenched, and called: 'An eye for an eye! An eye for an eye!'

From the flax a large brown dog rose to follow him as he leapt to a lower ledge and plunged into the thickness of mahoe and gleaming karaka.

TOM Mahler watched a small piece of cloud break from the line of the hills to drift alone, moving more quickly seaward. He rose with difficulty, using the boat for support, breathed deeply and then with new resolve fiercely shouldered the bow until the dory teetered on the brink — took hold of the transom and with a final lunge pushed the boat over the edge.

Slowly at first the stern rose like a humpback then, picking up speed, it dived, the soft branches of mahoe snapping like a popgun firing, spraying broad green leaves and shards of white bark over wiry manuka. Then silence as it plunged to a halt in impenetrable flax.

He clambered alongside the stern and with both hands stretching for the keel he heaved without success — not then nor on his second and third attempts. From the bow he braced himself against the bank, but though he raised it a small distance the boat could not be budged. He peered down a cliff so steep it was unimaginable so large an object should be hindered.

'You bastard,' he said quietly, and rested his cheek on the gunwale. 'You bastard!' and his eyes closed. Soon his head began to roll gently back and forth, back and forth, and occasionally one hand rose and banged the hull. A moaning rose from his lips and carried away over the brow of the hill — a funereal chant that prompted the dog that had suddenly appeared to howl until its own cry smothered the man's. As suddenly it stopped and a voice said: 'Too much noise here.'

Ringatu swung down and pointed. 'Go,' he commanded, and at once their combined efforts caused the boat to shift such that they were compelled to scramble.

'Here.' Ringatu indicated where Tom should stand while he pushed. 'Move up!' he shouted so his eyes bulged and the boat lunged, bouncing on the green rapids, skidding to left and right and rolling finally with a bone-splitting crack ten metres down.

'No!' Tom leaping to crouch beside the boat and Ringatu oblivious, turning his attention to the short drop to the grassy slope above the black sands. Coal-black sands hissing at small waves that marked the approach of the evening tide.

'This black stinking air,' he pronounced, then noticed with irritation the other man's efforts to swing the boat round the stump. 'Wait!' And before Tom could remove himself Ringatu seized the stern and lifted with reckless violence, launching the dory down leathery leaves that made a soft whistle. Tom was off balance and he fell as the boat passed, unable to avoid the chine shimmying his leg like a crosscut saw. He rolled tight, nursing his leg, and the dog hovered, anxiously licking his face. Tom did not see the extended hand as he gingerly lifted his trouser leg to examine the red-speckled gash.

'Cunt,' he said softly, and rising, limped.

'Yes it is,' said Ringatu, looking away; 'it may be the source of great pain.'

At which a bubble of insane laughter exploded in Mahler's head and a flock of grinning birds fell and floundered on their black and broken wings. Trancelike, the Maori continued to stare at the low line of green waves rising and falling. Green Tasman Sea, tumbling and subsiding in soft sighs on the black sands. The dog retiring to sit nearby, also looking out to sea — all looking across the empty beach to the distant water's edge.

'How?' asked Mahler wearily.

Ringatu cast around until he had two straight lengths of driftwood. He fitted one below the stem, then indicated the stern. 'Both of us here.'

Shoulder to shoulder they lifted and pushed until the boat slid across the log. 'Hold!' Ringatu returned to the bow to place the second log. Twice more this procedure was repeated until much of the boat was suspended above the sand. They rested, standing alongside their charge and breathing heavily.

'The boy is lost?'

Tom rolled his head from side to side and heard the roar rising, felt the heat and smelt the burning bush.

'The boy is lost?' Ringatu repeated, and then for a moment placed his hand on Tom's shoulder and understood the trembling in that man and how his head moved like that. He was wounded and the turehu were in him. As they were in Ringatu and like banshees they came flying from the quiet parts. 'Pagett is dead!' he said fiercely and taking Mahler by both shoulders he stared hard into the other man's eyes. 'I will *eat* that *fucker*!' Then he turned swiftly and with great venom began to rock the boat. Tom joined him, rocking until the boat pitched onto the sand and they scrambled down the orange clay and dragged it over the soft dry sand until they were at highwater.

'Still a couple of hours.' He motioned toward the waves. 'The tide ...'

'Yes.'

Ringatu gestured toward Tom's shin, to the dark blood on his boot.

'Nothing.' But Tom held the injured leg so the toe merely brushed the ground before he lowered himself and closed his eyes. Moments later he draped his arm over the dog, which sat close, laying its head across his knees, its large brown eyes blinking. The Maori sat too and rolled a cigarette. They listened to a pair of black oystercatchers, their quick red legs striding as they dug for tiny green crabs. Back and forth following the edge of the water they went with their short necks bobbing. Back and forth, calling and locked in the endless rhythm of ebb and flow.

They listened to the gulls stationary on updraughts high overhead as the tide inched, and felt the droplets of a gentle rain beginning to fall on the dull black sand etched by the steely sea.

Ringatu did not close his eyes. He watched gentle waves tumbling and he thought about the small boy running like a pale spirit — a turehu crying: *What use are you, Ringatu?*

Tom lifted his head and studied the sea for a long time. Toneless he said: 'We'll use the logs,' and climbed stiffly to his feet. The dog retreated, puzzled, picked up a small piece of driftwood and proffered it hopefully, like a cigar. But twenty minutes passed with no sound save the grunting of those men, the clunking of the hull on the wood and the surge of the approaching water.

Tom felt the cool wash around his ankles. 'One more,' he said, and the deadweight of two hours was plucked from their grasp and lurched sideways as the water embraced the boat and then receded. And then a second and a third surge pulled the boat into the small breaking waves.

With Ringatu holding, Tom unlashed an oar and fitted it to the port rowlock. His eyes were alight now, as he clambered over the side for the first time to sit on the centre thwart. The first time and he was trembling but not from cold. The dog splashing and barking with great excitement, jumping repeatedly so his large nails marked the new timber.

'I may hold you.'

'Fuck off!'

Ringatu gave the dory a final push to free the keel but still he held the gunwale, walking rapidly to keep pace, eyes fixed on the slight figure manoeuvring to keep the bow seaward.

'Come to my place.'

'Let go!'

Ringatu released the boat. 'Why do you die like the tarakihi?' The boat pulled away. 'Why?' Watching it lift over a breaking crest, up and over with a soft whump. 'We could die like the shark!' Out beyond the line of breakers the dory glided on the oily sea. 'Like the shark!' But the man in the boat rowed without pause.

'Go home then! Go to your home!' Ringatu stayed in the water until it was hard to discern the small figure against the glare of the dying sun. 'Go home!' he shouted, his eyes fierce and fingers extended like forks. Glaring across the water. 'We brought nothing into this world ...' he cried, and his head slumped onto his chest.

TOM watched the figure in the surf thrust its arms upward as though to throw him from the shore. Heard his cries and watched him walk across the sand to the bank, the dog turning repeatedly to gaze out to sea then hurrying after. He saw them climb onto the grass and the man turn to look out to sea, arm raised and held high for a minute or more. But Tom did not cease rowing and soon they disappeared in the flax.

THE rain stopped and from the western horizon a soft light fell on the tiny cottage and the crude shelter overlooking the beach. He looked to the north, to the smoking valley rising to the skyline, and was drawn to the huge tree with its seared arms outstretched. So tall that its highest branches retained tufts of foliage, but an uncanny glow appeared intermittently on the enormous trunk — sparkling lines of dying embers fanned by the breeze — and the smoke streamed far. A sob burst in his throat like grapeshot.

The lights of the tiny village to the south, with its sprinkling of houses, traced the cliffs down to the river mouth, and he wondered if he could make out the school in the darkness. He wondered whether he could see the old pohutukawa tree in the playground, still in crimson blossom even this late in the summer. A short cry, like a bird, escaped his lips. Like the gull sweeping by, peering unnoticed. Only the creak of the rowlocks once more — creaking wood and the swish of the blades in the calm sea. Creaking and swishing in the failing light, hour on hour.

Then the oars trailed and the boat glided aimlessly, puffed by the breeze on low swells. Staring into the heavens, into the starry southern sky, he filled his lungs and called, 'Here I am, Luke.' Gazing about that endless sea. 'Luke. Here I am.' But sinking, that forlorn sound, without trace in the dark water.

RINGATU paused on the narrow track that led from the grass into the trees. He watched the dog turning circles on the porch of Tom Mahler's cottage, its head high and the jersey dangling.

'Give it,' he said, and retrieved the pale polyester with its frayed cuffs and the word 'Firestone' in black lettering across the chest.

Ringatu slung the small garment over his shoulder and gazed out to sea.

'I ask them to extend their mana as long as he wants it,' he said. And he listened to the whispering in the trees and divined that his request had been heard.

The keys were in the ignition of Mahler's car. 'Get out,' he said, and pushed the dog with his boot. He drove quickly, heedless of the potholes in the track and anyone who might have been coming.

* * *

THE INFLIGHT MOVIE ended but Mary Chisholm barely noticed. High above the Pacific and thousands of miles to the southwest of Los Angeles, she felt she was doomed to fly for ever. Wondering how she would be received. Imagining how it would be if mystified eyes asked what it was she wanted.

She reached into her small travel bag and extracted a large envelope, from which she withdrew two neatly folded but dog-eared letters. She let them lie on her lap for some time before she began to read.

~ 29 August

Dear Mary

It is winter here. Though it is cold it is not nearly so brisk as Chicago. Sometimes I see the snow on a mountain called Taranaki across the bay. It appears to rise from the sea itself and is the most perfect cone I have ever seen.

I am sorry I have taken so long to write. This is truly a different place! At first I wanted to get the first flight home but I persevered. Or perhaps I simply couldn't face the notion of giving up. But where to start?

Uncle Henry's place is unbelievable and I know I would not have come if I had really understood what it is. I am living in the most rudimentary shack made entirely of tin called corrugated iron. It is wrinkled and painted red though the paint is not good. Not that it matters since it is stuck in the middle of nowhere. I am not kidding when I say this. The village of Mokau is in the middle of nowhere and then Henry's property is up the coast a bit all by itself. There is nothing here but forest! The only clear ground is round this old shack and there is no garden. It is a wild place and I do not mind admitting that I was afraid here for quite a time. I am not sure why since it is a peaceful place. I doubt that anything much has ever happened.

At first I didn't know what to do with myself and I crept around like a mouse. It took me some time to start exploring. I have never explored in my life before — not in a wilderness. I have been afraid at times but this is something utterly different.

I have made a friend. A large dog! This dog scared me to death but it is really gentle with big droopy ears and huge paws. We fight a lot but I am the smarter. We go fishing! Can you imagine? I have named him Chinook.

There is nothing in the village. A 'pub', that's a bar, a general store and a school. I started to paint. I am grateful for the paints by the way. I am painting landscapes, which I am finding to be very dramatic, and also some aspects of this tiny community.

AND, I am building the dory! I know you will find that amusing. I have made so many mistakes and as much as I progress I go backwards. But it is happening. I have an old shed with no sides, just a roof, out front. It is perfect for boat building though I have no idea what I am going to do when and if it gets finished. There is a steep hill down to the sea covered in trees and anyway, the sea here is very wild. It blows a lot and even the trees are contoured. Maybe it is even windier than home and that is saying a lot.

So, now I am adventurer, painter and boat builder! I am not totally sure, but I think I am beginning to enjoy being here. I am beginning to get a feeling about why Henry came and stayed. Incidentally, I have met his old friend's son. He is a Maori called Ringatu. He is an impressive guy though somewhat peculiar. If you met him in Chicago you would think you were in the wrong place at the wrong time! He has a tattoo that must have hurt like God knows what! A Maori is a native like a Sioux or Mohican. He said he is a Ngati Ruanui.

I think about us quite a lot. About you and me and Luke. I guess that's been one of the best things about coming here. I have been able to reflect about all sorts of things, for the first time really. I never had time before. I know you will say that was my choice but I think not entirely. I was doing what I did for us. I think a lot about the early years. They were very good. I really mean that and I miss them.

I trust you are well and that business is good. One day, perhaps, you will want to venture to this lost world. I will write again.

Tom

Mary studied the familiar handwriting as she had a hundred times already. She could hear his voice in the words. She could see his fine features, and his black eyes gleaming with that slight madness she had loved. She remembered when they met and how it had been. The fun and laughter and the sense of a huge adventure beginning and so it had been for many years. She tried to imagine him now and it was barely possible. Painting, building a dory! These were strange notions. He was in a 'lost world'. Or was it simply that he was lost? But what did that mean?

She refolded the letter and opened the second and the feeling returned. This was why she was here, winging her way to the ends of the earth.

~ January 9

Dear Mary

It has been a long time I think. I have been engrossed in things. But it has changed. I don't know what is happening but I hate it. That's strong isn't it? But it's true. There is something macabre about this place. I don't understand why things have changed. Yes I do — this is a primitive place. The coast is raw and the winds terrible.

I may leave soon, I don't know. I have met a boy. Did I tell you? He is helping me and I help him. I fear for him. Perhaps I fear for me. I am sorry if this sounds a bit wild but I am just writing my thoughts. I may not post this, I don't know.

The man does not deserve to be a father. But I suppose you will think that's ironic. I am unsure what to do but I think I will not let him. I cannot let it happen, Mary. Luke deserves more than that.

The dog is still here though he deserts me sometimes. I mentioned him didn't I? He keeps me sane. I can hear him now, on the porch. He is an ass — like me you would say. We are well suited.

Things have happened here that keep people apart. The Maori and the Pakeha I mean. That's what I am — a Pakeha. I became involved. The land next to me is contentious — and worse, has something to do with the boy's father.

I may come home, Mary. I don't know whether I will post this. I may be just suffering one of my 'moods'. But maybe not.

Are things good with you? I hope so. Life in the agency seems so far away. It could be on the moon. I look at it often. It fills the night sky sometimes but mostly it is so dark. I try to imagine I am looking at it back home but it looks different — bigger.

I don't know what to do about the boy. I guess I will think of something. Do you remember Mike and Doggitt? They're here.

Love from Tom

'Mike and Doggitt?' She shook her head as she unfolded the first letter and laid the two side by side. She compared the handwriting and noticed again, how different it was — the well-formed letters and tidy layout of the first. Everything legible. But the words and letters in the second were deformed by haste.

It still frightened her. For two weeks she had read and reread the letter and then written a response, but it remained unposted. She allowed Sophie to read Tom's letters and quizzed her remorselessly. 'Just go,' said Sophie. 'Just pack your bags and go. The café will be fine. I'll help.'

'I'm not his wife,' she had responded angrily.

But here she was. Trapped in interminable night high above the Pacific.

2

'I'M LATE TONIGHT. I was in town.' Rachel felt disappointed Pete hadn't started the milking without her. 'Funny bit of rain,' she called as she left the house for the milking shed below, clumping in her rubber boots and zipping her yellow smock. Looking appreciatively across the green valley with its shelter trees and neatly spaced fields.

For Rachel Lynch the grassy flats and the dark trees on the high hills were things of great beauty. And her cows were good friends. Each afternoon at four she called them into the shed, with its low-slung corrugated iron roof, to take their place side by side while she attached the milking cups to their udders. And she talked to them as the pneumatic pumps chugged and sucked. The fusion of scents of fresh milk and animal waste were as natural to her as cut hay and the sharp tang of the bush after rain.

'Come on then, hiyup!' she called, sometimes pushing on a large bony flank to get the last animal in position. And with enormous patience she walked up and down the shit-covered concrete trench, replacing cups that a cantankerous charge had dislodged with a hoof.

With seventy cows it was a small herd, so the job was often completed in a little over two hours, morning and night, day after day. Then she would set to cleaning with a high pressure hose, washing down the stony concrete yard and the trench, scrubbing the twenty sets of cups and hanging them to dry.

And all the time she dreamed. She looked across the yard to the river willows and up into the hills that were as mysterious still as the day she had arrived in the valley twenty years before. She dreamed of colours she imagined she might find in far-off lands — perhaps reds and white and ochre. The colours of dry places she had never visited and would never visit because her destiny was this farm in this wet river valley. Because Pete would never leave.

He dreamed too, but not like Rachel. He dreamed of things past and lost. He dreamed of young women he would never meet. He drank until the dreams were pressed under a swirling cloud in his head and he slept sitting in his chair next to the kitchen fire and waited for Rachel to return.

But Rachel loved Pete. She loved him despite the changes, and she knew how the farm had become a trap. He hated the wetness and the smells. He hated the cows and their stupid eyes. Sometimes he hated Rachel. Most of all, he hated himself.

The late sun caught a window on the Pagett farmhouse further up the valley. At this distance the farmhouse couldn't be seen clearly, though sometimes she would see a truck turning by the bottom gate as Trevor Pagett took delivery of animal carcases or loaded fattened pigs. On exceptionally clear days she was able to see a figure. But she had not spoken to Pagett in five years. Not since he shot Honey. Consequently they never sold him any of the cows that died during calving. Even in death, Rachel would feel she was betraying them if she gave them into the hands of this man. She chose not to think about him. But she knew what Pagett planned and it made her angry so that she tossed her head from time to time and frowned. And so she was when she heard the muffled bang echo down the valley — a flat report that rolled briefly in the gullies. She knew it to be a rifle shot. It disturbed her. It could be hunters but she instinctively felt it was not. Though it was not possible to be certain, she felt the shot came from the house on the hill.

The cups clattered from the udder of number 25 and she hurried to replace them, absently patting the cow's leg. Not noticing the raised tail, she was rewarded with a stream of green that splattered wild patterns down her smock. Rachel was undismayed.

By the time the last cow left the shed her thoughts had turned to the cutting of the hay.

'You're late.' Pete looked at her with bleary incomprehension.

'I told you, I was late back from town.'

'Well, that's just great.'

She began to clear a space on the kitchen bench, then paused. 'Did you hear anything earlier?'

'What?'

'Did you hear a bang?'

'What're you talking about, woman?'

'I thought I heard a rifle, before. At five — did you hear?'

'Nope. Have you got any fags?'

'In the bedroom.' She tipped minced meat and chopped onions into a pot. 'You didn't hear? It was quite clear. I think it came from up by Pagett's house.'

Pete stumped down the hall in his socks. Shortly he returned and lit a cigarette. 'So what?' He fell back into his chair by the window, inhaling deeply. He coughed.

'Well, I don't like rifles. It's a bad sound.' She threw some potatoes into the sink.

He grunted. 'Turn on the news,' he said.

'You turn it on, I'm busy. Oh, all right.' She wiped her hands on her pants and found the TV remote on the sofa. Almost immediately Pete closed his eyes, the cigarette hanging from his lips. A minute or two later she gently removed the butt and threw it out the window.

Perhaps we should cut the hay tomorrow, she thought as she undressed in her bedroom and walked across the hall to the shower. Haymaking was a good time of year. It was like being a squirrel with acorns, though she had never seen a squirrel and doubted she ever would.

Later, with her hair still wet and gleaming, and wrapped in her black silk bathrobe with the embroidered golden horse, Rachel stood outside with a cup of coffee and stared up the valley to the darkened house on the edge of the hill and wondered. It's probably nothing, she thought, and focused her thoughts on the soft blue river flats that were ripe for cutting. There were many more important things to be done, and she tossed the dregs into the garden.

* * *

A DARKER SHAPE in the brown water. Slow moving and wary, the eel in the early evening. Remembering something? Stay still, stay stone-still and that black pod will not see the danger. The sound of a kingfisher only, way over there. 'Keh, keh, keh.'

See that blunt black head coming on and sniffing. A good meal waiting for him, hanging there, in the brown water. Muzzling that line. Muzzling and thinking? And now another one, more urgent, the blunt snout opening as the second comes sliding, sniffing and pushing and eager to share. No — wanting it all. Come on then and yes, a dull tug and wondering to itself? What is that hard thing? Waiting a moment and pulling back.

Stuck in your mouth, you beauty. Come to me, and long slow pulling and coming up the slimy mud wriggling and writhing and a good meal too. And now chop him. Swift death but still writhing and not prepared to give life after all these years. But soon in pan that eel.

But what is that sound? Stay stone still above the brown water. Crouch next to that black pod slow-moving in the grass with his bleedy neck and smelling of river bottom. Crouch down in the willow wands and the misty light and listen. Listen to an animal coming but not a cow, nor a goat or a pig but a large animal coming on through the willows and so careful not to make much noise. Why? Why here where no one comes, way up here where only me? Not like that child-thing — this one too big and heavy but stepping lightly. Coming on through the willows brushing so quiet but coming on this way.

Stay stone-still and crouch down in the grass with that bleedy pod underfoot now and slow death arriving. Now silence, though the sound of breathing somewhere. Are we seen? Are we seen crouching but what then? Slide into brown water? Not with greedy pods waiting. Stay stone-still and think about nothing.

Him moving again. Further and stepping over that big log fallen in the storm when the brown water crept into own floor and made roaches climb. Walking towards water and stopping. Know that shape? Yes, and now afraid. Stay stone-still. Him holding something and throwing it into the water, splash and frightening those black pods back under the willow roots.

Him turning! Turning and staring with those eyes. Guts turning to water now. Did he hear? Staring through leaves like burning coals. Stay still and don't look. Feel him there. Angry? Need to piss. What's this? Moving again. Moving but down the river pushing willow wands and so quiet but moving away, swiftly. Stand and feel too many aches but stay still while light falling and listening. And him here ... throwing that rifle? Why here?

But piss now and okay. Yes and hungry. Black pod to fry.

* * *

THE FOLLOWING DAY the cloud had cleared, the sun was warm and a gentle breeze took the edge off the summer heat. Rachel brought a basket down to the flats by the river and they sat on a threadbare blanket and ate a lunch of freshly baked cheese scones with cold meat and pickle. Pete reckoned he would have it all cut by three o'clock.

'It feels good, doesn't it?' she said later when they were sitting on the front step of the house. 'I always love the smell of cut grass. It's clean too! I think this is the cleanest the farm's ever been. Remember how much weed we used to have? That ragwort everywhere? Now look — hardly one to be seen.' Rachel smiled to herself and glanced at Pete who was absorbed in a copy of *PC*.

'There's some great new gear,' he said; 'I might get one of these Compaqs.'

'What's wrong with the one we've got?' But he didn't hear. 'I hope there's no more rain this week.'

'Have we got any gin left?'

'Do you want one?' She rose, then paused on the doorstep. 'How can you read in this light? Come inside before it's dark. I'm going to serve dinner anyway.' She paused and peered up the valley and wondered why she felt uneasy. 'Strange that there's no light up there,' she said.

Pete didn't lift his head from the magazine so she walked inside as the phone rang and he heard her voice rise in sudden exclamation before the phone banged on the hook.

'I can't believe it!' she seethed, standing on the step with her hands to her face.

'What?'

'Pagett! He's burned the bush! After all that! He's ignored everyone and set fire — yesterday.' She shook her head and growled, unable to find words to express her indignation.

'It's his farm.'

'What? It's not! Well, yes — but he shouldn't!' She turned and stomped into the kitchen and slumped by the table. 'He's a wicked man!' she cried out so Pete would hear.

* * *

THE NEXT DAY was Friday and Matty Manuhuia and his brother Jake were fishing at the river mouth. They should have been at school but it was nearly the weekend and they had never seen it so calm in their young lives that they could be right out at the point where the river met the sea. Far out on the sandbar with a rod and spinner. They had caught a kahawai already and they could see more of the silver fish sprinting across the face of the small waves trying to push upriver.

'You know that Lucy?'

'Yeah.'

'I think she likes me.'

'She likes everyone.'

'Nah! You know what I mean. She thinks I'm good.'

'Who cares?' Jake hurled the spinner out across the water and began to retrieve. 'Hey, I nearly got one.'

'Well, where is it then? You can't catch nothing. Only me.'

'I'll catch one. I'll catch two. What's that?' He stopped winding and examined the large grey shape that had materialised in the river beyond his line. 'That's a shark! No, that's a boat! Look, Matty, that's a boat out there. Sunk!' He dropped the rod and ran to keep pace until the sea stopped his progress.

'It's a boat all right. I can see it. Sinking. Whose is it?' Matty held himself through his pants and jumped up and down.

The upturned hull of the boat ducked and rose as it entered the mouth where the waves were forming.

'It's that man, Tom! It's Painter Tom!'

'Whoa! He's sunk. Where is it?'

'I can't see it now. It's sunk. Out there.' He pointed. They stood like stone and stared until their eyes hurt. Once they thought they glimpsed the boat but then it was gone.

'You think we should tell someone?'

'I dunno. We'd have to say why we were here ...' They considered the implications.

'I think we could tell Uncle Louis. He'd know about it.'

'Yeah. He'd know about it.'

They returned for the rod. 'One more time?' said Jake.

'Nah. I think we better go. You might hook 'im.'

That was enough. Matty picked up his fish and Jake carried the rod. They walked silently for fifty metres, glancing at each other, then Matty broke into a run with Jake close behind. They ran along the shore, up from the shell-speckled black sand and onto the grass verge of a thin tar-sealed road.

'Man, this is too much.'

'Ha! You're not very fast.' Matty quickened his pace. 'Slow!' he yelled derisively and laughed. He jumped a ditch, swinging his fish wide in the air.

'Some good kai, you boys.'

'Yeah, it's mine,' Matty called to Mrs Walker weeding in her front garden. Red hollyhocks and cabbages mixed in front of her tiny green cottage, with an old brown chair by the front door.

They ran around the corner past a rusting Valiant with no wheels and in the gate. Matty dropped the fish on the verandah boards, panting heavily, and with his hands on his knees. Jake threw the rod on the grass and collapsed on his back.

'That's too much running,' he said.

The door opened and Uncle Louis appeared. His tweed trousers were suspended by a red-striped tie secured around his waist. The trousers had no fly and Uncle Louis was not wearing anything under them. Matty noticed but was unconcerned. Uncle Louis was old and often wore that Taranaki rugby jersey with the sleeves cut off above the elbow and all frayed at the ragged edge. Except when he was going 'Uptown'.

'What you boys doing here? You bring me that fish?'

'It's my fish,' said Matty straightening.

'Well what? You come to show off?'

Matty shook his head. 'Can we have a Coke?'

'A Coke! A Coke? I don't have any more of that stuff. But you come in and we'll see what we have.' And he turned inside. Shuffled down the narrow passage of ancient smells like cheese, into a tiny lean-to kitchen on the back of the house. It contained a table just large enough for two but there were three chairs. A creamy fridge ran fitfully in the corner, and from this Uncle Louis produced a jug of pale ginger beer. He filled two enamel mugs and placed them on the blue painted table. He sat and rolled a smoke while he watched the boys drink — watched those large eyes flicking above the rims, serious but alive to new possibilities.

'Lot of fish out there?' They both nodded. 'It's funny old weather. I don't remember such a calm for years. Not since before she died. And we caught plenty then. Much more than you will ever see today.'

Jake banged his mug down and his eyes widened. 'We saw a drowner!' he blurted.

'What drowner? Drowned? How did you know?'

'Not drowned, sunk,' rejoined Matty. 'He was sunk. That Painter Tom. Sunk out there.' And he pointed in the direction of the river mouth.

'The eels will be at him,' Jake said hoarsely, and his eyes rolled.

'You see his boat?'

'Yep! That's what we saw. Him and that old boat that he rows. Out there. We came straight up here. To you.' The whites of his eyes looked like the ring on a poached egg.

'You tell anyone else?'

'Nope! We came straight here. To you.'

'Ah. Well, we better be telling someone about this. In the river mouth you say? Well, we better be telling Mr Buchanan.'

'The police!'

'Yessir! This is what they do, my boy. That's their job. We better be going.'

'What about us?'

'You better come.'

'But we haven't been at school.' Jake's eyes widened more at this difficult disclosure.

'I don't think we worry about that. At this moment,' Uncle Louis finished mildly.

But this was less than reassurance. Two pairs of brown eyes were downcast and four sandy feet shuffled nervously. Uncle Louis lifted his battered bowler hat from a hook in the hallway. No one spoke as they walked two streets to the small building on the main street that was the office of Constable Brian Buchanan.

'Come,' said Uncle Louis, motioning with his hand as he sensed the widening gap. He frowned deeply, not because of his reluctant companions but because he saw Mrs Simes looking across the road from under the 'Superior Merchandising' sign. Bother about that, he thought, and was conscious that he was not in his uptown clothes.

'Hullo, Mr Ropata,' she called.

He returned an embarrassed smile and a quick wave and kept his pants turned the best way.

The presence of the police car indicated that the constable was in. In fact he was trying to read the sports page of the *Daily News*, but he was unable to concentrate. His thoughts returned to her all the day. At night she was there, in his head and in his loins. He could feel her kiss, almost, so close it might be real but never quite. And now the burn-off. He was not interested in Pagett's bloody bush. He did not want to have anything to do with that thing at this time.

'Louis?' he said suspiciously. 'How can I help?'

'Constable Buchanan,' Uncle Louis removed his hat and held it over his crotch. 'These boys have seen a boating mishap. That man, Tom Mahler — in the river.'

'Mahler?' Buchanan said sharply. 'What's he doing?'

'These boys have just seen him and his boat down at the river mouth. Sunk. That's what these boys came to tell me. We should get a search out.'

The constable walked around the desk, still frowning. 'The last time I saw you two was up at the reservoir. Not at school then either ...'

'That's when we were eeling,' Jake contributed helpfully. Buchanan almost smiled.

'Of course ... Well, what did you see just now?'

Without raising his head Matty said, 'We saw Painter Tom's boat, upside down in the river. Going out. Upside down.' Jake nodded.

'Anything else?' They shook their heads, then Jake said, 'And we saw Painter Tom, upside down in the water. Like the boat. They were sinking ... to the eels.'

The constable pulled his ginger moustache and frowned. The two pairs of earnest brown eyes held his gaze.

'Right!' He was brusque now, as he lifted the phone and ordered an immediate boat launch, advising of a possible drowning in the river mouth. He placed a second call to New Plymouth and filed a report, suggesting that a chopper might be necessary but that a boat was on its way out. He replaced the receiver and strode out the door. 'I'll need a full statement later, Louis.'

Two boats were waiting at the river, one already in the water. Constable Buchanan leapt into the red and white jetboat.

'River mouth, Fred. That bastard Mahler may have bought it.' And he experienced the strangest emotion: a strange swelling in his throat, almost like relief.

They found the boat a kilometre offshore but there was no sign of the occupant. Buchanan had the second boat take Mahler's craft in tow while he continued to search. He radioed New Plymouth and advised that he had the boat but no body. He requested the chopper urgently and was told it was already in the air.

Louis passed by the pub and broke the news, which was greeted with strained silence.

'Well, we got to find that bloke,' said Louis. One by one they shifted from their stools and filed out the door. Except Jim Harkness. 'I'm not wasting my time on that prick.' And he returned to his beer.

Soon, more than twenty people were searching. The chopper swept the river mouth and the oily sea out some five kilometres, but come darkness there was no sign and people trailed home.

'He'll turn up,' said Buchanan. 'The tide will bring him back.'

But as a precaution he drove up to Tom Mahler's cottage and confirmed he was not on his property. He stood in the doorway and flicked on the light. He called out but it was unnecessary. An hour later, he found Mahler's car parked near the willows by the river.

* * *

MARY HAD SEEN photographs of fiords and boiling mudpools, of snow-topped mountains and white sandy beaches. Nevertheless, the first sight of forested hills surrounding a huge harbour to the west of Auckland was unexpected. And so was the city off to the east, with a high telecommunications tower and bright-coloured houses stretching over an extraordinary area, and beyond, islands sprinkled on blue sea.

'No, I haven't been on a farm for many years,' she told the official. 'Does a city park count?'

She collected her luggage and elected to walk to the domestic terminal, following the blue line on the concrete path in the early morning and wondering if she looked as foreign as she felt. There were many brown-skinned people, in strangely coloured skirts some of them, and happy in their milling groups of all ages. A young man with a plaited black ponytail and shoulders like a young bull returned her gaze with a slight smile and she reminded herself not to stare.

No longer than her caféand with two tiny propellers, the commuter aeroplane was frightening. She had seen only three other airlines in the entire airport and now she was climbing onto one of the smallest aeroplanes she had ever seen. It was bizarre.

'How long will it take to get to New Plymouth?' she asked the woman seated next to her, though she knew already.

'About an hour. You're American?'

And they talked about America and how the woman loved New York and had landed in Chicago once with her husband, but now she was visiting her sister in New Plymouth who had a new baby. 'Do you have children?'

'No. At least I did, but he died — last year.'

'I'm so sorry.'

Mary was grateful for the rising roar of the engines and tried to lose herself in the landscape. 'What a beautiful coast,' she said. 'It's so wild.'

The woman told her about several wild places but was puzzled when Mary said she was visiting a tiny village called 'Moka'. She asked Mary to describe where it was exactly.

'Mokau! That will be Mokau,' she said triumphantly, pronouncing it 'Mo-cow'.

They laughed about that and agreed that foreign languages were difficult. Then the woman said that Mokau was not a tourist destination.

'Well, I'm not really a tourist. My name's Mary, by the way — Mary Chisholm.'

She liked the other woman with her warm green eyes and her summery complexion, and suddenly she wanted to tell her about everything. 'I've come to find someone. How crazy does that sound?' Gaye did not look as if she thought that was crazy. 'His name is Tom ...' And she talked about how she felt about leaving her home and her business to travel across the United States and beyond and how she thought the plane might never land. And though she laughed at herself the woman could see the fear was real enough.

'How should I say?' Mary said. 'Tom's been living alone, I think, in Mokau for a few months. But something has happened and I think he may be in trouble.' She hastened to explain: 'Not serious trouble — he came to New Zealand for a rest. Yes, that's what he wanted — a rest. After our son ... His uncle left him this property at Mokau, of all places. He was stationed here during the war. That's how he found it, I guess.'

The woman listened with interest to how Tom's uncle came home after the war and had an engineering business, then suddenly sold up and left and no one ever saw him again. Tom was only small when that happened, Mary said, and certainly had never known him. And then out of the blue, about a year ago a letter arrived from a solicitor saying that Uncle Henry had left Tom the property. Tom just told them to sell it but nothing happened. So then he decided to come over. To rest and think and things, and it had seemed to be going well.

'I got a nice letter — brighter than he had been for months. Yes ...' she trailed off. 'But then I got another and it was so different. Tom gets involved, sometimes in a way that's obsessive. And I know he's like a fish out of water. He hardly ever left downtown Chicago! And now he's way out here and I think something has happened and that's why I'm here.' Unconsciously she turned the pages of the magazine in her lap.

The woman smiled and said it was exactly the right thing to do, and Mary felt relieved. She marvelled at Taranaki's blue peak streaked with dazzling snow and thought about how it must have been for Tom, not so long ago.

After they disembarked the woman introduced Mary to her sister and the baby Jenna, and invited her to stay. When she declined, she shepherded Mary to her car and offered her advice about her trip.

I can't believe it, Mary thought as she concentrated on keeping left on the narrow highway heading north. I'm exhausted but I don't care a bit.

SHE passed through the village of Urenui and was reminded of swimming at Wailea. Remembered playing beach volleyball and eating baked crab in the warm Hawaiian evening.

Perhaps it was the sound of the word — 'Urenui'. She said it out loud. And perhaps too it was this landscape with its unexpected mix of undulating grassland and orchards. The rows of casuarina and Japanese cedar sheltering leafy vines, and all tucked in the shadow of steep, forested hills.

And the sea! How beautiful it is, she thought, and she parked on the brow of a hill to gaze northward. Such a short time ago in the chill Chicago winter wind, and now: 'Look at me now!' she called to the sea. With her face upturned and her eyes closed she focused on the song of a tiny bird somewhere high overhead. How much I am looking forward to seeing him, she thought, and she opened her eyes and smiled, spreading her arms from her sides and wondering whether to take flight.

Humming, she pulled away from the verge, then panicked at the blast of a horn and the shockwave of a bus. It barely slowed and was long out of sight before she moved again, driving slowly and with fierce attention.

* * *

BETH GILBERT SMILED as she read the story written in a random mix of capitals and lower case letters and with not one sentence able to be contained within two parallel lines. When she smiled her eyes glowed and a face that in repose appeared almost plain became in an instant extraordinary. It was a smile that children loved.

What a funny little girl, she thought and she wrote across the clear space below: 'I really like this story, Moana. You must tell me whether she finds her pony. I do hope so.'

Beth liked to mark at her classroom desk rather than take schoolwork home. She preferred to keep her school life separate from the rest of her life. At least, that had been her rule, but it had never been meant to cope with the events of these past few weeks.

Such strange days ... But she had seen an opportunity and seized it. That's what teachers had to do and that's what had happened that day. She knew that in him she had found a valuable resource and the children had enjoyed it. And so had she. But then she had felt the first of those delicious moments that told her something else was happening. Something she had barely wanted to acknowledge, and that had been exciting too. Something that she sensed was beginning to fill her in a way she had never experienced. But it was dangerous. She hated the pain she was causing and knew of no way to change things.

She rose and walked restlessly around her spacious classroom, its walls brightened by exuberant artwork, and paused by the boy's desk. She touched the wooden surface where hands had been busy doing many things for many many years, way before her time, and would do so way beyond. Small hands trailing and touching and moving restlessly. But latterly, the hand of the small boy and the man together, on this desk, exploring a world to which no one including herself had access. Their world it was, and how exciting that had been, and she had been instrumental in that transformation.

The polished linoleum beneath her bare feet was smooth and warm. Perhaps I am drunk, she thought, and she touched her throat and traced the outline. She felt hot, and opened her eyes with a start.

'Close your eyes all I will bite your neak,' she read, and smiled again as she recalled the author's impish eyes peering from behind the Dracula mask with its vivid red lips and white fangs, and its green ears like tubers.

More of that strange shouting down the road, and the sound of a helicopter. How long had that been going on? She had been absorbed but it was an unusual commotion and she felt she should investigate.

'Miss Gilbert! Miss Gilbert!' A small boy with straight red hair and the palest freckled face came in eagerly, peering with his usual startling intensity.

'You look like you've seen a ghost, Paul,' she said jovially. He shook his head, staring with solemn eyes.

'It's Painter Tom,' he said. 'He's drowned, Miss Gilbert. My dad's looking for him.'

Startled by her expression, the boy stepped back. 'Dad's got the helicopter and everything, Miss Gilbert. But they don't know where he's gone. Only the boat. That's what they found. I've got to go.' And he turned suddenly and ran out the door.

She followed. 'Mr Harkness!' She saw him near the intersection. 'Mr Harkness ...' Running down the road heedless of sharp stones, her voice shrill.

'He's lost!' the man exclaimed with grim satisfaction. 'Drowned, they say. Not that it would worry you?'

'What a horrible thing to say!' Harkness is a liar, she thought as she walked back towards the school. He is a troublemaker who wishes to see the worst, and he would like to hurt me. But she quickened her pace, turning into Soldiers Road and was nearly home when she cried out at the sight of a cat on the grass verge. Black and white, with its eyes closed and a tiny pink tongue protruding. Poor little Paul, she thought, and wondered whether he knew.

THERE were several people outside the police station and someone called out, but she knew instantly and drove on by, allowing her little blue Volkswagen to steer itself, up into the coast hills and down the winding gravel road to Tom Mahler's cottage.

* * *

THE GIRL HAD glimpsed a frightened face in the red car and understood the bus driver's agitation.

'Blind!' He glanced at her nervously. 'You'd think a bus was big enough.' She nodded agreement.

They swung around a bend that allowed her to see the village not far up the coast. I do not want to see them, she thought. Any of them, and least of all her, but it will only be a couple of days, and then gone for good. Or him perhaps?

Her jaw set and her eyes closed tight. And yet, she felt she was beginning to understand. He had not wanted to hurt her. During the night something had happened and he had become ... mad? She remembered his eyes and the things he said that made no sense. Her eyes clenched more tightly.

The driver changed down and the bus ground slowly up a hill. And was *he* still working on that dumb boat, she wondered? With that retard?

The bridge came into view and her gaze hardened as she looked at the small houses along the riverbank. The strip of green grass above the black road and the tufts of toetoe with their creamy tassles like the lances of knights riding.

'Home for the weekend?'

'This is not my home,' she said with finality as she leapt from the bus. The driver watched her walk across the road. Watched the swing of her hips and studied the head of the Bacardi bat showing in the small of her back. He thought about that tattoo all the way to Awakino.

The key and the earwigs were under the brick and the same two plastic bags gathered dust in the porch. The small orange house smelled just the same and was just as gloomy. But not for long, she thought as she made a cup of tea. She felt relieved at the silence. On the back step she lit a cigarette and blew a long stream into the still, warm air, and was amused to see Pelican jump from the top of the fence. 'Hullo, you greedy bugger,' she said, and rubbed under his chin. He dribbled on her hand.

The front gate clicked but she did not move. Sounds in the house, then the back door opened. That flat voice: 'So you've come back?'

'Nope. I'm just a figment.'

Silence, and then: 'Smart talking as always. Well, what're you here for? I thought we'd gone for good and glad of it? Don't tell me you're homesick?'

'I'm getting the rest of my things and then I'm going to Auckland.' Silence, then footsteps retreating. Melanie sighed. She stubbed the butt on the concrete and was about to rise when the shuffling footsteps returned. There was a pause.

'You know he's dead? Drowned. You knew that?'

'What?' She turned to look at her stepmother and saw triumph leaping in the small blue eyes. 'What?'

'You haven't heard?' Excited now.

'There's nothing round here I want to know about.' But she did not dare hold Trixie's gaze and the afternoon warmth became suffocatingly hot. She pushed the cat away.

'Him. That Yank. You didn't know he drowned? Course you couldn't have — you were on the bus. Well, he's gone.'

Melanie took the last cigarette and threw the packet onto the grass. The older woman remained in the doorway, blinking uncertainly at the girl's back.

'They've been searching this afternoon.' Trixie's words were softer.

'Good for them. Are my things where I left them?'

The woman had extended her hand towards Melanie's shoulder but it stopped in the air unseen and was withdrawn.

'You care more about that prick than you do about me.'

'Yes! Yes I do. You're pathetic.' She was pleased to see the woman cringe. 'He's far more than you'll ever be. He loves me.'

'Loves you?' A peal of shrill laughter. 'You idiot! He used you like the slut you are. Well, I'm glad!' She followed Melanie down the hall. 'I'm bloody glad!'

The door banged and Trixie stood heaving, frightened and alone. She tottered into the poky room filled with the junk of years and fell into her chair and cried.

* * *

THE SIGN OUTSIDE the general store said 'Superior Merchandising'. The ornate script highlighted the 'S' and the 'M', with a red stripe down the middle of the gold, but the colour was faded after so many years. The name had been Herb Simes's idea. He told his wife, 'You've gotta say what you're gonna do, Merle. You gotta aim where it is you're going in life.'

Merle became the sole proprietor when Herb died three years ago.

They had run Superior Merchandising together for eighteen years but now, since the girl had gone, it was only herself. The girl, Melanie, was pretty in a way and she knew about men. It was apparent in her eyes and the way she moved — with that bizarre tattoo on her back that went right down below her pants! But she had attracted trade, perhaps. Something had to explain the drop in sales.

Merle had hated being stuck out on this windswept coast and had wanted desperately to go back to Palmerston North. But now it seemed the most homely community of decent people. Except for the few ratbags who stole from her on occasion but there seemed nothing to be done. They were too clever, and used their numbers to distract. She sometimes suspected the girl knew what they were doing. Constable Buchanan did what he could, but then, what could one man do against several determined teenagers with time on their hands?

Otherwise, Mokau was a peaceful and pleasant place and Merle had long since stopped thinking about living anywhere else. Here in her store with its racks of goods and things right up to the ceiling — many of which Herb had hung there to remain just as he had placed them and never to be disturbed again. Paraffin lanterns in case the power lines went down, though that hadn't happened for years. And all the cooking implements you could want to start a commercial kitchen if you needed, and a cluster of possum traps though she hadn't sold one of those since Bert Polsen with his leg died. Fishing gear, seeds and fertilisers, a surfboard and preserving jars. But people were buying more of that stuff in New Plymouth, or they simply didn't do some things any more. Sometimes she thought she should get rid of it, though in a way it would seem like she was getting rid of Herb. So she didn't.

Merle absently dusted the tops of the jars that contained an assortment of boiled sweets. I should take another one from stock, she thought as a pink feather fell from the head of the worn duster and wafted gently out of sight behind the counter. Look at this thing; if it were a chicken it would be awful cold. She thought about other things. She thought about the times. Even before the horror of the drowning, people had been behaving strangely. Sometimes she wondered whether it was this weather. It was uncannily calm and hot. No one could explain why the westerly had simply stopped — not old Louis or John Reid, and he was a good farmer.

Perhaps that was why there had been that rowdy meeting with people shouting at each other. 'Don't touch our heritage' had been painted on the side of the fire station. The bush, they meant. Pagett's bit of bush that hardly anyone knew where to find. And that had been followed by: 'Farms for farming'. It was the first time anyone had defaced the fire station wall for years and it was no less unsettling now than then. Not since that young Sam Wherry went strange.

'We're all neighbours,' she told anyone who would listen.

The doorbell rang and a stranger peered in her door. A woman wearing a green trouser suit. Strange attire but it looked powerful, in a way, and Merle liked her high, clear cheekbones and the fine shape of her nose.

The woman said 'Hi' and that she was looking for someone, and she smiled pleasantly. Her accent caused Merle to press her hands on the smooth counter.

'Tom Mahler. An American?' Mary added, since the elderly woman appeared not to have heard the name at all. 'He hasn't been here long, but I assume he would have been a customer.'

She knew he must have been and wondered whether the woman was deaf or perhaps simple. 'I simply want to confirm that this road,' she gestured to the map in her hand, 'is where he lives.'

She placed the map on the counter and stared at the old woman, still pretty with her soft eyes and pink, translucent skin. Noticed the ornate silver brooch at her neck and the fine hairnet that enclosed most of the grey hair and had a sudden vision of her own mother.

Merle shook her head. 'I'm so sorry,' she frowned fiercely. 'I'm so sorry. Perhaps you should talk to the constable — to Constable Buchanan. That might be the —'

'Pardon? Talk to who? You do know Tom Mahler? Why are you looking like that?' The woman was frightened. 'What is it? Please, I've come a long way. A very long way and I'm very tired.'

'Mr Mahler ...'

'Yes?' Mary felt she should go out and come back in.

'Mr Mahler, is missing,' Merle managed at last. 'Yes. He's missing, from his boat. Down at the river. They've been looking for him. I'm so sorry.' Her hands moved in strange little motions on the glowing wood.

Mary stepped back, dislodging cans from a shelf behind her. She wheeled, 'I'm sorry,' she said automatically, and stooped as though to pick them up but stopped and rose again. 'Missing?' she asked faintly, and observed the tiny nod. 'Not ... drowned?'

'No! At least, he's not been found, but he might be. They're all looking. You should talk to the police. Just down the road on the left. I'm so sorry ... just down there, on the left.' Merle moved to the doorway and pointed. 'That's where the constable is.'

THE air was fresh and clean and the sun warmed her face instantly but it was not home. It was a far distant place where a strange boy with the straightest of ginger hair and a face as solemn as stone walked by. In his hand he held the tail of a dead cat and he was struggling to keep its head from touching the ground. She heard his swift intake of breath like a tiny curse whenever it bumped, but otherwise he too appeared unconscious of his surroundings. She stared at the animal, its legs stiff and pointing, and she wanted to cry. She wanted to touch the boy but he was soon gone.

A cattle truck drove by too fast and left a scent like nightshade, and the crunch of her shoes in the fine gravel on the side of the road hurt her ears. There was no response to her knocking on the polished desk or her calls, which echoed in a high voice that she did not recognise. She returned to the car.

'I must concentrate!' she said out loud and gripped the steering wheel so fiercely her hands began to ache. The sun no longer warmed and the high hills threatened to throw her back into the sea. A car flashed its lights and she realised she had strayed across the centre line. 'Slower,' she breathed as she left the highway and crept into a winding and unsealed lane in a narrow valley hemmed by forest.

A small blue car materialised and they were fortunate not to collide. Momentarily the two cars faced each other and Mary wanted to shout something. The other woman restarted her motor and accelerated recklessly past her and down the hill. Mary wound down her window and breathed deeply. Only the soft murmur of the engine intruded on the silence that seemed to deepen as a cloud drifted over and the folds in the hills disappeared.

A few minutes later, on the crest of a hill, she turned in by a large wooden gate that was hanging by a chain, off its hinges. She began to descend a twisting, pitted track that ended in a small seaward-facing clearing in which stood a red cottage.

'Tom?' she cried, fumbling with the doorlatch of the car. 'Tom?'

* * *

BILL MANUHUIA DROVE his old flatdeck home, grateful for the end of the week. He had heard about the drowning but he had stayed on the job until after five. The new road was way behind schedule. Some folks blamed the Maori. That was unfair, Bill thought. But sometimes he felt uneasy. Sometimes he wondered what it was all about. When they discovered the hangi stones it had been kind of exciting. He wasn't sure why; after all, he made a hangi often enough himself. But these stones were way up the highway where no one had lived in his memory. These stones must have been from way back. Tupuna — but which ones? That was the thing. Could have been Ngati Tama or Ngati Maniapoto. Could have been that bastard Te Rauparaha! Could have been his own whanau ... that would be something.

Bullshit! They were just old hangi stones. What did they have to do with anything? The job was to widen the road so the traffic could go better. That was today. That was what counted today. Not bloody old hangi stones that couldn't make the traffic go better. They couldn't make a difference to any damn thing. And he was the foreman on the roading company and it was his job to make sure things got along.

Bill drove south towards Awakino, alongside the winding river that had so little water this summer it was more a necklace of silver pools, winding through the high bush, the cicadas singing. He started to hum but it didn't seem right.

What had really pissed the boss off was those Patais coming along and making a noise. 'Bloody artists,' Merv had said scornfully. 'This is a job! This is not a carving or something. If they want those rocks in the museum, well, put them there.'

Merv Layton was a good bloke and a fair boss. Bill had known him all his life nearly and he knew that Merv wanted the same sorts of things for his kids as Bill did. Merv gave a lot to the community. He donated his time, and his machinery sometimes, to local projects. But he got pretty wound up about those stones!

And Tom Mahler? What an awful thing that was. He recalled Tom on Christmas Day when they had talked about stuff including Bill's job, and Tom had said he wanted to come out with Bill, to watch. And Bill was quite pleased about that. No one wanted to see what a roading foreman did. They had talked about Chicago, though Bill didn't know anything except the Bulls came from there and BB King.

Tom was interested in the hangi stones and said so. Merv Layton thought Mahler was queer and said so. 'What would he know about cooking stones?' But Bill thought Tom was okay and it seemed very bad that he should have drowned. It meant the sea would not be good for quite a while. Uncle Louis would sort that thing out so that nobody would go fishing. It would be a bad thing to be catching fish while that Tom Mahler was out there. God rest his soul.

Bill passed the Awakino pub and noted the empty carpark. He drove along the coast and caught the late afternoon rays on the white papa cliffs to the south. He could feel the white rock inside him. He could feel it as if it was part of his bones. The sight of those glowing cliffs made him feel whole.

He wondered about his boys. His boys liked Tom. Tom was a painter. Well, that was good. Bill's father had been a carver. That was good too. It was very good to be able to make things that told stories. He wondered about his boys when they grew up. Most likely they would want to leave like all the rest. Go to Auckland. They wouldn't want to work for an old roading company. They would want more money and bright lights and fast cars.

Bill smiled to himself. He might have liked those things once. That was how it was when you were a young buck. Get out and dust your broom. That was good. But only for a while and then you needed to do something else. You needed to do something that made more sense. Like working on the roads.

Alice Moorhead with her bright eyes and ready laugh came to his mind, even after so many years, and he wondered where she ended up. That was a fine woman.

He sighed and his thoughts returned to Tom Mahler, remembering him sitting on the back verandah on Boxing Day and singing along with everyone. That was what it was about. Sitting with your people and singing. That was what made sense. He frowned and in his heart he said a small prayer for Tom Mahler.

As he approached Mokau he saw a red car coming that was too close to the centre line. He flashed his lights twice and was reassured when it swerved back. He didn't recognise the woman.

3

THE DOG WAS tired, lying next to him with its head on its paws and eyes closed, long pink tongue protruding from the side of its jaws like an empty sock. It had worked hard, covering many times as much slope as he, investigated many more crevices and crooks in the gully.

But Ringatu was not despondent because he knew the magnitude of the task. He had asked the turehu only to provide a safeguard. It was not their obligation to join the search. He looked along the ridge to the right and calculated that he would need to do two traverses before he would know he had covered the required area. And darkness on this peculiar day was almost upon him.

He rose and the dog was instantly on its feet. For good measure Ringatu untied the small blue jersey on his neck and waved it at the dog, which attempted to take the garment in its own mouth but Ringatu whisked it away and retied it. Then he descended slowly into the bush, letting his eyes become accustomed to the gloom. Smelling the fern and listening into the dark gullies of the tiny flitting tomtit.

He remembered back to his childhood when he lived down by the river. Two houses along from old Louis. That old bastard. He recalled Louis chasing him and his brother along the road after he caught them in his back shed, drinking one of his beers. Nearly caught them too. Probably would have if Ringatu, already a master of strategy, hadn't shouted at his brother to head for the river while he sprinted for the town. That fooled old Louis and they made their escape, and laughed as the wild words floated along behind. He was good to the boys though, letting them come and go as they pleased and taking them fishing.

You needed old people like Louis to teach you things. Like how to live in the bush or kill a wild pig and where to find some food in places where most people would starve to death. You needed them to point out the big pa sites and tell who lived there and when: to tell you about the deeds of the ancestors. Now look — the old bastard rarely moved away from his cottage. That was all he had. Pissy little cottage with no TV and no carpets, just himself and never any underpants. Having a piss in his backyard and going to sleep on the front verandah, curled up like an old dog.

Ringatu shook his head. That's another thing that's not right, he thought, as he watched the dog quicken its pace through a grove of tree ferns: an old man like Louis should be respected. He was a kaumatua. But who cared now? Who gave a shit about the old ways? Old Louis was just a joke, asleep on his porch.

The dog returned and seemed to sense Ringatu's expectant gaze. It cocked its head, then wheeled downhill out of sight.

Ringatu remembered when Louis first saw his tattoo. When he got back from Auckland the first time. 'What's that thing on your face, boy?'

'This is Titokowaru,' he said tersely. He didn't feel he needed to give any explanation to the old man and was especially disinclined to tell him how he had changed his name.

'Oh,' said his uncle, clearly surprised. 'And how has that black eye got anything to do with that man?'

'He was blind in one eye,' said Ringatu. 'This is just to remind me of the musket ball.' He pictured the crescent moon under his eye and was okay about telling about Tito, but he kept the Ringatu symbol to himself.

'You're a mad boy. Why do you want to be thinking about him? Tito's past. He didn't get anything. You would do better to look into the future. Leave the past where it belongs.'

But Ringatu knew that Louis hated to say such a thing. He was hurting himself for his own failure. He knew he was right to remember and Tito needed to be remembered. The chief himself had said: 'I shall not die.' So he didn't argue with Louis because he knew where he was coming from. A brown Pakeha: that's what his uncle had become. Grovelling about. He'd lost everything, worst of all his dignity. That was something Tito never lost. His freedom and his eye but never his dignity. And sure enough, Louis went straight off and got drunk and fell in the garden and cried.

'I shall not die,' Ringatu said softly as he recalled the man Mahler rowing into the sunset, and he felt troubled. He wondered how Titokowaru would have dealt with all this. The warrior chief had tried cunning — a war of wits with the Pakeha — and that hadn't worked. Then he had tried force of arms and that nearly had. It bloody nearly had — those bastard settlers had been driven all the way to Wanganui and they were afraid. Ringatu paused and thought about Tito manoeuvring his tribe down the coast. His whole tribe with women and kids but still eluding the constabulary at will, setting ambush and trap so the soldiers were afraid to follow. He smiled. But it failed in the end. Tito grew tired and his enemies grew in number.

Louis said we had to move on but Ringatu believed that was not possible when a kaumatua slept on the verandah of a crappy cottage on his own riverbank, grateful to the Pakeha for leaving him alone but nothing more. All that was left of what had been. When all the riverflats and the hills and the sea belonged. It was not possible when the people were treated like losers unless they played the Pakeha game, as if that was the only way that meant anything. And building over everything. Building over the pa in that stinking Auckland. Digging and building like people possessed and with no respect. That's how they were — possessed with the need to change everything and eradicate any sign of the first people.

And still burning the bush ... Ringatu gripped a branch on the kawakawa and ripped it down, and his eyes gleamed and his body grew as hard as the tawa. But that bastard had paid. Now what? Someone else would occupy that land and bring cattle. Someone else would destroy in the ceaseless pursuit of money. What then? His eyes enlarged and his mouth twisted open. 'Exalt for Te Kooti,' he rasped, 'Te Kooti the bold!' And he took a step forward holding the branch before him, 'So fierce in the onset, so dauntless of old!' He twirled the branch and suddenly thrashed it against the trunk of a lancewood. 'Ha!' His eyes popped but they did not see. 'Ha!' And he lashed the trunk until the branch splintered and pieces flew into the fern and after a while he held the shaft and peered at it curiously as if he wondered from whence it came.

Then he relaxed and leaned against the tree, straight and hard that tree with bark like the sinews in his own brown flesh. A small smile came to his lips. He listened again to the bush and heard the dog off to the right, pushing through some fern. A fantail flitting a few feet away to catch the insects he was disturbing. He watched the tiny bird with its elaborate tail spread, dipping and diving through impossible spaces in the branches and with that little peeping sound all the time. That was good tactics. Flitting here and there and so difficult to catch. Not even a cat could catch such an acrobat. That was good tactics. That's why he was alone, and yet not. The ancestors were always there and they were pleased, talking softly those tupuna in the trees. Sometimes to him and sometimes not. Sometimes keeping those capricious turehu at bay.

Tom Mahler was alone. How strange that his father had known Mahler's uncle. They had been mates after his father saved Henry in a brawl. Down in Wellington during the war. It was a huge fight that had gone on for hours and if it hadn't been for Koro that man Henry might have been killed. No one wanted those smooth Yanks all about and talking up the local women. That's what his father said. 'Too smooth for us, those Yanks,' he said. 'Flowers and chocolates and God knows what!' and he laughed that big laugh.

But how strange that Henry had returned and then Tom. They weren't even alike: could have been from different families altogether, those Mahlers. Henry had married that Wetere woman and then gone AWOL, his father said. He was a good man but a bit peculiar. So was Tom. He was a bit peculiar. Building that dumb boat. And educated. Stuck way out here building a boat no one would want. Could have been making heaps back home but stuck here. Rooting that woman? That made some sense. But it was a long way to come for a root.

Now he was gone. Even hated by his own people. Gone into the deep. To rest. That would not be so bad ... to rest. But it was a mistake perhaps and he would miss that man. He would miss his crazy arguments. Ringatu shook his head.

Pushing on downhill, unable to see more than a few metres now, he continued to listen for the dog. Need to be careful here, he thought as he encountered the top of another bluff. No more than ten or so metres high but steep. They had to be navigated properly these rough limestone outcrops, with thick tangled supplejack vines and ponga ferns all around.

Then he heard the bark, once then several times, about fifty metres down and to the left now. Ringatu climbed to find a quicker way. Confident he was and pleased that they had kept their word; he followed a pig track through the young manuka that took him closer to the dog. Abruptly the trail gave out and in a split second the big man had grasped a slender branch that prevented him falling. 'Shit!' he said, but as he swung himself about, scrambling to regain his balance, he saw, and it was enough.

* * *

THERE WAS NO sound. Mary looked around the small room with its bare boards and yellowed window glass, a crude bench and table, and was repelled by the thin smell of cold ash. There were boat plans on the table and ancient unfamiliar pictures on the wall.

'Tom?' she said softly as she stepped into the dim passageway to the bedroom. She switched on the light and looked quickly around the tiny room and there, on the ledge by the rusty bedhead, an unframed photograph of Tom and Luke and herself, their arms about one another with Luke in the middle. Laughing with his white mop of hair sprayed in all directions.

'Yes!' she said. 'Oh, Tom. Oh, Luke!' And she fell forward onto the bed, clutching the photograph to her chest. Pushing her face into the pillow. 'I came and you're gone. You're gone! What am I going to do? What am I going to do?' and she cried as the dusk descended and the exhaustion of past days overwhelmed her, until she sank at last into the deepest sleep.

In the ancient macrocarpa near the beach a colony of shags with their white fronts and snaking necks made querulous noise for an hour, and on the top of a rewarewa a speckled thrush sang the evening song. Until all sound except the regular swish of waves on the sand faded away and the moon rose and moved steadily across the night sky and vanished behind the hill.

* * *

HE MOVED FASTER now, back to his left. Skidding on a deep drift of rotting vegetation he burst out of the waist-high astelia and hastened to the side of the boy. Uncertainty rising at the sight of the face so pale and the wound on the forehead. Pushing the dog aside, and with great gentleness manoeuvring long fingers under the boy's head and very slowly feeling his way back. Barely lifting or altering the boy's position, pausing frequently to assess, thinking and then proceeding as he reassured himself. Finally he straightened the short, muscular legs and sat back with a satisfied grunt. He watched the regular rise and fall of the boy's chest. The dog reclined and extended its nose until it just touched the boy's outstretched arm and the darkness deepened.

Ringatu cast around the ledge and gathered dead fern and other soft material into a bed near the foot of the escarpment. Onto this, and with the same great care, he laid the boy. He paused at the murmur. Nothing perhaps, so he rose and climbed down to a slow trickle of water. First he deepened a shallow bowl in the stones so it would accommodate his water bottle, and when it was near full he pulled a blue cloth from his back pocket and dunked it. Then he returned to wipe the dry blood from the boy's face.

When he was satisfied, he placed the bottle to the boy's lips and allowed the water to trickle into his mouth, all the while keeping the head slightly raised. Soon, the boy coughed and moved his hand such that the dog suddenly leaned forward and vigorously licked the small face. Ringatu pushed the dog aside and noted the eyes wide and staring.

'I asked the tupuna to watch over you,' said the man. 'And the dog found you.' The boy looked at the dog and may have smiled.

'Tom?'

Ringatu froze. 'What's that?' He peered intently but the boy's face was closed and Ringatu was doubtful. He waited a few seconds and then proffered the bottle. 'You said something?' Ringatu persisted, but the boy continued to drink and gave not the slightest sign he had heard the question. I must be hearing inside my head, Ringatu thought. The voices are getting very loud. 'We will have to stay tonight,' he said, and he began to assemble a small enclosure of stones into which he bundled kindling of dry fern and twigs. All the time as he worked he watched the boy and when he applied a match he could see consternation at the thin spiral of smoke.

'This will be a tiny thing, just for you and me. There is no need to be afraid of this little fire. It is not like the valley.'

Sean gestured in the familiar way. Ringatu frowned and looked up into the delicate canopy. Without looking at Sean, he pointed to the north. 'He is some distance,' he said. 'That man is in his boat.' The boy seemed satisfied.

Soon only the dog, the boy and the man showed in the feeble light of the fire. Caught in a circle of darkness, Ringatu waited until the boy had rested his head on his arm and closed his eyes. He waited for the regular breath of sleep then he lay down and closed his own eyes.

But he did not sleep. He listened to the chattering of the turehu in the tree ferns. Sometimes he could see them flitting through the leaves in the moonlight and then they were in his head.

'It is done,' he hissed fiercely into the darkness. 'Titokowaru has eaten the flesh of man.' The chattering subsided.

Once he thought about the girl.

The boy's sleep was not restful and twice during the night Ringatu held his head and dribbled water into the unconscious mouth and thought about the horror they had both seen.

* * *

MARY OPENED HER eyes and stared at the roughsawn timber walls with apprehension. 'Please help me,' she whispered.

There were wine stains on the table and a single sock lost under the edge of the sofa. She picked it up and sat at the table with the sock dangling over her knee and imagined how it might have been. Studying the boat plans and tracing the familiar handwriting with her finger, then touching the empty letter pad as though it might soon disclose a secret.

Unsteadily, she moved to the window to peer into the dawn light in the ghostly trees and wondered where the night had gone. On the floor near a simple wooden chest was a large ball of paper. She picked it up and spread it to reveal large words, crudely handwritten with a pastel or crayon: 'You are a fucking pedo. You are not wanted. Go back to your place. We will cut off your goolies.'

'God! What is this?' She hit the table with her fist. 'What is this?

Tom?' Sweeping the paper off the table onto the floor and pacing the room, frightened by the sound of her shoes. She turned the tap over the sink. At first nothing happened but as she moved away a gurgling deep in the pipes heralded water. She threw some on her face and then searched until she found a glass alongside several uncorked bottles of wine in the wire mesh safe.

They were surely intended for someone else, those words, and she found ways to be busy while the light changed from blue to mauve and birds sang into the morning.

Later, she stood on the edge of the verandah and gazed at the bay and all along the high ridges to the left and right. Back to the bay and the stark rocks peering from brilliant white foam. Around the small clearing enclosed by short scrubby trees and the lightless tunnel that was the beginning of the track back to the road. She ventured out on the grass and looked back over the cottage to the high hills. Deep in shade but with the first rays of the sun creating a golden glow in the very tops of the trees and everywhere the scent of wild herbs and flowers.

How utterly foreign, she mused in amazement. How utterly primitive, and she hastened to the trunk of her car to recover her baggage. She pulled on a red sweater that had been a birthday present so long ago she could barely remember. Rummaging further she found her small photo album and flicked rapidly through the pages.

This was you, Tom? She laid the album aside and surveyed the cluttered room. This was where you came? Oh, how I wish I had come sooner. How I wish ...' 'Tom?' Noticing the ball of paper on the floor where it had rolled, with sudden determination she looked for matches. Eventually a flame burst forth and flared in the grate and she glanced around as though she was seeing everything for the first time.

A book on the floor: two books, beneath the table that may have been knocked off or perhaps placed there. She knelt and reached for the larger: *The Dory Book*. She lowered herself to sit with her back to the wall. The book was well thumbed and, like the blueprints on the table, full of underlining and extensive annotation. Alongside a drawing of something resembling a trapdoor inside a boat, Tom's note: Ingenious! Then a photograph of a dory being launched from a bleak stony beach, decades before and somewhere on the coast of

New England she guessed. Next to the photograph the handwritten note said: This is it!

With little effort she imagined the man to be Tom and the woman herself. The other smaller person might have been Luke. The idea warmed her. What a funny man. He who had never built a thing in his life had built a Newfoundland dory, here on the other side of the world: built the dory for Luke and him. She closed her eyes and remembered the painting of the dory on a stormy sea — the men in sou'westers struggling with their fishing lines against the wind and the waves of the Grand Banks, and the single gull, forever fixed, its beak agape in silent exclamation hovering above. The picture that had remained pinned to the wall above Luke's bed for ten years at least. Moved once or twice to allow the addition of larger posters of musicians and glamorous girls, but never lost.

'Do you think we'll build it, Dad?' And Tom had answered, 'Hey! Does the sun shine?' But they hadn't. She closed the book and put it to one side, brought her knees to her chest with her arms wrapped around them. After a while she reached for the other book.

'Titokowaru,' she murmured, struggling with the complicated word. 'Titokowaru?' There was a name inside the front. A heavy hand in black, inscribed, 'Ringatu'.

'Ringatu,' she said. 'Who are you?'

And that was how she found the diary. Just beyond, on its edge, fallen between the wall and the short floorboards.

* * *

THE YELLOW STOCK truck, with the name 'Westfield' on the side in bright blue, wound up the slope above Mokau and followed the road along the river into the hills. Past the McCleods' where the road twisted into a gully full of green raupo reeds and an ancient stand of pine. Past the Lynchs' blue and white house on the edge of the low hill and a boxthorn for shelter, speckled with shining red berries on the northern side, and a straggling wire fence that led to the cowshed. Down the slope again on the narrow bitumen road with lichen growing on the centre strip and then up the last hill towards Pagett's place even as the morning sun touched the steel gate at the end of the road.

Joe Matarangi drove for Westfield Trucking. Collecting cattle, sheep and pigs from many farms from Waikawau down through Awakino, Mokau, Urenui and all the way to New Plymouth. He regularly collected fattened calves and pigs from the roadhead up the Mokau. But today there were no animals in the pen by the gate. Joe lit a smoke, leaned against the cab of his truck and appraised the river flats and hills. It was familiar and even quite pretty though it meant little enough. None of it ranked alongside a good golf course.

He listened to the regular ticking of metal cooling and the soft shuffling of hooves in the cage. Smelled the animals and the hot grease and decided to wait just five minutes more. He picked up a smooth stone with curious golden streaks, wiped it on his sleeve and then sent it spiralling close to a post twenty metres down the road. Sat on the step of the cab and thought about the game he expected to play that afternoon. 'Bugger,' he said out loud, then ground the butt beneath his boot and walked up the drive for the very first time.

He didn't know Pagett at all. The man never spoke. Just helped him put the squealing pigs into the truck then disappeared up this same track over the crest of the hill. Funny sort of bastard, with the blankest face Joe had ever come across. Not like it was reserved or something, just blank as though you weren't even there. Joe gave up trying to make some conversation a long time back. Pagett didn't even tell him to shut up! Nothing!

There had been a time when Joe had caught the smell though. It had been a fine morning and he was early. Pagett was still herding thirty head into the road pen and Joe had waited like today, leaning on his cab. And then the gentle breeze had assaulted his nose with the stench of putrefaction. It was a breeze that came down the valley but from over the crest he was now climbing. While it had lasted only a few seconds he knew it was much more than one rotting carcase. Not that it mattered. He had never smelled it again — until now.

Joe could see the house about a kilometre distant and beyond the small, cream weatherboard and red-roofed farmhouse there was a large unpainted stock shed and a timber implement shed. A tractor with a shovel extended in the air was parked next to a windblown walnut and several abandoned vehicles and pieces of agricultural machinery lay haphazardly around the house and sheds. A small number of bobby calves in a pen shifted restlessly and three dogs chained to 44-gallon drums placed on their side barked a furious warning. But it was not the sound of the dogs or the lack of human activity that made Joe uneasy. It was the dead. As he walked closer it became clear that the large lumps lying near the house and the shed were the skinned carcases of beasts, and around the carcases, chewing and squabbling were a hundred pigs, feeding.

'Sweet Jesus,' said Joe, as he was assailed by a stench that stopped him like he was pole-axed. The bloated animal nearby had been recently skinned and still shone bloody red, but many other carcases, with their abdomens split, rib bones white-tipped or hoary black, had lain for weeks. He took his hand from over his nose and mouth.

'Pagett!' he called. 'Pagett, it's Matarangi.' The sound echoed off the tin, the dogs jerked on their chains and a mob of small pigs wheeled suddenly from their gory meal to scamper across the field and over the brow of the hill. Joe stopped at the shed and peered into the gloom. 'Pagett!' he called. He turned to go, then paused uncertainly. The front door of the house was open. 'Are you there, Pagett?' His voice rang hollow in the bare hallway.

He stepped inside and took three paces to peer into a darkened sitting room. 'Hullo. Pagett. It's Joe Matarangi.' He turned to the kitchen. 'Holy mackerel!' he said and his voice caught in his throat.

He stared into Trevor Pagett's eyes and watched a bluebottle crawl out of the man's mouth. The body slumped on the floor against the kitchen bench with its hands outstretched and palms upwards. A wound in the chest, blackened with dry blood that had seeped through the chequered bush shirt.

'Man, oh man, what has happened here? What has happened? Are you dead? Are you dead?' And he came near that he might be determined that Pagett was truly dead, lying here on his own kitchen floor. That he might see the pool of slimy blood on the floor and with growing horror see words, smeared on the pale door of the sink cupboard, next to the man. 'Man oh man, what is this?' he asked softly, and he leaned forward, conscious of the vacant eyes and wanting to tear himself away but needing to see. '... the love of ...' he read, but was puzzled by a word that was barely decipherable, and he felt a chill creep over his scalp like a rash and wanted only to be outside.

Backing up, looking, listening and treading so quietly as he returned to the front door and the sun. Listening for any sound above the dogs and scanning quickly for any movement beyond the pigs which, like giant maggots, moved easily in the carcases. Then he returned to the kitchen and lifted the phone and dialled, but there was no answer. He hung up the receiver and hastened outside.

'Shit! I ain't waiting here.' And he started up the track towards the roadend. Started at the sharp barking of the dogs. Soon he was jogging and the air seemed to whistle in his ears so he might not hear and at the same time was the sound of a fiend coming. And he could see those strange words in his mind: 'For the love of ...' and the last word took shape in his mind, 'For the love of Mary'.

* * *

AT LEAST, IT appeared to be a diary, but as Mary flicked through the pages she noticed that while the early entries were dated, progressively the text became continuous with occasional dates only. She could see where a new entry began by some small difference in the script, and sometimes a black rather than blue pen had been used. She noticed too that the book was full. It was quite long — maybe fifty pages — and had simply stopped, or was that the last entry? She peered into the crack that had concealed the book and tentatively explored the space with her hand. It was empty, and nor was there anything else under the table.

Excited nonetheless, she opened the school exercise book. This was a chronicle. This was Tom's chronicle!

The first date was 4 July. Not much more than a month after he had left Chicago. She read:

~ God, but the waves crash against this place. And the wind! I thought home windy, but this is much worse. It is unrelenting. I am unsure why I am writing. Is it the beginning of a diary? Perhaps it is just a strange mood upon me because of this special day. We shall see.

Same day: I need to write something of what has happened to me. I think I need to contrast my feelings with how it was only a few weeks back. I am becoming accustomed to the wind and the trees and the sea. The people? Maybe. Before, I felt even the elements resented me.

I am trying to understand why it happened. What could have been done?

I celebrate Independence Day with a chicken and chardonnay and feel a loneliness I might never have imagined.

5 July

Well, here I am again already! 'Dear diary!' Good Lord, what would Gerry and John think about that? Undoubtedly, that I had 'lost it'. Maybe I have.

Luke dominates my thoughts. It has been so hard I have often thought I should just end it all. Certainly, I could not have remained in Chicago, and I am pleased now that I came here.

Why didn't he say something?

Mary frowned. Who? Luke? Tom had not been able to share. He had coped badly and much worse than she, who had soldiered on. In fact, the café had been essential, but Tom carried guilt that he should not. It angered her — as though his loss was the greater.

~ I bought my first Japanese car. I still don't feel safe though it is economical. And then this wilderness that is Henry's cottage — this is where he was, alone and for so many years. I try to understand what induced him to come so far. Of course he did not choose to train here. Somewhere up north — Western Springs they said. But he did choose to return. One day I will retrace his steps.

I wonder whether I am being punished. Yet it is diminishing though I still cry. Not since I was a child have I cried so much and I wonder what is happening in my head.

July 12

A small entry: Today I began the jig. It is looking good.

So much for resolve! Tonight I cooked two lamb chops, mashed potato, kumara and some green beans. 'Kumara.' What a splendid name for such a splendid, sweet potato!

I also cut myself. I am far from adept but it is early days. Lost a little skin but it hurt. I am unused to being hurt and not having anyone around. It was a sharp reminder of my isolation. The dog licked the wound dry.

I wonder whether a large meal of meat causes the dreams? I had pork last night.

July 18

I need to talk about my great accomplishment. I am building a dory. I never thought I would. Luke knew that. All those years and he knew. How I would turn back the clock. And yet I truly didn't have the time. Now, here, where the sea is so rough I would never dare to launch anything, I am building the boat. What for? I think he knows.

I am remembering 'Mike' and 'Doggitt'. Luke peering at me as serious as life and telling me how he and Mike and Doggitt could see the lions and giraffes in the undergrowth. And me saying I could see them too and him simply being pleased that we had shared this moment. And me wanting to squeeze him to death and laughing inside fit to bust.

He talked to them for years! How I miss that. How I miss that. Can you hear?

July 20

I went to a small timber yard in New Plymouth and the yardman knew of a dory! They are seldom seen here and yet they were the mainstay of the fishing fleet from Maine to Newfoundland. I imagined they were everywhere.

Now I have timber and tools! Who would believe? I can check any angle. I have tried many corners in the cottage and not one is square! And the 'plumb-bob'! There are no vertical walls in this cottage. The mysteries of construction revealed!

July 21
I have completed the jig on which the boat will be built in an inverted position. It is a very important structure. The plans are etched in my mind perhaps never to be erased. I do not remove them from my table because I need to 'feel' my way into this thing. They looked like another language with their lines and tiny annotations, as if prepared by someone who wanted them to be incomprehensible. But I eat on them, read next to them and watch them go yellow in the sun.

My drive south was my first adventure away from my retreat. I cannot deny the nature of my reclusive existence. I remembered little except for the methanol plant — surreal this jungle of pipes and smokestacks, perched in the midst of verdant pasture beside an expanse of ocean. Why did they do that?

I have to concentrate to keep left. This is a quaint custom and seems illogical. And while the traffic was light, nevertheless the road is narrow most of the way and one passes other vehicles perilously close. Someone blasted me with a horn and gave me the well-known international salute.

I ignored this intemperance.

'Just like me.' Mary smiled as she recalled.

~ I saw a herd of cows on the highway! I drove very cautiously and was rewarded with a symphony of flatulence such as I have never heard!

New Plymouth goes on for ever. Tiny shops and quiet as a churchyard. But then what is Mokau? What is my cottage out in the forest? I am truly in the land of peace and tranquillity. I spoke to an elderly man who fought in the Second World War and who knew many Americans at that time. But he did not know of Henry.

The air is so clean! I could see to Mokau. The white cliffs reflect the sun and look most striking. I should acquire a camera.

I was glad to return with my load of lumber. The boat builder at large!

July 25

I planned to start on the frames today but it is raining again. The dog is wet. I don't know what he has been doing. Later, I will say something about him.

All right — the dog. He is big and dark brown. I think he is sort of Labrador and something else sneaked in the backdoor. His ears are floppier. His eyes are almost black and I would be willing to make a small wager that he has limited English. He understands 'food', 'swim' and 'working', and there is no question about 'walk'. However, and I believe this is evidence of a cunning mind, he feigns ignorance of 'fuck off!'

I have named him Chinook — after the wind. He lives in my back porch, which is where I found him. He was not well but has since become very healthy. We have taken to exploring the valley in which we live and along the coast on the beach. He knows every tree and stone, and revisits each one as we go. When I work on the boat, he lies near and watches or sleeps. Though when I say 'sleep', he remains alert. I have to be quick to snatch whatever stick he happens to be treasuring! He has a big thing about sticks. I know that's a 'dog thing' but with him it's more. Like a chimp with a banana I would say. I have concluded the stick is not simply a brainless and frivolous diversion. The sticks are often larger when he is hungry. Or when he is feeling aggressive. This may result in an insight.

I am living alone! I have to say something about this. I nearly failed but I reminded myself that this was my uncle's home for thirty years. I am astonished to have discovered the old guy had a Maori wife though she died young. I imagine his last years might have been dreary. I wish now that I had known him.

This place spooked me. For days I jumped if I heard any sound — a mouse (and there are a few). When there is no moon I cannot see my hand and everywhere there is the menace of trees. Beyond my little clearing there's an impenetrable wall of vegetation. It would be intolerable without the sea. I sing 'Rocky Mountain High'.

At night the forest creeps closer and I hear birds mostly, though there is a furry animal I now know is a possum. It makes a horrific noise that sounds like strangulation. One jumped on the roof and created for me a defining moment! I realised that it was an animal but when I found him with my torch I was not reassured. I did not know whether it would be carnivorous (they are not). But they are a substantial size of an animal.

I have noticed I have begun to talk to myself. I expect that is natural enough. Sometimes, though, I am mildly embarrassed.

It has stopped raining.

August 4

My track becomes dangerously greasy in heavy rain. This morning I attempted to drive out and slid into the ditch. After a major effort involving my spade and pieces of wood I am proud to record that I extracted myself. Then I fell and my pullover has become impregnated with clay. Exercising discretion I retreated to the safety and comfort of a hot bath. I never had a dog and I have no association with one so big. The Chisholms' corgi hardly counts. Chinook is a proper dog with big limbs and teeth everywhere though he is quite gentle. I buy him Tux biscuits on Melanie's recommendation.

It is not an easy thing keeping one's mind on brands when she is helping though she is surely good branding for the store. I think Merle finds that a mixed blessing! From a marketing point of view, I would say Melanie is worth her weight in gold. I have made unnecessary trips and bought a variety of useless goods. I have a sink plunger, a lantern I do not know how to use and worst, FOUR packets of chocolate macaroons!

He is very clean which is another thing I like. I don't know where he shits but it is not on my grass. I am very tired today for some reason.

Aug 7
I woke last night on the grass with no recollection of getting there. But the dog was with me. A truly crashing headache today and I would gladly trade my head for a baseball.

Aug 10
Screw the boat! I cannot build. Why did I think I could do this? Who is the condescending ponce who designed this thing? What is a 'rocker'?

Gunwales and shores and scarphs! Archaic terms designed to exclude. I was so pleased when I finished the jig but now I am seeing it is rudimentary compared to what has to be done. The step between understanding plans and making wayward bits of timber come to look like they should and be the right dimension is huge.

I am beginning to dislike this place. Dark trees and a stupid boat. Human flotsam washed up here. Cannot get John Denver out of my head!!

Experienced a pronounced fit of ill humour today that caused me to hit the boat with such force that I broke the handle of the spade and drove a splinter into my hand! The object of my aggression, though, was barely damaged! In fact, the whole thing barely quivered, giving rise to elation and dancing on the grass — Luke and me. The boat is much stronger than the appearance of light frames would suggest. I have reread the use of 'shores' and know now where I goofed. I am resolved to try again.

Went to town for supplies. Merle is as sweet and straightforward as a child. She has lived here for years and knew Henry reasonably well. He kept to himself and I gather tended to associate with his partner's family mostly. She said he was 'a man of few words'. So in that respect, I guess we're not very similar.

Little by little I am beginning to see below the surface. She said some things are not so good now: some division in the community — between Maori and Pakeha. That is the native word for whites — Pakeha. I am trying it on. Maybe it is simply the outcome of different people struggling to get along or maybe it is more? She is not an analytical thinker and I have insufficient information. Or interest?

I was also given a long introduction to Herbie though he is dead as a stone. I do empathise though. Memories can be as much a hazard as a source of pleasure.

It is exactly ten o'clock and I don't know what day it is! Only a few months ago I would have been in the office for three hours — and here I'm sitting on my front porch, looking out to sea like some old mariner and eating my breakfast. I never ate breakfast! But now I take an hour sometimes. Muesli, toast and jam, and coffee mostly though I may treat myself to eggs and bacon from time to time. I watch birds fishing. They're called gannets which is a daft name though I think we exceed that with 'boobies'! Diving into the sea from a great height, their vision must be truly extraordinary, and their skulls! They deserve a more edifying name and I think to call them steeleyes.

They remind me that I should try to catch a fish. There is a rod here and some hooks. I will try one of these days, off the rocks at the end of the beach. It is too cold to swim. I wonder what it will be like in summer? But I doubt I will be here then. The Reids' home is on a 'No Exit' road. 'No Exit'! I wondered whether it meant I would not be allowed to leave!

The house itself is charming. It is a 'colonial villa' and has a wide porch on three sides, several gables and ornate filigree around the upper edges of the porch. Inside, huge drapes and old-fashioned carpets that still look great despite many years.

The most beautiful piano and several pieces of furniture that I could have coveted at one time. Such a contrast to my own residence. My dog box!

My fellow guests were the Watts, Taylors and McCleods. All very nice people who made me feel most welcome. In fact I have been offered similar hospitality at all three homes, so I may need to commence a social diary as well. They are farmers and are surprisingly informed.

The Watts, like the Reids, farm on the coast and the others are in the river valley. The dairy cows tend to be in the valley and the sheep are raised on the coast.

No one knew Henry?? They knew of him but were not acquainted! I do not understand how that can be in a community so small.

We talked about the States and I felt keenly how much I would like to be home, though I appreciated their warmth and hospitality.

Coming from a country so large I have never given much thought to the fact that for these people every sneeze in the US in an economic sense must seem like a tornado! I was embarrassed to learn of a tariff on New Zealand lamb. Perhaps when I return I will call my congressman.

It was difficult telling these people about Luke. They were sympathetic but I don't want to talk. I have been offered horse rides should I feel so inclined, use of small 'quads' — a type of mini four-wheel farm machine — and free range over the farms.

After dinner, which concluded with a superb sticky date dessert, we talked about Mokau. This is less the agrarian paradise than I had thought. 'Pakeha' is not a well-liked term and theft is common. John Reid catalogued losses that he totalled at thousands of dollars. Jocelyn said there is a 'handout mentality' here. I said that this is not an issue restricted to New Zealand.

They spoke of someone called Pagett. He has land near to me and apparently is intent on clearing it of forest. I expressed some concern but they said it was some distance off and would not affect me. They also said there is a madman who has shot a number of cattle beasts on Pagett's land. I said maybe the land was better left as forest, but this was not well-received!

'Maoris don't think like us!' An interesting proposition but supported by numerous examples. They do not understand economics (who does?), technology or development. What is the issue here? Are they children?

I returned to my humble cottage after midnight and slept better than I have since I arrived.

Today I ventured around the headland and discovered another bay somewhat larger than my own. It is completely forested and is less steep and I am resolved to explore it properly. I have also spied a tree of huge proportions near the back of the valley that may be a hundred feet high and several feet across. It is a giant among trees! Strangely, there is no other like it anywhere in the valley. It is a patriarch. Why it should be so distinctive is a mystery but whatever the reason, I am captivated. It has much vegetation, it appears, hanging from its limbs. Almost like clothing. It is a complex tree. When I compare it to conifers or cypresses they are like a flute to the orchestra. This tree is a symphony with not one part the same as another.

Is it Luke's? He talked many times of the Normus Tree where he and Mike and Doggitt went. And of the flying elephants! Perhaps I have found it. We must go together. It is surely the Last of the Mohicans. I will call it the Mohican.

The lines in the drawing were fine and deliberate, with elaborate shading to give depth and texture. She could feel the power of the tree even as it had affected him — a truly grand tree of unfamiliar construction and not in the least bit symmetrical. And she marvelled as had he at the hanging gardens on every huge limb. It was easy to imagine many creatures making a home in that profusion of growth.

'Where is that tree?' she asked him one time, and Luke rolled his eyes as he brought it to life in his mind and pronounced in the most serious and deliberate way that the Normus Tree was only where he and Mike and Doggitt went. 'That's where. Only at that place.'

'Maybe at the Botanic Gardens?' she prompted helpfully. But he shook his head emphatically. 'That's not the place. It is a long, long way away.' And he stretched his arms out and pushed one way and then the other, 'And you can only fly there.'

She glanced at the drawing and imagined Tom sitting alone as she now was, thinking about that little boy they loved so much but who was gone. But that was when he was so little. He had nearly grown up. What happened in between? Did he lose him so long ago?

'We're all alone. All alone,' she said softly and had to stand abruptly and walk the room, blinking furiously and peering from the window into the morning.

On a ledge next to the stove sat two tins, unmarked but soon to disclose loose-leaf tea and ground coffee. She had never known Tom to drink tea.

A small cupboard under the sink yielded a coffee plunger and a small quantity of ancient crockery. She turned on the element, filled the kettle and then studied anew the plans for the boat. More alive now they seemed, more real and even comprehensible. As though learning of Tom's work imbued them with meaning, hitherto unseen meaning.

~ Today I met some less desirable locals. I returned from an expedition into town to find a carload of youths on my porch! They were pretty drunk. Said they always drank up here. I said not any more and was abused. I threatened to call the police though I can't get any reception. In hindsight, I regret being so peremptory but their presence disturbed me much more than I might have imagined. They left but didn't take their empties.

I think I might like to meet them again in more suitable circumstances. We have not gotten off to a good start.

Nonetheless, I need to install a gate. I don't like the notion that anyone can simply drive down. I will investigate.

Aug 21
The weather has deteriorated again and the wind is ferocious. It woke me with its howling and the panes rattle like mad tympanies. Cold rain is coming in sleety showers off the sea and beyond occasional glimpses of white and grey I can see nothing. The flax thrashes and sounds like a frenetic machine but causes the wind to veer so I get less of the blast than I might. The chimney leaks too, though I guess it doesn't matter much.

It is ideal weather in which to paint. So many years but too busy then. Too busy for anything and anyone. And she gave me these paints! The irony. I'm sure she knew.

I am painting the estuary at the river mouth from memory. I don't care much about literal accuracy for it is the colours and texture that intrigue me. When I arrived I found the way things were — like the colour of leaves and the forest, and the sea and the clays — were intimidating. As though the landscape was saying, 'Go home, you who do not belong.' But I have persevered. Now, I am painting what it is I feel about this place. It is wild and raw and I'm still afraid (perhaps that's the wrong word) of the forest.

The estuary is quite beautiful but not in a classical way. It is brooding and a violent mix of light and shade, black and whites and greens. I am intrigued by small brown boys playing at the edge. It is easy to imagine times long past when they were the only inhabitants? They appear quite primitive as though out of time. I wonder what they do? I have yet to speak with one. They are Maoris.

Chinook came back during the night. I truly wish he had been here when I was invaded. I wonder where he goes. The rain has stopped and the wind is dropping. There is even a hint of sunshine though it looks ill, trying to sneak through low, roiling clouds.

I will see about a gate today. I have nothing to purchase but I might call at the store. I am sure I can find some useless article.

My garden is planted. I hope it is warm enough now. Nineteen sunflowers along the side wall. One for each year, one for me and one for Mary. I hope he likes them.

'Oh!' she cried, and ran to the window, and there in the morning sun, gently waving on slender stalks, a row of gold. Through the front door and almost falling from the porch she ran, around the side of the house and almost into them. Her hands extended to feel the rough stem and then the flower. Moving right to the next and the next, caressing petals and laughing and crying.

~ Aug 24

I have seen the madman! Even now, here in my cottage and after a drink and some food, I feel disturbed and I know it has tempered my desire to explore. He is a Maori. He did not see me but I saw him. He is big and wears a ponytail.

So that is where he is — in this dense forest. We set out this morning for the Mohican and got perhaps halfway when we heard the shot. A cataclysmic sound such as I have never experienced. And then the beast!

We didn't see it clearly, but it was red or orange and huge. We saw part of it through the undergrowth from no more than thirty yards. Crashing through the trees, branches and whole trees even, snapping like pretzels and this orange monster smashing its way down the hill. What a terrible thing! We held the dog and didn't dare move, but Chinook? Utterly nonchalant as though a bird had flown by instead of a monster in its death throes. His attitude gave us fortitude. And then, through a tiny gap and only for a split second we saw the madman. I am confident he was unaware of our presence.

The crawl home was excruciating. Creeping and creeping. I said this is how it must have been in Vietnam. Anyway, we are sure we do not want to get any closer. Luke said he was like Geronimo. I am wondering whether to inform the constable.

But if this is Pagett's land it is only a valley away! If it is the same land it also contains the Mohican! What to do?

It is under way — the gate. Ham Skinnard will build it. A bucolic fellow with a truly ancient beret that might be grafted to his head. I met him in the 'pub'. Not lucid exactly but I think we understand each other. I felt I was inspected and found wanting! I don't think I will mention that I am a creative director. How would I know what sort of hinge a gate needs?

He was insistent that a galvanised steel gate would be best. I was equally insistent that timber was what I wanted. I told him I liked the 'aesthetics' of timber and he replied that he didn't care if I liked the way it looked! 'Steel's the trick,' he said, and I said not this time, and he said, 'It's not keeping up with modern times.' This from a man who has no phone!

The pub is not too good. Everyone smokes and the conversation is not deep. I talked Harleys with a guy called Harkness. Due principally to the extent of my knowledge and interest, this conversation did not last long.

I was informed about the All Blacks. I felt it reasonable to assume this was a Maori team but met with raucous rebuttal. It is mostly white! I will have to read about them, or better still, I could watch a game. I have seen games being played on a field nearby.

I determined that 'whitebait' are tiny fish with an eye as big as their head. They bung them in a sort of omelette and that seems to be a big deal around here. I will ask my friend Merle about this.

It was hard to warm to Harkness. One of those sour types with the worst perspectives on everything. And the foulest mouth I've heard in years — maybe ever. If he removed the expletives, he would say maybe a dozen words of English in an evening. He spent some time making out with a woman called Trixie. I think she flirted with me. I was fascinated and repelled.

I asked about Pagett's land and no one seemed certain where it was but neither did they care. They said it was his business what he did. I am unsure why I am concerned as I do not expect to stay. I hardly feel like an 'owner'.

I wonder who the madman is? I wonder what he thinks he is

doing? I am perturbed at the notion that he may actually be nuts. That could be dangerous. And yet, I have this sneaky sense of sympathy. It is troubling.

If you are here, you cannot be gone, Tom. I have you here, and she hugged the book to her chest under fiercely crossed arms but it was not sufficient. With sudden and the most vivid clarity she saw him deep in the sea and grief rose like lava.

A blackbird dropped from the trees and prospected, its beady eye cocked as it listened first with one side and then the other. Hopping along the line of the flax and stopping suddenly to commence a furious digging that resulted in a short but inevitable struggle with a worm. It looked at her as though it spied a rival, contorted there on the sofa ready to leap and it fled with a shrill cry.

I must go into the village, she thought. I must do something, and wiped the eyes that burned.

4

'MURDERED? SHOT?'

'HELL!'

The ceiling fan with one twisted blade made its rhythmical whunk, whunk, whunk and barely disturbed the mushroom of cigarette smoke over the group perched around the end of the bar. It was a bombshell such as few had experienced. Not some newspaper report of a remote incident, but Jim Harkness bursting through the door and shouting, 'There's been a murder!' And all unable to speak at first, then a babble as they tried to find out who and where, and then silence.

'Murder?' Whispering and heads shaking in utter incomprehension.

'Home invasion ...' said Porter.

'Home invasion?' echoed Terry Cotterel. His glass missed his lips.

'Why Pagett?' said someone, but received no response.

'Hardly knew him,' Derek said.

'Good bloke though?' And they tried to remember.

'What's home invasion?'

'Don't you read anything? Shit!'

'But murder ...' It was difficult to catch anyone's eye.

'And a drowning ...'

And they all wondered what was happening in this place where big news was the whitebait run and the beach horse race.

'And shot?' Each one trying to imagine the horror of a shooting and the savagery of a bullet in a man's kitchen.

'You only know the half of it.' Turning towards Harkness, whose eyes gleamed with the light of dark satisfaction. 'Matarangi says it's like a meatworks up there. Dead animals everywhere, he said. And pigs getting fat on the carcases.'

'Queer.' And they tried to imagine the dead lying on the land like a battlefield. One of them said it was probably robbery. There could have been a lot of cash, he said, but Harkness said it was something else, then made them wait.

'It's about that kid,' he said. They were unsure about this but

Harkness reminded them. 'I think so,' said Harkness evenly, and despite their doubts they had to agree that he might be touching on something and they felt uneasy. 'But there's more … evidence.'

'Evidence? What?'

'Matarangi said something was written … in blood.' He enjoyed their stunned expressions. 'Yeah. Written in his own blood — on the wall …' And his voice dropped to a whisper.

'Jesus!'

And the babble rose while Harkness sipped his beer. He placed the pint glass down as gently as if it had been gossamer.

'Matarangi said it said: "For the love of Mary".'

Voices rose as one, then subsided. 'I don't know any more about that than you but I can make an educated guess. That's what Matarangi read and that's that. But if you put a few things together you start to get a picture. Like, that's an expression that's to do with the Virgin? Well, who would say something like that but some bastard has a serious issue with Pagett? Like Mahler, for instance …'

'But maybe it was Pagett himself …'

'Matarangi says it was written by someone else.'

'How would he know?'

'He was there.'

'But what's it mean? Why would anyone say that?'

Harkness frowned and sipped from his glass. 'Why would he say that, Terry? Why would any insane bastard say anything? But think about his hobbies …'

They sat thinking silently until Derek said: 'If he was molestering, he might sort of try to justify it in the Lord's name? Like priests?'

'Now you're on to it, Derek. See?' Harkness gleamed with satisfaction. 'Only the bastard's gone and drowned himself. And why? Remorse! And that poor prick Pagett has paid a horrible price for having his son molested.'

'Jesus.'

But the one called Porter was dismissive. 'It's nothing to do with that prick. Simple prick just drowned. It's the other thing, ain't it, Gert? It's the burn-off. It's utu.'

'What about the boy?' she asked without looking at him.

'Don't know, Gertie. Don't know,' said Derek.

New pints were placed on the table.

'Thanks, Pluggy. What? You think it's revenge?' Harkness considered this. 'By crikes, if it is there'll be hell to pay. Hell to pay ...' and Harkness switched horses as easily as a champion jockey.

'Queer anyhow — that Mahler. Playing around with that poor little bastard.' Derek laughed uneasily.

'He wouldn't be the first,' said Gertie quietly.

'Like putting it to young Melanie?' Porter sang her name.

'Like you'd all like to if you had the chance.' She rose and collected her flax kete.

'Seeya, Gert.'

Whunk, whunk, whunk.

GERTIE Ngahere blinked in the bright sunshine and started the long walk down the road. Bowed forward and with a brown shawl pulled over her head to keep the sharp rays at bay, but enjoying the smell of the summery hay and the hum of bees in the clover.

Gertie was tired. Not physically tired but the bone weariness that comes from depression of the spirit. Pulled down to the ground by a murder and the loss of a little boy. Then the drowning of a man she thought was much more good than bad. But she didn't know Tom Mahler well, and what of that boy? Not a whole lot either, and as for Pagett? What was the Lord thinking? She terminated this blasphemous thought abruptly and determined to put the horror from her mind.

She decided to stop at the creek for some fresh cress, to go with the sweetcorn and some fine new potatoes from her own garden, with a roast leg of mutton. That's what her boys liked. She glanced at some wild blackberry on the road cutting and saw there were many berries but they would not be ripe till March. Hard and green they were and not yet enticing to birds or people, but soon ... Maybe she would make a pie anyway. Perhaps an apple pie with some ice-cream. That would make those brown eyes pop!

Pausing in the shade of an ancient puriri, with its dark, wrinkled leaves and papery bark. Red berries were falling and a soft plopping sound alerted her to something high up in the branches. She shifted a little and spied the brilliant white breast of the kereru. Gertie watched for a few moments and remembered the taste of that fat pigeon with warm appreciation. Back in the time when many fed in the huge puriri and the feathery miro — back in the time when they had preserved those fat birds in skins of bull kelp — but not now. There were so few and they were protected. That was sad and good.

Things past ... things like kereru and plump running weka. Things like feasts for visitors and singing and games. Even when Gertie was small there were still feasts and games for visitors coming up the coast. But not like the old days, her father told her. Not like those days when the tribes still held together and mana was great.

She sighed and started on down the road. The sound of motorbikes made her pause and she felt the shockwave as they passed. Some of those from up north who were living near Betty's, and him with a cross tattooed on his cheek just stared at her and then gone. She waited until the noise had faded.

That Porter was not a good man, she reflected. But nor was he bad, though he liked to be spiteful at times, so much so she thought she might not drink there any more. But maybe he was right? Who could tell what some young fullas full of drink or what else might have done? Many had been angry about the burn-off. She frowned under her old brown shawl and shrugged those thoughts away too.

What had they done to Pagett? She shivered and stopped and became aware of the skylark hovering far above. 'What did you see, you little bird?' She nodded knowingly and moved on, her flat shoes padding soft grass. Shot that man. That Pagett that had that young woman way back. Came and went and who could blame her? Stuck with that Pagett but left that little boy. She shook her head and wondered about a woman who could run off from her little boy and leave him with a man like that. Like what? Just a man. Just another man working on the land. Mean spirited, some said, but who was to say? Maybe just lonely? Alone all these years with just that boy.

She clambered down the thin track through the swishing green rye with long ears beginning to ripen and carefully laid her shawl beside her kete. Removed her shoes and tucked up her floral skirt so it would not get wet, then waded into the clear water, gurgling over grey stones and as clear as light. Picking some crisp cress and placing it in the grass at her side, and looking up the creek to see the long-legged bird peering back at she who was intruding in its home here among the cress and reeds. 'I don't want to eat you, you old pukeko,' she managed a chuckle. She remembered eating that fowl once upon a time. But she had all her teeth then.

Flicking white tail moving away up the creek bed out of sight, like that little boy with his white hair all over the place. Whitest she'd ever seen in her life. Like that pukeko's behind it was and flicking about just the same. Going here and there. Always going somewhere, as though searching and searching for God knew what. 'The Walker Boy', that's what her boys called him. He came home once or twice but he didn't speak, not a word. Never a single sound when Gertie asked him would he like shortbread but he ate it just the same. And those blue eyes staring at her and at Bill.

Not that his soundlessness bothered Matty and Jake. They went eeling with that Walker Boy, sometimes, up the valley. They talked enough for five! They said the boy was 'as fast as a weasel'. They liked him but it seemed they met more by chance than anything. They just happened to meet him down on the beach or up the valley by the river or across at the dam. Then they did things together for a while before the boy wandered off. But he didn't come into the town much except to go to school.

She gathered her cress and placed it carefully in her kete, pulled on her shoes and replaced the shawl over her head. But that Pagett — he hardly ever came into town at all. Cannot remember even the sound of his voice, she thought as she climbed back to the road. What did he do up there? No folks around — just a few animals and that little boy? It wasn't any wonder he was just walking all over. And now where was he? He might have seen his dad shot dead. The thought made Gertie's lip tremble and she blinked as she looked out to sea. Surely not? That would be more than any child should have to bear.

She heard a car slowing and then tires on the gravel crunching along behind. Creeping up on her. She turned to see a red car coming almost to a standstill a few paces back and then accelerating in a jerking fashion until it was beside her. The nearside window wound down and the woman leaned across.

'Can I give you a ride? I'm going into town ...'

Gertie didn't know this person but she liked her face and her feet were weary.

'Thank you,' she said as she climbed in, holding her kete on her lap.

'I'm just going into the village. Is that where you are going? Oh!' The car leapt forward so Gertie's head jerked. 'Sorry! I'm not used to this.' The woman was flustered and glanced at Gertie apologetically as they proceeded along the highway. 'I have to remember about your road rules.'

And Gertie knew who she was and was troubled. 'My old legs get tired walking across the road these days. Too old, that's the trouble all right. Soon I won't be able to catch my boys before they get out the door. I'll need a crook.'

They drove into the main street and Mary slowed. 'Where can I drop you off?'

'Oh, anywhere will be good. You just stop wherever you want.'

'I'm going to the precinct — the police. Over there.' Her face was pinched and Gertie could see a lot of fighting going on in that face and she felt a deep sorrow for this woman.

'I don't know that you'll find anyone there. I think the constable may be up the valley. I think he may be somewhere else. We only have Constable Buchanan in this little place and I think he has his hands full right now ...'

Mary still held the wheel and stared straight ahead. 'What will I do?' she whispered to herself.

'You look like you could use a cup of tea. Why don't you come home to my place and I'll make us a cup of tea and we can see what we can do. My name is Gertie. But if you would prefer not, well, that's all right.'

Mary turned to her passenger and looked at her for the first time. She examined the dark brown eyes surrounded by myriad wrinkles and the lips that were almost mauve, lifting into a warm smile. Mary could not check the tears that were welling. They streamed down her face and tickled her neck but she did not care, and when the old woman placed her hand gently on her arm it was as though she was touching deep inside her and her whole body began to shake.

'I'm sorry, I'm sorry.'

'It's never no mind,' said Gertie gently. 'Never you mind. Why don't we drive down the river? That's where my old house is and we'll see what we can do.'

Mary dried her face with her handkerchief and drove as she was directed. Happy not to have to make any decision about anything. Happy just to have a companion.

'TOM sat right where you are and sang. You know he sang ... now what was it?'

'Not "Rocky Mountain High"?'

'Yes! That was it, and very good too.' And they laughed sitting there in the sun with tea and some sweet apricot biscuits. And Gertie was careful not to talk too much but she instinctively knew this woman would want to hear about that poor man.

'Go away, you boys!' she remonstrated with Matty and Jake who loitered at the end of the verandah.

'He sang Rocky Mountains,' said Jake and glanced at Mary. When she smiled he continued, 'He's Painter Tom.'

'Go away,' Gertie repeated, 'I'm telling you if you want your dinner.'

'Don't send them away,' said Mary quickly. 'Why do you call him that?'

The boys immediately came closer while avoiding Gertie's glare.

'Cos he painted all the time. In our class he was always painting. He ...'

'He drew more like,' interjected Matty. 'He drew stuff, like horses and animals and trees and skypokers and all sorts of stuff.'

'I know, that's what I was saying. He drew all the stuff you could think of. Frogs ...'

'Yep, his frogs were good.'

'And his horses and elephants.'

'Yep!'

Mary felt light as she imagined Tom in a classroom with these boys and other children. It was an image that was totally new and yet was immediately among her most precious. 'He talked about a boy called … Sean?'

'That's Walker Boy. That's who that is. He's our mate. We do stuff with him.'

'Yeah, we catch eels and stuff. He's pretty good,' Jake nodded gravely.

'Perhaps he lives around here?'

They shook their heads and Gertie interceded. 'No, Mrs Mahler. That boy lives up the valley.' She glared at Jake but too late.

'His dad's been killed!'

'Jake!'

Mary dropped her cup and it broke in several pieces on the verandah planks. 'I'm sorry,' she said quickly.

'It's nothing. Just a bit of old china. It's nothing at all. Here —' and she gestured at the boys. 'Pick up these pieces and do something useful,' and they saw that this was a time to do as they were asked. 'They're such bigmouths — yes, it's you I'm talking about! Go on with you and be hoping your dad doesn't get to know about all your mouthiness.' And the boys retreated inside with the broken crockery.

Gertie glanced at Mary and could see she knew some things but far from all. But nor do I, she reminded herself. Who knows? There's a murderer out there and we don't know. She shook her head and the blackness she had experienced at the pub returned. 'It's a very bad time, Mrs Mahler.'

'Please call me Mary.' But neither spoke for some time. Then Mary said: 'Was something happening …' She broke off and placed her head in her hands, her nails digging into her forehead. 'What I mean … Gertie … was Tom accused of something here?'

She looked up quickly and found strength in the warm expression on the old woman's face, but no answer. 'Do you know what I am referring to?' Gertie nodded slowly in response. 'I found this note,' Mary continued, 'in his cottage. It was horrible. A horrible thing and it said — it accused him of something monstrous that I simply don't believe … but why? Where did it come from?'

Gertie looked up into the sky and seemed to reflect. 'Maybe I have an idea about that but then again maybe not. Some things have been said that shouldn't be said. That's how some folks are. And your husband, well, he was not from around here and some folks have some difficulties with that. Yes.' She nodded slowly to herself. 'He was different from us. He's American ... but it wasn't that exactly ... I think some people found him hard to understand. More than old Henry. Old Henry, well he was a mechanical man. He made things work and he was a no-nonsense sort of man and that's what folks can understand. But your Tom ... he was sort of refined. He was a painter. That's why those foolish boys called him that name. He was a painter and maybe he was a bit stand-offish. Folks don't understand that so well.' She continued to nod gently, looking up into the sky.

'But this wasn't about being stand-offish, Gertie. This was something else. This was about ... children.' Her voice choked on the word and she was afraid when she saw no change in the old woman's demeanour.

'Yes. I understand what you're saying. I understand that thing.' Gertie pursed her lips and glanced slowly around the verandah and over her shoulder into the hallway before continuing: 'There are some mean folks that think Tom was messing about with that boy. There, I've said it, though God knows I don't want to and I never believed it for an instant. But some folks have that sort of a mind. They're not the best sort of folks but maybe they're just sort of jealous, or afraid. Yes. That could be it. They were afraid and jealous of your Tom. He just came and was living away up there and then he got near to that boy and that was good, but some folks look at the world in a whole different sort of way than you and me.'

'But surely?' Mary cried, hotly shaking her head. 'That's evil thinking. Is that all it takes? To become friends with a little boy?' She stared at Gertie so hard the old woman put out her hand and laid it on her own. Mary flinched. 'Is that all? Gertie?'

'I'm going to make us another cup of tea.' Gertie stood. 'You stay there and enjoy this sun. I'll be coming right back.'

And a grey heron flew on by, going up the river with its long legs trailing like straw and its neck tucked up, and across the river a cow cried out for no apparent reason and Mary liked that sound. She was calmed momentarily: being told what to do by Gertie here on Gertie's verandah in this strange land. She could hear the old woman talking to her boys out the back and soon they came running around the side of the house and cast curious glances at her. And one of them gave her a quick wave so that she impulsively waved back and they shared something in that moment that she liked. Then they shouted loudly as they ran out the gate and down the road.

'I'll be the first. I'll be the magic boy!'

'Nope! You'll be last!' And their voices trailed off as they dropped out of sight down the riverbank.

'They're the noisy ones all right,' said Gertie as she returned to place a fresh cup of tea on the arm of Mary's chair.

'You're very kind.'

'Ha! That's not what those boys say when I'm on the warpath! But I have to be or else they would be getting totally out of control.'

They sat and sipped their tea and Mary experienced an unwelcome apprehension. 'You need to tell me something else, Gertie. You're not telling me everything and that's maybe because you think I might not handle it too well. But I need to know everything.' She looked steadfastly across the river at the meandering cow that resembled, curiously, the one elk she had ever seen.

'That's a curious thing. That's a curious thing in my mind. To know everything. Sometimes it seems the only way and other times it seems the road to nothing. Only the Lord knows everything, and the bits we know, maybe that's all he wants us to know because we're weak things. We truly are. But ...'

'I only want to know what happened to Tom. And you haven't told me enough to account for that.'

'That's the truth! That's certainly the truth.' She looked at Mary. 'Now, when I say this I want you to understand that I don't have all the facts. I only know what some folks have been saying ...'

Mary nodded. Gertie sipped her tea, then put the cup on the verandah boards. 'There's two things that seem to be something about this, Mary. There's this girl, here. Her name is Melanie and she's a fine looker of a girl. She reminds me a great deal of the girl who old Henry up and married many years ago. And that girl, well, she is like a flower around here and you know what a flower is attracting ... and so she does. But she wasn't interested in these boys around here — most of them good for nothing and layabouts but not too bad. But that's how it is. And then here comes your Tom ...'

'We divorced many years ago, Gertie.' Mary heard her voice harden involuntarily. 'So, is that it? Was he having ... an affair with this girl? Ugh!'

'Ah, well, I don't know the answer to that. According to some folks there was more going on that just some talking. But that's not my business and not theirs either — but that's how some folks are.' Mary nodded and they sat silently.

'You said there were two things.'

'Ah. And so I did.' Gertie looked truly uncomfortable.

'Please tell me.'

Gertie sighed deeply, and then said, 'We have a good man here who is the constable. He's a good man but not a Frank Sinatra. Not a Dean Martin, you might say. He looks out for my boys and stuff like that and makes sure they get a clip behind the ears when they play hookey. And they are needing that. That's what Mr Buchanan does. And he's been good when things have got a little touchy between folks from time to time. Yes. And that Mr Buchanan is engaged to our teacher-lady. That's Beth, and she's a fine young woman. She's a fine teacher-lady and we're lucky to have her here. Yes we are ...'

She paused as a car drove by and she returned a wave. 'Well, the fact is, Mary, that folks are saying that your Tom has stolen Beth away. And I don't know the truth about that either, but I do know that Mr Buchanan has been looking like a dog bit a part of him he would not want bit. There — that's all I'm knowing.'

Mary sighed and massaged her forehead. At last she said, 'I'm not greatly surprised by what you've told me, Gertie.'

'Ah. Well, some men are like that. And your Tom? He's a good looker and he's interesting, being American and all those things, and a painter. And he's a bit mysterious and that's always like a honey pot for some women. But that's not his fault and I don't blame him for anything like that. That's just Nature.'

'Maybe. But you're saying Tom has made some enemies here? I can see how that could happen.' Gertie nodded and they sat silently for while.

'And now what are you going to do?'

'I'm going back to the cottage,' said Mary firmly, and was surprised at her conviction. 'I have things to think about and anyway, I need to wait a little while ...'

'Yes. Well, you know that if you want to talk at any moment then you can come here. And if you want to eat something, well, you don't even slow down but come right here to this house! Even if you want to sleep.'

'You're so very kind. I feel so lucky to have met you —'

'Ha! That's not what my boys are thinking when I catch them with their hands in the pantry.'

'They're good boys.'

'Tell me that when they're late for their dinner. Ratbags!' And she gave Mary a hug on the steps.

MARY stopped by Superior Merchandising and purchased a frozen steak, some bright apples, green beans and potatoes. 'If I can do anything, Mrs Mahler, you just let me know,' Merle told her and refused to take any payment. Mary then proceeded to the police station and wrote a note to the constable.

I wonder what I'm doing? she asked herself as she drove back into the coast hills towards the red cottage. And she thought about Tom and the girl Melanie and the woman Beth and that made her angry.

* * *

'THIS IS UNBELIEVABLE, Buchanan. Didn't anyone know?' Detective Sergeant Andrew Barker gestured with disgust.

'No, sir. He kept to himself, and as far as I know, Matarangi was the first to come up here.' Barker turned from Buchanan and spoke to one of his CIB colleagues about the requirements of the house search.

Buchanan recalled Mahler shouting: 'It's a charnel house up there!' But Buchanan didn't want to know anything from that bloody Yank.

'I called for a bulldozer.'

'What?'

'I called for a bulldozer, sir, to clean this up ...' He gestured at the carcases.

Barker looked like he might bite: 'You will cancel that then, won't you.' His voice sank ominously lower, 'Because we need a bulldozer like we need a bomb. Everyone who needs them will be issued with a mask. Get some Vicks!' He turned away.

Buchanan waited uncertainly, like a little kid. He should have been here as part of the CIB squad. Instead this bastard lectured him because he had driven his car up to the house. What the hell else should he have done? 'Freezing the scene means freezing the bloody scene, not driving all over the evidence!' Barker had articulated as though his audience was retarded. The arrogant bastard and now he was ripping into the young detective in charge — the OC Scene — because Barker had just learned that the pathologist was on vacation.

'Well, find another one, Milligan! That body is melting!' Barker turned to Buchanan. 'Show Milligan where you and the guy who found him have been. Where you walked, what you touched. Try not to increase the contamination, would you?' And as an afterthought, 'And where is he?'

'Sir?'

'The Maori who found him. Where is he?'

Buchanan felt the heat rising. 'He's gone back. He had a load of animals ...'

'You let the guy go home — to where?' Barker stepped into Buchanan's space. 'I suggest you get him back here right away.' He said quietly, 'I don't care where he is or how many animals he's got. I want to interview that man today. Do you understand me?'

To his immense relief Matarangi was little more than an hour away. 'Sure, Mr Buchanan. After what I've seen today, man, my game's just rubbish!'

'Got him,' Buchanan said to Milligan and motioned the detective to follow him towards the house where he pointed to where he and Matarangi had walked or where they might have touched something.

'His bark's worse than his bite.' Milligan nodded towards Barker who was apparently locked in debate on his mobile phone. 'But he's a good cop.'

5

~ Sep 5

I am still shaking. He ran straight in front. I wasn't looking. He ran after a ball and I turned when I heard the woman. I saw his eyes. I saw inside him in a split second. Right inside his head. I saw Luke. There in front of my car. His eyes so wide and his mouth a perfect 'O' and there was my little boy. My Luke. Who am I? What am I? I know, a dog. I see the faces of people who greet me and I know them not and they not me. Merle says hullo to whom? Who does she see? Does she think I am normal? That I hide in these foreign hills and build something that will never float? Yes it will.

The teacher said I was lucky! Lucky? Lucky that I might see the death of my little boy? Thank God he's safe. The Lord? Thank the Lord? Thy bloody will be done!

Mary shut her eyes tight. Then she reluctantly examined the crude drawings. Of eyes wide and bits of faces, mouths agape, head turned, hair flying forward. The pen left deep imprints in the page.

Recognised the frail figure with its arms outstretched above its head and a look of such desperation. Like the body, twisting as it ran. But surely it would fall? Not looking where it was going. Just running.

Did Luke, she wondered? Did he see the truck? Probably not, they said. The truck driver said the car veered so quickly there could not have been time. He did not have time. It just happened. All so fast. He must have fallen asleep, they said. It was a terrible accident.

She placed her hands on the page, touching the strange image with her fingertips, and could see Tom now, in their garden with Luke. Under the chestnut, holding Luke and spinning in circles around the lawn. Both laughing joyously and little Luke's pure white hair streaming like a halo in the golden sunlight. She felt a warmth flow through her hands, through her chest. She allowed the warmth to flow into the figure. 'I am with you, Tom,' she murmured, and she felt stronger. She opened her eyes and turned the page.

~ I am feeling so homesick. What a feeble word! How childish. But I have been here four months and suddenly it seems an eternity. I am simply staying alive. I eat and sleep. I fool around with the dory but progress is slow. For every advance, I make two mistakes. Sometimes the day seems it will never end. I lose track of the hour and the sun does not move.

I am thinking about home so much lately and it hurts. I think about the office and my colleagues. Gerry, that pain in the arse. I love Gerry. And Jill? How she looked after me — protecting me and Gerry too. I miss her flowers and the coffee. I am missing many clients. Donut Harrison. If ever you could prescribe the perfect client it would be he. And I miss Mary. All three of us, in those faroff days. And whose fault?

The writing stopped and there was a substantial space before the next entry, as though something was to be added, perhaps at a later time.

'You bastard!' she said out loud. 'Whose fault?'

She rose from the couch and stepped onto the thick kikuyu, enjoying the feel of the springy grass on her bare feet. She walked to the shelter where he had constructed the dory and the jig with its rough sawcuts and protruding nails. A few creamy wood shavings lodged where the wind had not been able to carry, and the square. She felt happy suddenly to find this tool, rusting already in the grass but just as he described, and she imagined him checking the angles in the cottage.

'You built a boat?' And she shook her head in admiration and bewilderment. Here, under this rough iron roof held by four knotted posts. She stroked the smooth silver wood and thought about him labouring for many days. Labouring for many weeks amidst bad weather and frustration at his lack of skill.

But the afternoon was warm and calm and she felt drowsiness like the humming of bees in the bushes with their tiny white flowers.

I'm so tired, she thought, so tired, and she carried the book inside. Perhaps just a little while, she thought as she lay down.

THE sun had moved far out to sea and the light was softer when she woke. She sat on the edge of the verandah and watched a trail of tiny ants emerge from a crack in the boards and disappear down another. She became conscious of an expanse of ocean such as she had rarely seen. Blue water stretching without end. By comparison the lake was a mere pond and yet it had seemed infinite when she was a child. Yachting with her family on Michigan. Picnicking. Friends ...

I will bathe, she thought suddenly. Henry bathed here, and Tom. I can bathe here, and she suppressed her immediate distaste at the worn enamel of the ancient bathtub, and found cleaner and cloth in a bucket behind the door. Undressing on the cracked, mouldering linoleum was not a pleasure, but lying in the deep tub of steaming water was bliss.

The sun touched the far horizon and fired a glittering beam across the sea and up the hill to the cottage. The yellow light illuminated the dust and cobwebs of decades on windowpanes of wrinkled glass. Wrinkled glass and dusty, unpainted boards. She wondered whether any inhabitant of this unworldly refuge could not go mad.

~ The gate is finished! Ham has done a fantastic job. He brought a young guy with ears like a wingnut. They worked all the day and concreted the posts and erected exactly the right sort of wooden gate. It is so robust. And yet it swings with just the slightest touch. Silent as a hawk it swung, and bang right in that dog's arse. He actually looked embarrassed! I am sure he understands the concept. That dopey grin, and he won't look at me.

I have put a lock on the chain. It will be much less convenient but on the other hand I feel I have 'secured' my retreat.

It is the valley of the Mohican! How far? Perhaps two miles but what if a fire got out of control? Should it happen anyway? It seems anachronistic that anyone should be clearing forest, but then, is it? It is his land after all, and I have no notion of whether I have any rights in this. I am merely a visitor though the thought of that tree being felled or burned appals me. Am I being sentimental? I need to think some more on this.

This has surely been my most eventful day! First, I encountered the madman properly. If coming face to face in so strange a manner can be described in that way. I was about to return home when he approached from the bay to the south, striding towards me in a long coat and with his hair loose, black and wide across his shoulders. He is tall and seemed to flow as he walked. I prepared myself for a meeting and continued across the rocks towards the sand.

And his face — below one eye there is a large black mark. If I used one word to describe his appearance, it would be 'warrior'. I felt a little menaced, but without cause since he walked past me as though I did not exist. I was a mere coincidence and he ignored me, and yet when I say that, to be ignored implies one has been noticed in the first place. I do not know that he ever saw me!

When I realised he was not deviating I did not move since he would pass a good ten yards from where I stood. Closer he came, and I thought to catch his eye. I even started to raise my hand in greeting but somehow it seemed a ridiculous gesture and I allowed it to fall.

And Chinook! Not a sound. Not a hackle raised — nothing! Just as it had been in the forest. He seemed completely comfortable with this strangest of interludes. In fact, as the man progressed towards the far end of the beach, never looking back, the dog had already begun to amuse himself with seaweed. I am considerably puzzled.

That was the signal event and indeed it has seldom left my thoughts. I am no longer alone in my valley. I am sharing with a lunatic! However, in the end there was nothing about his demeanour or deportment that suggested hostility. I am unsure what steps to take, if any.

Recording my first fish seems an anticlimax, though I was wildly excited at the time. My first 'casts' were disastrous. I could not get the sinker more than a few yards away from the rocks and at one point had a considerable mess of nylon on my hands. But when I managed a quite respectable cast, the line was only in the water a few minutes when I got the most terrific tug and then what a battle! Unfortunately, Chinook had a fit and at the penultimate moment, when we could see this beautiful fish in the pool below — disaster! The idiot crashed me off the rock into the water. It was awful! So cold!!! And I couldn't see with the water stinging my eyes and the dog scratched me down my neck and chest with his claws. I didn't drop the rod though, and when I managed to pull myself out, at the cost of scraped knees and elbows, I still had it firmly grasped. And … the fish was still on the line! So, the fishing expedition was a success and a mess! Luke said he was just a dog and we should forgive him. I suppose that's true.

It looks a lot like a salmon but it is a kahawai. What a beautiful name for such a beautiful fish — kahawai. I am not sure I pronounce it correctly, but it sounds good to me. I have said it several times today and I will do so again. It has a huge eye, large scales and the body is silver and streamlined. There were little greeny dots on the side but they have faded.

My cuts hurt and woke me in the night. I made ample use of the antiseptic and that seemed to fix things. The unforeseen hazards! I did not go back to sleep for a long time. I had a very clear image of him striding towards me and away and I wonder whether I should feel insulted or grateful for his complete indifference. By the time dawn came, I felt relaxed again. For reasons I am unable to crystallise, I do not feel afraid.

Today I described Chicago for Melanie. She can think of little but how and when she will escape Mokau and is not charitable in her views. It's the curse of small towns for those with bigger horizons. I told her this.

She hates everything! Her stepmother, neighbours, boys, her life … I realised that my lot is not so bad. At least I am doing what I like?

But she is unusual and would never fit in this tiny community. She is half-caste and it would be hard to imagine a finer outcome though her eyes are almost too large. She has the thickest hair I've ever seen — long and jet black.

I think I am an 'exotic' presence. She talks to me about dreams and desires that she appears unable to share with her friends. Or maybe she does?

Naturally, she wishes to act. I told her the road to Hollywood was paved with misery. She just laughed. It would not be like that for her. She was too tough, she said. She mimed herself making a sale — she is a talented girl.

Also this morning, I washed my clothes. I do this by hand in the two concrete basins in my back porch, stirring the garments by hand and wringing them repeatedly. I am reminded of women on the banks of the Ganges. Here am I, creative director Tom Mahler, of Sturgess & Linkwater, handwashing my laundry in ancient concrete tubs!

Sep 16

I find it difficult to shake the idea that I am the first on this wild coast. I walk the beach below my cottage and mine are the only footprints at any time. I am Crusoe! Can there be anywhere left on earth where this is possible? It is peculiar that in this small country (that is nowhere near as small as I had thought) one can be lost in such a wilderness.

I love to explore the rocks. Soft blue and brown rocks with mussels. Has anyone ever picked them? God, how strong is their attachment! I guess they have to be. Most of the time they are subject to a wild battering from huge and relentless green waves that bang and bang. And how sharp the barnacles? My arms are covered in cuts and grazes I did not even feel. I intend to steam the mussels with a little wine and garlic. I will report.

But the sun is so warm and the air so fresh and clean! And the silence no longer disturbs me. I think I would find the clamour of downtown a painful and intolerable intrusion! Ha! That is how I am adapting. As though a switch has flicked in my head. I am feeling excitement and the urge to explore further afield. I am marvelling at all this.

I do not want to call Gerry.

A splendid day in my garden. The sunflowers are bright. Chinook too interested in my weeding so I was finally obliged to hurl a pot of cold water but he merely laughed.

My bubble burst. I am not the first. I have found two caves, and in the caves, drawings — or carvings. Glyphs is the word that came to mind. Cave drawings nonetheless. Of feet!! Very peculiar in that all the drawings appear to be of feet, only with a varying number of toes. Some three, some six, one with eight!

But of course mine is an egocentric view. Perhaps it was Henry passing the time. Merle described him as 'eccentric'. I am suspecting now that she was charitable. I ponder the meaning of the feet. What did he wish to depict? Or, if not him, who? Maoris perhaps? Maybe these are an important archaeological find? I am wondering whether to report it to someone. But who?

I hate this place. I hate this tin shed with the ghost of a madman I never knew. Have I wasted so many years? Have I wasted something more precious? In the mirror I fear I see the worm of self-aggrandisement.

To walk into the forest, perhaps into the sea and never to look back, but I have not the courage to do even that.

The dory is the thing. When it is finished I will leave. I am here for a reason and it is to build the dory lest I fail this last test as surely as I failed the first. Tomorrow, I will redouble my efforts.

I wonder whether it is saleable? This wasteland in the name of Mahler.

Sep 23
Progress! I have clad one side of the boat and I feel powerful. We all do. Chinook knew too, forever helpful, digging me in the leg with his sticks. He appears to think that if he has a stick in his foolish mouth, that he is superior to me.

It is not easy. I am sure that a large sheet of plywood was not intended to be cut with a handsaw, though I have done it. Securing the planks to the frames was one of the most nerve-racking things I have done in my life! At first they appeared too large, and then as I clamped them to the frames, too small. But finally, I got each one nailed, and with the exception of a small gap that I can fill with glue, it is near perfect. Ha!

I gave Chinook the steak I intended for myself while we ate a large can of salmon with potatoes (mashed) and green peas, all washed down with an excellent local chardonnay. Mildly drunk. By nine we were well-matched.

I discuss many aspects of the cladding with Luke and that is helpful. Now that I am resolved on my Purpose, I am finding we are enjoying each other's company all the more.

But my back! I am conscious of my back in ways I have never been. I do not imagine for a moment that the solid, competent boat builder in my book ever feels this way.

The pig is large and black and runs helter-skelter down that valley and it knows I am watching. Banging recklessly through the wire fences and ramming trees. It ran at me but then lay at my feet, looking up with its cunning eye. It is not a relationship I want. If I could only kill it.

I was obliged to visit the village this afternoon and was pleased to find Melanie in residence. We talked animatedly for perhaps half an hour. That surly fellow Harkness came. She said he fancied her. She said all the men did. I asked her how she felt about that and she just shrugged as though it were the most natural thing in the world and said they were all 'losers'. Except for me! Ha! She said she would come to visit — to inspect my project. Well, I daresay I would take a break from my busy schedule to show her around the boatyard!

Two more planks secured on the dory. It is beginning more than ever to look like a boat! Indeed it begins to resemble the illustrations in my book. Luke says I should be the 'motorman'. He said he would be the sail trimmer. I don't have plans to put a sail on her so I will have to burst his bubble. He can row.

My interactions with Melanie remind me strongly that I am not a natural celibate. I am tired of this abstinence. I do not believe it is either natural or edifying.

The sunflowers are two feet tall!

Mary closed the book in her lap and remembered. She remembered the good times when he had clambered so impatiently — in the early days when it was a shuddering affair of no finesse. But that had been fine — she had been just as needy. She remembered the times he had pulled the car over on a country road near her parents' home and they had run into the trees, half undressed before they had found a place of concealment. So many years ...

~ Tomorrow, we will try to catch a fish.

Too windy. It blows and blows so that at times the sound from the cracks in the iron seems like the voices of Hell!

Instead, I baked my first loaves of bread! The dog has eaten most of one and I have had three slices. It is more a wholemeal brick and he is not looking good. I let it rise twice but I wonder whether it was sufficiently warm? The temperature has dipped again and I am back to having a fire.

A fire ... For a moment she was home. Home in the kitchen of the big old house where no floor was even and everything was finished in dark polished timber and whitewash. Where a fire burned in the kitchen grate all the winter and neighbours called by with a jar of preserves or a smoked trout and always a little gossip.

She stared into the grate where the paper ash lay black tinged grey, and wished it were a cold day.

~ I set up my easel and eagerly awaited the bell that heralds the children spilling across this small field. There is a rope trapeze out of a large tree and today I watched a small boy in crisis. Perhaps it was his first time for he hung on the edge of the platform, petrified, and despite many exhortations seemed neither able to jump nor to return to the ladder. Maybe he slipped or was pushed. It is possible. He shouted all the way down as though stabbed.

I spent the remainder of the day in town. Bought a sunhat with a wide brim as I can feel my face starting to burn. I did not see my friend Melanie but I did meet Pete Lynch. He is a farmer up the valley. He told me that if I contemplated buying property I should be careful. I said I already owned property and mentioned my recent encounter in the forest but he did not appear interested or maybe he didn't understand? He didn't have much time for Trevor Pagett, he said, but if the man wanted to clear some scrub, well, that's what he should be able to do. 'Clear some scrub …' An innocuous expression that sounds increasingly to me to be no less ambiguous than 'surgical strike.'

There is a row of tiny houses by the river that look very poor. As far as I can tell, they're all Maori. They do not look particularly friendly, though I guess they just ignore me. I wonder what that piece of land means to those people. Surely it is even more remote from them.

I treated myself to an afternoon pint and introduced myself to a group of regulars. Gertie (a Maori!), Derek, Terry and Porter.

We talked about home and Mokau. It did not last long, though I liked Gertie. She knew Henry and told me to stop by.

Derek has the most angular features and is altogether one of life's unfortunates. I wonder why some can be genetically blessed and others more like unsuccessful experiments. His hair sticks out and he has tufts protruding everywhere. His eyebrows are like feather dusters. But when he laughs there seems a light inside and I quite warm to him.

Porter I did not like. Where Derek's laugh redeemed an unfortunate visage, Porter's seemed malicious.

Terry is at least seventeen stone! When I was introduced he shook my hand, somewhat bashfully, and caught my eye for a split second only. But my hand disappeared as though up a drainpipe and was clamped so that I had little hope of retrieving it until he released me. One might have expected he would be the natural leader in this or in many groups, but the opposite appeared to be true. When he spoke it was mostly to agree with someone else. And he agreed with them all.

I am sure I was studied. Two or three times the old woman caught my eye and I think we exchanged a 'secret' smile! She lives down by the river and did not appear the least bit primitive.

The dory is fully clad! We marvel at the shape. Sometimes we kick it just to feel the strength. It is like steel. We are very pleased with ourselves. It is truly a pleasure to sit on my porch with a glass of wine and to admire my handiwork. Luke wonders whether it will be possible, somehow, to launch the dory upon the sea but I said we'll take it to the river.

He says it will need to be painted red. We argued but he is insistent! Once I would not have given way so easily. This is how I am changing.

Melanie will cut my hair! Even if she gives me a 'Number One' I am sure it will be a pleasure.

Oct 5
Strange things are happening in the life of the 'American hermit'. The teacher is excited by my painting. Her name is Beth. She teaches everything from math to art — only she knows nothing of art and has asked me to help! I left my easel and accompanied her to her classroom and was at once the object of the most unabashed scrutiny. After observing them for so long, it was I now who was the exhibit.

They have been studying the wetlands and were representing their discoveries. I saw creatures that would terrify the strongest man — frogs and birds that more resembled the inhabitants of nightmares but comical too. Penelope introduced me to her family of frogs. All riding bicycles and each with a hat. For sunburn!

I can't say I helped anyone in the slightest.

I am looking forward to my haircut.

We have had a glorious spell of spring weather. Hardly a breeze, warm and a cloudless sky. And I have used a spokeshave for the first time. What a splendid tool! I wish my father could see. I wonder why he never used tools. When I think about my youth it seems to me now that we lived a cosseted existence. We read, he played music and we visited friends in similarly cultivated surroundings and went to church. Perhaps his profession had something to do with it, though personally I know many lawyers who I don't think are as austere. On reflection, I feel I did not know him well. I think that was why I wanted so much more for Luke and me but then what did I do? Almost the same goddam thing.

I see I digress more often than not. There is no discipline! But so what? Perhaps I might wake in another time and place. I feel anything is possible.

What a day! Asleep on the front porch and woken by Melanie. Staggered to feet, missed footing and fell onto the grass! Oh, the great creative director! Then suffered the double indignity of a face licking by the idiot dog.

She had not the slightest hesitation about invading my premises, or thought for my sensibilities. My dirty laundry scattered about my bedroom and dishes yet to be washed. But she loves the dory and my sunflowers.

I sat on one of my kitchen chairs, out here on the porch, admiring a view without peer while she used scissors and comb on my unruly locks. I told her she should think about attending a drama school of some sort. She said there are two or three here so that seems a good start. I think that this at least is good advice.

I made a superb whitebait omelette. Like a local! An old hand, or a loquacious host on a culinary show. Today more than ever I was reminded of how it is to have company. She mimed. The 'schoolmarm' and 'the drunk' are brilliant.

I walked her to the gate where she had left her motorbike. A dirt bike she called it, and I told her any time she wanted to call she was welcome. I could see she was pleased.

I am still distracted. Went for a long walk on the beach and threw stones into the sea.

Mary frowned at the drawing. From behind, a thick plume of straight hair that if an accurate rendition must be magnificent. A long, slender leg, outstretched, unconnected. She turned the page.

~ What do I expect? With hair like snow and blue eyes exactly the same. He did not see me and nor did he do anything. Not speak to anyone and nor did he address his paper. So much activity all about but he just stared at empty paper. What could he see?

Despite the temperature his feet were bare. But his demeanour — utterly motionless with his head in his hands. All around him wriggling, talking and laughing and him like stone.

I asked him what he was going to draw and a boy announced, 'Sean doesn't talk.' Sean — so alike and yet not.

I told him I believed there was something in his paper waiting to get out and I drew a running horse. I drew the horse with eyes so large and its mouth open and mane streaming. I told him the horse was running to escape the mountain lion. I asked him whether he could see the lion — said it was indistinct to me — I suggested it was camouflaged. But there was nothing. What do I expect?

Beth said he is mute and his name is Sean Pagett. Strange ... he is the son of the man who owns the land next door. The domain of the mad Maori. Strange that this boy ... like a wraith, wandering the district. Over farms, up the river — everywhere — nearly always all by himself. Sometimes with the Maori boys.

I want to help but do not know how. What do I expect to do? I returned to my painting but could not concentrate.

I called Mary today. From the top of the hill and left a message. I wonder what she will think. I had fifteen messages! But I have responded to Mary alone. For some reason I feel the others are not real.

Mary stretched her neck and rubbed her eyes. I'm trapped, she thought. I'm trapped in Tom's head but I don't mind. I don't want to be anywhere else.

She rose and refilled the kettle and then, yielding to hunger, unpacked her groceries. Thinking about the boy as she sliced vegetables, imagining how it must have been. This boy that he referred to in the letter — that he likened to Luke, she mused. What had happened? Did he become confused? Were you so lonely, she wondered, and bit her lip.

She recalled the little Maori boy's remark with sudden clarity. 'His dad's been killed.' An accident presumably, she thought, but how horrible. Is this what life really is? Is it little more than endless suffering and misfortune with a few short interludes of happiness? Would I be happy to have Luke back? To have Tom back? Yes, Oh yes!

She realised she was looking unconcernedly at a mouse under the chair in the corner, with its tiny bright eyes and twitching nose, advancing, retreating and advancing.

Does that mean, she wondered with a jolt, that I might never be happy again?

* * *

BILL DID NOT struggle long.

'I'm tuckered out! Get off!'

'You're the giant!'

'And you're the chimp! Get off! It's been a long drive. I've been all the way to Te Kuiti.' He released Jake from a headlock. 'Is your auntie in?'

They squirmed from under their large father and sat panting from their exertions.

'Yeah! But let's wrestle, Dad.' Matty launched himself at his father's head. He batted the boy aside. 'Goddammit! Aren't you listening to me? What about Mr Mahler? What happened today?

'Nobody's seen him.' Jake climbed over his brother to stare into his dad's eyes so their noses near touched. Bill calmly pinned the other boy beneath his leg.

'Quiet now, boy. Let me hear.'

Though he squirmed unsuccessfully, Matty competed with Jake to tell how they had searched all day but no one had seen anything.

'Maybe he was eaten by a shark!'

'That's no way to talk. That's a very bad thing that's happened.' Bill clambered to his feet. He glared and they hung back until he had gone inside. 'That's very bad news, Gertie,' he said. 'No sign of that man. That's bad and I liked that fulla.'

'Us too. We like him, don't we, Matty?'

'It's a bad thing,' said Gertie quietly.

'He showed us how to paint and stuff.'

'Painter Tom! That's what we call him.'

Bill helped himself to a beer from the fridge. 'We're nearly out. I'll stop by the store tomorrow.' He flicked the cap at Jake. 'Maybe I should go down to the beach.'

'You could, but there's folks been down there a long time now and it's nearly time for tea. Maybe you should go after.'

'Everyone's been searching. They all know we were the ones who seen him!'

'Go outside. I don't know about all this, Gertie.' He sat heavily and watched her, quietly efficient — graceful — at the bench. 'One day I'm talking to that man and he's saying he'll come to see me up the road and now this. It don't make sense to me at all. I wonder who's looking out now. I wonder who's looking about the place and seeing who might be needing help.'

'The Lord is looking, Bill Manuhuia. What do you expect? You're just a common-garden man!'

He was surprised by her vehemence. 'What did I say?'

'It's worse news. It's worse.'

'What is it? What's happened?'

She dried her hands on her apron and sat down across the table from him. 'Trevor Pagett's been murdered. Yes, he's been murdered in his house — up there.' She nodded towards the hills. 'He's been shot.' Bill opened his mouth and then closed it. 'I heard this morning,' she said softly.

'Murdered?' he whispered.

She nodded. 'That man Mahler drowned and now this. Joe Matarangi found him.' They stared at each other for a long time.

'Who did it?'

She pulled a face of incomprehension and opened her hands.

'Good bloody grief,' he said quietly. 'Good bloody grief.'

'I don't know. I just don't know ... you got a smoke?'

He rolled her a cigarette and passed it across the table, then made another for himself. They smoked in silence. Then he said: 'That bushfire ... that was bad. I wonder ...'

'Well don't!'

'Gertie,' he chided gently. 'You know what I mean. Some young fullas might have gotten something stupid into their heads. You know what I mean?'

She ground the butt in a paua shell. 'I know full well what you mean and I don't believe it for a second. Not for a second! Not you or anyone with a sane thought would do that! Not anyone I knows around here would have done that! That's wickedness beyond anything I've ever heard. I don't even want to think about that thing.'

She seemed to be struggling with something inside. At length she looked up and said: 'They're saying something else. They're saying that Joe saw some words there written with that man's own blood.' She sighed deeply. 'They said it was written on the wall and it said, "For the love of Mary".' She watched him closely.

'Man alive! That's what it said? Man alive.' Bill shook his head. 'What's coming on?'

'And I met Mary Mahler,' she said flatly.

6

'DID YOU HEAR? Someone's topped that bastard Pagett.'

Saying it out loud like that was strange. It sounded crude and inhuman and she wasn't impressed with her choice of words and yet she found she savoured the sound. Peta Patai studied her partner's face, but with characteristic, sometimes infuriating, implacability George didn't miss a blow with his mallet. He did not even raise his eyes from the carving that stretched four metres across three trestles.

'Is that so?' he said.

'Is that so? Is that so?' she mimicked him. 'You big smart prick! Did you hear what I said? Well, I don't like anybody dying —' She paused abruptly to contemplate that too — a heart stilled and a brain turning cold and meaningless as deep stone. Then she tossed her head. 'But I don't feel much sympathy for him.' She walked to the open door that looked out across the gleaming Tasman Sea. 'He was shot.'

She raised her arms above her head and closed her eyes. 'I should feel horrified. I should feel stricken, George.' He didn't reply and she continued, 'That a man's been killed right here in our valley. Someone who's lived here for so many years. Eating, thinking, fucking even. Must have. And then someone has taken it all away ...' Her voice trailed off as she tried to imagine that moment when death visited Trevor Pagett. 'He was a boy once.' She frowned at this thought and shook her head involuntarily because she could not tie an image of Trevor Pagett to boyhood.

'He has that boy. What's happened to him?'

She opened her eyes and turned. 'I know. That's bad. They don't know where he is. There's talk about him and Tom Mahler but I don't believe that shit! You know the media will be here?'

'So?'

'So? Why don't you come out of your trance just once, George Ngataki, and recognise an opportunity when it smacks you in the face. The media — probably television — and here in Mokau! That is an opportunity. This is a chance to tell people the truth.'

'Which is?'

'Which is that Pagett is not an innocent victim. That what people around here think about him is bullshit. That what he did is just an extension of the bullshit that has gone on here for a hundred and fifty years!'

George straightened slowly. 'It would be best, I think, that you do not refer directly to Pagett. I never liked what he did, but I'm sure he didn't deserve this.' She considered his words and found nothing to dispute. 'What did happen?' he asked.

'I dunno. That guy Matarangi who drives a stock truck found him. Been dead for a couple of days they say. Now the cops are up there. It's all sealed off. Whatd'ya think?' She walked past him, not waiting for a contribution. 'Shot dead. Man, that's bad! That's a bad scene, isn't it, George. Bad! Well?' She spun on the balls of her feet, her bare arms buried in the pockets of her khaki overalls.

George frowned and rested his mallet. 'I think,' he said so slowly she wanted to leap at him, 'I think this is going to be a difficult time.'

'Difficult!' She pushed near to him and stared up into his face. 'Difficult! More than before? Is that what you mean? More than with him burning our ground? More than having the land stolen from under your nose? What's more difficult? Tell me that!' And her dark eyes sparked with indignation.

'A man's been killed.'

'Many men have been killed. And many much less deserving than him! All over this coast — all over this land. Don't tell me about one man! Don't tell me about one man who ignored all of us and just went ahead with his evil.'

'I'm not. But he's dead now. Just over there.' He nodded to the south. 'And that's murder.'

She took her hands from her pockets and massaged her face. 'I'm getting all wound up. I'm wound up like a spring.'

'I know. And many will be. A man is dead and that's a time when thinking can be crooked. Maybe there's been some crooked thinking already.'

She cast an admiring glance at the big man with arms like hams, who was as gentle as a lamb. 'You think I'm stupid?'

'Not at all. I think you're a bit of an incendiary. But that's okay with me. Come here.'

'Think you've got the wood on me, George Ngataki? Have another think!' But she allowed him to wrap her in his arms, towering over her. 'Well, maybe you have. But there's no one else, that's for sure.'

'I only think how lucky I am to have such a talented ...' and he kissed her lightly on the nose, 'good-looking ... feisty ... woman.'

'You're full of bullshit, aren't you?'

'No higher than the top of my head.'

They stood silently for a time and gazed out the door, her with her back to him and not objecting when he slid his hands under her overalls.

'Cheeky bastard! Get out!' But she didn't move. 'Already people are saying it's a home invasion,' she said. 'Home invasion!' She snorted. 'And guess who the home invaders are?'

'Some brown fullas?'

'That's right! It's convenient, isn't it? But that's only part and you're right. There are some who think it's utu for the burning. Gertie said that's the gossip in the pub. Either that or Mahler — and he was no murderer. No suggestion the bastard's been killed by any number of the Pakeha he's probably cheated. Oh no, whichever way they look at it, this is a Maori.'

'I really hope it is not. I really hope not.'

She pulled away. 'Well, I'm not going to stand by and listen to that bullshit laid on my people. He did some bad things here. He wanted to hurt us and for some reason the bad has come back to him. Well,' her voice dropped, 'I bet the TV won't know anything about that land. They'll only hear about Pakeha afraid to lie in their beds at night and poor Trevor Pagett being an innocent victim. Well, they're going to hear the other side of the story.'

'How are you going to do that?' George took up his mallet and addressed the curious blend of traditional and modern in his carving.

'I'm going to wait down there until the cameras show up. Then I'll introduce myself.'

'I bet you will.' He placed the razor edge in the red totara and delicately tapped the back of the chisel. 'What about Mahler?' He didn't look up.

'Nothing. Louis said the boys saw him with the boat but he's not sure about it. But they haven't found him. That's a sad thing. That's a real sad thing. Those bastards have him to answer for as well. Louis's doing the rahui. There'll be no fishing on the coast for a time. And they'll hate that too.'

'I am very sorry about that. He seemed okay.'

'Yeah, well don't be forgetting it's the same where he came from — maybe worse. It's the common lot of indigenous people. The common lot. But he seemed nice. But that's a part of it, George,' she said reflectively. 'That's a part of it. People being nice while they get what they really want. That's the pattern.'

'Some of them are just plain nice.'

'You're a bit soft. But I know what you mean. I think I just get angry when I see how they will not accept there's more to it. Not even a simple acknowledgement. Steal the land then tell us to forget about it and get on. Get on!' Her voice was savage with scorn. 'Get on with what? That's all, George. A simple acknowledgement that wrong was done, but even that's too hard. Like those stones.' She walked out the door then came back in. He tapped at the wood unperturbed. 'Shame, isn't it?' she continued vehemently. 'We didn't just conveniently fade away, did we? We're still here like we've been for hundreds of years!' She kicked a hay bale and a startled bantam flew across the barn. Peta watched it exploring a dark corner, then she looked up into the gloomy rafters. 'But we were robbed blind while the missionaries were up our skirts. The bastards! Well, they have to face it. And I will make them face it.'

'You be careful. You got some work to finish yet.'

'You think it's coming along?'

'I think that sculpture will make the name of Peta Patai.'

She grinned appreciatively. 'You hoping for something, Ngataki? Well, you might get lucky. See ya.' She swung her hips provocatively as she walked out the door.

* * *

EVERY QUESTION FORCED him to reveal something that made him appear not just foolish but culpable. There was a boy, Buchanan told Barker, and no, he had no idea where he might be.

He tried to imagine what Paul would think, seeing his dad, the Mokau policeman, being interviewed like a suspect.

The boy's name was Sean and he was ten years old or thereabouts, but he didn't know much about him except he was mute. The schoolteacher, Beth Gilbert, was the one to talk to, he suggested, and knew his face must be that of the red-handed thief.

There were transients in the town, he hastened to tell them. Recent arrivals who he hadn't had the chance to get to know but nor had there seemed any urgent reason. He thought they'd come down from Auckland or somewhere and he had been thinking about going to visit them, and he agreed it would have been better to know what they were doing. They would catch up with them in the morning, Barker said, and Milligan affirmed he was working on the Area Canvas questionnaire.

Buchanan knew almost nothing about Trevor Pagett and silently cursed his complacency. Pagett preferred to stay up here on the farm and that was not so unusual, he said, though he felt now that the extent of Pagett's self-imposed isolation was. Then Barker was called away and Milligan said he needed to finish the questionnaire that his team would use in house-to-house interviews.

What did that weird message mean? Buchanan brought to mind the words smeared on Pagett's cupboard. '*For the love of Mary*'. That was a weird thing for the killer to write. They were speculating about some sort of religious connotation, though Barker wanted to know the names of every woman of that name who had lived in the district over the past ten years. Buchanan could bring one woman to mind — Mary McDonald. She had been a schoolteacher in Mokau when he first arrived but he knew she was dead. Died at least two years ago and never taught the boy. No link whatsoever that he could recall. But Barker hadn't assigned him anything anyway. He was redundant as far as this investigation went.

* * *

HE PULLED INTO the drive of his cream weatherboard cottage and turned off the headlights.

'That is not a good programme. I've told you that!' Buchanan switched off the television set, regretting his sharp tone. 'Have you had your tea?' The small boy nodded and looked at his father with big round eyes. Buchanan softened. 'I'm sorry I've been so long but it's a big investigation.'

'I told Miss Gilbert,' the boy said.

Buchanan turned away, and in the mirror above the mantle he noticed the darkness under his eyes accentuated in the dim light. 'What did she say?'

'Nothing.'

'Nothing? She must have said something — what?' He crashed into his favourite chair and pulled off his tie, laying it carefully on the arm. 'What did she say, Shorty?'

Paul cocked his head on one side and frowned. 'I think she said that was ... fine?'

'Don't be daft! Don't you listen to anything? How can you expect to grow up to be a policeman if you don't listen?' He drummed his fingers on the arm of the chair. 'Did she ... look different?'

The boy tried hard to figure what his father wanted to hear. 'Yes. She was different. She looked different.'

He nodded as though this was the correct answer, and they listened to the Molloys' dog barking, then he said: 'The Pagett boy, Sean — is he at school?'

Paul shook his head.

'Not yesterday?'

'I don't remember. There's lots of days he doesn't talk to me.'

Buchanan felt his unease return. 'He can't talk ... Shorty? When that man came to the classroom, the man who painted? You know?'

'Painter Tom?'

'Yeah. When he came. What did he do, exactly?'

'I don't know.'

'Course you know. Did he talk to you? Or to the other kids?'

Paul blinked and yawned. 'He talked lots. Me sometimes. Me and him talked about horses because that's what I want.'

'I know — but what about Sean Pagett? Did he talk to him a lot — more than you or the others? Did he ever touch ...' He stopped suddenly and bit his lip. Paul looked at his dad without the slightest comprehension. 'No,' Buchanan said flatly, and felt unwell.

'Dad?'

'Yep?'

'Sooty got runned over and I've taken him to the toolshed.' A tear rolled down the little boy's cheek. Buchanan lurched from his chair and embraced his boy, feeling the trembling.

'I'm real sorry. I'm real sorry.' Buchanan felt he was apologising for many things. 'Are you okay?' he said after a while, and felt the head nod. 'Shorty,' he said gently, 'what would you think if your dad wasn't a cop? Like if he was something else?'

There was a long silence, then: 'That would be okay.'

'Would it?' Buchanan gulped and forced his thoughts to clear. 'You want a story?'

The boy clambered quickly off the sofa and ran down the hallway. He reappeared with a thin book and sat next to his father. '*The Happy Prince*,' he said. 'Sooty liked this story.' Buchanan was about to ask him to get something different but stopped. The boy lifted his father's arm and placed it across his own chest then waited.

'High above the city, on a tall column, stood the statue of the Happy Prince ...' Buchanan read.

* * *

THE FLAMES FLICKERED in the dark like an orange star. Piled high were twisted logs and limbs that had been flushed from the hills by torrential rains and brought to the beach by westerly winds. Bonfires and picnics and fires for no particular reason — just to be near, even when the weather was warm. A fire in the night made a cocoon where friends could gather and exclude the rest of the world.

It was where Sly Harkness and his mates gathered many times. They brought a boom box and played SirMixaLot. Sly particularly liked 'Baby Got Back'.

He delighted in singing: '*I like em round and big! I'm long, I'm strong and I wanna get the friction on ...*'

And his best mate Napper would sing right back, *'I like a big sweaty butt, no bimbos, only flojos'*, and then they would join together and roar, *'She's sweat, she's wet and she's going like a turbo vet!'* And they would bounce their arses off each other to see who would hit the sand first. And it was nearly always Napper since he was half a head shorter than Sly.

And Mitch or Headcase would laugh and cry, 'Loser!' But they got sick of that too.

Mostly they wouldn't say much at all. Just drink and sit silently listening, and finally go to sleep on the sand. There wasn't much to talk about. Cars mostly, but they didn't have money. Just enough to keep the old Corolla in gas and they'd dump that heap if they could. They talked about jobs for a short time when Mitch got work at an engineering firm in New Plymouth but that didn't last long. He said it sucked. Working all day for not much. Crawling around the air-conditioning in old buildings full of pigeon shit. He said he told the boss what he could do with his job. He said he put sugar in the tank of the firm's ute. 'What happened?' they asked. Mitch said the ute blew up. 'Bullshit!' they said, so he threw a bottle onto the road to smash like glittering confetti.

But leaving Mokau — that was a good thing to talk about. Maybe for Auckland ... maybe for Australia. Just leaving this dunghole and never coming back. Maybe burning the school or something before they went. Sly told his mates he was going to Auckland soon. He had been saying that for a long time so they didn't take much notice any more. He didn't know how he would go or what he would do. But the idea buoyed him when he felt the hills crushing him with their dark, sneering silence. He told his dad he was going, and hated it when Harkness senior asked about where the money was coming from. 'Can't even afford a bus ticket,' his old man said. 'Whotcha gonna do anyhow? Fuck all.' And Sly told him, 'I'm going, that's all. The further the better.' He had said that five, maybe six times.

They talked about girls. Hoping they could get their end in and boasting. Pouring derision on anyone who made it with Patsy on account of her size. Probably you were in line after her piebald. They used to talk about Melanie Blackman a lot but not now. Sly reckoned he'd made it but the others didn't know whether to believe him or not.

They were dead envious anyway. She was so cool, with those tits and everything. Class. She had so much class. The legendary Bacardi bat. She wouldn't open for Sly, they thought, but maybe she had.

Sometimes they even talked about their folks, but not much because they were generally a pain big time. Sly's dad was a huge loser. He shouted at Sly about this and that, work and stuff, but what had he ever done? Drew a sickness benefit for some make-believe thing to do with his lungs. Couldn't even keep his mum home. Where had she gone? No one knew. Things were getting worse and even being here on the beach was pretty useless.

'Who brought the bourbon? Who's got my bourbon? I'll scrag ya, Headcase, if you've touched my bourbon   here, give it over.' Sly wrenched the bottle away and took a long swig. 'Man, that stuff's the best. I don't like whisky. It's utter crap! But I like this.' And he swigged heavily and pretended he enjoyed the hot burning in his throat because he knew no one else liked to swig on that stuff. He listened to SirMixaLot and sensed a kindred spirit.

'Far out, man, that spade's the shit of all time. Listen to that! "I like big butts!"'

And full of the need to distract himself, Sly hauled his trousers down and in the flickering light of the fire thrust his big white moons at his companions. 'Big butt, baby, I gotta big butt. "*Even white boys got to shout, Baby got Back!*"' And they laughed hugely as Sly collapsed on the sand and pulled his pants on. He suddenly felt talkative. Anything to fill the void in his gut. 'Man,' he said, 'I'm bored off my arse. And there's cops all over. Like a disease. And they won't find that prick. I'll bet they don't find no one.'

'The cops are dumb as. My old man says that prick is drowned and he did it. But they can't find him anyway. We should have fixed him.'

Sly regarded Napper appreciatively: 'Yeah. But I don't reckon that Mahler had the balls. I don't reckon he would've gone up there, to old Pagett, and shot him just like that. He didn't have the guts. Pagett would've hung him out to dry. I reckon it was some blacks.' He tasted some meanness. 'Like you, Headcase, a black like you!' But there was no response from Headcase who merely stared into the flames of the fire and nursed his beer.

'Hey!' said Napper, changing the subject. 'I saw a Charger today. Mint as. Orange with a black stripe. Those Valiants are the best. Be cool if we had one.'

'Yeah, it'd be cool. If you had any money but you don't. No one's got any money.' Sly was not pleased with this change of subject. He wasn't finished. 'Except pricks like Mahler. Comes from the States just to mess with little boys. Doesn't do no work or fuck-all. He had money.'

'Screwed Blackman. That's who she was screwing.'

A sudden silence, and Sly turned to stare dangerously at Headcase. 'What'd you say?'

'Just saying,' Headcase repeated mildly, but sidelong he watched carefully as Sly stood slowly and deliberately with his arms hanging loose like he had seen. He faced Headcase in the half-light of the flickering fire and thought about words. 'You can piss off, you brown arsehole. Now!' Keeping his voice low and controlled. He tensed his arms so he imagined they were like curved scimitars, and his legs were slightly bowed.

'Don't worry.' Headcase rolled over and wandered off into the dark. Sly had to straighten up because it was uncomfortable, and the others sat by the fire and nursed their drinks and were disappointed that nothing happened. And Sly felt even more dissatisfied. He wished he had hurt Headcase and lamented the missed opportunity. Even more he wished he had hurt Mahler. 'Little prick,' he said, referring to both, and flopped down on the sand. The whole thing was crap, he thought. But it hadn't been like that when Melanie was around. Things had been good when she was there. For the first time that he could remember, it seemed like. She knew some things. She knew about leaving and he believed her and secretly he had hoped they would go together. Things had seemed clearer or something. He shook his head. But then Mahler had come and she had gone. And he was right back and it was piss poor. Hanging out wasn't the same.

Then Napper said: 'Wonder what'll happen to it?'

'Happen to what?'

'The money. Now he's gone down?' They looked at him bemused. 'Mahler must have had money.' He repeated, 'Wonder if it's all in the bank?'

'Or in his wallet?' said Mitch quietly.

'Yeah. Like he could easily have kept some in his wallet rather than go to town to the bank all the time.'

'Especially when you live way the hell out there ...'

They lapsed into silence and pondered the implications.

'We'll go look. Just in case. We'll go look, tomorrow.' And he lay back and thought about Melanie Blackman and tried to decipher his anger.

* * *

RACHEL WAS SURPRISED when Pete said he was going to help her milk. 'No,' she said kindly, 'you stay in bed. It's Sunday!'

'So what?' And he insisted he was going to help. They were late but Rachel knew they wouldn't see the milk truck for four hours.

'What's gotten into you?' She felt surprised and pleased, and the sight of her 'girls' gathered near the gate cheered her too. 'My girls,' she called. 'See, Pete, my girls are all waiting patiently, aren't you?' She swung the gate. 'Come on then, hiiiyup! Hiiyup!'

Pete leaned against the rail and lit up, dragging deeply and squinting into the warm early sun. He watched his wife pushing the cows into the stall. He watched her firm behind beneath thin linen.

'There's my 144,' he said. 'I fed her from a calf, didn't I, old girl.' And he patted the nose of the big black and white animal and returned the docile, gentle gaze with untypical fondness. 'They're good old cows, aren't they, Rachel? Good old girls.' He lit another cigarette. 'What about Rastus? I must go see Rastus.'

He made his way across the concrete yard, struggling to climb the ancient, lichen-covered concrete wall.

'Rastus,' he called. 'Where are you, you fat bastard?!' There was an immediate oink, from beneath a battered sheet of iron leaning against the wall on the field side. 'What are you up to, you bloody ratbag? Come on out to see your old dad.'

There was a shuffling and the iron moved a little before a small, stout, black and tan pig staggered into the sun. It grunted with enthusiasm.

'Look at you — fat bugger, aren't you. But I brought you something.'

He swung his leg over the wall and dropped onto the churned clay that had set like rock in the summer dry. 'Here you are, old pig.' Pete proffered an apple, which was eagerly investigated and then not too delicately removed from his hand. 'That's my Rastus. You know who's your mate, don't you now? You know who rescued you. You'd be bacon fat now if it weren't for me. You know that.' He rubbed behind the pig's ears and patted the thick hairy back.

'Solid little bugger, aren't you? Like a barrel.' He stood and listened to the pig snuffle the remains of the apple in the grass and looked across the valley towards the Pagett farm. He could just make out a small group of people near the edge of the hill. The police were busy. It's not a bad view, he thought, and at the same moment realised that his perspective had improved because of the news he had received only yesterday. The hill had been 'cleansed'. Pete felt a momentary stab of guilt at the thought but brushed it aside. It was a fact. Pagett was an arsehole and he felt no compassion for his death. There was no doubting that his passing had lifted his spirits in a way he had not recognised until that instant.

He turned to the pig, which was sniffing his boots. 'We don't care at all, do we, Rastus? We don't care. In fact, we're pleased.' He grabbed the pig by both jowls to give it an exuberant shake and was bitten on the arm for his troubles, with sharp teeth and a small but powerful tweak of the pig's tusk.

'You bit me! You bit me, you bastard!' Pete lurched backwards and the pig peered shortsightedly at his retreating benefactor. He examined the slight wound and to his horror discovered the sharp incisors had drawn a little blood.

'Rachel! Rachel! The bugger bit me.' He climbed the wall and hastened to his wife who was engrossed in cupping the second run of cows. 'Rachel, the damned pig bit me, here.' And he thrust his arm towards her.

'Let me see,' she said soothingly. 'Poor old Petey, let me kiss it better.'

'I gave him an apple and then he just whipped onto me. He's got sharp teeth that little bugger,' he said proudly. 'Hey, what about a kiss?' And they paused to exchange a perfunctory, unpractised pressing of lips.

'Not now, Pete. I've got cows to milk.'

'They'll wait,' he said as he pushed his hand down her trousers.

'No, Pete, not now.' But she was giggling, 'They'll see!'

'They know what it's about,' he said, pulling her trousers to her knees, and she moved back to lean against the railing and undid his belt.

'You're not wearing underwear!' She laughed. 'You planned this.' And she felt happy, bucking about against the railing with the sun streaming down and the smell of fresh milk in the air. 'Come on then, you big brute, come on then,' and she applied strong, expert fingers to him and massaged like it was a teat. But Pete stopped rubbing her chest. Stopped trying to get his hand under her bra. Suddenly he was scrambling to pull his trousers up. She did the same.

'What?' She was alarmed. 'What's the matter?' Turning quickly to see what he could see. Four people walking across the paddock less than a stone's throw away. Dressed in dark, shapeless clothing with hoods covering their faces on this hot summer morning.

Pete jerking clear of her and hurrying to the concrete wall. Hesitating, then shouting: 'Hey! Hey, this is private property. Hey, where do you think you're going?' But it was as if he didn't exist, as if his call went up into the air and vanished. The four plodded on without turning, reached the fence at the same mechanical pace, climbed over with a squeaking of wires, and moved on down the hill. Soon they were out of sight.

Rachel joined him at the wall. 'They saw! How embarrassing! They watched!' She covered her mouth with her hands.

'Bastards! They're bastards. That's all.'

'Where're they going?'

'How the hell would I know!' He was angry at their complete disdain. 'They're the people you're always going on about! Walking all over other people's property. They're the ones you feel sorry for!'

And she felt shaken by their chilling silence.

* * *

'THEY'VE FINALLY GONE too far.'

'Who?'

'Those activists. That's what they think they are. But they're just criminals.'

'You don't know that, John. You're just guessing. The police don't know.'

'Don't be so naive. I've seen it a mile away, and ever since Pagett decided to do the burn-off it was inevitable.'

'But this is murder!' Prue Reid shuddered and thought of their three children safe in their boarding schools.

'Yes, it's murder. And that's what happens when you keep nursing grudges that have nothing to do with today and everything to do with some sort of misguided wish to turn back the clock! How many times do we have to be robbed? How much gear do we have to lose off the farm because no one will stand up and call it what it is? It might have been us — you know that?'

'I can't believe it.'

'I'm not suggesting it's all of them.' He paced the large kitchen where Prue made conserves from bright tamarillos. Looking down on the sea through ancient wisteria and a bed of orange and yellow roses. 'And the stock! The thing's got to be sorted out. Pagett stood up to them and this is what happens. Well, it's not going to happen here!' He smacked a large fist into his open hand and then almost bashfully caught her gaze.

Not so long ago, she thought, the notion of locking the farmhouse would have seemed absurd.

'Why is Brian coming to talk to us?' she asked.

'Because he has to talk to everyone who knew Pagett. Not that I know much about the man.' He heard the car and he broke off to hold the front door.

'Tea?' Prue poured four cups. How different these two men are, she thought. Brian Buchanan who they had known for years, stolid and almost good-looking — a thoroughly dependable person who they were pleased to have as their local constable. But Andrew Barker was different. The way he had glanced around her home, at her and then John, as though they were exhibits. Robotic almost, and yet surprisingly patient though the fact was, there was not much to add. They hadn't seen anyone suspicious or anything out of the ordinary leading up to or after the event. But then, John Reid had been repairing fencing, he said meaningfully, on the other end of the farm. And Prue had just returned from a visit to their daughter's school in Stratford.

'Tell me a bit more about the land.' Barker was interested.

'Pagett's? Well, it's a coastal block of second growth scrub, mostly, out beyond Awakino. He bought it years ago but didn't do anything with it. Then this year, apparently, he decided to clear it for run-off for dry stock. That stirred things up. And not just the Maoris, but the greenies as well. There was a meeting, not that Pagett went, and some bastard, excuse me, had shot a few stock he had on the place. Just killing it and leaving it to rot. But you never found out who, Brian ...'

Buchanan shook his head, conscious of Barker's critical gaze.

'We'll talk about that, constable. So what happened?' Barker prompted Reid.

'Pagett went ahead and burned it two days ago. That's all.'

'That's coincidental.'

'That's what I think. There's a lot of emotion about land — I don't think city people know how much, and not just here — all through — my brother farms down the coast and it's just the same. You would know ...'

Barker gave no sign. 'We'll look at it,' he said. 'Now ... Tom Mahler? Did you know him?'

Reid looked surprised. 'Know him? Not really, but what's he got to do with anything? Surely you're not suggesting he's ... No! That's daft!'

'The Pagett boy is also missing. We have yet to find Mahler, or the boy. You haven't seen either of them?'

'Not for a long time. He came here once ... but I had heard some things. He had something to do with the boy ... I'm not sure.' Reid looked as though this was an unpleasant subject. 'And a girl — a teenager, I understand. I don't go down to the pub much. But I had heard that someone was a bit upset that he was at the school all the time. He's an artist, I think. I think he helped the kid, or kids. Do you know, Prue?'

'Only that. I know he did some work at the school — artwork, anyway.' A silence descended. Barker appeared to be thinking about other things, as if he were alone in the room. Then he said:

'But he's not — wasn't a teacher, was he?'

'I don't know,' said Prue, 'but I think he helped Beth Gilbert ... I'm really not sure.' She glanced at Buchanan but his gaze remained fixed on the wall.

'We'll talk to Miss Gilbert.' Barker paused and looked as if he might speak, then gazed around the room. 'Nice view,' he said at last, and indicated they would see themselves out.

Barker's mobile rang as they walked to the car.

'Is that right?' he said. 'I'll be there shortly.'

* * *

THIS IS MORE than just a murder story, the reporter told her editor. He asked whether she had the pics for the evening bulletin and she told him they had done a camera piece next to the police roadblock.

'What about the other thing?' he asked.

'I've met a local Maori artist who says that the farmer may have set himself up,' she replied. She told him she was going to interview her shortly and then send it through.

'What about a chopper?' she asked. The editor said he would think about it.

* * *

THE THREE POLICEMEN looked down the hill at the back of Pagett's farm. They peered at the edge of the recently turned soil where two forensic officers worked with trowels.

'Right there, sir. That's where it came out.'

'Why wasn't it discovered way back then? Bloody amazing, isn't it? Seven years too late. The dental records will do it.'

'You know the pigs fed here too?'

'Fuck's sake, Milligan, do you think I need reminding!'

Overhead a skylark trilled. But no one noticed.

* * *

IT TOOK RINGATU a little over an hour to reach the ridge. Pushing through the deep fern in the half-light and stumbling sometimes in the dry creek bed with its mossy stones. Occasionally he loosened the boy's grip on his neck but he was pleased with the strength he could feel in the small arms.

At one point the whirring of wings and the unexpected sight of a pheasant caused him to pause and remember another time. Louis, himself and his own father hunting far up the river. A pheasant had come like a bright star in the trees and him, only fourteen, lifting the 12-gauge and blind with excitement, firing both barrels and hitting Sam. He would never forget that sound or how he had begged to carry Sam out but his father put a bullet behind the old dog's ear. No one spoke about that. Not then and never since. The dog was born the same year and given the same name, and he'd killed him.

He sat on a sun-bleached log on the ridge and stared out to sea. Gazing over the devastation that stretched down to the mouth of the stream. A tangle of twisted black shapes covering both sides of the valley and the heat still rising. Hundreds of hectares and there, defiant still, the charred remnant of a giant tree. 'The Last of the Mohicans', that man Tom had called it. In his own strange way he had appropriate respect for that tree.

The boy trembled.

'It is the work of an evil man,' Ringatu said softly. 'It is the work of a man who had no understanding. But it will recover. Tane will bring the forest back to this place. It is not the end.' He prised the boy's fingers apart and lowered him to the ground. Scanning the horizon through the thin haze as though he might yet see a dory. At length he said: 'Tom has gone far out. He has taken the dory far out — beyond our eyes. It is no use asking.' He pointed in the direction of the horizon. Sean stared at the sea for a long time, and though he made several gestures, Ringatu did not respond.

'He might be fishing,' added Ringatu after a while. They continued to stare out across the deepening blue sea. 'Or he might be looking for something ... The Promised Land?' And he gave out a short, mirthless laugh. The boy looked at him with an intense frown and Ringatu opened his hands and shrugged. 'Who can tell?' he said.

The boy studied the man's face as though he might see some answers in the black crescent or the bridge of his nose. Ringatu ignored this scrutiny, though his eyes slid sideways once to catch the boy's gaze. A slight smile sprang to his lips but the boy remained steadfastly solemn. After a few minutes he turned away from Ringatu and peered around the ground, turning two or three times with his head lowered. Turning his back on the sea and the blackened slopes and finally curling into a ball with his arms wrapped around his head. Soon he was asleep.

Ringatu lit a smoke and closed his eyes. Carried far off into the past. Seeing a pa on the headland with many people working and playing. Hearing songs drifting up from the women working on the panels of tukutuku. Hearing the clash of taiaha where the young men practised the arts of war. Hearing the children laughing under their kites high in the blue sky, with creamy toetoe tails. Hearing the chanting of fishermen hauling the canoes back onto the beach. He sighed and opened his eyes to behold the hellish landscape. 'What is left now?' he said quietly. 'What is left that is worth anything at all?'

He pictured the man, Pagett, slumped in shock, and the blood splashing. 'What were you? What were you that was worth anything? Less than one of these stumps now. What were you?'

A magpie flew low overhead but when it came across the blackened ground it wheeled sharply and hastened back to the green trees. Ringatu studied the Mohican. It was a rimu but he understood what Mahler had meant. It was truly the last of its kind here on the coast. Missed maybe — or spared by the loggers so many years ago. Perhaps then its mauri had been stronger. Perhaps the turehu had been more vigilant. Now though, it was gone. The spirit of the tree had been given up to the flames and all that remained was a skeleton that would subside into the scorched earth. Ringatu heard the cry of the tree and it pierced him keenly.The sun crept above the ridge and cast the deep shadows aside. 'If we have food and clothing with these we shall be content,' he murmured. 'But those who desire to be rich fall into temptation ... into many senseless and hurtful desires.' His head began shaking from side to side. 'Into many hurtful and senseless desires ... that plunge men into ruin and destruction.'

He studied the burning cigarette balanced between two fingers of his left hand: 'What is the price?' he asked. Slowly he raised the cigarette and pushed it into the centre of his cheek until it extinguished with a hiss. And his eyes remained open and his lips barely trembled.

* * *

THE POLICE TEAM waited patiently for Andrew Barker to finish his phone call. Sitting in the motel room that was the temporary HQ, with its cream concrete block walls, red formica table and all the windows that were too small. He rang off, apparently satisfied, and sat silently shuffling some notes on his lap.

Brian Buchanan forced himself to concentrate, but it was not easy. He was thinking about his conversation with his son, Paul. He was wondering about how it would be to be in civvies again.

'Review.' Barker began without looking up. 'We believe the victim was killed at almost exactly five on Wednesday evening. The Lynch woman heard what she took to be a shot and noted the time. The pathologist agrees and says it was a rifle, most likely a .243, but we don't have the weapon. We do know the victim owned a rifle but it has not been found either. We also know that the killer used the victim's blood to write a message on the cupboard door after he/she had shot him. The message said "For the love of Mary".' Unconsciously Barker showed his distaste. Then he continued: 'At about 2 p.m. yesterday, Joe Matarangi found the body, and we were called in a half-hour later. We know the victim's only son was not at school on Thursday or Friday and is missing. But we also know he was often absent and apparently wandered alone all over the district.

'At about 11 a.m. Friday, two boys saw a boat and its occupant in the river mouth. The boat was recovered by the Coastguard an hour later but we do not have the occupant, who is thought to be a Tom Mahler — an American visitor who has lived here for about seven months. We now believe that Mahler had some sort of special relationship with the boy. All the more peculiar given his opposition to the victim's plans to clear land near Mahler's residence.

'We have also learned that Mahler's objections were not isolated. The victim was pretty unpopular with the tangata whenua and others for his treatment of said block of land, which he burned off on Wednesday.

'We know the victim was cash rich, despite appearances, but we cannot know, at this stage, whether robbery was a motive. In this regard, we also know that there are a number of transients in the area of whom at least two are known to us.'

He paused to take a breath. 'And we now know that the victim's wife, Adele, who disappeared seven years ago, was buried at the back of the farm. At this stage we don't know how she died. That's what we know. Now ...' He looked around the room. 'We have also learned that things in this little piece of heartland New Zealand are anything but sweetness and light.

'Local non-Maori think this was done by home invaders after money — consistent with, I am led to understand, habitual thieving, or because Pagett burned some bush and upset Maori. Maori, on the other hand, see it as simple burglary gone wrong, and a few on both sides think it was Mahler because he had a disagreement with Pagett about the bush and the nature of his relationship with the man's son. The local teacher and several others are equally adamant that that's crap. We shall see.

'We also know that a person or persons unknown had been shooting the victim's stock on the coast block for some months.

'So, what can we conclude at this point? Maybe the victim disturbed burglars, who used his own or their own gun on him — or maybe it was the missing Mr Mahler.' Barker frowned and put his notes to one side. 'But the Mahler thing ... let's think about this. He helped kids or he was a molester. Depends who we talk to. He allegedly had relations with a girl who, if she wasn't under age, must be close to it. Except her stepmother doesn't know exactly how old she is anyway. Still, if he's dead, and that looks likely, it won't matter too much. Yes, Milligan?'

'Possible some or one of the local hotheads confronted him about the fire and things went wrong? Or then again, it may be someone who isn't in the frame at all.'

Barker stared as though he had not heard. 'I'm still talking about Mahler,' he said mildly.

'Yes, Sarge.'

'The boy is missing. What was Mahler doing?' Barker strode to the wall and spun around. 'If he was genuinely helping kids in an art class as the teacher says he was — what was it that was happening with the Pagett kid? According to Beth Gilbert, whose perspective I suspect is not entirely unbiased, Mahler had a special relationship with the boy. An unfortunate choice of words, I pointed out, but she didn't appreciate my little irony. What makes this all the more interesting is that the kid is mute and largely illiterate. Now that makes him a pretty suitable target for someone with certain proclivities — that, Wilmshurst, means he might have liked little boys.'

'Yes, Sarge. I knew that.'

'Good man. Just the look on your face ... anyway, apparently the kid was a good-looking little tyke. Blue eyes, blond, well-built etc., etc. If we are to assume that Mahler was plucking the strawberry, then a confrontation with the father could well have got out of control. But here's the snag. What's the snag, Milligan?' Barker stared at the constable.

'Ah, the snag. The snag with that, is why Mahler would go up to the farm? Especially after the fire. What would be the point?'

'Yes?'

'Well, I would expect him to avoid the victim.'

'And, yes?'

'Sarge?'

'If he did commit this crime, why would he write a message on the cupboard door, Milligan? Why would he do that?'

'I have no idea.'

'No. And nor have I. Why would someone who would have every reason to fear another go so far out of his way to meet with him? My experience of molesters does not conform with this situation. So, while I do not dismiss this as a possibility, it is not highly ranked. Are we agreed?'

'Yes, Sarge.'

Barker began to pace backwards and forwards, causing Spencer to hastily shift his chair. 'Burglary or a revenge killing. Or accident precipitated by either of those circumstances,' he said. 'Now, what's the problem with the burglary motive? Wilmshurst? Speak to me.'

Wilmshurst frowned and placed his coffee cup on the floor. 'No evidence?'

'No evidence of what?'

'No evidence of a theft, Sarge. We don't know whether anything has been taken — except for the rifle — and we're not yet sure about that either.'

'Good. No evidence of theft and yet if the bastard had left bunches of dollar bills lying around and those bunches are now gone — we're none the bloody wiser. So, we cannot dismiss burglary, in my humble opinion. Which brings me back to revenge.' He pulled out his chair and reversed it so he could sit and lean his forearms on the back. 'Revenge. Tell me something about that, Spencer.'

'From what we have been told, the victim was not a popular man. But nor was he particularly unpopular,' he reflected. 'It appears that no one knew him much at all. He came off the place to pick up dead animals for their hides but never talked to anyone — well, not in any normal way. He stuck to himself. So, it would be difficult to find something that would suggest a revenge motive — at least from his business dealings, which seem to have been straightforward ... excepting perhaps the way he ran the property. But no one knew about that either.' Spencer paused. 'Then we get to the land issue. There seems little question that in the burn-off he created enemies. It appears he didn't much care about Maori or conservation sensitivities — '

'He didn't give a shit! Spencer!' Barker paced impatiently. 'And you know why? Because I believe this bastard nailed his own wife! And the fact that local Maori claim there was a burial ground out there, for this bastard, was a matter of supreme inconsequence. Is that what you were going to say, Spencer?'

'Pretty much, Sarge.'

'Well say it! This bastard may have topped his wife and blatantly ignored every other prick so he could burn the bloody bush! That's what we're looking at here. Do you think so, Milligan?'

'I do.'

'Good!' Barker's sudden colour subsided. 'So one or two go up to have it out. The man's dropped diesel everywhere and then thrown a match into it. For people who have tried everything to make it clear that this is an unacceptable action, that would seem to me to be pretty provocative! Wouldn't you? And put it on top of what has obviously been a fairly contentious issue around here for quite some time — '

'Sarge?'

'What?'

'You mean the other things? Like the land thing, you mean?'

'That's precisely what I mean. That's precisely what I mean. I think burglary is an outside shot. I think you can keep Mahler in the picture — but mostly what I think is that Pagett was confronted by at least one, and maybe more, Maori hotheads.'

'And the message, Sarge?'

Barker gazed out the window and thought for a moment. 'That, I admit, is an arse, and yet it might be consistent ... The alternative is to assume that our attacker was either a complete stranger to the victim, or that the victim has had a significant interaction with someone called Mary, who was also known to the killer. Now taking the former case, it is unlikely, I think, that a stranger would use that or any expression as an afterthought. Especially after an accidental death. On the other hand, one might say "For the love of Mary" to suggest that this is what the victim deserved in a general sort of way, or to mean that the victim was guilty, in the eyes of the killer, of some specific transgression. What do you think?'

'It's sort of like an epitaph.' Spencer spoke slowly. 'For whoever wrote it, the words must have been meaningful. It's hard to imagine any other reason. It seems too deliberate. And if they killed the victim deliberately, then they wanted to say why. Not necessarily for us. Maybe just for the record — like signing off.'

'And if that is the case,' Milligan cut in quickly, 'then the killer is almost certainly local. And if the woman's name is actually a real person, again, the killer is likely to be local and probably known to the victim. That could also explain why the shooting took place inside.'

'True, true. But the shooting may have taken place inside simply to reduce the possibility of the killer being seen. But I like your analysis of the message and I am inclined to agree. We cannot discount the chance that we are searching for a deranged opportunist who happened to be in the area, but the evidence points towards someone with a serious grudge. What we don't know is whether we are looking at perhaps a religious statement or a statement linked to a person by the name of Mary.'

'But one thing, Sarge.'

'Spencer?'

'The fact he was shot in his kitchen? It's possible he may have been shot by someone unexpected?'

Barker screwed up his face. 'Spencer, of course he did not expect it! If he had expected to be shot he would probably have taken strenuous evasive action!'

'I mean, Sarge, that he may have been shot by someone who he presumed posed no threat. In other words, he turned around, and bang.'

'Bang! That's what there was. Incontrovertibly! But I am following you. The victim is in his kitchen eating or doing the dishes. He hears a sound, turns to see someone he knows, and the shot is fired. But that would mean that the someone, if he/she was not carrying their own weapon, knew where to get his gun and probably was moving about in a perfectly normal fashion. Which would lead us, not unnaturally, to the questions of who and for what motive. Quite a long shot, Spencer. Forgive the pun.'

'Yes, Sarge. But there is the boy ...' Barker stared hard at the constable but Spencer would not be browbeaten. 'You did ask for possibilities.'

'I did indeed. And you gave one. The possibility that a ten-year-old kid who may have been molested by Mahler shoots his dad and then writes an unintelligible message in an adult hand, and then disposes of the weapon before racing off to hide in the bush! Excellent! Now, let me put this to you. Pagett is accosted, verbally, at his front door. Either he feels sufficiently threatened that he says to the intruders he is going for his gun, and is followed in, or, he is disturbed, gets his gun and goes to the front door only to be attacked and disarmed.' He took a breath. 'Or, the assailant or assailants have a gun, and the victim is shepherded back inside before being shot in cold blood.'

'Possible.'

'Yes it is, isn't it?' Barker paced out a circle. 'And then, and quite separately, Mahler is on the river in his rowboat with or without the boy — fishing? Who knows? Gets in trouble and he or both go in.'

'No bodies.'

'An astute observation, Wilmshurst. But true enough. We can't find one, let alone two. Now, let's assume Mahler drowned and in fact was on his own. We know he did this from time to time, rowing about on the river. We'll find him. However, we also know that the boy is not the full quid and that he lived some sort of strange nomadic existence wandering all over the countryside by himself. Having seen his home I think we can understand why. This being the case, it is entirely likely we're going to turn him up at any time now — possibly unaware his father is even dead. Possible?'

'Yes, Sarge.'

'I think so. I think so. That being the case, I think we can agree we have several fertile lines of enquiry.' He turned to Milligan. 'How far are we on the Area Canvass?'

'Maybe half. We should complete it by tomorrow evening latest.'

'Good. And the search for the boy?'

'No sign but we've got the dog handler out there still. Bit of a problem with that. Lot of dead ends so far and now the uniformed branch is pushing for a full-scale search.'

'They would. But I don't want it yet. Might as well run a digger over the place.'

'Yes, Sarge. I told them that.'

'All right.' Barker leaned against the wall. 'We may need to look at an aerial search but we'll make a decision on that at the end of the day.' His face became animated. 'I'm bloody hungry! Have you ordered anything in, Milligan? What about some pies?' Satisfied, he frowned and checked his notes. 'Oh, and the local ground search?'

'We've covered all round the house, the sheds and down to the bottom of the hill, sir. No sign of the weapon. I think we'll need to go for the river.'

'Have you called the divers?'

'They're on their way.'

'Good.'

* * *

MERLE CLOSED THE door and through her side window watched Constable Milligan cross the road to his car. She could see he was speaking, although he was alone in the car, which was quite strange, though he was a nice man. He had asked her a lot of questions. So many, she told him, it made her head swim. But she did her very best and she told him that, and he said he could certainly see that and was most grateful.

She told him she didn't think that she could tell him anything valuable, even useful. She was old and she was sure he could see that too. And he said some of the best witnesses were elderly because they 'observed'. And she had felt a bit funny to be called a witness but she didn't say anything about that but racked her brain for any tiny detail that might be helpful. And she told him how the things that had happened were not like Mokau. These things were not like anything she had ever seen. They were an 'aberration', she said, and was immensely pleased at that word and used it several times. She didn't know why that word had come to her, it just did.

She sat in her easy chair and looked at the street as she often did when she was not in her shop. She liked to see passing traffic and people wandering by. She was a witness.

I wish he were here now, Merle thought. Herb Simes, I wish you were in that chair right this instant. She gazed tenderly at the orange reclining chair with the colourful rug she had knitted him many years before. The chair sat, as always, on that side of the fireplace where he could watch the little TV tucked on the corner ledge. Next to his prized collection of beer mugs. At least forty mugs on two shelves, from bars from Germany to Samoa.

The single light bulb mounted on a flexible coiled steel stem also remained, clipped to the back of the chair so Herb could read. In those later years he had spent a good part of each day sitting there, watching TV or reading a book. He was a book man. He was the biggest user of the mobile library service from Urenui to Awakino.

They made him a little presentation once. He was made a life member of the library. Not that she read herself — too busy. I was always the busy one and he was the quiet thinking one, she reflected, and he called me his 'busy little bee'. She smiled at the thought and sipped her second cup of tea. Sitting in the patch of sun that streamed through the window. It was nice to relax for a while and just remember things.

'Herbie. I do wish you were here today. But I know you can't be. All the same, I know you're listening.' She smiled again and promised to make a fruit cake because that was his favourite.

The cat door clicked and she turned with pleasure to watch the approach of her fluffy grey cat with its stubby tail. 'There you are, you naughty boy. Where have you been then? Mummy and Daddy have been waiting all the time. Yes they have.' The cat rubbed against her stockinged leg and she stroked its head. 'Do you miss old Herb, Porgie, do you? Do you miss him like your Mummy does? Course you do.' She lapsed into silence as the cat left for the kitchen to lick its bowl around the floor.

It would have been a great comfort to have Herbie, just sitting so she could share her concerns. What about that woman who came into the shop? That was such a shock. She hadn't known what to say, she told the constable. Fancy that man being her husband. That was so peculiar. She had never imagined that that sort of person would be married. How could they be? It was so unnatural. It was worse than the drunken boys, it was evil. She had prayed specifically about Tom Mahler. And yet, the peculiar thing was that she had liked him at first. He had seemed gentle and thoughtful. But that was probably how he managed to do what he did.

But should he have died in the river? Was that the Lord's way of cleansing him? She was comforted by this thought. But what happened to his poor wife? Or was she? Did people share such hideousness? she asked Constable Milligan. He thought not, which was reassuring.

And Constable Milligan was very interested and asked a lot about that little boy, Sean, and Mr Mahler, and Merle said it got like it was kidnapping in the end. She told him how Mr Mahler got very excited in the store one time and said Mr Pagett was a 'beast'. That was the word, and she would never forget because it had really stunned her, though she didn't show it because that's how you were in 'retail'. And no, she couldn't remember why he had said that. That's where Herbie would have been useful but of course he hadn't served for years, due to his condition.

She watched Trixie Blackman walking by on the opposite side of the street, wearing those awful slacks. She was certainly the person in Mokau with the least dress sense of anyone. Stopping and looking across the road she was, probably wondering whether the shop was open, but she would know this was Merle's lunchtime and she wouldn't open until two o'clock. Her face bore that gloomy, rundown expression. So unlike her stepdaughter she was. And now the boys didn't hang around so much. That was good. They were like dogs, really, sniffing up and down the street. Always on heat is what Herb called it. She shuddered. Sometimes he was unnecessarily coarse. She suspected from time to time that it was intentional.

Constable Milligan asked her a lot of things about Melanie, including her age, but Merle didn't know though she thought about sixteen or seventeen. She told him to ask Trixie. She told him that Melanie had been friends with Mr Mahler, which she had thought was a good thing at first.

Trixie was coming across the road straight towards Merle's door. She had seen Merle in the window and smiled a nervous sort of smile and mouthed 'Hullo' or something like. She smoked so much her face was going yellow, Merle thought sadly, and rose to go to the door.

'You haven't talked to Melanie?' Trixie was clearly upset and her eyes darted from side to side. Merle said no, and was surprised because she thought Melanie had gone to New Plymouth. She was surprised that she had come back, and anyway, she hadn't seen her.

'Is there something important?' But Trixie seemed very distracted and was twisting her hands this way and that and just mumbled thanks and went on her way.

What a sad woman she is, Merle thought, and she watched a petrol tanker rumble through. She heard motorbikes approaching and presently two swung into view across the road and parked, and when they stopped their engines it seemed very quiet. And then those two boys, Matty and Jake, appeared and stood near the motorbikes staring. They were good boys, Bill Manuhuia's boys. Louis's boys too really ... standing there next to those bikes and talking to the men. She didn't know who they were but they leaned against the Meltons' fence and lit cigarettes. The boys climbed onto the motorbikes and pretended to be riding, and they were laughing so their teeth gleamed and that amused the men who offered the boys a cigarette! But the boys shook their heads and Merle was very pleased. Until Jake suddenly put out his hand and accepted one and then Matty did the same and they put the things in their pockets. Then she felt angry and she went to her door.

The men looked up with no more than passing interest, though their casual demeanour changed a little when they realised she was coming at them.

'You shouldn't be doing that — you shouldn't be giving those boys cigarettes. Shame on you!'

After a momentary silence they laughed. At least the one with the cross on his cheek laughed, and then he told her to 'Fuck off.' But she didn't. She went closer and asked them their names, even though she felt apprehensive, and Matty and Jake climbed off the bikes and moved silently backward down the street.

'We got nothing about you,' the man said and turned away from her.

'Well, I've got a problem with what you just did. I don't sell children cigarettes because it's against the law and so is what you did.' Merle felt very hot, and she wondered what had given this man such a hard face.

'We're sorry for that,' said the other in a most surprising voice; 'We just weren't thinking.' He smiled and Merle felt slightly better. Though the other would not look at her, she softened: 'I just thought I should tell you,' she said. 'It is the worst thing that can happen to a child almost.'

'I'm glad you mentioned it,' the man said, and smiled again. 'We won't tempt them again.' Merle stared at him a bit suspiciously but he seemed sincere, with his frank, open eyes and pleasant smile. So she said thank you and returned to her house and sat in her window, and she saw they could see her there. And the one flashed a big smile again, but the other who told her that frightful word said some things that she could not understand, but she sensed they were not good.

She wondered where they came from. There never used to be strangers in Mokau but now ... and when they came into the store it wasn't the same. They were menacing, some of them. Not that she was afraid. This was her town where she had been so long. But it was not nice of them to be like that as though she had done something. They were not like the Manuhuias at all.

And now some talked about the land as though that was a new thing when in fact it was so old no one knew what they meant even. They certainly had talked about it when they were criticising Mr Pagett, she recalled. What good would come of it? Everyone was upset. What good was it to shout about Mr Pagett when the poor man was simply trying to farm? But now he was dead. Murdered. She told Constable Milligan that the devil was loose. 'He comes in many forms,' she told him, and she could see he knew.

The motorbikes started with a roar and moved off, and Merle noticed Louis Ropata coming across the road. She rose hastily and smoothed her hair.

Louis had changed into his button-up blue shirt without a single stain and his good black jeans. His silver hair was brushed across and covered most of that bald place.

'Good afternoon, Mr Ropata,' she said cheerfully as the doorbell tinkled.

'Good afternoon to you, Mrs Simes. Though there's much that isn't, eh?' He made his way along the aisle where the freezer chugged.

'There's been no word?'

'No word. No word. That's correct.' He rummaged in the cabinet and produced a package of sausages.

'It's a terrible time, Mr Ropata. I cannot remember any such time. Can I wrap that?'

'Thank you kindly.' Louis placed the sausages on the polished counter. 'Yes siree. Yes siree ... ' He gave her a small and polite smile and she nodded encouragingly.

'I saw some men giving cigarettes to your boys. I gave them a piece of my mind.'

'Ah. Thank you for that, Mrs Simes. Thank you for that. There's so much, so much ...' and he sighed and adjusted his shirt at the front where the lower button had gone missing.

'That's a nice shirt, if you don't mind my saying,' she added quickly and presented the wrapped package.

'Well, thank you. It's nearly twenty years old but it goes.' And he smiled. 'It's a lovely day but there's little enough. I've been thinking about that Tom Mahler. A good man.'

She frowned. 'Yes,' she said a little uncertainly. 'Yes, in a *way*.'

They stood silently for a time and listened to the clock on the wall behind.

'Well, I best be getting along. Let you get on with your work.'

'Oh, I don't have much to do today. Everything's shipshape and it's so quiet.'

'Yes.' He picked up his parcel. 'Well, it's good to see you in good health.'

'And you, I'm sure.'

Louis raised his hand in farewell and shuffled to the door. 'Let's hope we get some good news soon.' And the doorbell jumped and tinkled above his head.

* * *

GERTIE NGAHERE CHOPPED cress. She threw it into a large aluminium pot on the electric stove that had three good elements and one that hadn't worked since Matty repaired it with a hammer. On one of the other elements, potatoes boiled briskly. She opened the oven, standing back as a swirl of hot, misty vapour mushroomed towards the ceiling, and she stabbed the leg of mutton with a long fork. Juices flowed and the colour was just right. She closed the door and turned the temperature down.

Those boys will be back soon, she thought. They will be hungry like little pigs. Turning to the split timber table, she worked the pastry on her breadboard and then moved to the bench by the sink and added brown sugar from the bin to the sliced apple. She placed the pot on the free element and cocked an ear to the high-pitched tremolo of the oystercatcher flying low along the riverbank. And beyond that the sound of boys. She smiled. They're coming up the road, past Louis and the Treblicos any moment now. She wiped her hands on her apron and turned to the hallway. A commotion was occurring outside.

Ratbags, she thought, feeling in her pocket and producing two wrapped lollies. She hid them in her right hand as she walked to open the front door.

'Hey! What's all this noise out here? You boys trying to waken the dead or what are you?'

'He's been stealing my pencil again, Auntie. Here give it back to me, Jake, or I'll bust your neck!' Matty scragged his smaller brother around the neck and pulled him to the ground.

'You're a liar! Auntie, he's lying. It's my pencil. He stole mine last week. Ouch!'

'Anyone want a sweet?'

'What?'

'I've got a sweet for the boy who gets here first.' Matty released his brother and leapt towards the verandah. 'Keep your old pencil!' he shouted. 'Thanks, Auntie.'

'And me?' Jake widened his eyes until they might fall out, in what he assumed was his most winning expression.

'And you? And you, little eel? Well, there might be another. Come and look.' And she held her hands behind her back. He paused.

'The right! It's the right one, Jake. The right!'

'Left!' shouted Jake without hesitation and Gertie slipped the sweet from her right to her left and presented it to him.

'Ha! See!' He grasped the sweet and threw himself off the verandah onto the grass and rolled about while he removed the wrapper.

'Dinner's nearly ready now. You almost missed it you so late. I was going to throw that old meat to the chickens. So come on.' She led the way to the kitchen and took the meat from the oven. 'Stand back, stand back.' She placed it on the bench, then removed the cress from the stove and drained the water into the sink, followed by the potatoes.

'Who's going to mash these spuds?'

'Me!'

'All right. Here's the masher and here's some butter. Ka pai.'

'And who is going to cut this meat?'

'That's me. I'm the meat man, aren't I, Auntie?'

'Yes, Matty, you the meat-man all right. Just don't eat any or I'll bust your head.'

She set four plates and knives and forks on the table and served the cress. Then she put the apple in the pie dish and placed the rolled pastry carefully over the top and put it in the hot oven. 'Your dad should be home soon. You didn't see him?'

'Nah. He's working on the other side of the bridge. We went up the valley.'

'Oh, did you? When your dad said not to. He'll be giving you an earful.'

'But we only went just past the Lynchs'. We went with Jimmy!'

'That ratbag?'

'Yeah. He's okay. He said it was a *good job*!'

'That's a wicked thing to say.'

'A *good job*!' echoed Jake. 'All mashed,' he announced, handing her the pot.

'Well, I don't want that sort of talking around here. And what did you see?'

'Cops! So many! And a chopper!'

'A what?'

'A helicopter, Auntie, that's what we call choppers. We saw the chopper go all over the place. It was TV!'

'Sit up to the table.' She watched them reflect, their mouths full of meat and potato. 'You're going to choke on that meat one of these days and I'll be saying I told you.'

'Miss Gilbert was a bit funny today. She was all ... red! We saw her down the store.'

'Red?'

'Nooo, not red, Jake, she was sort of sad or something. I seen it in her eyes when she was telling me off about that pie.'

'No! Red!'

'What pie was this?'

'Oh!' He frowned at the inadvertent disclosure. 'Nothing.'

'Yes! It was something, Auntie,' Jake said gleefully. 'He took Samuel McCleod's pie and ate it.'

'Not! I did not. I took a small bite that's all. You're a liar!'

'What? You bad boy, Matty Manuhuia. What do you think your dad's going to say to you? Probably belt your bottom,' she threatened with a twinkle in her eye. 'Why did you take that boy's pie?'

'He was being cheeky. He said we were lying about Painter Tom and that he never did drown in the river. He said he has taken that boy Sean away somewhere. He said Painter Tom was a *prefect*.'

'A prefect? What's that?'

'I dunno, but he said that's what his folks called Painter Tom. A *prefect* who does things to people — boys, or something. So I grabbed his ole pie and took a big bite. That's what happened.' He grinned at his aunt, then quickly lifted his plate and licked the gravy.

7

THE YOUNG REPORTER appeared on channel 3, standing in front of a police roadblock on a country road a short distance, she said, from the farm where a man was found shot to death. The police had now confirmed his identity as longstanding resident Trevor Pagett. They were treating the case as homicide, she said, and they had found a rifle they believed to be the murder weapon in the nearby river. Earlier, she reported, her news team had flown over the area to gain a better perspective. Images showed the red-roofed farmhouse and the working sheds. Then the helicopter had flown down over the willow-lined banks of the river where the rifle was found by police divers.

'I talked to the detective in charge of the case,' the reporter continued, 'and he said there were no immediate suspects. The first priority was to find the deceased man's ten-year-old son, Sean Pagett.' A grainy image of a snowy-haired boy with large dark eyes and a solemn expression appeared on the screen.

There followed a brief interview with Detective Andrew Barker in which he made it clear that he had not drawn any connection between the homicide enquiry and the missing American.

This was one of the strange coincidences in the case, the reporter said. The American, a Mr Tom Mahler, had been in Mokau for just seven months, living on land formerly owned by his uncle. Mr Mahler was visiting the property and had been staying, apparently indefinitely, although it was not known what he did.

Then the camera zoomed in to capture the reporter's grave expression. 'There is another dimension to the events in Mokau that we have discovered just this afternoon,' she said. New footage showed the chopper's perspective of the smoking, blackened valley and headland on the coast.

'This land was owned by the deceased farmer. It lies a little to the north of Mokau and we are informed that it was recently burned off by the deceased to increase his cattle run. However, we are also informed that the burning of this land caused a great deal of controversy in this small community, effectively splitting it into those who supported the farmer's right to clear his land and those who claimed it was wilful destruction of environmentally important forest. Further to that, we understand that the land has some spiritual significance to local Maori, who campaigned to have the burn-off halted. In fact, we understand that an injunction was in the process of being sought at the time the forest was set on fire. We talked to Ms Peta Patai, an artist who lives near the farm.'

'Prue! Come in here — quick!' John Reid rose from his favourite chair and watched in amazement as Peta Patai appeared on the TV screen. She was being interviewed near the school library.

Prue hurried in from the kitchen and they stood together listening to Peta telling the reporter that it was sad about the death of Pagett, but that what he had done had stirred deep feelings in Mokau. She said that Pagett's actions, which were supported by many Pakeha, were no different from what had been occurring since the Pakeha had arrived to falsely obtain land in much of the Mokau area. There were many people in the community who deliberately chose not to know about the history of the land and the rights of the tangata whenua, she said. Maori were tired of the attitude that they should just get on with their lives as though the events of a few generations past could simply be washed away. Especially as it was the Maori who now found they had nothing, after a century of colonial looting.

'Could the burning of sacred ground have prompted a violent retaliation?'

Peta looked directly into the camera and paused. 'People are very angry,' she said. She had nothing more to add about that, she said.

The reporter returned to the camera: 'And there it is. A murder enquiry, a missing man, presumed drowned, and a boy who has not been seen for several days. And against this tragedy, land issues that stretch back to the nineteenth century but which are as alive now as they have ever been. A series of events that are shaking this tiny community to its roots.'

Reid switched off the sound. 'Good grief! What the hell is going on in this place? *Sacred ground!* What the hell is she doing on TV saying that crap? How unbalanced is that?'

'I don't understand it. She's ...'

'Why don't they talk about the theft and intimidation? Why don't they talk about the laying about doing absolutely nothing instead of working?' Reid strode ferociously up and down the lounge. 'Why don't they ask what justifies *murder*?' He stopped and glared at his wife. 'What do they want? For the whole country to go back to bush? Why do they want to live in the past, for God's sake? What do they think? That everything will be fine when they're catching bloody eels and carving bloody planks? Good bloody grief!'

'I don't think she's typical, John, she's ...'

'Oh, no? Oh, no? Don't you believe it! You won't find any of them getting on there and saying Peta Patai doesn't speak for me. They'll be over the moon!'

He slumped into his chair and glared out the window, staring at the pale evening sky and wondering how these things had come to be.

'Did I tell you about Henderson? About the sand?' She nodded but he continued anyway. 'Henderson went down to the river mouth for a trailer-load of sand and some young bastards told him he couldn't take it! They told him it was Maori sand! Can you believe that?'

'Who were they?'

'Some of those young guys who have been turning up from God knows where. From the city, can't get any work there so they come back to bludge. And then they have the cheek to say that!'

'What happened?'

'Well, he told them if they wanted an argument with his spade to just get in the way.'

'And did they?'

He snorted. 'Of course not! They're just troublemakers with nothing else to think about.' He steepled his hands and recalled Joe McCleod's comment: 'These bastards are growing up thinking we should give everything back. Look what's happening in Zimbabwe.' Reid had said that could only happen in Africa.

'What?' he asked, becoming aware that his wife had spoken.

'I said, I think she's just grandstanding, Peta Patai. And of course the TV people are going to love that. It's what makes news. But I'm sure it will blow over.'

'Prue. Prue. That is so ...' He shook his head. 'Blow over? It's getting worse every year. It's not blowing anywhere but up our noses!'

Prue flushed, then said firmly: 'I'm not sure that land should have been burned. I don't think he had the right to burn it. With the burial ground there. It was wrong.'

'No right! No right? Bullshit! He had every right.' Reid leapt to his feet and towered above his diminutive wife, but she stared back without wavering: 'He *owns* that land. That's what freehold means. How the hell can you farm a property ... effectively, if you can't do what's necessary?'

She was unsure how to respond to his grim expression and he became suddenly aware that he was shouting. 'What if we decided to clear the bottom end?' he demanded more quietly. 'What would you say then?'

'I'd say, no.'

There was a pause in which his agitation grew and then as suddenly subsided. 'Yeah, I know.' And he turned away. 'I *don't* know. I just don't bloody know. It's all getting so complicated. It seems like every bastard who wants a say in anything can have it. I can't cut a tree without permission! I can't plant bloody pines without permission. That's not how we made this country but that's where we're going. And what are the bloody politicians doing? Nothing!'

She stepped behind him and wrapped her arms around his waist. 'We'll be all right. You do the right things.'

They didn't move for several minutes. Finally he said: 'I'm going out on the search again in the morning.'

'That's a good idea,' she said. 'Poor little boy. I do hope you find him.'

* * *

BUCHANAN DROVE SLOWLY to his office and closed the door before sinking into the chair he kept in the corner for 'time out'. He noticed a piece of paper under his desk. At first he just stared at it while he reflected on events and his own future. Almost certainly he and Paul would have to leave Mokau, and he wondered in what direction they might head. Wondered with a thrill of apprehension what he would do. He was well trained — but for police work. What could he do? And when he confronted the hard reality of leaving the Force, he realised how much he was bound to it. He liked being the local cop. Maybe the CIB thing didn't matter so much any more. Being the local cop was a good job.

He thought about the past few years, the people and the incidents. Nothing very serious in terms of crime, and his relationships with the locals were good. He acknowledged that perhaps he had become a little complacent. But how could he not? The odd burglary and domestic — otherwise, it had been routine. Dull?

Then he recalled the times with her and the plans he had made, and a powerful sense of failure swept over him like the smell of dog turd. For a time he buried his face in his hands and when he opened his eyes he was looking again at the paper under the desk. He reached for it and read: 'Mr Buchanan. I am staying at Tom Mahler's cottage. I understand you are searching for Tom. Please contact me. Mary Mahler.'

Buchanan stared at the note for some minutes. He wondered how the note came to be under his desk and how long it had sat there. He wondered about her name and his mind raced at the possibilities. 'It's him!'

* * *

MELANIE BLACKMAN WAITED until the sun sank into the sea and the purply hues of dusk deepened. She waited in the sandhills above the beach, sitting in the wiry marram grass with her feet tucked under the soft sand. Then she walked where she was sure she would avoid people coming up from the beach. Further down towards the river mouth she could see a fire, and she heard the strains of rap. She headed north and away, enjoying the feel of the sand on her bare feet sliding in the dunes. When she was sure the beach was empty she made her way across the hard sand to the water's edge and let the water wash up her legs, heedless of her jeans. She stood in the soft foamy water, now black as pitch, and stared out to sea. Thinking about that man who listened to her dreams without sniggers or derisory remarks. Telling her about America and the people and the cities and everything.

A solitary cloud crossed the new moon and the sea disappeared into the night, but the stars winked and after a while she could see even those small lights upon the smooth water.

How strange that she should come back on this very day. How strange. An omen, clearly. She had not cried. Not one time since that woman told her. Gloating like a beast of some sort. Horrible gloating beast. She would not cry now either. Perhaps never. What would that do? Bring him back?

The moon emerged and she could see far again. Far out to sea and far up the coast. She turned to look back at the dunes rolling like waves themselves and then up into the high hills. Moonlight so bright she could see silver trees. The water rose to her knees and she was conscious of that. She looked about her in the swirling water and wondered if he was near. Whether he might suddenly bump into her as she stood. She would not mind. She would be glad if she found him. He was out there somewhere. Somewhere in that black sea. Why?

She walked slowly back onto dry sand and sat with her arms about her drawn up legs to her chin for a long time. Watching the tide and remembering things. Then she rose and pulled her sweater over her head. She unclasped her bra and allowed it to fall. Then she undid her belt and peeled off her jeans, nearly falling as the wet cloth stuck on her ankles. She removed her pants and stepped away from her clothes. And then she began to dance. She swung her arms away from her and prescribed slow circles on the sand there on the empty beach in the moonlight. She swung so her hair streamed out and she lifted her hands above her head and made pirouettes, lifting a leg so she spun on just one and swept across the sand in wide arcs. And all the time her face was serious and composed. After a time a tiny smile came to her lips that were open from her exertion but still she swung and bowed, leapt and froze in graceful positions and when she did she said: 'I am dancing for you.' But only the black oystercatcher, hidden in the darkness at the edge of the tide, could see.

At last she stopped and stood still, feeling like a little girl. Sadness and loneliness swept over her and she crossed her arms and squeezed tightly lest tears should come. Then walking down to the sea with eyes glazed, unseeing, feeling the water lap her ankles and then her knees and coming up between but she barely shivered. In the black sea.

* * *

BUCHANAN PACKED PAUL'S lunch. He included two cheese and jam sandwiches because those were his favourite.

'Doing anything special today, Shorty?'

The boy rolled his eyes and held a spoonful of cereal just below his open mouth. 'Swimming,' he said and inserted the spoon in his mouth. 'It's Monday so it's swimming.'

'That's good. I packed you two of these.' He waved the sandwiches and enjoyed the grin he received.

'You doing anything special?'

'Oh, I'm working on the investigation.'

'I know. You going to catch anyone today?'

'Maybe. But investigations can take a long time.'

'Mmm. Can I have a piece of toast with honey?'

'Sure you can.' He glanced at his watch. 'But we have to hurry now.'

A few minutes later he bundled Paul out the door with his bag in one hand and toast in the other. 'Shorty ...' he said. He crouched suddenly and looked into the boy's big eyes and suddenly remembered the boy's mother. 'Nothing.' And he gave him a huge hug. 'Get away and learn some things.' Then he drove north towards Mahler's cottage.

* * *

BILL WAS PUZZLED to see the digger being driven from its overnight park against the grey and yellow streaked clay. He parked his flatdeck and peered through the dusty windscreen. No one else had arrived. Only the boss was here at the roadworks on this beautiful Monday morning. Only Merv Layton and him, and here was Merv in the digger and something was wrong.

Bill climbed from the truck, throwing the lunch Gertie had prepared back onto the seat. The digger reversed towards him, stopped, and then lurched to the area that would eventually be the new road. Not yet though. Things hadn't been sorted out, but that was where Merv Layton was heading.

Bill broke into a trot, following the big yellow Komatsu, seeing it wheel until it faced the hummocky ground that had been cordoned off with orange plastic tape. Still unable to believe his fears, he felt his mouth open with amazement as the shovel dropped and the motor roared, lunging through the bright plastic cordon and deep into the soil.

'Hey!' Bill yelled and began to run; 'Hey!' He dropped his tobacco and sprinted as the bucket jumped and clanked and the big machine shuddered like an angry rhino. He ran alongside as Merv reversed with the shovel rising, swinging the machine forward to the edge of the bank and tipping the shovel so the contents crashed down the bank into the edge of the thick bush.

Bill could see Merv in the cab and he waved his arms. 'Hey! Merv! Stop, man! Hey!' But the machine reversed rapidly back across the level ground, spun violently and roared back through the broken line and ploughed into the trench.

From the corner of his eye Bill saw two of his workers arrive and stall, mesmerised by the strange spectacle. He tried to jump onto the steps of the digger but Merv was already moving. 'Merv! You can't do this! Merv!' Again the fresh earth and rock crashed down the slope into the broken foliage.

'Bastard!' said Bill and he ran to his flatdeck. Another car arrived, stopping violently to avoid being hit as Bill raced across the lumpy ground to cut the digger off. As he braked close in behind, Merv glanced back and there was great anger in his face.

'Get out of the road, Bill, or I'll crush that thing!' Merv jumped to the ground.

'You've got no right to do that! You know you've got no right.' The other men gathered, silent and curious.

'No right? Don't tell me my rights. I'm sick up to here with rights! Two months we've been on this job and we can't finish it because there's some old cooking stones in the way. Well, not any more!'

'That's a dangerous thing you're doing. Those stones are tapu. Only Louis can lift that.'

'Dangerous! Don't make me laugh. Old Louis! Get off, Bill, I thought you had a few more clues.'

'But why?'

'Didn't you see it last night — on TV? You didn't see it? That radical bitch ranting about Pakeha stealing her land? You didn't see that?' Bill shook his head. 'Well, that's why. I am sick of that shit up to here! We're in the twenty-first century in case anyone hadn't noticed, and in my view that means getting on with things. Not pissing around with old rocks like they were your girlfriend's tits!'

'Whatever she said, that doesn't give you the right.'

'Is that so? Well, I've got other views on that! Old Louis can come and chant all he likes but this road will get built — today!' He swung back onto the steps of the digger, 'And if your wagon stays there, Bill, it'll be fucking scrap!'

Bill leapt forward and grabbed his boss's arm.

'Get the fuck off!' Merv swung his arm, lost his footing and fell. When he rose there was madness in his eyes. The men retreated as he lunged at his antagonist and caught him a blow to the shoulder. Moments later they were toe to toe, slugging.

The roar in Bill's head obliterated Merv's hits and he was barely conscious of his own pumping arms. The roar and grunting. The heat and the feel of the bigger man so close. The heavy breathing and pushing. Huge body blows delivered both ways, wordlessly. He felt the edge of the digger's wheel sharp in his back and an explosion in his right ear.

'Stop the bastards — they'll kill each other!'

Suddenly the melee involved everyone. Arms thrusting and pulling, wild fists swinging, bodies banging against the digger and the flatdeck. Shouting and the smell of sweat and excitement. And as quickly it stopped.

Bill wiped the back of his hand across his mouth, glanced curiously at the bright smear and wondered why the only sound he could hear was a kingfisher so far off it must be near to the sea. He looked at

Merv, who was touching his own face and scowling. The men watched nervously, jittery like sheep near the dog.

'Best you pack your bag, Manuhuia.' Without waiting for a reaction Merv turned on his small workforce. 'This is a roading project. Anyone who doesn't want to get this road under way can leave.' He stared balefully at the group who shuffled away, eyes for the most part downcast. 'Now get on with it.' Merv strode towards the site office. The others hesitated.

'Sorry, Bill.'

'That's okay, Mike. You got to do your job.' Bill climbed into his flatdeck. He paused to watch the men straggle over to their tools, tall like Simmons, fat like McConachie and brown like Wetere. His head felt hot and was starting to hurt — like his back. He drove slowly down the road to Mokau. He didn't hear the cicadas and he didn't see the hitchhiker with the sign saying 'New Plym'. He saw a dark gorge as wide as the Tasman and a sound in his head like a train coming.

* * *

IT WAS NOT what he expected. She was not what he expected.

'I'm Constable Buchanan. You left a note for me. I'm sorry I've been so long.'

'Oh! Well, thank you. Would you mind waiting a moment?'

So he sat carefully on the sofa on the verandah and looked out to sea. Glistening pale blue and the faint scent of seaweed even up here. A perfect morning to fish but there was the rahui.

He stood as she came back out onto the verandah. She was beautiful. Even like that. That black hair and skin like silk. Slim … why had he left her? Perhaps she was a shrew … but more likely he was a prick. She said she was glad he'd come because she didn't want to go back into town.

He apologised for the delay. 'Actually your note fell off my desk so I didn't find it until last night.'

'Oh! Well, perhaps that's good …' He could see she'd been crying.

'I don't have any news. I'm sorry, Mrs Mahler.'

She nodded and gestured to the sofa. 'Actually it's Chisholm, but I figured that wouldn't make much sense. Please sit.' She sat on the arm at the other end and looked into the distance. She seemed quite calm. 'I guess I hoped. At least while I was up here and no one called, I could hope ... But I have to face it, sooner or later.'

'We haven't given up,' he lied.

'You're still searching?'

Buchanan flushed. 'Not exactly, you see it's been five days now. We're keeping an eye out.'

'For the body?' she said flatly, and smoothed her trousers as though an unseemly crease had appeared. 'Would you like a coffee? Please do — I'm going to have one myself.' She walked past him, 'Come in if you like.'

But he preferred to stay outside. What a balls-up! he thought angrily. Such a fine-looking woman stuck in this hole, wondering about her dead husband and I shouldn't be here. Barker will want to see her.

'Milk?'

'And two sugars, thanks.'

'I'll see what we've got.' She disappeared.

And the chances are the guy's gone nuts, he reflected, and committed murder. In her name! Good bloody grief! He was out here for months. A Yank from the city, stuck out here in this. He looked around the sagging and unpainted verandah boards and at the paint-peeled corrugated iron with its popping nails. With that boy — out here all alone and then things got out of hand. A terrible accident? Maybe, but then he goes and writes that thing. What did he want to say for chrissakes?

'I don't take it myself but I found some.' She offered a small jar with a teaspoon and noticed how ill at ease he appeared to be. 'Can you tell me anything? About the accident?'

'Not much.' He sounded like a possum trap going off and he noticed her surprise. 'I'm sorry. I'm a bit ...'

'That's okay. I guess even for a policeman it's a difficult task.'

He nodded and told her how sorry he was about it all and she nodded. Said it was like a nightmare that wouldn't end. They sat awkwardly sipping their coffee and listening to seabirds as though there was nothing else more interesting.

She finished her cup and put it on the arm of the sofa. 'Constable?'

He turned unwillingly. 'I would like to know about an accusation made against Tom.'

'Look, Mrs Chisholm, I came in response to your note. I should really be letting my superior know you're here so that you can … talk formally. It would be best.'

'Tell me about the boy,' she said firmly. 'I need to know more about the boy.'

'They're rumours,' he said, and explained some of what he knew. He told her the police would treat them as nothing more than that.

She seemed to be satisfied with that so he made to move.

'I want to tell you, Constable,' her words were clipped and measured, 'that the possibility of Tom being what these … *bastards* have said is absolutely *zero*!' She flushed with anger. 'Absolutely zero!'

'I'm …'

'My ex husband was not perfect, Constable, but nor was he a criminal. He most certainly was not a child molester.'

'There was a note.' It came out so quickly.

'Where?' She imagined the note she had burned.

'At the scene …' and he realised she did not know; 'I must go.' He rose, knocking his hat to the grass. Before he reached it she cut him off, so swift he was astonished, and nearly as tall as he.

'What note? What scene?' she hissed, and he stepped back.

He recovered his composure but she stood between him and his car. 'A man was murdered, Mrs Chisholm.' He assumed his official tone. 'On Thursday morning. About the time we think Mr Mahler went missing. The man was the boy's father.' His eyes blinked owlishly.

'My God!' She shrank into the sofa. 'Now this … now this …'

'Will you be all right?'

Her head moved from side to side as though she expected to see some answer in the grass. 'You said there was a note. What was that?'

'I shouldn't tell you. I …'

'Tell me!' she lunged forward and grasped the verandah post and he feared she might attack him.

'There was a note next to the dead man, Mrs Chisholm. It said, "For the love of …" Shit! I can't say this.'

'Tell me!'

I'm fucked, he thought savagely. 'It said, "For the love of Mary".'

She stared in blank incomprehension. 'For the love of Mary?' Her voice dropped to a whisper. 'For the love of *Mary*?'

She's going to fall, he thought, and stepped forward. 'Are you okay?'

'Okay? *Okay?* Am I okay, Constable ... what's your name? Buchanan? I'm ...' and she slid slowly to the step and hid her face in her arms.

Buchanan felt the sun hot on his cheek and the sweat running inside his collar. He looked down at the woman and wished more fervently than anything in the world that he could change things for her. He thought about the magnitude of the screw-up that was his life at this time. And he had a glimmering of the size of the fuck-up that was hers.

* * *

BARKER KNEW THESE guys. Not personally or even by name, but the type. Near a couple of hundred grand's worth of Harleys parked outside and all owned by people drawing the dole.

It was uncomfortable standing there in the mid-morning heat with not even a breeze to help. Milligan was taking notes. Monday morning and the two of them sweating while these bastards sat nonchalant as you like in the shade of the verandah. Lounging on the verandah of this clapped-out house that undoubtedly was not theirs. The tribe's, or someone who was doing time, quite likely. No paint for years and rotting wooden piles making it sag towards one end. What did they care? Sitting there with a beer and their stupid bloody hoods on a day any sane person would be in shorts at most. Or working, but that's how they were. Hiding in oversize jackets and hoods.

'You were having a party then? All afternoon? Until what time would that be? Four ... five?' He waited, staring into the eyes of the man with the cross on his cheek who was called Mercury.

'Midnight,' the man said. 'Or after that, sometime ... dunno.'

'And not finishing until around midnight,' confirmed Barker. 'And did anyone leave in that time?' Mercury shook his head almost imperceptibly, but he was raising his bottle so it might have been something else. The dark eyes gleamed. He did not know Pagett, he had said. He did not want to know. Did not care what had happened to him. 'Dead, eh? That's what happens.' And he leaned back against the wall and looked somewhere else.

'What about you?' Barker stared at the thin man with a moustache and a greenstone pendant hanging from his ear.

'He was with us. I told you.'

'I was asking him.'

'I was here drinking piss and fucking.' A toneless, soft voice with an educated accent that surprised Barker though he did not show it. The others grinned. Barker decided he was wasting time. For the present.

'I'll be back.' They looked away.

'Hey! Another beer out here.' Shouted into the dark doorway at someone unseen. Barker turned to his car.

'Get a warrant,' he said to Milligan as they drove away. 'Arrogant bastards! Shit it's hot!'

* * *

UNCLE LOUIS WAS sitting on the back door step. He did not answer the knock on his front door and he ignored Bill's greeting as he came around the side of the little house, pushing his way through the blue and purple hydrangeas. Bill sat on the pile of bricks and waited silently — plucking stalks of dry grass through the cracks and glancing at the old man who continued to stare at the ancient wooden palings of the fence. Three empty beer bottles lay on the grass at his feet and half a dozen cigarette butts were scattered around. Bill opened his mouth to speak then hesitated. Instead he studied the old man's face. He could see signs of great strain. Louis was nursing another beer but was clearly far, far away.

'You okay?' Bill asked at length. Louis nodded as in slow motion and pursed his lips. 'You don't look it,' said Bill. 'You look like you heard some bad news.'

Louis turned to look at the mossy weatherboards of Mrs Ogden's yellow house and did not answer. 'You want to know why I'm home early?'

'Nope.' Louis coughed after a time. 'No doubt you got your reasons.'

Silence descended again.

'Well, Merv and me had a fight.'

Dispassionately, Louis studied Bill's face for the first time. 'How does he look?'

'Not so good.'

'That's okay then.' He picked up his tobacco, sighed, and began to roll a fresh cigarette. Most of the tobacco fell from his clumsy fingers but he continued to roll the paper.

'You've got something on your mind.'

The lips pursed again and Louis lit the cigarette. The near-empty paper flared and he looked at it in surprise and then dropped it. 'What were you fighting about?'

'Oh ... fuck all. We don't always see eye to eye, Merv and me. Today it got a bit out of hand, that's all.'

Louis nodded. 'Bullshit,' he said mildly.

They stared past one another until at last Bill rose, 'I best go clean up. You coming over for dinner?' Louis nodded and looked up in time to see his nephew limping as he rounded the corner. The sight made him feel more despondent.

What am I going to do? he asked himself. It's a sunny day and I feel like I'm under the ground. Perhaps that's where I should be. Perhaps I've done my time. He put the bottle down and it fell over and drained into the grass. He made to kick it but his foot waved gently in the air. He sat still.

'It's not a pretty sight, is it?' the detective had said. But to Louis the photographs had not seemed real. They seemed like they had come from a story of some kind ... out of a magazine. Yet there he was, Pagett, lying in his own blood and in his own kitchen. And there were those words. There were those words smeared on the cupboard door just as Matarangi had said. And Louis had felt a weight of darkness fall over him at that instant that had not lifted.

It had been hard, even for someone with many years' practice keeping cool. 'Nope,' he told the detective. 'I hardly ever spoke to this man ... and I don't know why anyone would want to do this thing.'

And all the time his eyes shifted back to the photograph of those words and his old heart beat faster despite himself and he had to turn away so the detective wouldn't notice. Perhaps the detective already knew but Louis suspected not. He had asked a general question about Sam Wherry and Louis let it slide by without difficulty. He told him he hadn't seen Sam for a year, almost. That's how long, and he thought he'd gone back to Auckland. Somewhere up there. 'Working for a builder or something. Maybe a sparky.' Then the detective had asked him about the newcomers and suggested Louis might help to get some cooperation from them. Louis was grateful to talk about them instead of Sam and promised to help.

What am I going to do? he asked himself, and clenched his hands together. How long would it be before the police cottoned on? How long before they realised those words did not say anything about 'Mary'? How long before they found some handwriting to match, though that might not be so easy. How long before someone put two and two together and remembered all the sermonising? That wasn't so long ago and written on the wall of the fire station for all to see.

What to do? Murder was murder. How could it be? And yet, perhaps it was obvious — perhaps he should have seen it coming for a long time.

'You stupid — old — useless — bastard!' he said. 'You stupid — blind — useless — old ... bastard!' He stared at the back fence and remembered the graffiti on the fire station wall those years ago. Then he said out loud, though quiet: 'For the love of money ... is the root of all evil.' He glanced around anxiously, then his head sank into his hands. 'Sam, Sam, Sam ...' he said softly.

8

THE NEWS ABOUT Manuhuia and the destruction of the hangi stones spread quickly. Down at the pub people listened quietly, then some finished their beer and left, walking with a sense of indignation rising and feeling a deeper hurt. And they were watched by others who raised their glasses in salute to Merv Layton.

Up at the marae people weeding gardens and repainting the sleeping quarters came together in an incredulous silence as they heard. And then cries came like gulls flocking. Wails and angry exclamations, some staying and some leaving but the work finished for that day.

And on the verandah of the old house on the edge of the town, Mercury listened without opening his eyes while that silly young Headcase, whose real name was Jimmy, talked. He talked about how Uncle Louis had declared the stones could not be moved until the tapu had been lifted. That would mean something bad would come down on Merv Layton. That would mean he would get sick or something.

'Fuck!' said Mercury with a sigh. And the boy looked quickly at the scornful face and felt foolish.

'I don't believe that stuff. That's for weirdos,' Jimmy said. 'I might do something.'

'Yeah. You do something.'

Jimmy poked the dirt by the steps with his stick and tried to think of something better. He told how the bush had been burned by Pagett. 'No one wanted that,' he said. 'That's where the tupuna lie. Out there ...' and he gestured vaguely with his stick. He glanced at Mercury and admired the cross on his cheek and vowed to get one just the same. 'That's what's happening. Some serious stuff like that.'

'That is what is happening,' Mercury repeated. 'Some serious stuff.' And the way he smiled when he said those words made Jimmy thrill and he knew he had been right to tell.

* * *

DESPITE THE HEAT the door of the red cottage remained closed and silence reigned as the sun rose high, beating on the iron and making the sunflowers wilt. At two o'clock a magpie landed and bobbed around the grass until it spied the gleam of the stoat's eye, and with a sharp cry it scudded like a chequered dart over the languid flax.

In the gloom of the tiny living room with its ragged sofa and uneven table all covered with curled and fading plans, a mouse explored around the stove, near the fridge and under the table, its pink ears listening. Listening all the while to the restlessness that remained in another room. And the shaft of bright sunlight moved across the floor until it made the ashes in the grate glow with renewed energy.

All the while the woman curled under the thin grey blanket shivered and dreamed and cried sometimes. Deep in the drugged sleep of exhaustion and red wine, yet sometimes so lucid the air itself was visible and the taste of the iron walls so bitter she caught her head in her caliper hands.

At four o'clock she reached out and saw her frail fingers unfurl like pale petals in the darkness, and she called: 'Take my hand. Please take my hand.'

* * *

IN THE NORTHERN hills the dogs led the men through the valleys beyond the Lynch farm to the ridge and down the other side. They started in the early morning and came together in their small teams at midday to decide their new course and to eat a sandwich. Calling sometimes and listening, but finding no trace and nursing private misgivings and dark thoughts about the strange times and circumstances in which they found themselves. And being grateful sometimes for the fatigue that comes with an unselfish task but wondering all the same whether the day could ever end in triumph.

John Reid and Pete Lynch, George Ngataki, Harold Watts and his two boys, and many others also, strung out through the bush behind the police dog handlers.

'We'll finish tonight at the trig,' the constable said and they made that point at nine o'clock as the sun sank into the sea. The men exchanged quiet looks of disappointment.

'Tomorrow we'll head away towards the coast,' the policeman said, and tried to sound like that was exactly where they should be.

* * *

THE SINGING OF frogs. Down at McCleod's dam the croaking had been increasing for days as tadpoles made their strange journey. Now they crept to the edge of the raupo in liveries of green and gold and sang and sang, and their call was a magnet for other creatures. And the grey heron stalked the edges of the rushes, gliding on spindly legs to spear the unwary singer. And deep in the rushes the brown bittern, impossible to see when it did not move, lanced passers-by as effortlessly as if they were ripe fruit hanging. Even the clumsy pukeko in its brazen blue and red stalked with ease and frogs were gulped, skewered, macerated and wounded all around the pond. But many survived, and the singing would rise and fall, rise and fall.

And the sound carried down the creek that left the dam to wind its way through the gully below the homestead and past the pine trees near the road and under the culvert. It carried to the ears of other creatures with an intense interest. Dangerous creatures that carried long sticks whittled from lancewood, sharpened to a point and charred in a fire so the smooth tip was as hard as glass. They listened to the croaking coming from the dam and they sat on the low concrete parapet above the culvert in which '1946' was cast, and they deliberated. But they had not noticed the date and it would have been as meaningless to them as any hieroglyph. They were listening and thinking. They were thinking how much they would like to get near to that dam so they could spear a frog with spears newly forged and as yet unblooded. Waiting impatiently all the school day and hearing that song as powerful as any siren. They sat and dangled their brown legs over the culvert, side by side, and stared into the trickling water edged by cress and under which they knew small eels would be sheltering. But they had been after eels last Monday and got three. They were not interested in eels today. Only frogs. But the frogs were up at the dam and the dam was near the house and the house was the McCleods'.

So they sat silently and stared into the clear water, noticing small larvae swimming and a large dragonfly hovering with its two pairs of gauzy wings beating so they looked like shimmering lights. And beyond the frogs they heard the tremulous quavering of the tiny grey warbler in the boxthorn that was the hedge along the side of the road that you needed to be careful about, because that was a thorn that could really hurt your foot. And the sun beat down on bare backs and that was good and it didn't matter much if you didn't move because that was just a good feeling. But the frogs were singing louder than ever and calling.

'It's the best place,' said Jake, matter of factly.

'I know.'

'If we went through the pines and stayed on that side.'

'Yep.'

The legs swung lazily in unison below the culvert and the dragonfly darted six inches and then hovered. A spear drew back as though to throw, then slowly moved until it poked into a bare foot.

'That's sharp.'

'I know.'

The grey warbler sang and the sun beat down.

'If we were on the other side of the raupo.'

'No one could see us.'

'I know.'

They sat silently and then Matty rose and Jake did likewise and followed without another word, off the culvert and through the gap in the boxthorn, but stepping very carefully, and through the slack hanging wire on the old fence. Standing exposed in the field on the wrong side and needing to go low, so Matty ran down the slope to the edge of the creek and leapt over where there was a narrow bit and ran along the bank towards the pines.

'Now we're safe.'

'Yep.'

Looking about in the dim light under the close-planted trees with their thick bed of silent needles like a carpet everywhere. They approached a ring of red and white spotted toadstools and examined them without speaking. Then Matty drew back a few paces and raised the spear above his head and hurled it at the largest. The long stick missed the toadstool and stood quivering. Jake stood in the same place, poised, raised his spear and sent it clean through the toadstool so it broke in half.

'Fluke!'

'Nope.'

Several throws later and all the toadstools but one small specimen with a strange wrinkle on its edge were smashed into large fragments. They looked like bloodied snow on the ground.

The spear tips were carefully cleaned on the dry needles and examined for damage.

'Mine's hardly dented.'

'Same.'

Matty led the way through the trees towards the end nearest the dam and paused at the edge. The croaking was so loud now it filled the air and was intoxicating in its allure so that the spears were given one or two unconscious jerks in hands already visualising the kill. But there was a long stretch of open ground between the trees and the bottom of the dam. Exposed for a good run. They stared at each other and frowned, then Matty ran and was immediately followed by his brother. Heads down and running fast, leaping from place to place along the line of the meandering creek and startling a wool blind sheep that ran helter-skelter into a wire fence that twanged and squeaked to make four brown eyes pop and four brown legs run even faster.

And then headlong into the edge of the raupo so the frog chorus stopped as if a switch had been thrown and a pukeko squawked and leapt into awkward flapping flight to the other end of the dam. Then all was silent except for the panting of the hunters. Listening. Then one frog way back, a tentative beginning uuururp, uuururp. And then another across the other side, and then another. And soon many singing and so close now.

'So many.' Whispered.

'I know.'

'Round this way.'

Matty creeping forward with his spear raised and Jake following, and hidden from the purview of the house on the hill, by the tall raupo reeds that rustled mysteriously though there was no breeze.

'Watch out for a pukeko.' A nod and a meaningful shiver of the spear and the squinting of a hunter's eye taking aim at an imaginary target. Feet in warm water at the edge of the dam and croaking all around; feet stopping and bodies frozen as eyes searched the green sedges and brown water for the two shiny beads that would indicate the presence of a half-submerged quarry. An arm moving back and a sudden throw, and the spear dashing forward to hit the stem of a reed and a splash as the brilliant frog leapt to safety. Silence nearby, but frogs further over undeterred.

'Missed.'

'I know.' Retrieving the spear and examining the tip. 'Close though.'

'My turn.' Creeping past Matty and edging forward, listening and eyes straining because that croaking is so loud that frog must be almost on my foot. An arm poised above for an age so it begins to feel an ache, and surely that frog must be so close, and there he is. Not even looking but throat swelling so you can see it even from behind and that strange sound coming into the reeds and filling your head so there is no other sound anywhere in the world. And then hurling so that white stick flashes through the green and stabs the frog into the swamp, then lunging forward with a whoop to procure the prize. Wriggling feebly with its guts hanging out and its golden eyes already shut tight.

'Ha! That was a good throw. One of my best. Look how far.'

'Not that far.'

'Heaps. My first. I'll get another.'

'I'm going to try more round. You make too much noise.' A little disconsolate, Matty walking to the edge and wondering how come his first throw missed because it had been closer but not by that much. But still ... and then another sound. Boots. Large boots coming quickly and a thrill of alarm and even panic.

'Run for it!' Breaking from concealment and running through the raupo and Jake stumbling and crashing headlong and hearing a shout. An angry shout and deep, of someone big coming.

'Wait!' Jake crying out and scrambling along and sprinting and another shout and the big boots running too, around the left to cut off the way down the creek to the pines. And bursting out of the raupo straight at the man standing with a stick in his hand and a red face and outraged teeth everywhere and shouting. The stick raised in the air and loud words: 'Little bastards! Stop!'

But neither slowing, and splitting one left and one right and dashing by even as a stick swished but missed and fleeing as though a horror was on them. Hearing a heavy tread for a short while and then stopping: 'Black bastards! Keep off! Thieving little bastards! I'll get you!' Reaching the pines, scrambling and risking a backward glance and seeing it would be okay but not pausing.

Through the fence without a glance for boxthorn and out onto the road and running for a hundred yards to the grove of cabbage trees and plunging into them and falling to the ground out of sight of the road. Heaving chests for an age and an occasional foot poking the other but no words and then a glance and finally a grin and then laughing.

'You were shit-scared.'

'You! You falling over like an old 'un and screaming out!'

'Both of us.'

'Yep.'

Lying under the cabbage trees and peace returning and listening to the rubbing of those spiky leaves on stalks and a cicada just up the trunk that might become a target in due course. Listening and thinking.

'You black bastard.' Said softly and experimentally, and glancing at Matty who frowned.

'Thieving black bastard.' Frowning and then rolling over and examining the dirt. At last: 'Did he mean you or me?' Looking at each other and feeling peculiar.

'That was Joe McCleod.'

'I know.'

They lay in the sun and thought about how he looked. With his angry red mouth and harsh voice. They talked about how scary it had been.

'Someone's coming!'

They watched through the bracken and then relaxed. They watched the gangling youth coming up the road swinging a baseball bat and occasionally pausing to hit a homer.

'It's Jimmy.' They climbed from their hiding place and Jimmy froze with the bat extended in a two-handed grip and his smoke protruding like a signal from his thin brown face. He removed the smoke and said, 'You shouldn't do that! Creeping out like that — I could smack you with this bat.' He allowed it to fall. 'What're you doing?'

'Nothing. We been hunting.'

Jimmy smirked. 'Hunting,' he said scornfully. 'Frogs, more like. That's for kids.'

'What're you doing then?' asked Matty, chastened.

Jimmy looked mysterious then drew on his smoke and blew a cloud that the boys watched as it writhed and suddenly disappeared. 'You want one?'

'Nah.'

'Yep. I do.' Matty stepped towards him and held out his hand. 'One of those big guys gave us one.'

'Did you smoke it?'

'Nope. We were going to but we lost them.'

Jimmy smirked again. 'All right. But yous got to smoke it here.' He dug in his trousers and produced a packet, pulled out two cigarettes and gave them to his companions. 'Go on then.' He struck a match and watched Matty and Jake suck and cough. He laughed loudly then picked up his bat and smacked it into the cabbage tree with a thunk. 'I'm making plans,' he said. 'I'm going to do something ...'

They came close. 'What? What're you going to do?'

'Oh, something about what that cunt up there did ...' He watched their eyes widen and grinned. 'I hang out with Mercury and the boys now. Not that loser Harkness. And we got something going down! You know what I mean?'

They shook their heads and he snorted. 'Course not — you're only kids! Can't even smoke or nothing!'

'Who's Mercury?'

'Ha! Don't even know! He's the number one man, that's who he is. And he knows I'm going to do something. Maybe tonight ... maybe tomorrow. I'm still planning something big.'

'Can we come?'

'Ha!' Jimmy dropped his butt and ground it into the road. 'Kids!' And he hit the trunk of the tree again. 'But I s'pose you got to learn some time,' he said, turning. 'Otherwise yous'll be green all your goddam lives! But I got to go.'

'What about us?'

'You come round later. Then we'll see.' And he strode off up the road leaving the two boys staring after and thinking how good it was to be changing from green into something else.

* * *

RACHEL WALKED AROUND the side of the house, enjoying the warm breeze coming down the valley that barely ruffled her irises, blue and gold against the pale grey of the wall. She could not see the colours in the moonlight but it did not matter. Bright enough tonight to see across the river flats and up into the bush hills. Bright enough to see a possum sitting on one of the power poles fifty metres away. Motionless as stone, sitting up there in the night. Enjoying the stillness, like her perhaps.

She sat at the wooden barbecue table that Pete had built many years ago but which hadn't seen a barbecue since ... two summers? When her cousins came for Christmas? That long? She lit a cigarette and remembered when there had been four little kids milling about. Shouting and playing. Falling in her flowers, but she hadn't minded. Not at all, she told the anxious mother. Let them play. Falling and fighting and chasing. She loved to watch them. She wished they were hers. And pushed the thought from her mind.

It's not so bad, she told herself. Life's not so bad. Even when the terrible things happened, it was still better to be alive than not. What's my life? She pondered. Not too much really. The cows. Looking after the land. Looking after Pete. Not much else. But did that matter? Some things weren't so good but many people were much worse off.

Even rich people. Their money hadn't made them better, or happier — sometimes just the opposite. She had read this.

She thought about the fight that had occurred up at the roadworks. It was mostly gossip, she supposed, but it was sad if it was true. Even partly true — that Bill Manuhuia had attacked Merv Layton. That was a sad thing. She didn't know Bill well, or Merv really for that matter. Not much more than to say hullo to either of them down in the town. Pete knew them both. He said Merv was a good guy. He said Bill was okay too. But then he attacked Merv on the job, they said. Tried to run him down in his flatdeck. She shook her head slowly and tried to imagine what would prompt such strange behaviour. Perhaps it was the weather. Men were susceptible to the weather. She remembered when they were younger Pete had always got randier if the wind was strong. Like clockwork it had been. She had had to prepare herself as the wind got up. When she could hear it in the pines across the gully, she knew he would pounce. That was good. She dragged on her cigarette and remembered. The pines were gone now though. And sometimes it didn't seem to matter how hard the wind blew.

She wondered why things in the town were not so good. She tried to think about whether it was a new thing or a trend or just coincidence. Were people worse? Were people unhappier or what? Someone said Bill had road rage, and then they had fought until they were both knocked out. She shook her head. Surely it must be the weather?

The window rattled up behind her and a butt flew out onto the grass. The tip still glowed but faded quickly. She stubbed out her own and walked back in the front door and made her way to the darkened bedroom.

'I was thinking about Bill and Merv,' she said. 'Why they were fighting and why people seem to be unhappy.'

'That's just how it is.'

She pulled back the sheet and slid in next to Pete.

'I don't know. There seems to be something wrong. We've lived here all these years and I don't remember anything like this. Friends fighting. All that thing about Pagett's land and him murdered.' She shuddered. 'Now that man drowned. And the little boy ... it seems too much. I'm frightened.'

Pete lit another cigarette and thought about Melanie Blackman. He thought about her long legs and her breasts, tight and perky as turnips. He thought about Mahler fucking her and felt envious. Bloody prick, he thought.

'Why can't we do something, Pete?'

Pete wondered what it must have been like. When she was naked and wrapping those long legs around you. That would have to be something. That prick. How did he manage that?

'Pete?'

'What?'

'Why can't we do something?'

'About what?' he said crossly.

'About all the things going on. About the problems people are having with each other. We are a community after all but we don't seem to act like one. It's like no one seems to care about anyone else.' Pete grunted. Perhaps he paid her? That was possible. Big-time yank with lots of cash and living out there — out of sight. That must be it — the bastard! 'Pete?'

'What?'

'Do you care?'

'Not much.'

Rachel lay quietly and wondered whether it mattered. Pete didn't care.

'I think we should. Care, I mean. I think we have a responsibility to do something.'

Pete sighed. 'Like what? Woman? What do you think you're going to do? Set up a soup kitchen?'

'Oh, I don't know. But I think we should think about it instead of simply accepting that things are bad.'

'They're always bad. They stink! Things always stink!'

'No they don't,' and she laughed. A clear, happy laugh. She was amused because things never stank. They could be troublesome but while she had her cows and her flowers they could never possibly stink. 'You are such an old gripe.'

Pete listened to her laugh and unaccountably felt better. He remembered that laugh. She had laughed that way since he had known her and it was a good sound. He turned towards her and said: 'I was thinking about screwing Melanie Blackman.'

She laughed again. 'Pete? What?' And she continued to laugh. 'You are so awful. I should kick you out! You're such a lecherous, horrible man!' And she knew he was telling her the truth but it didn't matter.

'Don't you want to hit me or something?'

'What for? You can't help being crazy. You're an old goat!'

He slid an arm across her stomach and squeezed. 'You're a mad woman, aren't you? Any other woman would shoot me. But not you. I'm lucky, aren't I?'

'I don't know. I don't know.' And she laughed softly. 'You're all I have and it's enough.'

Pete looked at her profile in the moonlight. At the curve of her nose and her cheeks. They hadn't changed much after all these years. He ran his hand over her breast, gently.

'You're a fine woman, Rachel. I'm not good enough for you.'

'You're an old goat.'

'You think you can put up with an old goat?'

'I keep hoping the wind will get up ...' She turned and looked into the gleam of his eyes. 'You think it might?'

'I think so. I think this might be a windy old night. Give me a hand.'

Outside the possum looked the other way. High up on his pole in the warm air with scarcely a sound anywhere. He looked down the valley towards the sea. Scarcely a sound except for that rocking in the house. From that black square in the side of the house. A rocking noise coming from there but not dangerous. Just a rocking sound like branches knocking together in the wind.

* * *

THE REID HOMESTEAD gleamed in the moonlight. The Tasman Sea gleamed and sheep were near as visible as by day. Still eating, even now, late in the evening they wandered, heads down and grazing. A peculiar wrenching sound as they tore short tufts of dry grass with their sharp teeth. Crunch, crunch, crunch.

The sprinkler on the front garden spun rhythmically. Swish, swish, swish. And the people in the sitting room talked.

The sounds of the night. Peaceful sounds as they had been for many years. For many decades. The dogs sat silently in their kennels with their beady eyes and occasionally an ear would cock when a cat wandered arrogantly by or a hedgehog snuffled in the mulch.

And people talked about children at school and their grades and the prices of wool and mutton. The prices of cattle and the American burger market and the Chinese woollen industry. But only when they needed respite from talking about the search or Merv Layton and Bill Manuhuia, and agreeing that Merv had done the right thing. Some drank a toast to Merv and they agreed a stand had to be taken lest Mokau started to go backwards. To sink back into the bush and no one in their right mind would want to come and it wouldn't be worth farming if things weren't sorted out soon. And in the room it was as though a valve had been opened and the steam hissed strongly.

Someone said it was probably just a half a dozen shit-stirrers, if that. Might be only two or three. Peta Patai was named. She was definitely one of them, and better educated too — that was a strange thing. They all needed to be better educated then when one was — look what happened?

But look at old Louis, someone said. He was not a shit-stirrer. Good old guy and always was — pleasant and polite and they all used to be like that. Really pleasant and polite and good-natured — that was the thing you noticed mostly. Talk to him down the whitebait stands any time and share a cuppa. That was so true! Never had any trouble a few years ago, but now ...

Someone asked, 'How safe is it?' The police still hadn't arrested anyone. What if it was not a personal thing but a weird political act? Someone said, 'Hauhau', and the room fell momentarily silent. 'Don't be bloody daft!'

'The Hauhau were mad. What's to say it hasn't started again?'

'That was the nineteenth century, for God's sake!' But the men agreed that it was best to keep a rifle handy regardless.

Someone said their fathers would simply not have believed it was possible for all this to have happened. When we were kids we all played together, went eeling and stuff like that. Haymaking and shearing — you name it. Played rugby — what the hell had happened? It was like a disease or something had got into people.

Someone said it was the politicians, and there was general agreement that they had raised 'expectations'. You can't keep agreeing that people had been disadvantaged without getting them all excited and anti everything you've built up. Instead of seeing that you have to get on and do things yourself, every Maori with a grievance can waste the country's time arguing for a hand-out. A whole generation growing up thinking they were owed.

Hot sausage rolls and asparagus sandwiches were passed around and were well received.

'What if it was Mahler? No, seriously, it just might be.' It seemed too much coincidence that the two things should happen together.

'That's ridiculous. He had dinner here. He was perfectly pleasant — urbane.' 'What's that?' 'Don't be a pain, Geoff.'

'But that's the thing with those sorts of people — you just don't know. Doctors, lawyers, judges even. It was well known. It was a worldwide thing involving all sorts of people you would never suspect. Business people ...'

'Men! Well, yes, mostly men, probably. No probably about it!'

'So it could be ... Mahler? Yes. He seemed a bit, what's that word ... like feminine?' 'Rubbish! He wasn't a farmer that's all, and he was having an affair!' A momentary silence again.

'Yeah, well — the bastard deserved something for what he's done to Buchanan. That's my view.'

'That's typical! You don't know anything about it. You don't know anything about what happened or about Beth Gilbert.'

'Well it bloody shouldn't! And Mr Bloody-Lily-White was at the girl as well.'

'Lucky bastard!'

'You are disgusting!'

'Just kidding ... sorry.'

AND the moon cleared the macrocarpas and washed the garden with its silver light and the white roses shone like stars. A small group stood on the verandah to smoke and listened silently to the conversation flowing through the open French doors.

'It's more likely it's the Maoris. It's more likely some of those who still believe that crap about the spirits. Like it's all very well being respectful — about cemeteries and things like that — but a burial ground hundreds of years old? And hidden under the bush? No one ever went out there with flowers, for chrissakes. I'll bet no one even knew who was buried there!'

'They bloody ate each other and that's a fact.'

'I'd like to know where's the boy? I fear for that boy.'

'We searched all day. Covered a huge amount of ground but not a trace.'

'Poor little beggar ... if he's been ... you know ...'

'Damn right!'

Inside someone asked, 'Is anyone going to the funeral?'

* * *

'WHAT WOULD YOU think if I said we should move?'

'Move? What do you mean? Where to?'

'Australia. Gold Coast maybe.' Merv Layton returned his wife's gaze until it became uncomfortable. 'What?' he demanded, 'I'm just thinking.' He raised his beer and stared across the dark valley with a few lights sprinkled like fireflies. Never in the ten years since he'd built this house had he felt more uncomfortable than he did tonight.

'Well, don't! Is it the thing with Bill?'

'A bit. A bit it is. But it's been building up. Sometimes I think I'd like a change. I get a bit sick of the same old stuff. The roadworks, the rain ...'

'I don't believe you. You've never said that before.'

'Well, that's because I just get on with the job, that's all.'

'It's the business with Bill Manuhuia,' she repeated flatly.

Merv sighed. 'I guess so. But more than that. There's the thing with Pagett and then that looney Patai woman on TV. It all seems to be going screwball. We used to just do things. You know what I mean?

We all just got on with it and now it seems the further we get the more we go backwards. Pulled back to a time I don't even understand. I'm not even interested. You know what I mean?'

'Yes. I do,' she said slowly, 'I do know but I don't let it bother me. We have a good life, Merv. You have a good life.'

'Maybe. At least I always thought that way but just lately ... with Bill and all that. It really pisses me off. I can't for the life of me understand how we got to be fighting. Him and me? Crazy!'

'Yes it is. But I think you did the right thing.'

They stared into the night.

'Maybe. But I've been thinking about a shift for a while. There's plenty of contracting work around Brisbane. We could easily make a go of it there and be shot of all this.'

She didn't respond for a while, wondering how best to deal with this unexpected agitation.

'I don't know ...' She placed her hand on his arm and he covered it with his. 'This is our home and it would be a big jolt for the kids. Moving them from their schools. I don't think that would be good and I'm certainly not going to leave them here.'

'Do you think they would find it so hard?'

'I do! I really do, Merv. All their friends are here. They're settled in and doing well. I doubt you could drag them away. Patrick wouldn't move!'

'No. He'd be difficult.' Merv felt proud. Patrick was a sportsman. Better than his dad, but then that's the sort of opportunities he'd gained at a private school. I never had that, he thought, and that's what I've given him. But it hadn't happened by accident. He had worked hard to build a damned good business.

'What about Bill?'

'Fuck him!'

'There's no need for that language!' But it was a soft reproof.

A long silence ensued and far back in the hills in impenetrable darkness, they heard the roll of thunder. Merv breathed deeply and wondered at the strange confusion in his head. He needed to say something but it was not taking any clear form.

'Something happened that day,' he said at last. She looked at him sharply. 'With Manuhuia. Something's changed ...' He frowned heavily and rubbed his forehead with his free hand. It's sort of like nothing looks quite the same. You know what I mean? The hills, the river, the road even. The same but not. I can't figure it.' He sighed and sat up. 'Strange, eh?'

'I don't know what you're talking about.' Her voice was strained.

'Me neither. It's just that I drive to work and I look at things and they seem different. Sort of like they just appeared. Sounds daft but it's like I know them but then I don't.'

She fidgeted. 'Are you feeling all right? You're not feeling a bit off-colour?'

His loud laugh, abrupt like a bark, was disconcerting. Neither spoke for a while and she hoped that whatever it was would pass.

'Ill? I don't think so.' He felt embarrassed that she should think he was unwell. 'I've never felt like this before,' he said slowly. 'That's why it sounds daft. Like Bill ... I don't even know who he is.' And as he exhaled he knew he had said something that disturbed him deeply. 'That's the thing — I don't even know who Bill Manuhuia is! Known him all my life but he seems foreign. Shit!' He sat forward suddenly and felt an unpleasant sensation bubbling in his chest. 'That's daft! Why don't you come to bed? Why ...'

'Just listen a moment!' He looked at her fiercely and was startled by the strength of his own turmoil. 'I'm not unwell! Bloody hell! Something's bothering me, that's all. And it started after that bloody fight.' He rose and walked to the edge of the deck, then turned towards her. 'People thinking I'm great and all that bullshit! And then the whole place ... I wonder ... I've lived here all my life. It's my place. All this,' he swung his arm around the unseen horizon. 'The hills and the sea and everything. It's where I come from. But now, something's happened. I don't know Bill Manuhuia. I'm not even sure about ... me.' He lapsed into silence and crashed back into his chair. She came to stand behind him and began to massage his broad neck. Those huge dependable shoulders. Her lips compressed at the many splintery thoughts flying.

The long wail of the fire siren pierced the sultry air and even before it finished they could see car headlights racing in the direction of the fire station. They watched for several minutes in silence. Watching to see in which direction the fire engine would go, and as always she said: 'Someone's world is coming down. Oh do be quick.'

'It's going up the valley,' he said with misgiving. 'The Lynchs' or the McCleods'. Or Pagett's,' he said with the certainty of afterthought.

9

~ Oct 20

Ringatu. He is considerably younger than I. Early thirties maybe more. The tattoo is quite weird and there is something about the man's face that inspires circumspection. I wondered whether he could speak English. Though it was warm he wore the same long brown coat and his hair was tied back the way I had seen in the forest. At that moment, staring at each other on the rocks on that remote coast, I felt like the first Pakeha! And the bloody dog licked him.

I asked him what he wanted and received no response. In fact, I think he had the temerity to be amused. Then he asked me what I was going to do with my fish! He said kahawai needed to be treated properly, and without the slightest concession on my part, strode over, took the fish and in a moment had slit it from tail to gills. I have never encountered a situation like this and I decided that discretion was advised. Nevertheless, following him up the beach to my own track — like a kid, with the dog acting all the while as though the man was a friend was a tough call.

I told him we were on my property — that it was my track but again received no response. He is an arrogant bastard.

At my cottage he threw the fish on the grass and began gathering twigs from the undergrowth. He lit a fire — right there on my lawn — and then asked for salt and pepper. He wasn't threatening at all, but I felt I had little option. He split the fish into two wings, rubbed in the salt and pepper and lay the fish on the edge of the coals. A surly waiter, I produced plates, wine, bread and butter!

He placed one wing on my plate and the other on his and seated himself on the edge of the porch.

'I'm Ringatu,' he said. I introduced myself and remarked about his apparent relationship with my dog.

'Your dog?' he said without the slightest surprise. 'Your dog has been my dog since he was a rat. But he can be your dog if you want.' It makes sense.

I asked him about his activities on Pagett's land but he refused 'to speak of such matters while I am enjoying such a fine meal, lest it give me indigestion'. The truth is, the fish was delicious, and despite the simplicity of preparation it tasted far better than my previous efforts.

When he had finished he produced tobacco and proceeded to roll a cigarette. He did not offer any, but I no longer felt uncomfortable.

'You ask why I kill cattle?' he said. 'What would you do if someone pissed on your father's grave?'

I didn't answer and he said: 'This land, that you sit upon is the resting place. It is simple enough'.

When I asked him to explain, he quoted some scripture! Old Testament I am guessing, and then he said that his task was to listen to the turehu! I recalled Gertie using this word and when I suggested that it meant a spirit of the forest he seemed appreciative.

And that was that. He thanked me for the wine and strode off down the hill and, to my consternation, was followed by Chinook. I am unsure that he is not deranged. In some way he seems to be two personalities — the other being that of a zealot. He might seem educated at any time and then reveals he is as superstitious as a fairground shyster.

But this — not a word about my dory!

It seems to me that this encounter is no mere coincidence. The resemblance to Luke is uncanny and the fact that he should be here? I am unsure what to do next though I am eager to see his face again.

I have continued to use the spokeshave on the dory planking and it is coming along well. I have also completed the nailing along the seams. It looks extremely professional, with the rows of nails and the red glue giving it the appearance of a surgical operation. And I do feel like a surgeon. I will contemplate my work for a while. I no longer feel such haste.

I have decided to return to my painting tomorrow and hope that Beth might invite me again. I have been reflecting on yesterday's encounter with Ringatu. For some reason I do not yet understand, I feel pleased.

Melanie appeared this morning. She was 'just out riding'. I do not believe her. I had been preparing to go into town to recommence my painting. I asked her whether she knew Sean and while at first she said not, when I described him she was immediately aware. The 'Walker Boy', she called him. He was 'dumb', she said. I told her he was mute. She said yes but quickly lost interest.

I said I was going to paint. She was quite put out that I should leave so soon and I swear she attempted to provoke me. Not that that is difficult, she moves the way only a few girls ever learn to do — or is it simply instinctive with some? Like a cat, and I have to say I would be pleased to give her a stroke! I suggested she might come back for a meal some time. She was petulant at first but pleased nonetheless. She puts it on but then reverts to a natural demeanour that is charming. I think she realises that affectation is unlikely to work with someone so venerable. Ha!

In the event, I did not get to the school because I ran into Pete again and he insisted I accompany him to his farm. I met his wife Rachel who is delightful but shy. She failed to catch my eye for at least an hour, but when we went to the cowshed to milk, she became much more animated and talked quite freely about 'her girls'. It is amazing to be so close to such large animals, with their huge eyes and strength. And the smell! God, it is unlike anything I have ever encountered. But it is not unpleasant at all — just intense.

They are a very nice couple, although my impression of Pete is that he is restless. He couldn't stay with one thing —

sometimes talking to us, interrupting sometimes, and then disappearing to do something in a nearby shed. His wife seems to pain him in some indefinable way. Working with those cows, pushing them about, operating the milking machinery and yet all the time talking about the hills and the farm as though she was seeing them for the very first time. I think she is admirable.

Pete was enthusiastic about a pig! My first! I have never touched a pig before and in fact it was not what I expected. This smallish animal, which he calls Rastus, is very hairy and HARD. It has tusks! Pete said it was a wild pig that a local boy captured as a piglet. We fed it an apple and it seemed most appreciative but I took care not to get close to its mouth. It looks unpredictable to me. It is much shorter than my pig, which is an excessively long beast with cunning eyes.

Rachel insisted I stay for dinner and I am very glad. A delicious meat pie that reminded me how rudimentary my own cuisine has become. By nine o'clock it was apparent Pete was quite drunk and I could sense Rachel's discomfort. I promised to come again. By that time, I am quite sure Pete had not the faintest idea who I was.

The louts I ordered from my property were outside the store. They are not attractive and seem to have nothing else to do. But then, who am I to criticise?

* * *

THREE OF THEM in the night creeping like commandos. Creeping across the dry grass and all the while eyeing the house on the edge of the hill. Grateful when a cloud stole the light so they hastened forward, but stopping frequently and listening to their own excited breathing and feeling the pumping in their chests like a kicking animal.

Hearing cars on the highway far down the valley and their eyes glowing, and smelling the fresh-cut grass and feeling like warriors. But freezing when a cow cantered away in the gloom making a noise on the hard ground like a car with no tyres, and saying 'Shit!' in a harsh whisper.

Creeping forward to the base of the hill and standing close to listen and gaze, eyes straining to see and thinking how it would be. Climbing in single file on hands and knees because the slope was steep and the dry grass slippery as soap, and the tin can being carefully placed by the tallest one, not wanting to share — wanting to carry that precious burden by himself.

Listening for any sound of someone on the other side where the light remained all through the night but hearing nothing. And then the one with the can moving forward alone and sliding up to the bottom of the house, unscrewing the top and being overwhelmed by the thrilling monstrousness of that smell. With shaking hands and his head hammering like tympanies that surely could be heard across the other side of the valley, spilling the contents along the ground and splashing them onto the painted boards.

Then a dog barking like artillery going off and a shout in the still night, surely bringing them all. Soft urgent cries down the hill but knowing the mission was not yet done. And the sound of footsteps round the other side, crunching on the gravel, and then the voice of the enemy calling out.

'Who's about?'

Fumbling in the dark but finding the packet and dropping it and nearly wetting his pants but it would be done. It would be done, and striking the match and tossing it at the boards and *Whoosh!*

Light all over the sky and flames flashing everywhere, across the grass and right up his leg and him screaming in fear and falling back, hitting at his legs and falling back over the side of the hill and rolling down like a catherine wheel spinning.

The sky burning and two running across the field leaping and stumbling and looking back and seeing flames high above the roof of the house and a man momentarily on the edge and then jumping down the slope after them.

'Jimmy!'

And hearing the screams of the human candle at the base of the hill, the bigger one turning to run back but stopping and seeing the constable in a cocoon of bad light, beating Jimmy with his jacket until the flames were gone. Wrapping the boy and cradling him while high above the wood exploded and the iron blew into the freaking sky.

And two boys sprinted across the field to the road with the fire siren coming at them like a death dragon.

'Jimmy's dead!' Jake screamed. And the oystercatcher cried shrilly as it sped down the river towards the sea.

* * *

~ Something happened! Today I went directly to her classroom and felt the most unaccountable excitement. Of course he was oblivious to my presence. Or not? He turned though I had made not a sound and nor had I been seen. He just turned and looked at me for a moment and something changed in his face. I am savouring that glance still.

The kids clearly adore Beth and she has the most radiant smile. It was apparent though that something was making her especially cheerful. She took me into her small office at the side of the room.

'Sit down, Painter Tom!' That's what she said, and she produced my horse but there on the paper, behind the horse, was another creature. As hideous a monster as I have seen, and coming from a crayon wielded by a small boy it was unsettling. It might conceivably have been a spider since there appeared to be several legs, but the body was more the elongate thorax of a beetle. And its eyes were not those of an insect but a human. The mouth that clearly intended to bite the horse contained many long, pointed teeth like those of a shark. The creature was simple in design but the in-fill colour was crude and often broke the outline of the animal. The whole gave a feeling of intensity and danger.

I found the depiction disturbing and I still do, but Beth seemed delighted that something had appeared where previously his paper had remained stubbornly blank. She told me they would do some more art in about a half-hour, so I could wait or come back. But she was adamant that I must spend some more time with Sean. I couldn't have wished for more.

I visited 'Superior Merchandising' and talked to Melanie. She is as melodramatic as anyone I have met — pronouncing her life to be 'death'. She demands to know why I am here and when I will leave. I diverted her with difficulty. Notwithstanding, she told me she was coming to visit in the morning.

I watched them depict 'Life in the city', but not Sean. While skyscrapers and a multitude of cars and people (of equal size in many cases) sprang to life all around him, he remained motionless.

I will mention Jake and Matty, for it was they who coined my new nickname — 'Painter Tom'. Jake termed his tall buildings 'sky-pokers'! This seems apposite, but as evidence of his complete misunderstanding, he had drawn a fowl sitting on top that, if all were to scale, would have weighed all of a hundred tons! He told me a fowl runs a long way without its head. He said he speared a fowl and I said I believed him. I drew the line at his claim to have also speared a hippo — up at the McCleods' dam!

There seemed nothing I could say that made the slightest impression on Sean and it pained me in a way I found hard to bear. I so wanted to share something. Perhaps that's why Luke came to me then. I pictured the tree I have named the Mohican — but with Luke, and Mike and Doggitt — and I began to tell this boy. I described the Mohican where the elephants fly. I told him how they go there to learn what is happening in the forest. How they talk to the Mohican and hear her thoughts in the breeze. She is the oldest thing in all the world and has seen everything from the time even before the animals, and she tells them what to do when life is hard. When there's not enough food and she alone knows the direction in which they should go. Sometimes to the Mango Island itself! That's when the elephants are so important. They carry the animals across the water or they bring food back to those who are unable to travel far. I told him this.

I told him how Luke and Mike and Doggitt were the best

friends of the Mohican, even closer than the elephants. But how they all had to be careful about the Blackness — a sly and evil beast with cunning eyes that crashed about in the forest, terrifying many animals and breaking many worthwhile things and scorching the earth with its evil breath.

And he touched my arm! Even now, as I recall, I am excited. He reached out and I was there. I was there just as I was so long ago. Now it can be different!

I drew the Mohican for him and no sooner did my hand come to rest than he took the pencil from me and commenced to draw.

Now I know. Now I know why I am building the dory. And yet maybe the mystery of my existence has grown by many orders of magnitude. I have prayed for Luke and he is here.

Mary closed her eyes and ran her hands, so gently across his handwriting. She could see him crouching by the small boy. She could feel the struggle to make sense of things he had avoided all his life. She studied the new sketch of the Mohican that had the addition of many elaborate animals around and above it. She frowned at the leering creature she knew must be the 'Blackness'. She turned the page.

~ I know I cannot turn back the clock but even if I could, I am not sure I would not do the same again. Am I an evil man?

I am so tired now. We walked far up the coast, Chinook and I. There was a dead seal but I could not tell why it had died. How many miles of ocean had it travelled only to lie, pecked by gulls and sinking into the wet sands on this lonely coast? Who had it known? What strange things had it seen?

Death apart, some things, I think, cannot be avoided. But how am I going to get my stores? Drive all the way to Urenui to avoid her?

There were tears frozen in its eyes.

Nov 2
I have invented a track to the Mohican. There are many routes through the forest but I have discovered a way that takes me from the ridge, across the valley and up almost to the horizon.

It is everything I imagined. An utterly complex organism covered in many others. Everything perfect, every tiny piece of lichen or moss or fungus. Every piece of bark, and the epiphytes — perfect! No gardener could improve on this!

I am impatient for school to be in. I will take him to the tree at some time.

I saw several beautiful birds that I assume are species of pigeon. They are much larger than I have seen previously and more colourful, and with the whitest breast! I watched one feeding from no more than fifteen feet for at least twenty minutes. I am sure it could see me but it was totally unconcerned. When the sun caught its neck and back it revealed the most extraordinary range of colours — as though it had feathers of burnished copper. Except these were natural and needed no earthly embellishment. I had to wrench myself away.

In the tree itself there are several species of bird. Some quite large (not as big as the pigeon) and black but with a small blob of white on their throats. I was intrigued by this but more so by their song. A truly extraordinary array of notes and whistles, and sometimes like chimes or bells — singing that I first mistook for several birds of different kinds. I felt a peace here I have not discovered for many months.

Domestics: I have concerned myself with cleaning — something I have neglected. I hammered my laundry in the concrete tubs, swept the entire cottage, cleaned the bath and basin (ugly) and aired my bedding. My spirits that had become somewhat depressed during my long contemplation have risen. The temperature also is rising and I can feel the spring advancing.

I cooked a steak and had a little more of the red than I ought. But I am far from being drunk. I have not been so since that day.

Sometimes I lie close to the sand and then I see how many different colours there really are. But at a glance the whole is a bluish ebony. I remember well my early distaste. But like so many other things, I see now how many stereotypes I have carried in my head. I lie on the hot black sand and I love its sultry darkness. Maybe tomorrow I will do so again. I might fish.

She brought vibrancy to my stark existence in this tin bolt-hole that girl, that I could not have imagined.

We shared a snapper today, which R. prepared in his inimitable fashion. It was a glorious evening with a light westerly off the sea and definitely warmer. We talked, or at least I talked about home. I described the Great Plains, which I love and which I look forward to seeing very much. I told him how my forebears had come to New England and then migrated west to the Great Lakes area. Mostly settling in or around Chicago. Not much more than a shanty town on the southern edge of Lake Michigan then. My father's family established the first saddlery in Chicago.

He asked me about the Indians. I am not particularly familiar with the native history and I felt at once at a disadvantage. He knew it. He asked how I thought the Indians might have regarded the Great Plains and Lakes. I said I expected, for I did not know, that they would have loved it as much as me. And how much was that, he persisted.

In the feeling of having roots, I said. 'Roots?' he said. 'Blackberry has roots. Do you think the land is pleased to have that spiky, smothering thing?' I said it was possible for anyone to develop a feeling of belonging, even affection, for the place they inhabited. He called me a 'shiftless Pakeha', to which I retorted he was a 'myopic Maori'. The moment hung in the balance.

He quizzed me then about how we shared the Great Plains and the Great Lakes today. I said I didn't know, and then he said this: 'Do you trust me?' I was nonplussed but said, 'Yes of course', and at that he smiled. 'You are right and you are wrong. You are right to trust me now, for I mean you well. But never trust a Maori. Some day I may remember that I have lost all my land and that you are the cause — and at that moment I shall be your enemy. Do not forget what I say.' Then he laughed loudly, ferociously, and I saw a dangerous adversary.

He mocked my discomfort and said he merely quoted his ancestor. A man who said that very same thing to a white soldier more than a hundred and fifty years before. And that is how R. is. Sometimes I feel I am talking with someone who has stepped right out of the past, who is there still, perhaps?

He told me the chiefs of Taranaki compromised with the Pakeha and conceded land for settlers' use, but it was never enough. How, he asked me, did that resemble the fate of the Indian? But even before I might frame an answer, he laughed rather unkindly and said, 'But of course you do not know.'

I said that all of us need to look to the future, not back in anger or pain at past wrongs — if that is what they were. He leapt to his feet, his eyes quite demonic. 'Is it not right,' he demanded, 'when a thief is recognised, however long it has been, to demand of him restitution?'

I was in a quandary. This issue is clearly so personal for the man that conversing sensibly about social migration and economics is out of the question. But I did say that the taking of land was not an exclusively white preoccupation, and that I was aware that Maori had fought Maori over land, in this very area. Just as Indian fought Indian. Tactically, this was another mistake.

'Oh yes,' he sneered. 'It is easy to consider the contest for kai moana among the peoples as being the same, but it is not. The creeping confiscation of our land was for the sole benefit of a few greedy Pakeha, obtained by lying and cheating. It is,' he said, and I shall never forget the bitterness in his voice and eyes, or the fact that his words suddenly became present tense, 'the action of cowards who manipulate the laws they make and then break in order to have what they will. And they do not remember, Tom Mahler, they do not like to remember!' And at that he picked up his kit and disappeared into the trees.

I was considerably disturbed by this exchange and I felt compelled to record our discussion immediately. It has left me feeling (even more) contemplative.

I am in no mood to write today. Hit my shin with a log while splitting wood.

Is it mere guilt that I feel? I wonder how I might have resisted such temptation in any circumstance and the truth is I know I would not have succumbed were I home. What does that mean? Has my moral fibre disintegrated with my isolation? Was it an unnatural act? Did I fall simply for one delicious moment knowing I would send her away?

December 3
Christmas is approaching. His eyes were so bright they burned. Like lights. Laughing and laughing. All of us. But he is not at school. She presumed he could be unwell — or helping his father. She invited me to have a coffee after school but I declined. I felt too upset. I had anticipated seeing him so much.

I slept until well after noon.

I have sketched bits of coast, the sea, rocks and forest. Depictions as wild as the land and seascapes themselves. But I feel I am marking time.

The weather has deteriorated again.

What is happening? Still he is not at school. It is all I can do not to visit his home but I think I cannot. The weather is abominable. It strikes at me here.

I have had a horrible night. I am now convinced something is seriously wrong. I intend to talk to Beth about it but she does not seem concerned. Flu, she says, is likely. Flu? I wish I could do something.

A turning point! R. and I sitting on the porch when Melanie arrived. I was so pleased. Perhaps it doesn't matter after all. It was a mistake and we move on.

She baked a chocolate cake and seemed quite happy and even seemed to like R. though I think he did not address a single comment to her at any time. He refused her cake. He is less approachable than a sheer wall of rock!

But what a pleasure it was to have their company. Odd couple extraordinaire but then to which pair do I refer?

If only they could have known one another. If only they could have been friends. Today I wished I had his space rocket jersey, with its Tintin replica in black and white on vivid blue. Like his eyes. How I laughed when I saw him in that jersey. The memory will remain with me until I die, and it is all I could want.

It is not! I want my boy. I want my boy.

She closed her eyes and recalled Luke at sixteen. Loose-limbed and handsome, with strong regular features and a truly disarming smile. A little shy, but with a dry sense of humour. He attracted others like a magnet though he often seemed so offhand. She smiled at the recollection of friends playing cards in their sitting room, patiently waiting for him to wake. She guessed it was because he was 'solid'. They knew where they were with Luke. They felt secure around someone who was indifferent to peer arrangements or social circumstance. Maybe that was a reason Tom had neglected the teenage relationship because Luke was so undemanding? Tom had taken him for granted but she had not. Luke and she had been the very best of friends always.

'I could have exposed you to your own blindness,' she said angrily into the flames. 'You short-changed both of us, you bastard! And now what have you done?'

She rose and paced the room. Kicked a small cushion and leaned against the sink bench, then opened the front door and peered into the night. Listened to the waves on the beach and saw the glittering tail of the moon on the sea. This cannot be, she thought. It cannot be that he has come so far to perish here, in this foreign wasteland. In this terrifying wasteland so far from home it almost dropped off the earth. It could not be. Everyone deserved to breathe their last where they lived — where they grew up. Where they were loved ...

She closed the door on the darkness and wandered aimlessly. Spied a broom and swept through the living room and into the hall. Sweeping the bedroom and then the bathroom and knowing all the while that it made little difference. From under the kitchen bench she took a cleaning cloth and started on the benchtop and stove and was revolted. I would be closed in a split second flat, if anyone found my café like this, she thought.

* * *

BARKER STARED AT the water stain and thought how much it looked like a troll. A huge troll sitting sideways and dripping from its jaw. Or a pig? He looked around at his colleagues. At Milligan with his pencil in his mouth and a permanent frown. At Spencer writing in his notepad and Wilmshurst with his eyes closed. At Buchanan quiet as stone and staring into space.

'What a shit of a night.'

'Yes, Sarge.'

Barker walked to the sink and poured himself a glass of water. He swallowed it without pause. 'How's the kid?'

'He should be okay. Burns on his legs and shocked but okay. Priddock left him at Base.'

Barker nodded and sighed. 'Fucking kid. Loony fucking kid.'

'Yep.'

'Where's Priddock?'

'He's turned in, Sarge. I posted Matheson.'

Barker laughed. A short sound as hard as his name. 'That's terrific! What's he looking after? The dog kennels?' He laughed again and sat down in his vinyl easy chair. 'Give me a beer.'

Milligan looked surprised. 'Sarge?'

'Oh, don't bloody *Sarge* me, Milligan; give me one of those beers.' He reviewed the troll and decided that in fact it was Len MacDonnell in HQ. 'What a place. What a bloody place! There's only three hundred people here — less — and it's like a fireworks factory full of smokers! Thanks.' He took the beer and thought about the disastrous beginning to the day. 'I can't believe that prick of a contractor would do that. Responsible member of the community my arse! The place is boiling over with this enquiry and he has to throw his bottle out of his playpen about bloody hangi stones! Unbelievable!'

'Yep.'

Buchanan listened without comment. We'd still have Pagett's house were it not for Layton, he thought, and we wouldn't have that poor little prick in hospital with burns and a pending prosecution. What got into Layton? Known him these past six years. Played rugby with him. Drank with him. His kids were friends with Paul. *On my patch*, he thought angrily.

And the boy, Jimmy? No dad — it was that simple. Over and over again he'd seen crazy kids and nearly every time the same old formula. No dad. They made him sick. Pricks who absconded, or if they were there at all, had no balls. Had no idea what it was to be a father and didn't have the gumption to find out. Jimmy wasn't bad, he just needed a firm hand. He just needed someone who took an interest, for God's sake, but it had been denied him. I'll go see him, he thought, soon as the investigation's over.

'What did you find?' Barker had asked him in the late afternoon after Buchanan had foot-slogged over about five hundred hectares of coastal bush. 'Well, you're the man with the local knowledge, Buchanan,' he said.

Buchanan was dog-tired. He was dog-tired because he had traversed some steep country without a whiff of anything and he was dog-tired because of the way he felt about Beth. The thought that she wanted to feel that other bastard wound him up like a spring. But he was now having to confront the uncomfortable idea that it might not be Mohler. Mohler had gone up there once and had a shouting match with Pagett. But had he gone again? Had he gone a second time and got so carried away he killed? He recalled with a flush the conversation with the woman. He recalled her distress and the way she carried herself. He recalled her vehemence and it was persuasive.

But she had to believe he was innocent. What would she say when she was interviewed by Barker?

He turned to the detective whose eyes had closed and studied his superior's face. In repose it looked tired and ordinary. He hesitated.

'Sergeant.'

Barker opened his eyes. 'Does my having a nap offend you, constable? What?'

Buchanan swallowed. 'I talked to Mary Mahler today ... this morning.' He braced himself.

Barker's eyes narrowed and he sat forward. 'You spoke to Mary Mahler?'

'Yes. She left me a note and I went up there first thing. She didn't know about the enquiry. I told her you would be wanting to talk to her.'

'Did you?' said Barker slowly. 'Did you now?' He turned thoughtfully. 'Wilmshurst went to find her this afternoon but didn't.' He frowned. 'Wilmshurst!'

'Sarge?'

'Why didn't you bring Mrs Mahler to see me?' He sounded bemused, as though he had discovered sugar in his tea.

Wilmshurst looked uncomfortable. 'I got halfway there and had the flat. And that's when I got a call to pick up Priddock. Then with the rifle and things ...'

'You forgot?'

'You might say that, Sarge. Sorry.'

Barker leaned back and wondered who he should kick. Wilmshurst, Buchanan or himself? Or Milligan? Good grief, he thought wearily, what an arse of a day. Well, she would be there in the morning. 'Wilmshurst?'

'Yes, Sarge?'

'Can I count on you to fetch Mrs Mahler in the morning?'

'Definitely.'

'Thank you.' And he leaned back and closed his eyes.

Buchanan closed his eyes in wonderment. That was it? Thank you, Lord, he thought wryly. His thoughts returned to the task ahead. He'd keep working his way north, towards the burn-off. The boy was clearly dead. What'd Barker think? That a ten-year-old boy could survive for days out in the bush? And why would he stay out there anyway? No one wanted to think about that.

And if I knew what I was looking for, he mused, that would be really helpful. What a waste of time: a murder enquiry, and he was footslogging looking for someone who had probably departed months ago. Someone who had shot some of Pagett's cattle. So bloody what?

'Buchanan ... are you with us?'

Buchanan looked up, startled to see faces staring at him.

'Sorry.'

'I was saying that you can have a couple of hours from the chopper tomorrow afternoon. We'll concentrate on the ground search for the boy in the morning.'

'I don't think we're going to find him.' Too late Buchanan realised his mistake.

'No?' Barker snapped. 'Well, let me tell you this! We will work on the assumption that we will, until I fucking say so! Have you got that?'

'Yep.' Buchanan held his superior's gaze for a few moments and then dropped his eyes to the floor. 'Yes, Sarge.'

Barker scowled and put his bottle down. 'I'm turning in.'

BUCHANAN drove slowly home and quietly let himself into his son's bedroom. In the light of the moon he could see the boy's face and remembered with a pang that they hadn't buried Sooty. He lay down on the floor with his hands behind his head and closed his eyes. The events of the long day came crowding in and he pushed them away. He thought about Beth and remembered her sitting on the couch reading to Shorty, and him preparing cheese on toast for all of them. He remembered swimming at the beach and touching her while Shorty swam. But she was gone.

He winced and thought about the search for the Pagett boy, and imagined if it had been his own boy they could not find. We're not going to find him either. Not alive anyway, regardless of what Barker thinks. He's drowned. Another kid down, and even worse, the poor little bastard had been abused.

The moon shone brightly in the window and illuminated the wall. Buchanan felt his spirits lift in familiar pride at the sight of Shorty's artwork. There was the new one he'd done only last week, before all this happened. It was a strange painting for Shorty in that it was just words. He was learning to use words well, but not before had he used them in a painting. Big words across the paper saying: 'The black cat is my cat. His name is Sooty.' Painted in big childish strokes with white paint on a dark blue background. Big words painted like ... Buchanan frowned and wondered what it reminded him of. Those words — like that. Like ... graffiti. That was it. They looked like graffiti on a wall. Unusual in my town, but some places ... Auckland ... bloody graffiti everywhere. But not here. He rubbed his eyes and detected a peculiar idea way back in his mind. Connected to Shorty's painting, though elusive, but growing in some way. And connected ...

Buchanan sat bolt upright and stared out the window into the night. 'Jesus!' he said and clambered to his feet. He let himself quietly out of the room, walked to the kitchen and made himself a coffee. He could not sit down and with the cup only half finished he returned to check on his son before letting himself out into the night.

* * *

~ I fear that I can no longer trust myself — in what I do or what I say. How I wish for Mary but I am alone. I know I have harboured increasingly dark thoughts about the father. Perhaps it was simply that.

He was so pleased to see me and that should have been reward enough. At first we drew many things though I do not like his pigs. They have gaping, grinning mouths that are disproportionately large and they are always the same. I drew a happy pig for him but he crossed it out and replaced it with another of his ugly beasts. They disturb me. Perhaps it was that too?

Whatever happened, the story seemed to materialise without rhyme or reason, and yet I did nothing to divert it. Nothing.

I drew the four of them — Luke, Mike, Doggitt and Sean marching, with Luke at the front, then Mike and Doggitt, and Sean bringing up the rear. Like Christopher Robin but much different. Doggitt rending that large stick so the fragments flew and the two boys bowed under weighty packs. Luke wearing his blue jersey and red pants and on his feet his big hiking boots. Sean in his leafgreen suit and a straw sombrero on his head (he instantly held a green crayon towards me). Still I could see he was pleased.

Mike, the 'sandyman', rising out of the beach where he lives, as black as the ironsand itself but with large white eyes. A part of the earth, he is, and knowing when the earth is unhappy and when the earth is unhappy he is a creature to be feared.

He pointed to his right eye — Yes, I said, he is just like Ringatu …

My thoughts were surely bending inwards to things that have been troubling me and to which this boy is inextricably linked. I am in thrall to the passion which is Ringatu's and I have grown to loathe a man I have never met. I hate what he has done to this boy and his abominable plan to burn the forest. Is that rational? Yesterday, I may have said yes, but then yesterday I think I would not have thought to ask the question. At best I am unsure. Yet I see it is distorting my view of the world. I am inventing things that have no place in my mind and certainly not in his.

With his hands he asked: 'Where?' I swept on with reckless abandon. They travelled to the Mohican, I said, to ask about 'The Worst-of-all-Fires'. How melodramatic. But the idea consumes me.

Raging and crackling through the forest it came and soon there were few places in which to escape the heat and burning, and all the time the Blackness followed, smothering the landscape and savagely consuming the weary and the unwary alike.

Did I know he was becoming unsettled? How could he not? In my own mind that shadowy figure is Pagett. He appeared as I spoke, here in my story, as a fiend with arms reaching to engulf the valley.

That was my last opportunity but I continued with a reckless abandon, even when he turned to stare out the window in the direction of his own home. I had become so absorbed, so self-righteous perhaps. What satisfaction could I derive from allowing him to think as I? Even when I became aware that other children had gathered. That Beth had stopped to listen.

The animals thought they must have done something dreadfully wrong, I said, and they fled before the flames to seek the forgiveness of the Mohican. Gathered around the great tree they were — the wolves and the horses lying together, and the sheep and the dogs and the mice and the cats. All waiting in the shade of the Mohican. All the forest animals, lying hopefully in the shade. In desperation.

So it was, I said, that it fell to Sean to ask the Mohican for its advice, because the animals cannot talk. His hand touched his mouth. Blue eyes fixed on me, puzzled, and his hand raised. Beth sought to interrupt but I ignored her!

He asked the Mohican why the Fire was coming and from whence it came. He asked what the animals should do since they would surely die of thirst if they were not first incinerated, and they listened anxiously, even the earth listened as though her existence depended on it.

The slightest of breezes moved the leaves of the Mohican as she began to speak. The treely sort of whisper that only special sorts of people can understand.

'The Worst-of-all-Fires is happening because the Blackness has broken the First Law that says all animals will do according to their true nature and never more than that. The Blackness was a good animal once,' she said and all the animals gasped, 'but he has fallen into evil that is learned and that evil is greed. The Blackness can only be stopped when greed is banished. The Fire will not stop while the Blackness stalks the land.'

Was that bad?

'The Blackness is here in this valley,' I whispered.

Then Matty said: 'His dad burns the bush like that. Walker Boy's dad.' Then Beth clapped her hands and directed them all to their desks and gave me the most peculiar look. It was fear in her eyes.

And Sean? He tore the paper into pieces. Expressionless, methodical destruction of our artwork. From side to side tearing and dropping the pieces on the floor and they seemed to me to crash like lumps of lead. Each one crashing at my feet. Nothing I could say. His hands covering his ears and my world collapsed in a moment. He ran from the room.

I do not want even so much as to see the boat. I think of destroying it.

Beth came to see me but I was drunk. I tried to explain. Can I expect her to forgive me? Him? I do not know what to do.

Mary closed her eyes. Were you always mad? She remembered the ad in the *Tribune*. 'Let it be known,' it said, 'that I, Tom Washington Mahler, hereby apologize unreservedly and without qualification to my dear wife Mary. I have sinned ...' How could you be so idiotic, she demanded? How could you tell the whole world about this? 'I think I was pissed,' he said with that grin she found endearing, but she hit him all the same. 'Never again!' she told him. And that wedding anniversary was the only one he ever forgot, but maybe it had turned out to be the best.

She opened her eyes. 'You are a lunatic! You are fortunate I have come.' She looked around the room, 'Tom?' But there was no sound in the cottage. How will I know? she asked herself. When will I know?

10

A MOREPORK HOOTED in the tree above, hidden in dense foliage beyond the soft envelope of firelight. The bird's call reminded him of the death and his restlessness increased.

The night was unusually calm but it was alive. Disturbed, they were, and he could feel their restlessness. He shared their displeasure and yet maybe he was the object. He rose and strode back and forth through the fern, back and forth, thinking. Am I trapped? he asked himself, or am I free? If I am free, where am I going? If I am trapped who is the jailer? If I am trapped will I escape? He pictured the one-eyed general who put the fear in the land grabbers. What would Tito do? What would he do now? For the first time he could see no clear direction and was alarmed.

Asking forgiveness of the turehu for his failure and requesting guidance. Pacing in the darkness and trying to divine the outline of his unfinished task. He thought of Te Kooti in the east. Leading the people into the Land of Canaan. Forming the Ringatu Church for the chosen people. 'Exalt for Te Kooti!' Ringatu stopped and raised his hands to his head as Te Kooti swung the axe that took off her head. Titokowaru, eyes slyly grinning, feasting on his enemy and all around the ghostly turehu stabbing and screaming.

'Off! Off!' He shouted and flailed at the night. 'I am Ringatu! I am Ringatu!' The dog barked and pushed him with its paw. Ringatu felt the dog and stopped moving. Stood trembling as he looked around the formless trees and the small flickering fire and saw the boy sitting watching, solemn as a gnome. The dog barked again.

'Fuck off,' he said suddenly, and pulled its ear.

The boy gestured. 'It's nothing,' said the man, and crouched on the opposite side of the fire and felt the throb of the burn on his cheek. He glanced at the boy and remembered how they played together. The drums. They had beat the drums together and it had been good. The boy liked the drums. Beating for an hour, maybe more. That was good.

'Lie down and sleep,' he said, and the boy lay down in the fern but his eyes remained open, watching. 'Close your eyes,' commanded Ringatu. A possum rustled along the floor of the bush and cackled.

Ringatu frowned and thought about food. He thought about Mahler's cottage. It was not far.

The dog raised its head and watched the man intently.

'You stay with that boy,' he said, and strode into the darkness.

* * *

THEY LOOKED UP at the starry night in silence. Uncle Louis, Gertie, her sister's son Manu and Bill, sipping the tea Gertie had brought them and munching her shortbread. She glanced at Louis and then nudged Bill. He nodded and cleared his throat.

'You talked to the detective, Louis?'

'It was nothing.'

'You don't seem yourself tonight. That's all I was noticing. Hardly ate your dinner either.'

'Stop your noticing.' Louis pushed his cup away. 'I'm going to bed.' He picked up his hat and shuffled off into the dark. They called but there was no response.

'He's been real moody today. Something's happened.'

'All of us come to that. All of us moody in some respect.'

'But there's something more for Louis. He was pissed when I got home and wouldn't talk then either.'

'Why would he want to talk to a public brawler?'

Bill sighed. 'I am not a public brawler.'

'I wouldn't want to talk to a public brawler if I was Louis. Fine example!' She picked up her knitting and peered at it. 'I can hardly see.'

The sound of muffled talk came from within and Bill was grateful for the interruption. He padded in his socks down the hall, pushed open the door and looked at the two boys on the floor with their bedclothes all around. They stared in wide-eyed amazement.

'You young fullas should be asleep by now.'

'We were just talking.'

'Yeah. We were just talking.' They fell silent.

'Well, stop talking or I'll warm your backsides.'

Bill closed the door and waited for a few seconds. Whispering started almost immediately. Good grief, he thought and returned to the verandah.

'You notice anything about those two tonight?'

'They very quiet. At least till now. That's what I noticed.'

Bill hitched his pants as he sat. 'Something going on in there. Talking but not to me. They haven't been in trouble?'

'Not more than normal.'

There was no response. At length Manu said: 'What's going to happen about that whitey bastard?'

Bill sat heavily. 'Nothing! That's what.'

'I don't care for that language,' Gertie interjected firmly.

'He has it coming.'

Gertie compressed her lips, and poked Bill with her needles.

'Things are not too good,' he said at last. 'Manu?' He looked at the young man who had recently returned from Auckland. Hardly recognised him after two years. So much bigger and his face had changed. The boy had been like one of his own sons when he was young. 'I had a fight about those hangi stones but I wish I hadn't. I don't mean that I shouldn't have tried to stop Layton doing what he did. But this fighting's no good.'

Manu looked away. 'They started all this. Doing that stuff on your job. Burning this place.'

Bill felt vexed. 'I don't want any more of that talk. Are you hearing me?'

'I hear you.'

'I don't want any more of it.'

'You said that — but it's not just up to you.'

The night air seemed suddenly to grow thick.

'It's up to me all right and I'm telling you! And don't you go giving me lip ...'

'Somebody's got to stand up. I thought you were staunch.'

'You're wrong! And don't ask me to repeat myself. None of it! I don't want any more of it.'

Manu rose abruptly and stood outside the circle of light from the bulb under the eaves. 'Something has started and it isn't finished,' he said, and before there could be a response he jumped the fence and disappeared into the night.

Bill hit the boards with his clenched fist. 'Young bastard!'

'What do you expect? Public brawler for an uncle and everything.' Gertie laid her knitting on her lap and stared into the night. 'You going to talk to Merv Layton?'

'What for? You want me in another fight?'

'Well, what's going to happen here? You two going to be lifelong enemies now or what? You two going to live here in Mokau and avoid each other? What?'

He reflected in silence. A car drove too quickly through the town and faded into the night heading north. 'Maybe we should go north — to Auckland?' But he hated the idea.

'Sure. Sure we could go to Auckland with no money or any damn thing and put these boys into some big Auckland school and you doing what? Working in some god-awful factory somewhere on the other side of that place and we never seeing you. Sure.' The needles started to click impatiently.

'Well, maybe Hawke's Bay? Meatworks maybe ...'

'Sure,' said Gertie. 'Meatworks! Sure and that'll be closed like all the others.'

'Well, you got any bright ideas? Full of this and that!'

'Why don't you talk to that man?'

'Right back where we were, Auntie. Right back.'

'I'm angry about him. I'm angry about that Merv Layton, make no mistake about that! I'll be giving him a piece of my mind for sure, but we've known him a long time,' she said, 'and what's the harm in talking? That's what I'm saying, Bill Manuhuia. What's the harm? Unless you two blockheads just want to fight so you can have a swollen lump on the other side of your blockheads?'

Bill massaged his scalp. 'I don't know if he'd listen.'

'Well, we've got to think,' continued Gertie. 'But let's not be waiting till we all drop down dead!'

'I'm going for a leak,' Bill said. When he returned, Gertie patted the boards next to her.

'This is surely the strangest weather,' he said.

'Yep.' She sighed. 'That poor woman. You know who I mean?' He nodded and she continued, 'That poor woman. Coming from America to see her husband and he's dead.' She shook her head. 'I talked to Merle. But she wasn't much help. She's never been a full kete, that Merle. A few holes in that basket but you think Louis can see that? But she said that woman came and asked where to find Painter Tom and she told her he was drowned. A mountain of tact, that Merle. She said the woman knocked over half the store before she stumbled out. What's she expect? Lord!'

'This is a bad time.'

'It's a bad time all right. You are right about that, William Manuhuia. Now that boy of ours comes home from the big smoke and finds his uncle fighting with his boss and all. Surely there's more brains in a yard full of chickens.' And the knitting needles clicked in the night.

Bill sighed. 'The funeral is in the morning,' he ventured.

'Not many Maori at that thing, I'm expecting.'

'Nope.'

'I would expect that man wore out his welcome before he left. God rest his soul.' Gertie put her knitting aside and looked up into the sky. 'We have to believe that the Lord is looking out for all of us. Without favour, though sometimes it's a test.' She shook her head and sucked through the gap in her teeth so there was a little whistle.

'I know. Maybe we have to remember that.'

'That's the truth, Bill Manuhuia.'

* * *

BUCHANAN TURNED ON the light. Even as he drove down to the station he knew but he needed to see. He needed to see it right now and he went directly to his filing cabinet, unlocked it and began flicking through the files with impatient fingers.

He withdrew a manila folder, took it to his desk and opened it eagerly. Neatly clipped sheets of paper numbered and dated. An incident report from four years back, and attached to the report a handwritten note. He knew pretty much what it said but he read it again just the same, and with increasing certainty he knew who was out in the hills this night.

In his own handwriting the page was headed: 'Graffiti. Friday 23rd November.' He recalled now how bemused he had been. They all had. How peculiar he had thought it after becoming accustomed to the unintelligible tagging all around Auckland — this was so different. This was plain nuts! This was a misdemeanour only because it was sprayed on the wall of the fire station. On a sign outside a church it would have been regarded as more than acceptable, but not in this context. In this context it was a sinister exhortation and he was nuts and that was a fact. And he'd been gone for a long while since. He was back though, of that there could be no doubt. And not only was he back but he was a bloody murderer! Buchanan felt a savage thrill, and even while he considered the options he knew what he would do. He expected Barker to get fingerprints off the rifle, but that wouldn't be till the end of the following day at soonest. Maybe not until Wednesday even. There was plenty of time.

He looked at the piece of paper again and shook his head. 'You mad bastard,' he said out loud and read silently: *'Those who desire to be rich fall into temptation. For the love of money is the root of all evil.'*

'You dumb bastard!' he said. 'You big, dumb bastard.' He even knew how he'd find the bastard. This would be enough.

'For the love of Mary!' he said incredulously as he drove home. 'Good bloody grief!'

* * *

~ 14 Dec

How did he find me! He walked but it is many miles. Appearing at my door carrying a small bag with his drawings. Drawings we have shared and some of his own.

I explained everything. I showed him the plans and we sat on the grass alongside the boat and I showed him what I have done and what yet remains. I even prompted a grin! Ha! I think he is unsure when I am joking and watches me closely for clues. If I laugh loudly he smiles. If I am earnest so is he.

We spent an hour sanding and planing the hull. He liked this and it is so good to share the task with him. And of course he loves Chinook who he greets like an old friend. It is so strange to watch him with the dog, ruffling its ears and playing with a stick but not a sound — not a word at any time. Always I am expecting to hear something. I catch myself listening for Luke. Luke, who spoke incessantly, describing everything — but this boy is silent as stone.

But it does not matter. I am garrulous. I am like a parrot, chirping and I know he listens. He tells me things with his hands but I know there is much I do not understand. I know when he means he is hungry or tired. He stood at the edge of the porch and peed on the grass!

We prepared a dinner. He washed and sliced vegetables and I grilled some steak. He hums when he is happy! Does that mean words are near? I must be patient. After dinner, I read to him. I am being very careful. Actually I read from The Dory Book! I cannot imagine anything much less absorbing for a small boy but he gave every appearance of listening. Then he went to sleep — right there on my sofa so I covered him with a rug and spent the remainder of the evening thinking and listening and now, writing.

I can hear a mouse rustling and a morepork calling and I listen as though to old friends! I listen as though these peculiar sounds were as natural to me as the sounds of downtown once were — only now, when I pause to reflect, it is those other things that seem a meaningless cacophony.

I have conceived an excellent plan! I will have Melanie, Sean and R. here for Xmas. I will buy a turkey. I will buy him something very special.

Today we painted, worked on the boat and walked to the Mohican. Bliss! It took us nearly an hour and a half but he seemed not the slightest bit tired. He tried to climb the tree from every direction but it is so big. I am sure he was imagining the animals high in the branches. I mimicked his actions and he nodded so strenuously, peering up into the high foliage, that I almost came to believe.

He explores in a way I do not, finding crevices and creatures

I would never notice. Even a huge brown armoured insect. He was utterly entranced and lay examining that thing for half an hour. Sometimes he touched it so its long, spiky legs reared up and I couldn't help feeling apprehensive but he was neither afraid nor did he mean it any harm. Sometimes he shared his discoveries but mostly he was deeply absorbed in a private world. I felt so alive! When he invites me to share I try to conceive of anything I ever did in my business life that was as significant and know now there was nothing.

We stayed for hours exploring, listening, and me talking from time to time. I told him how the Mohican had come to be. How she had been the tiniest seed carried by an eagle from a faraway country. How the eagle searched the land from high in the sky, near the sun, looking for just the right place for so precious a seed. Searching for a valley near the ocean and knowing when he looked down he had found the very place just here.

And he acted it all, flying and searching and then swooping to the ground. I felt so contented, watching him place the seed so carefully.

We ate a small picnic at the foot of the tree and looked up into the high branches where the birds flit in and out of a profusion of epiphytes such as I have never seen.

I cannot believe this man leaves his son in this way. I wonder when I will confront him.

My cottage seems so empty now. I have tried to paint but without success. I am bewildered and confused. I do not understand why I have lost Luke and yet this man has Sean. I do not understand.

R. came by! We drank beer on my porch and he talked about the river, the Mokau — as though it is his blood. It is peculiar to hear this sad monologue about a muddy stream. It is obvious he does not much care whether I listen or not but I like to. He does not look at me and occasionally will rise to his feet and stride about the lawn while he talks. 'Rants' is the wrong word but at times it seems a diatribe.

I am learning many things, and for some reason I find his soliloquy reassuring. It is adding a depth and colour to these wild hills and coast that I must otherwise invent.

He is, he says, descended from the Tainui and the Tokomaru. Ancient canoes — huge they must have been, and it is strangely exciting to hear him speak of these craft coming across thousands of miles of ocean to this land. To this very coast on which not a living soul had stepped.

I imagine 'Tainui' to be Tynooee and 'Kawhia' to be Carfeea. I am imagining words as though they were Greek or North American Indian or just gibberish. Perhaps all three. These Maori words are strange — but pretty. Even though I do not know their meaning they seem much more descriptive of this wild place than such mundane epithets as 'Shag Rock'.

He told me that there were seven great canoes that came to New Zealand many centuries ago. A thousand years, he said when I pressed him. 'A thousand … twelve hundreds, what does it matter?' And I guess that is true. 'Ahi ka!' he said. This means 'Keeping the home fires burning'. I like this expression. I told him that that is what I am doing but he became quite angry. He insisted I could not do that here. I can only do that where I came from. It is he who is maintaining ahi ka in this place. It is his turangawaewae. And he strode close to me, pushing his face into mine.

'Each one has his place to stand!' He shouted this twice and then laughed at my discomfiture.

This was the land of the Ngati Maniapoto and some other tribe but I forget. R. is partly this tribe and partly from the Nga Ruahine — a tribe that held much of Taranaki to the south. I am revising my perception of this place. I saw a wild and untamed land, recently discovered and broken in. I saw a landscape untouched in many respects indeed, so naive was my perspective I could imagine mine to be the first footprint! Unfortunately I disclosed this view to R. and was rewarded with a smile of pure condescension. 'That is how it is with you Pakeha,' he said. 'Yours is a narrow world of your own making. You do not like to see beyond your own footprint in case you see something older and larger.'

I refuted this strongly and caused him to stride my lawn again. For some minutes he did not speak but I am used to this and I have learned to allow him time to calm himself. When he sat at my porch again I offered him a meal but unexpectedly and quite sullenly, he refused.

Shortly after he left and I plunged into desolation.

The wind returned this afternoon and I confined myself to my cottage. At four I was surprised by a knock at my door. This is a sound that now fills me with soaring expectation or ill-defined dread.

It was Beth and I was pleased to see her. She wanted to talk — seemed quite distracted. Life and goals and 'growing up'. I don't know what she is talking about. She confirmed that I am no longer held in high regard in 'some circles'. I said I didn't much care but I do.

She said that people were thinking the worst. She wanted reassurance that I felt no obligation to give. She left soon after and I wonder whether I have lost her too. It is possible.

The boat is good. But I wonder what to do next. I think I am procrastinating on the hull for this reason.

I wonder where Melanie is. I would like to see her.

Days pass like litter and I have seen no one. I feel less and less inclined to go into the village. Oh, how I wish to be walking one of my grimy city streets. To listen to buskers, the idiocy of a cabbie, the traffic.

I should not be deterred by local gossip but I am feeling uncomfortable about even leaving the cottage. But I would like to see Luke. I would like to see Beth too. The Lynchs even. I am thinking and sleeping. I miss my boy so much.

I am unsure about my Xmas Day plan. R. seems to have withdrawn from me in some way though God knows we are hardly friends. And Melanie has become an infrequent visitor.

Mary started and opened her eyes, staring at the feeble, unshaded light bulb. She listened to the rustling of small animals and the breeze that had sprung up in the trees. It was not a comforting sound. She longed to see Sophie with such intensity it hurt. She longed to be in her bed at home so much she would have given her café for it. Maybe more.

'Oh Sophie,' she said aloud. 'I want to come home,' and she turned her face into the arm of the sofa and began to sob. 'I want to come home.'

Tomorrow, she thought, wiping away the tears. Tomorrow I'll drive straight back to New Plymouth and leave. The thought made her feel stronger, imagining the flight then the joy of landing at O'Hare. God, how good that would be. Just to get on the plane would be paradise.

'Tomorrow, I promise.' She looked at the book, which had fallen to her feet. With its curled corners and peculiar contents. All that remained of so many years. She opened it again and realised there were only a few pages remaining. Curious, she turned to the last page and saw that he had written to the last line.

She leafed back.

~ Many nights. I don't know. Glimpses of unwelcome days. I have slept and I have been very drunk. Don't know where the dog is. He, too, has deserted. But so what? I have no notion any more of what day is what. And does it matter?

A change in the weather? And I caught my first tarakihi. It is a truly beautiful fish. I killed it there on the rocks with my knife and gilled and gutted it as I have seen R. do. I gave thanks for the life of this fish. This single fish. This minor creature in the scheme of things, but not so. Not solitary at all but one of Tangaroa's children, he says. Do I become as superstitious?

He has One God and many it appears. And yet the sun shone and I am better resolved.

I spent the most hours on the dory that I have in weeks, and have finished planing the transom. I am sure Luke will be here soon and it would not be satisfactory to present him with the spectacle of our project in disrepair.

Beth returned. She is troubled. She is to marry the policeman Brian Buchanan but I sense she has many doubts. I wonder why she is confiding in me? We had lunch together on the porch. It is my place of hospitality. I prepared a salad and pancakes. They were outrageously successful. We lay in the sun after a coffee and talked about her engagement. (Is she doing the right thing?) I told her she would know deep in her heart. I don't know why I said this. It sounded appropriate but no sooner said than I felt it to be trite and absurd. She seized upon it as though it were my most profound utterance. Like most women she is searching. But aren't we all? Me too, if I'm honest.

I found myself telling her how I courted Mary. 'Courted!' Yes I did. I called on her. I escorted her to the prom. She was a childhood sweetheart. Beth thought this so romantic. Mary is the only woman I have ever courted. The rest were laid.

'True love persists,' she said. How naive. I suspect she reads many women's magazines, but nevertheless her words caused me a considerable pang. I think much of Mary. Of the warmth of her smile and voice that I so blithely took for granted, and the secrets in her eye that were invisible to all but me. Such is vanity.

She had seen similar depictions over many years. Mostly the disjointed caricatures that exaggerated his ears and arms and had always made her laugh, but now she felt a deep sadness. The eyes were melancholic and an air of dejection and resignation cloaked the figure sitting on the log. Mary touched the fragile figure.

~ Today I rowed the river. I am inspired by R.'s description and was in constant expectation of a waka full of bloodthirsty warriors. If he is to be believed this river swarmed with waka at one time. Perhaps for centuries? It is hard for me to grasp and I am not sure how much he fabricates. As I rowed upstream all I saw was dense rainforest covering high hills and right to the water's edge. It did not look as if it had been disturbed in a thousand years. But I looked also for the pa sites he described. Where did they live? Where did they go, these Ngati Maniapoto?

I rowed many miles upstream and just as I had explained to R. it felt to me that I was discovering an unknown land. I called to mind his fierce admonition that I was 'The last seagull to peck at the rotting whale.' I have not previously pictured myself in this way. He has a considerable talent for insult.

Consulting my map I found I had rowed to the Whakaroa or lower rapids. They did not look too daunting but I do not think I would be able to move my boat past this point unaided. Anyway, it is not much more than a punt and not very well built at that. Nevertheless, I calculated I had progressed at least eight miles from the coast and much further as the river rambled.

I was excited by my discovery of three pa sites on promontories above the river. Of course, given the vegetation I could not be certain, but everything about those places suggested they would have been admirable vantages. Why was I excited? It is hard to say. I think the idea that many people lived and played where I felt alone and isolated was uppermost. The idea that this fastness was home to a people with an economy and a culture utterly alien to my own was profoundly affecting. I strained to hear the cries of that picturesque tongue. Perhaps a sighting of the war chief Titokowaru or Wiremu. Or Te Kooti? On the other hand, perhaps I am grateful they are long gone.

I sense ambivalence in R. when he describes Te Whiti. This chief was an advocate of passive resistance, he said, which is a fascinating notion in itself. But I sensed R.'s admiration for his leadership was diminished in some way. It is Titokowaru and Te Kooti (about whom I am learning ominous things) who are R.'s guiding lights. He said: 'Tito understood that the time comes for action. Tito understood that it is necessary to eat the flesh of an enemy before he takes your own.' The Maori was a cannibal! This is a less endearing attribute. It is easy to imbue this vanquished race with a nobility of sorts, but it is well to remind oneself that they ate each other without compunction and warred incessantly. I do not think the Indians were cannibals. But I am resolved I will learn more of these things.

That Te Whiti was an exponent of passive resistance might indicate considerable sophistication. I know something of Gandhi and I am intrigued that this Te Whiti pre-empted him by nearly a hundred years. On the other hand, I wonder whether passive resistance might not have been a very obvious, though astute, direction for a besieged people unable to protect themselves by force of arms?

I do know that I would not like to have R. as an enemy.

I am very tired now. I enjoyed rowing down the current. I hid the boat in the willows and took care to avoid the locals and skulked across the fields. Drove directly without stopping.

I notice I am becoming less diligent about this diary — if that is what it is. I am missing many days on end where once I was religious. Two nights ago I woke in the bush far below the cottage and I have no idea how I came to be there. It was good to see Chinook.

What has become of me? I am labelled a 'pedo' by these illiterate morons! I cannot believe this. I returned from the beach to find a poster on my door. It is gross and comical. I assume it is the handiwork of those creeps. I am thinking of taking it to the police. But does it really matter? And yet it is monstrous. But then, is it possible it is merely the manifestation of jealousy? Melanie was the pin-up girl for the whole coast I imagine. But where is she?

It is Xmas Eve and there is no one. Only the dog. The cottage looks ugly, the trees rude and abandoned. The sea is unruly and unfriendly. All is waste. I have caught myself listening, hoping. But there is nothing. So much for my plans. The thought of waiting out these next two days is grotesque. I have been drinking since mid morning. I can feel I am sliding and I am pleased by this. I write now for by midday I expect to be blind.

I hate the smell. It is musty and old and I wonder whether he died in here? Fell on the floor and wasn't discovered for weeks. Or in the bed? Did he die there? Rotting away in that old bed. Like me. The smell creaks about this place. Cold ash and mildew. I am thinking about home. I am thinking about all the parties that will be going on. Here it is just one day after another and I wake and I am not grateful.

Perhaps I will fall into the sea.

Ho! How a simple contact changes the world! Ho! I am invited to Xmas dinner! Ho, ho! Tom Mahler, the well-known child molester, has been summonsed by a child! Ho! Those little boys from Gertie's. Those boys who gave me my nickname! They came and asked me to have Xmas dinner at their house!

Lying on the porch with my wine I was, when I heard my name proclaimed: 'Painter Tom!' Ha!

'Yes,' I answered, looking at the sky and expecting to see the One, peering, ready to deliver judgement. 'Will you come to dinner?'

I will, I said. We will eat human flesh! 'No,' said the voice. 'We eat pork!' And then I detected that the voice came from my left and I rolled over and there they were. Small boys with big brown eyes, and grinning. What a surprise! Just the sight of those faces made me feel glad. I am to appear whenever it suits me and I will be welcome! Ha! Welcome! Ha!

I am going to bed. All things considered, I do not feel that good, though an invitation such as this may be savoured aplenty.

Boxing Day

What a day! What a day I have had. Was it only yesterday?

I arrived at Gertie's at ten and it was as though I was a favoured family member! A prodigal son perhaps? Gertie gave me a big hug and so did several women I recognised but did not know! And the men, shaking my hand and old Uncle Louis giving me a hongi! Nose to nose, a hongi! I knew what he was doing but still, I must have resembled a marionette. And yet I was so pleased. There were about thirty I should say and all spilling in and out of Gertie's little place. And singing and games. All the day I felt I was in a warm cocoon.

And in the back garden the men prepared the huge cooking pit that is called a hangi. I arrived as they were spreading extremely hot rocks in the cavernous depression in the garden! Not your typical use of suburban lawn! The fire must have been lit hours before. Gertie and her helpers placed so many parcels of food wrapped in foil on the stones, and the men laid wet sacks and then covered the whole thing with earth! I have never seen anything like this hangi. It filled me with a huge sense of anticipation and I felt privy to a most extraordinary occurrence. The FDA I am sure would collectively melt down at the sight of such a method! And yet the outcome surpassed even the expectations of sharpened curiosity. Sublime!

I did not have the slightest interest in getting drunk and I am pleased to record that I did not. I talked and looked and listened and played with those kids. I had no choice. Matty and Jake and Alice I know well but there were older kids I have not seen. And we threw a ball around and wrestled and I found myself on the bottom of a melee! I bear many bruises that are badges of honour!

I talked extensively with Louis and Bill and George. I must go up to his place to see his carving.

I mentioned R. to Louis and remarked a very peculiar happenstance. As smooth as silk Louis steered the conversation on to fishing as though I had not spoken, and yet I am certain he understood me. I am certain he heard me but his old face brooked no reversal. I am curious. Perhaps R. is a pariah? I should not be surprised as he is most certainly an eccentric individual.

I met the local 'firebrand!' George's partner Peta. She is an artist so we talked about art for a time. I am very keen to see her work — and she mine! I find it hard to imagine her as a dangerous radical though she is aloof. Maybe 'arrogant' is a good word.

We talked about the land, and unlike R. who seems lost in the past altogether, Peta is very much in the future. I suggested that a future predicated on the past could be a considerable constraint. How would any meaningful development occur if the use of the land was dictated not just by the attitudes of ancestors but by the belief in some sort of life force in inanimate objects? Indeed, what relevance can ancestors really have to the here and now beyond the sentimental?

Of course, and much as I expected, she was scornful of my 'Pakeha notions of land use', which she bluntly characterised as 'greedy exploitation'. The fact is they do think differently! But is that right or wrong? I am unsure. It seems to me that Maori too must have developed natural resources, albeit with much lesser impact. But surely that was because it was effectively a stone-age culture? I have some sympathy with John Reid, even Pagett, on this.

Though her notions might give rise to nostalgia for a more simple existence, reality is a modern capitalist world. I write that and now I feel uneasy: as if I have just articulated a prepared script! I need to think some more on this.

There is mockery, a challenge perhaps, in her eyes that is quite disconcerting. Similar and yet not the same as R. He, I suspect, truly cannot divine reality from the phantoms he sees everywhere.

We talked about Pagett and I have to say I was unperturbed to hear her describe him in unfavourable terms. She said they would stop him. She said they were going to the courts and she was confident. I guess I am pleased at that news.

She has seen Sean many times. Apparently he ranges over many farms at will. How curious to hear him described by someone else as their visitor. I feel a little jealous. She believes he should be taken away from Pagett. An interesting thought.

The food was delicious and I overdid my consumption considerably. We sat at a long table in the garden covered with white paper — the most practical tablecloth! After Louis said grace we ate for an hour. Maybe more. Pork, eels and fish, and pumpkin and kumara and many other things.

This excessive consumption was followed by a near universal collapse around the garden, though a creditable guitar was played and many songs were sung. Everyone joined in whenever they could and then most of us went to sleep. At one point we were assaulted with water bombs! And that young fellow who played the guitar lit off after those kids and the noise they made!

We continued our siesta until late afternoon when the tea trolley arrived and we were revived with black tea and the most excellent Xmas cake! My God! Full! And then I said I should be getting along because I thought I might be overstaying my welcome, and such a fuss!

So that was how I came to stay all night. Allocated a space, sleeping bag and a piece of foam rubber on the porch!

In the evening there was more singing and a new fire was lit where the hangi had been. Louis made a long speech, some of which was in Maori. He is quite a wit and made his family and friends laugh. I gathered, from the concert of giggling glances and the mischief in that old guy's eye, that he made some reference to me. He did say how pleased they were to be able to provide me with hospitality in response to my efforts at the school! Ha!

For my part I thanked them for the best Xmas Day I could remember and led an outstanding version of 'Rocky Mountain High' to a great ovation! That was Xmas!

This morning, we had a breakfast so large one might have supposed the catering team thought we had not eaten for a week! Bacon and eggs and more tea. Then, without ceremony, people drifted away until there were only a few of us left.

This place is beautiful. We have been blessed with sun and only a little wind, and the hills all around look magnificent. And that Gertie! She told me much about Henry and a young Maori woman called Georgina. She was the prettiest girl around and there were many 'looking for her favour'. Gertie laughed about this. Gertie said she was 'wiggling herself all around', and Henry won her in a beach race! She moved in with him and they married shortly after. They never had kids and when Georgina was only forty-three she died of cancer. Henry seldom came down to the village after that. He was heartbroken, she said. He just stayed up there at the cottage for years and years.

In the early years he was a big help in the community. He made lots of things and helped people build houses and do up their cars. But he was a changed man after Georgina.

I found it the most natural thing in the world to tell her about Luke.

It was hard to leave.

Basking in the afterglow of my Xmas experience when Beth arrived. I was pleased to see her, not least because she brought me a book and a tin of home-made biscuits. Unfortunately I had not thought to have something for her but she didn't care.

I showed her my recent paintings though I haven't done any work for some time. She is most supportive and made me promise to keep going. She said she would be back soon and expected progress. It is possible.

I learned nothing of Sean and she is against my plans to visit Pagett. Surely it could not be dangerous?

She stayed a long time today and I was not sorry.

New Year's Day and no invitations to save me from myself. I should make a resolution perhaps. I think I am resolved that I will finish the dory by the end of the month and then I will go home. I am tired of this place. I do not belong.

Jan ??
I am so self-absorbed that I allowed her to talk and I simply didn't see. And then she was so close and in a way that left me in no doubt. I reacted abruptly, I think and she was a little upset. Fortunately we soon made amends and carried on as though nothing had happened. I do enjoy her company and I would hate to hurt her in any way.

Who wrote the horror note? Could it be Pagett? The man is becoming an ogre in my mind.

Almost the end of this book I see — of this diary cum confession. How strange. I will need another.

Mary turned the last page and below a depiction of children in a classroom found just two lines.

I must find Sean. He may be trapped. He may be hurt? I will go to the farm and I must go soon. I need to cook something and I have run out of wine.

Mary flicked back through the pages. She paused at some of the drawings: no more than unintelligible doodles many, others finely executed. She leafed through the pages and thought about the unforeseen and unexpected illumination she had received. So many insights into the heart of the man she had loved for many years and yet, here, evidence of how much she did not know. It was strange chance.

She closed the book and rubbed her eyes, leaned back and massaged her neck. She wondered whether she would find the second diary close by and hoped so.

For a long time she prayed for Tom Mahler and then she slept.

THE crash shook her so much she thought she had been physically hit. A huge bang on the roof, followed by several smaller clatters. She clamped her hands to her ears and stared wildly, trying desperately to locate herself.

'What is it?' But her words were drowned by another crash and another and at each successive blow she pushed further into the sofa. 'Stop! I'm in here. Please stop.' Laughter and another rock crashing. She fell to the floor and crawled to the light switch. Feeling for the door lock in the darkness, sliding it across and holding her breath at the squeak of the rusty bolt.

And then a tremendous crash against the door so that she launched herself away with a cry. Scrabbling on hands and knees she pressed herself into the corner below the bench and wrapped her arms around herself. Silence again, then hearing the back door opening. She stumbled against the table but heard the footsteps in the hall. Fumbling desperately she wrenched the front door open even as he rushed.

Three near the car, startled faces in the half-light. She leapt to the grass and ran to the edge of the hill. Cascading recklessly down the slope but reaching the sand and running blindly.

Staring at a black man. Directly in front — a huge man with a black crescent eye. She pitched forward.

'Ringatu!' she screamed. 'Ringatu!' Soft waves tumbling close and swishing across the sand. Seabirds calling and her own gasping but not moving now. Voices echoing in the thin light and the roar of a car engine but as soon diminishing. Soon, nothing but the sea in the dawn. She lay motionless and did not care.

The squeak of sand underfoot and a hand under her arm. He crouched near, studying. Exactly as Tom had described.

'Thank you, thank you,' she managed. 'I will stand.' He helped her to her feet and towered head and shoulders above. 'I'm so grateful. So grateful ... I'm so frightened.' She covered her face. 'I'm sorry ...' Wiping her eyes. 'Who? They just attacked me ... Oh, God.'

'They're gone.'

She nodded and wiped her face on her sleeve. 'Gone?'

He nodded. 'Not very brave.'

'Oh, you cannot believe how grateful I am. I'm so grateful.'

He looked away. 'I'll take you back.'

'Ringatu?' she said, but he did not turn and she followed, struggling to stay close. Scrambling over the same steps she had taken three at a time and gasping at the pain in her leg. Fearfully, looking around the clearing in the pale light. Seeing the rocks on the porch and the skid marks on the grass.

'They're gone?' She reassured herself, limping to the porch to sit. 'Why did they do that? What would have happened?' She smoothed her cheeks. 'I must see the police. I must.'

He did not respond. Still studying her but in a way that was not alarming.

'You want something? A drink?'

'Yes. A coffee. I need a coffee. And I'll make it.' She attempted to rise.

'Stay,' he said, and went inside. She could hear the kettle filling and the clink of crockery.

'You were just there.' She received the coffee and inhaled the warmth deeply. 'Thank you. You were just walking ...'

'I was coming.'

'What?'

'I wanted food.'

'Oh.' She sipped the hot drink.

'You knew who I was,' he said at length.

'Yes. I knew when I saw your ...' She indicated on her own cheek, touching beneath her right eye. 'Tom described you.' The look of bemusement she had seen when she cried his name returned. 'Tom kept a diary. Everything ...' She remembered. 'They knew who I was ...'

'A dangerous thing that diary.'

She did not understand. 'Oh, you mean, about you? I'll keep it safe. I don't want to destroy it but I won't mention it to anyone.'

He regarded her impassively. 'It is your right,' he said at last. 'Do you want me to stay for a while?'

'I would be grateful. I don't know what to do. Perhaps ...'

'I will stay. I will stay for a while.' And he lay down on the porch with his hands behind his head. It was apparent the conversation had ended. Mary rose and stood in the doorway, looking down at the large man whose eyes were closed now.

'Thank you, Ringatu.' She closed the door and walked towards the little hallway, paused to collect the diary then closed the bedroom door. She pulled back the bed cover and climbed in, pulled it over her ears and closed her eyes.

11

IT WAS SUPERB weather and Merv enjoyed the view across the valley as much as he ever had. Should be out fishing, he thought as he drove towards the roadworks, except that poor bastard was out there drowned. Best time of the year and there was a rahui down. More mumbo-jumbo. Not that it would be good to hook a corpse! That could give a man's love of fishing a bit of a knock. He smiled wryly. But it was also a mark of respect and there was nothing wrong with that. A man could live with the rahui.

He recalled the previous evening with some discomfort. A bout of 'nerves', his wife called it. Good grief! Like a woman! But then came the compliments — the admiration and approval of friends and neighbours.

He wound the window down and enjoyed the song of summer in the valley. You missed the cicadas when everything was cold and wet and the ground turned to mud. It reminded you just how good summer was. Wouldn't mind a swim in the river. Might suggest it to the boys at smoko.

But Pagett's house burning? That had been a real shock until they discovered it was that silly kid, Jimmy. Kids did some pretty dumb things. He had done some pretty far out things himself, he recalled, and a slight embarrassment swept over him at the thought of the haybarn. To this day no one knew, though he wondered whether his dad had tumbled him. And what about Fred Johnson's truck in the hedge? Merv laughed out loud. 'That was a bloody great night!' Him and Ted Johnson and Bill ...

He frowned. Those were the days when there was no 'boss' or anything. Just mates. Just rugby mates who knocked around sinking a few beers and chasing tail. What a bloody pain, he thought. He's such a good foreman. The men like him and, in fact, Merv contemplated with renewed wonder, I like him. Hell! he thought, why'd the stupid bastard have to go like that? If he'd just backed off they would've talked about it and Bill would have come around. He wasn't an extremist or anything. Straight as a die, mostly. Stupid bastard had to get all emotional just when his boss was feeling a bit antsy. He recalled the sudden flurry of blows and grinned. By cripes Manuhuia could throw a few. But he landed some good'uns himself. Sometimes a man just had to take a stand.

Merv pulled onto the shaded parking area next to his office. It would get bloody hot by about ten when the sun came over the hill. Best to get the paperwork done early.

He noticed a small cluster of men near the digger, and they looked excited when his truck appeared. Reminiscing I'll bet, he thought. Talking about who got hit where and the hardest. He glanced in the rear view mirror and frowned at the bruise. Dumb buggers. He was about to head into the shed when he was called.

'What's up?' he asked as he got close. No response! Just opened a space in front of the digger so he could see the damage. The injectors smashed. The fuel filter smashed. The air intake buckled uselessly. Paint lost from the block where a heavy implement had struck glancing blows, and two of the tyres slashed.

Merv restrained himself. 'Looks like you guys will be using the shovel a bit more today.' But he felt hollow. 'Well, we don't need to stand around all day gawking at this pathetic shit, do we? Work to be done,' he said.

'Some nasty little pricks have smashed my digger,' he told Buchanan on the phone. 'What're you going to do about it?'

* * *

JOHN REID LOOKED back at the small congregation, caught one or two eyes and nodded. This is a sad way to go, he thought. Less than twenty people gathered to say goodbye to a man they hardly knew. Many of them perhaps had never even spoken to him, and Reid tried to remember the last time he had seen Pagett. At least three years, he thought with surprise. Standing on the road talking to Joe McCleod when Pagett had appeared in his old Ford Zephyr. Reid had to move his car over and as he did, Joe attempted to engage Pagett in conversation. 'That's got to be the leeriest bastard I've ever met,' he told Reid after Pagett had disappeared up the hill.

Now here they were, at his funeral. At the funeral of the leeriest bastard between here and New Plymouth. But someone had killed him and now they'd burned his house down. Why? What were the police doing? It was a bloody joke. A kid just walked up and burned the place down!

'THIS is horrible,' whispered Rachel Lynch. Pete nodded and remained silent. She watched the minister turn the pages of the Bible and slip in a marker. 'I wish he'd get on with it.' She fiddled with her scarf.

'Yep.'

She thought of the afternoon that now seemed like months ago, when she had heard that shot. Then the shock of discovering that she had heard the shot that killed him ... the shot that no one else had heard ... an unwanted link to this dead man. She remembered asking Pete whether he had heard, and she remained envious that he had not. She and only she had heard someone pull the trigger. She had heard the instant a bullet took this man's life. All the while now, all the time she was milking she thought about that moment when someone just up the road, within earshot, was inside that man's home and intent on killing him. She tried to imagine who? Or what? What fiend had so much hatred they would callously kill any man? She pulled the knot of her scarf so it felt less close about her neck.

'What is he waiting for?' she whispered, but Pete just shrugged.

Perhaps that little boy? She remembered him so clearly, wandering down the lane or across their bottom paddock, but they didn't ever mind that. Only twice she had actually talked to him — or at him, for he never responded. So serious he had been. Barely any expression on his wan face with those bright blue eyes staring in a way that did not remind her so much of a child. Not shy or mischievous, just staring as though they had already seen everything. What had they seen? Were they seeing anything now? And she felt pain rise in her throat. The police must be losing hope. Everyone was losing hope. What a dreadfully sad time in our lives, she thought. 'I do wish he would get on with it,' she whispered. Pete did not answer.

What's the bloody point of it? he thought. None of us liked the bastard, though he felt ashamed of the satisfaction he had felt looking up the valley the day after. How he had thought a kind of darkness had disappeared. But now even the house was gone, and he pictured the raging flames lighting up the night and experienced again that terrible sense of helplessness. It was him that shot our dog, he thought, and it was him that chose to stay locked away up there on his farm. He was a mean bastard! I liked that dog.

John Reid turned to see three latecomers seat themselves in the back row. Old Louis and Bill Manuhuia he thought with surprise, and that old woman.

'*They're* here — can you believe that?' he whispered to his wife and gave her a gentle nudge. She ignored him and stared determinedly at the front of the church.

'I welcome you all here today, on this sad occasion, to say goodbye to a longstanding member of the community.'

We had to come, Reid thought, but they didn't. They probably hate the bastard and yet they've come.

'This is an unhappy time in our small community,' continued the vicar. 'This is a time when, more than ever, we must think of the infinite love of the Lord our Father. It is a time when we would do well not to dwell on the affairs of men, but on the love of God. It is a time when we must draw on each other's strength and come together as one.'

How can we be one when there's a murderer out there? wondered Reid. Maybe murderers? Maybe a whole bunch of people who know what happened? Maybe a whole bunch who are glad?

'This unhappy man, Trevor Pagett. Not well known in our community because he chose a private life and yet a man who lived among us, quietly and peacefully, only to come to a terrible and untimely end.'

'Leery!' Reid recalled. Who knows what the man was like? He was a pretty strange-looking bastard altogether.

'The father of the boy Sean … the little boy who we must not give up hope will soon be found safe and sound. The little boy who has been left without a father and who, tragically, has no relative that we know, will need us to support him, to love and care for him.'

Rachel cried when she thought of that boy so alone in the world. She lamented she had not tried harder when she had had the opportunity. I am a poor excuse for a human being, she thought. I could have helped in some way.

And Beth Gilbert remembered the one time Pagett had come to the school. 'This is the boy,' he had said, without so much as a glance at Sean. 'The boy!' She recalled her discomfort at the expression. No pride or affection, no warmth for the little boy who stared with his blue eyes. Who had no mother, and a father who seemed to regard him as little more than one of his working dogs. A little boy who wandered for miles and miles. Searching. He must have been searching, she thought, and her head sank lower. And then Tom Mahler came and maybe they found something together and now he was gone too. God, she thought, what is happening here? What is going to happen yet?

'More than ever, in this time of great tribulation we must put our faith in the infinite wisdom and love of the Lord Almighty ...'

The Lord knows, Louis thought as he looked towards the small stained glass windows above the altar. The morning sunlight made the image of Christ glow so Louis might hear the pain, and he knew that Christ and the Lord were staring down at him at this very moment with the greatest reproach. Staring down on this man who knew bad things. Things that were weighing him down inside so he felt he could barely muster the strength to walk. Coming to this place had seemed the longest of journeys.

He joined in the psalm without enthusiasm and listened to the vicar farewell the murdered man with growing agitation. He listened to the prayer and burned with the knowledge of a hardened sinner. I've got to find that boy, he thought. He allowed Gertie to shepherd him into the aisle just as soon as the pallbearers had assembled, and they left the church as silently as they had come.

* * *

MARY WAS STARTLED at the sound of the book hitting the floor. Hours had passed and now bright sunshine streamed onto her face like fire. She winced when she stepped on the floor, but hastened to the bathroom to splash cold water over her face, briefly examined herself in the mirror and was mortified.

The ashes were cold in the grate and her coffee mug lay on the floor. She limped to the front door and eagerly swung it open. 'Ringatu?' She hastened to the end of the verandah and glanced about the clearing.

Where to now? she thought. What am I going to do? I need to call someone. Sophie? Anyone. I will need to go back to Mokau. It should be safe. They wouldn't dare …

I want the other diary. Then I will leave this benighted place and never return. She walked slowly around the room then crawled under the table and confirmed that the slot at the foot of the wall held nothing. She continued along the wall, feeling and examining every inch, and with distaste discovered a white bobby sock that she flicked to one side. She shifted the sofa, rummaged through a stack of old newspapers and emptied a few seed potatoes and a bottle out of a cardboard carton.

'Don't be daft,' she said out loud as she opened the oven door. 'God!' And quickly closed it.

The bedroom next. She searched under the bed and lifted the mattress. Dumped the covers in the corner and hauled the clothes in the wardrobe aside.

'Damn, damn! Tom!'

She explored the back porch, the laundry tubs and the toilet, then returned to the sitting room and plumped herself down on the sofa. If not here, why not? He took it with him? Someone else has it? She considered these options. Why would he take a diary, especially if it was as big as the first? It would be inconvenient and useless.

Not Ringatu, certainly. The boy? But would he be able to read it? She narrowed her search: more likely to be someone who wanted it for sentimental reasons or to hide something. As fearful perhaps as Ringatu? Someone who could be embarrassed in a small community? A teacher engaged to a policeman …

The woman in the little blue car going much too quickly …

She went out to the car, drove cautiously up the gravel track, through the open gate and onto the narrow road that led to Mokau.

* * *

BUCHANAN WATCHED BILL and Gertie hug the old man then walk to their own house. A few minutes later he entered Louis's front garden and knocked loudly.

He did not remove his hat as he was ushered into the narrow passage, and he declined the offer of a cup of tea.

'Louis, you know why I'm here.' He studied the old man's face and was gratified. 'We know about the words. We know about them and we know why they were there ... and you know too.' Buchanan carefully placed his hat on the table, and wondered which way the old man would go. It didn't matter.

Louis broke into a coughing fit that allowed him to turn. Buchanan waited patiently.

'I don't know what you might be speaking of, Constable Buchanan.' Louis rummaged in his pocket for his tobacco pouch. 'Maybe you can tell me some more about this?'

'Don't bullshit me!' The old man's head jerked but he continued to roll the cigarette. 'We're talking about murder, Louis, and we're going to get him one way or another. But I need to know where he is.' His voice softened. 'He needs help, old man. He needs your help. We've both got a responsibility here. He needs your help, and I can find him.'

The fingers stopped moving and the paper and tobacco fell onto the table. Louis's eyes had closed.

'Louis ...' Buchanan spoke softly now. 'Imagine the armed offenders going in there ... Barker and co going in there after him ... choppers ... rifles. You don't want that.'

Buchanan heard the squeak of the front gate but Louis had not. 'Louis! Where is he?' He leaned forward and grasped the old man's arm. 'I promise there'll only be me. Tell me.' He held his breath and heard a footstep on the verandah.

There were tears in Louis's eyes. 'He's on the pa ...' He coughed, and at the same moment there was a knock at the door.

'The headland?' asked Buchanan urgently. 'The headland?' The second knock was louder and Louis registered the sound. *'Louis?'* The old man nodded and looked confused.

Buchanan rose. 'Thank you, Louis. You've done the right thing.' He walked into the hall and could see it was just one of the boys framed in the leadlight at the end of the hall. 'Good morning, young fella,' he said as he passed and made for his car. He did not look back.

'The police!' Matty followed Louis back to the kitchen.

'Eh? The police? Just Constable Buchanan.'

'What's he doing here? Is he gonna arrest you?'

Louis sat, and as the boy crowded close he put his hand on his grandfather's shoulder.

'Me? No. He's not going to arrest me ...'

'Well who? He must be gonna arrest someone. Jake?' The boy's eyes widened hopefully.

Louis frowned and he rubbed his temples. 'Where's your dad?' he said slowly. 'Is he still at home?' The boy nodded. 'Well, what about you get back there and tell him I need him. You tell him I need him real quick.' And he waved the boy in the direction of the gate. 'You be quick.' The boy ran up the hall. 'You tell him to bring the flatdeck!' he called as an afterthought.

* * *

GERTIE WATCHED THE big green Falcon coming slowly down the road. It was creeping. That's what caught her attention. She paused from her work in the front garden. She was weeding around her chrysanthemums. The car stopped on the other side of the narrow road then pulled onto the grass verge above the river. Gertie recognised the woman — Lynch. Maybe a 'hullo' at the store or something like that. Maybe a quick exchange at the school fair when Gertie had brought along two ginger cakes. Yes. She was from up the valley, she thought. She was a dairy farmer.

The car door opened and Rachel stepped into the bright sunlight.

Hullo, Gertie thought, I do believe she's coming here. She peeled off her rubber gardening gloves and laid them on the handle of the spade.

'Mrs Ngahere?'

'That's right.'

Rachel stopped on the other side of the fence and looked slightly embarrassed.

'I'm Rachel Lynch.'

'My name's Gertie.'

'You're probably wondering …'

'Nope! I don't wonder about much.' Gertie studied the fair face and the auburn hair tied back. The blue shirt: one of her husband's? 'Would you like to come on in. I'm only doing some old gardening. I'm getting mighty bored of it too.' She gestured to the gate. 'Perhaps you'd like a cup of tea? I'm going to make one for myself.'

'That would be kind.'

'Well, why don't you sit yourself down here and I'll go make it.'

Well, Gertie Ngahere, she said to herself, this is a different sort of tea party on your verandah, and that's for sure. Why do you suppose this lady has come to visit? I don't know. I truly don't know. She searched for her best crockery and found the silver teapot she hadn't used for years. That thing could use a good polish all right, but never mind.

On the verandah, Rachel silently studied the slow-flowing, mid-summer river. She looked at the old Charger sitting on boxes with no wheels and rust eating the door panels from one end to the other and she glanced at her own car and wondered. And Gertie? She had a nice face, but that old petticoat hanging down below her old brown dress? And the woollen socks!

She studied the garden. What pretty chrysanthemums, with orange heads like sunshine all along the fence, she thought. I should plant some of those. I should plant some next to the cowshed. That would be really nice. How nice it is to be here. She glanced along the riverbank. I love that river, she thought with a sigh. Oily old brown thing it looks, but I love it. I love the way it comes winding out of the hills from far away. I love it when it swells in the winter and it's so dangerous. It's not to be taken lightly then! Sometimes it rushes clear across the flats and the cows and everything have to be taken up the hill for safety. She hummed to herself and realised she wanted to ask Gertie about her flowers. She wanted to ask how her little boys were getting on. She liked those cheeky little boys.

'Here we are.' Gertie placed a tray on the old green chair and pulled a broken deckchair towards the ancient church pew. 'Get away out of it!' she said loudly so that Rachel jumped and then laughed nervously when she saw the huge rooster that had come sneaking around the side of the house and jumped onto the end of the verandah. 'Look at that bird! He'd be into my kitchen if I gave him a second. I should talk to him about the axe!' She laughed. 'White or black?' she asked.

They sipped their tea in silence and the sun was warm and the green hills looked as pretty as any picture. A small white cloud served only to remind them how blue was that summer sky.

At last, Rachel put down her cup and thanked her host.

'It's just that old Choysa!' said Gertie. And Rachel said how delicious the cake was. 'Oh, that's just that old date loaf.' And they smiled.

'Well, I suppose you're wondering why I've come? Uninvited and everything.' Gertie stared across the river and thought, this is an interesting thing to tell Bill. Wherever he's gone, that brawling man. Rushed out the door and not a word. 'Well, it's like this — Gertie,' Rachel said. 'Last night, after that awful thing, you know?'

'Oh, yes! I know about that thing!'

'Well, naturally we're all talking about things — the things that have been happening ...'

'They certainly have! There most certainly have been a few things happening.'

'Yes. Well, people are angry and ... I don't know ... confused. Yes, I would say confused, about things.' Rachel fidgeted with the cuff of Pete's shirt.

'Well, here's another one of them coincidences — I was sitting out here, right here last night with my nephew and Old Louis and we were talking about those very same things. Things happening and no one knowing what's it all about.'

They glanced at each other and shared a silent pleasure at how things had begun.

'Those are such beautiful flowers,' Rachel said wistfully.

'Oh, that's just those old chrissies. I need to plant some roses.'

'No, they're beautiful. I'd like to have them all along my cowshed. It would be like having the sun even on the rainy mornings.'

'That's the truth. Those chrissies are like the sun itself. That's what

I think. And I'm going to give you some.' Gertie was not easily deterred, rising to gather her gloves and trowel that instant until Rachel persuaded her to wait. They smiled companionably.

At last Gertie said: 'There it is then, a coincidence. There was my Bill wondering why his boss had done what he did after knowing him all these years, but not knowing because no one was talking. I can tell you that I'm pretty hot about what Merv Layton did. I don't mind that man. He does lots of good things for the school and that. But that don't excuse him. What was he about? Did he have some kind of a stroke? That's what we were thinking and then you ... you all were thinking too?'

'Yes. We were thinking about those things. But all the things like the burn-off. And the other stuff ... the farmhouse ...' Rachel paused, uncertain how to proceed.

'I know. It's a big bother, all right.' Gertie coughed. A brown car drove by and hooted. She waved.

'And the other stuff ...' Rachel paused and sensed a sudden awkwardness.

Gertie peered at her shrewdly. 'Those kids stealing, you mean? Those kids! There's some bad ones. A few of them. There's a few wants a good kick up the jacksy. I don't know. I don't know where they're coming from.' She shook her head and compressed her lips. 'You know kids!'

Rachel nodded but thought that she didn't really. 'Are yours good — I mean, are they coming along? I like those boys.'

'Ah! Yes, those boys are coming along all right. I would say so. They don't do everything that their old auntie wants but they're coming along.' She smiled.

'And they saw Tom Mahler. That must have been so awful?'

'Yes. That was awful, all right. That man, Tom. He was okay. I liked him, but now look. I wonder what's going on about all this. And that boy ... I wonder about that boy.' She gazed across the valley at the hills. 'Some folks is saying he was doing some bad things. Well, I don't know but it doesn't seem right to me. It doesn't seem to be the nature of the man, but I don't know, I really don't. But where has he gone? That boy? I don't know.'

'I know.' They lapsed into silence.

'My boys don't know.'

'No.'

'The police don't know.'

Rachel nodded. 'Gertie? Last night I said to Pete, that's my husband, that people should be talking more … like this, like we are.'

'Ah. I like to talk.'

'Yes, but people don't want to talk. They're afraid.'

'That's what they are. Everyone is and no one making any sense. Not Merv Layton. Not that public brawler, Bill Manuhuia! Not that man Pagett that's dead! He didn't want to talk and now look.'

They caught each other's eye and felt there was an understanding. But what? Rachel wondered.

'Gertie …'

'Would you like some more tea? Cake? Here, have some more of this cake — it's just my old date loaf.'

'No thanks. It's great but that's enough. No, what I wanted to say is, what should we do? About … things? About talking, or having more people talking? I don't know.' She shook her head helplessly and at the sheer frustration of trying to put into words what she felt in her heart.

'Talking! That's a good thing. Not like those brawling men! They don't talk, oh no! Well, you can call by any old time. I'm always here and I like to talk.'

'Thank you.' Rachel thought about this and wondered what it meant. She decided she needed to think some more. She was unsure what she wanted exactly, but she felt it had been worthwhile coming to visit Gertie Ngahere. She spoke of her garden and said Gertie should come and see it. Gertie agreed that was a fine idea and she would love to. Rachel said she would be happy for those boys to go eeling on the farm any time. She knew they did anyway but it didn't hurt to say. Gertie was appreciative and said she would give Rachel some of her smoked eel next time. Rachel said she had better go to the store for some supplies and get back to the farm, or else Pete would be wondering.

Gertie laughed and said wasn't that the way with men. Always wondering but never talking. Rachel said she talked to her cows more than to Pete and they both laughed.

Gertie touched Rachel's arm when they said goodbye and Rachel felt that lightest of touches all the way home.

Gertie watched Rachel drive off down the road and then took the tray and padded back into her little hallway, humming a song about the Heavenly Gates. 'Talking!' she said out loud as she clattered about in her kitchen. 'That's a good thing.'

* * *

A SCREAM IN the bush like a hunting hawk. Ringatu tucked himself away and ran back into the clearing where the boy sat upright and motionless.

'You are a little warrior,' he said softly. The boy did not hear. His breathing was rapid. At length he looked around and saw Ringatu, leaning against the rock wall. He fixed his gaze on the man for a long time and then with his hands he said: 'Frightened.'

Ringatu nodded in the gloomy light beneath the trees. 'You are seeing the past. It is okay. The past need not be feared. It is okay.' The small hands moved again. Ringatu sighed. 'He's in his boat. He's still in his boat.'

Whether or not the boy comprehended, he seemed to relax and after a while he signalled that he was hungry.

'I haven't got anything. It's no use asking.' The boy lay down on the fern and tucked his head under his arm. 'We'll go hunting.' Ringatu knew the eyes were open — he could see the gleam and he pondered how it would be. How he could carry the death? He pondered the day. He pondered the chopper sweeping to and fro over the black valley. They had come to search, at last. It had taken them so long. The faintest smile appeared and vanished. What did they want? The beast was dead and the boy was safe. What did they want?

He thought of Mary Mahler and tried to see that woman and Tom together. She had come a very long way. From America, and here she was in that old cottage waiting for a dead man. With her long black hair and green eyes. She was a handsome sort of a woman, and tall.

He glanced at the sun coming through a hole in the canopy and reached for his staff. 'Go for a possum,' he said, and the dog turned two or three excited circles and the boy came to the dog and they bumped each other about. 'Where's that woman gone off to?' he asked himself and Sean pointed down towards the sea. Ringatu grunted and led the way back into the valley. 'Maybe she'll bring something,' he said.

They made their way along a narrow animal track near the dry creek bed, the dog snuffling in front and the boy following behind Ringatu. Periodically they paused to examine an empty snare and twice Ringatu reset the loop. The boy watched intently and the dog interfered. 'Fuck off!' said Ringatu peremptorily but it made no difference. The boy caught hold of the dog's tail and without difficulty hauled the uncomplaining animal aside. 'That's the way,' said Ringatu. 'Damned animal getting out of control,' and they grinned.

He wondered what that woman would do. Now that she was here in that cottage. She must know, he reasoned, she must have asked down in the town and someone would have told her. She had come and found he was gone. He crouched to inspect another snare and the boy came close and placed a hand on his shoulder. Ringatu looked up with surprise but the hand stayed. For a moment he looked into those strange blue eyes and he felt puzzlement and warmth. 'Nothing here,' he said gruffly and the boy nodded and withdrew his hand so Ringatu could stand.

The three of them stood facing each other under the tree ferns and Ringatu said, 'This is a piss-poor morning. Not one of those things here.' They stared back and the boy signalled that he was hungry. He signalled that the dog also was hungry. 'All of us,' said Ringatu. 'That's what I said. We'll go up the ridge.' He led off and the dog immediately overtook him and sped up through the trees.

He wondered whether he should have stayed longer and talked to that woman. But what to say? That the man had gone to sea in his daft boat like a tarakihi?

The dog barked.

'There he is. He has come to our table.' Ringatu pointed to the possum struggling in the snare at the base of the mahoe and swung his boot at the dog. The possum was using all four feet to try to pull its head from the loop of flax that was tightening around its neck. The body curiously contorted, bunched in the air, and the tail outstretched and quivering.

They watched in silence for several seconds. Ringatu finished his smoke and again, poked the dog away.

The boy was advancing towards the animal. He studied the writhing that caused tufts of fur to break away and float around the agitated circle of the snare then he cast about, looking for something, and stooped below the track. Ringatu watched the tight, determined features. He noticed the fist-size rock in the wiry hands. He watched the boy raise the rock and crash it onto the head of the possum. He struck again and again until, silently, the animal subsided. Ringatu laughed.

'Give thanks for death.' He cut the snare and lifted the body, its legs poking like tines. 'For how else would we live?' The dog tried to bite the head. 'Fuck off!' said Ringatu.

* * *

BETH WALKED SLOWLY back to her sitting room. Those freesias are dead, she thought. Tom is dead. Brian and I are dead. She sat dumbly and stared at the red book. Touched it and then pushed it away.

'I don't think I want to know,' she said, but her fingers crept and felt the edge. Why do I not just burn it? What use is it now? She rose and walked around the table and stared at the book that seemed to cry out. She closed her eyes and remembered them sitting on the front verandah in the sun laughing. Remembered the feeling she had when she watched him and the children engrossed in their art. I will start, she thought, and with a deep breath she reached for the book and opened it.

~ Jan 25

A new book but not a new beginning. I have not seen the dog for days. Where is that bastard?

Luke came back last night. He was thin and cold. I fed him soup and bread. He looked at me with his huge blue eyes and did not once speak. I asked him about Mike and Doggitt but he just shook his head sadly. I fear the worst.

She was startled by a knock on her front door but did not move and she heard someone move away. Not Brian at all, she saw through the curtains but a woman: a stranger in jeans and a cream top who stopped uncertainly at the gate to stare at Beth's car.

Beth went to the door.

'Hullo?' she said, and saw sharp green eyes and a fine nose. An intelligent face with long black hair pulled into a ponytail. And the red car she had seen on Friday afternoon. 'You're looking for someone?'

A woman in her late thirties, handsome but stern at this moment and tired undoubtedly, with lines of strain around her eyes.

'I'm looking for Beth Gilbert.'

Beth nodded dumbly and stepped back, gesturing into her home. 'Come in — Mary?'

Mary extended her hand. 'I'm pleased to meet you.'

'I'm making a cup of tea — or would you prefer coffee?' Beth hovered uncertainly, then walked through to her sitting room. 'Please,' she drew a chair out from the table then busied herself in the little kitchenette.

'Have you been here long?'

'I arrived on ... Friday, I think. I'm losing track. And I stayed at Tom's cottage. But I saw you, didn't I? In the blue car?' And each clink of the crockery as she washed it seemed to Beth to be a cannon report. 'You and Tom — you were good friends?' Mary continued, 'I am pleased. Tom needed some friends, I think.'

Beth bit her lip. 'Yes, Tom and I were friends.' She banged the pantry door. 'Oh, where's that blasted coffee?' she cried.

Mary rose. 'It's okay,' she said quietly.

Beth remained facing the cupboards. 'Is it? I hardly know what to think, since he disappeared. And now he's gone. Did you know?' She turned. 'Of course you do, how stupid. The children called him —'

'Painter Tom,' Mary smiled.

'Oh!'

'There are many things I know and many that I do not. That's why I've come.' Mary's hand hovered at the edge of the table. She restrained herself. 'I've been reading Tom's diary ...'

The younger woman flushed. 'I knew there was another.'

'And so did I. We each have one.' Mary looked at the red book on the table and the kettle whistled.

'I went to collect it because I knew Brian would find it. That's what the police do —' her voice suddenly hard. 'And there are things that I ... didn't want him to see.' She gestured towards the book. 'But it's yours ... tea or coffee? I'm sorry, I don't recall.'

'I don't know that I have any more right than you, actually. But I think there is much that is unanswered for me that might be in these pages. Tea will be great.'

'Then please do. Please take it away. I really only wanted to hide it. You won't tell him?'

'No, I won't. But I can't guarantee I will not divulge anything that might be important — for Tom. He's been accused of things I do not believe. And I will disprove them,' she paused, 'if I can.'

Beth brought two cups to the table with sugar in a small silver bowl. 'My grandmother's.'

'It's very beautiful.'

'Yes, it is,' and she wondered how Tom and this woman managed to have a boy with snow-white hair. Then she spoke about the events that led to Tom's disappearance and angrily about the accusations about Tom and Sean. She described how he had helped all the children. How he had rescued the boy from a sort of prison in his own mind. She told about people who had believed and spread the horrid rumours, and concluded by declaring that she didn't care at all about Pagett's death.

Mary felt her spirits rise. 'I knew as much, Beth. I knew this but it is so good to hear you say it. I am grateful. I met some of those ... thugs, last night. I presume they're the same ones. I was rescued by Ringatu.'

Beth looked puzzled. 'Ringatu?'

'Had it not been for him — but he was gone this morning. I would very much have liked to talk with him.'

'Ringatu? I don't know ...'

'The Maori?' Mary was surprised. 'Tom saw him many times and they talked about all sorts of things. He must have mentioned it?'

Beth shook her head. 'You must tell Brian — the police. You must tell them.'

'I don't think I can involve him, for other reasons. And I doubt I could even identify them — the men. It was dark and I was inside mostly. But I think I will talk to the police. All I want is to stuff those evil words down this town's throat!'

'You have every right!' They fell silent and Beth continued to stir her tea until she became conscious of the clinking spoon. 'Mary, what are you going to do? I mean — do you want to stay here? It's only small but you can't go back up there ... I would be happy ... I can take you to Brian.'

She showed Mary a tiny bedroom with a single bed and old-fashioned rose print wallpaper. A tiny wooden table stood next to the bed, which had a cream duvet and a blue floral pillow. The one small window looked onto the back garden with its two apple trees and a lemon covered in fruit.

'It's lovely. Thank you.'

She listened to the front door close but before she could settle it opened again. Moments later Beth knocked and, with an apology, produced a small blue vase in which she had put two red roses. 'Off my climber,' she said. 'I thought you might like them.'

* * *

'YOU TOLD HIM Sam was up at the pa?'

'Yep. I did.'

Bill nodded as he drove with both hands seizing the wheel and his foot hard down but the flatdeck was not fast. Like a goddam bicycle. Like an old tractor, this grindy old thing.

'At the headland?'

'Yep.'

'He'd know about that?'

'Yep. He'd know.'

Bill glanced at Louis. 'You okay?'

'Yep.'

'I can't believe you never told me. I can't believe that.'

Louis did not answer. He looked straight up the road. He looked straight up the dotted white lines and thought it looked like a trail that led directly to Sam Wherry. Anyone could follow the trail laid by Sam's own uncle, Louis Ropata, directly to him. Constable Buchanan was following that very trail. He would find Sam at the end of that trail and Sam would be trapped.

The flatdeck barely slowed as Bill threw it into the corner that led from the highway onto the gravel road but Louis could still see that white line as clear as day. Leading right on up into the hills and the ancient pa.

Bill struggled to find the right words. At last he said, 'You think he did it?' He rammed the gearshift and the flatdeck slid around a sharp corner. He hoped they wouldn't meet anyone because there wasn't any room, not to pass and not to stop. 'You hear me?'

'I hear you.' Louis held onto the door with two hands. 'He was there. I'm pretty sure about that. And so's the police.'

Bill winced. 'Which track?'

'The ridge. That's where Buchanan will go.'

* * *

~ Jan 25

A new book but not a new beginning. I have not seen the dog for days. Where is that bastard?

Luke came back last night. He was thin and cold. I fed him soup and bread. He looked at me with his huge blue eyes and did not once speak. I asked him about Mike and Doggitt but he just shook his head sadly. I fear the worst.

The dog disappears for long periods. I am sure he goes to Ringatu. Does Melanie? I should not be jealous but I am. I am lonely and I wish to leave. The wind hates me. It has not stopped for days and it cools nothing. I paint dark scenes and I cry out to Luke but he is gone. I know I deserve his indifference. I have not cooked. I am at low ebb.

I read my words and see no meaning. I am an intruder who understands little. By dint of my exotic accent I am attractive to some and repugnant to others.

Yet he is imbalanced surely? Caught between the Old Testament and a plethora of local gods! That we should seek permission of Tane before felling a tree, lest we injure our tupuna? Ha! That we give thanks for the life of a fish?

'Respect evil,' he says, until it interferes with good and then it is right to enlist the aid of all to defeat it. To restore the balance? It is madness and yet there is something in that idea that is beguiling.

But he is so arrogant. So bloody arrogant! What can he know of these things? What can he know of what Sean is to me? 'Do you love him or yourself?' he demanded. Bastard!

Thank God for Beth! Oh, bountiful Beth! Laden with food and goodwill. We have had a splendid feast and she insisted on tidying my squalid little nest. But still no news. She looks at me strangely. Perhaps I am changing?

I climbed to the Mohican today but did not stay. The trees seemed less friendly. Today I heard the turehu and I am unsure how they feel about me. Perhaps they see the pig too.

Chinook returned. He lives two lives, that dog. We played the GAME and I enjoyed myself more than for an age. I gave him a piece of my steak and I think it was greatly appreciated.

I rose this morning determined to turn the dory. I cannot wait on the chance that R. will appear. But it was no use. It is very heavy and I am afraid I may damage the gunwale. Nevertheless, I may have to.

I have been down to the beach with the intention of swimming.

My gate has been lifted from its hinges and cast down the bank. What have I done to these people?

At last R.! Together we lifted the dory and sat it on the grass as it is meant to be. We are restoring the balance, I told him. We have breathed life into the timber and now we have a living boat!

'You are no different from the other Pakeha,' he said with infuriating incivility and left.

I am concluding that he is not so different either — they are all of them short of a marble.

I am so tired.

The pain will not diminish. Not wine, not resignation will dull the ache that tears my guts and spears my heart. All morning a chopper roved the valley dropping diesel! The smell is abominable! That monstrous bastard intends to destroy this land.

I will go tomorrow.

Mary closed the book and threw the bed covers aside. My God, she breathed, surely ... My God.

~ February 4

Now have I seen the pigs with grinning faces! Ghoulish pigs with bloodied jaws and entrails hauled from within. Here in Paradise a vile carnage!

Despite my revulsion I persevered and beheld at last the beast. A brutish face and complexion that reflect his loathsome trade. Eyes too small for so large a space and quite without human emotion.

I demanded to see Sean and was prepared for the worst but he walked into the shed and banged the door. For several minutes I waited with growing apprehension but for nothing. Not a sound from within, and then I noticed several small holes in the iron on the shed and I suspected I was being studied. At length I hailed him but still there was no response. I stepped up to the shed and kicked it repeatedly. The iron crashed loudly and even the pigs were disturbed. Nothing!

Backwards I walked for twenty yards before I turned

adjacent to the house. A crude, unlovable dwelling with cream paint peeling and no decorative thing of any description. I jumped up the steps and called in the open door.

What is in the mind of this man? A sound behind caused me to spin and there he was, racing towards me. His face! Jowls bulging and purple almost. He came very fast, though not in a direct line but in strange swerves — almost, on reflection, like a threatening dog. Momentarily I considered standing my ground but I knew I was not dealing with sanity. I ran down the track, more angry than frightened and confident I would outrun him.

I went directly to the police station but he was not there. Now I am filled with dread.

Buchanan will do nothing. Everything about the man's demeanour suggests he is closed to anything I might say. I wrote a formal complaint and left it with him. Could I go higher? I must think.

I searched for R. Why is he skulking in the forest?

I have lost three days. I am ill and I suspect a virus of some sort. The thought occurred to me that I may have contracted some horrible thing at that charnel house. I have sweated a great deal and been feverish but though I feel like shit I am improving. The black pig plagues as ever. The brute makes hideous overtures of friendship.

Beth was horrified though I suspect she thinks I hallucinate. Is it possible? I cannot recall leaving here.

Buchanan promises to visit Pagett but will not allow me to accompany him.

We have had such a day. Such a day! There is no wind and it is so hot. By midday it was unbearable in the cottage and we languished in the shade of the trees. And swam. He played in the dory! I fitted the oars and he rowed and rowed. I think he wanted to launch the huge thing down the cliff to the sea! Ha! I have to buy a trailer.

If only I could know where he has been and what he has been doing.

It is as I suspected. Melanie is with R.

I cannot understand why Luke does not return. I cannot understand. I wonder whether I have offended him in some way. I told him he could not have a dog for his birthday. He was upset but I think I was right. Our section is too small. I asked him whether it was fair to have a dog when we were all away all of the day. I know nothing of keeping a dog and I'm not sure I wish to find out. It is annoying how they shit on the grass. I told him he could have a new bike or a trip perhaps. I suggested Disneyland. I have not been there and I am sure we would have fun. But when? We have a very busy period coming up.

I would like to sleep but the night seems so close. I know I will be too tired in the morning and I have an important meeting. Perhaps Gerry will cover for me?

Luke has not seen the dory since we turned it over. I am sure he will be very excited. I will ask him about the colour — he can choose. Yes! If he wants red that is what it shall be. But I might steer him gently towards white. I don't know.

Tonight I made a cake! Chocolate. I would like to eat a piece but I am restraining myself. The cake is for Luke. It is a pity there were only four candles but I will suggest they represent the four winds. Or Mike and Doggitt, Luke and me! I am sure that will suffice and in fact it seems more appropriate. I am sure he will come tomorrow.

I told him how tired I am of attending meetings with his teachers. I am tired of his aimlessness and disaffection —

his rebellion. Why? We have given him everything it is possible to give.

How many times must I tell him about setting goals? I set goals. I set the goddam things every day, I told him. If I didn't, we wouldn't live where we do. We wouldn't vacation the way we do. He wouldn't have the advantages of the best education in the goddam city! He looks at me with blank indifference. What is it with this boy?

I am not feeling good. It is late and the valley seems completely deserted. I cannot hear any animal. I cannot hear the shags down at the macrocarpas and there is not a single steeleye circling the bay. Where have they all gone? Mary said something about Halloween. I do not remember. Was I supposed to be there? Was I supposed to have taken all the kids somewhere? I have a nasty feeling about this.

I have eaten a slice of the cake. It is quite good though it is not so light as my mother made.

Mary studied the drawing of the birthday party with eight children around a big square table and in the middle a cake resplendent with flaming candles. And such laughter! All the children with mouths wide, laughing. And each one wearing a birthday hat with a serrated top and streamers falling everywhere. And a man standing at the end of the table with his hands on his hips and laughing too.

Her eyes closed. She wished so much to be in the midst of the party. To take the man by the hand and to slip out the door while they played. A bird of some sort was singing outside her window. The sweetest sound, a gentle, tremulous sound ... if she could just slip quietly away.

A door banged and she listened to Beth moving about in the living room. Beth who was in these pages. Who had been there ... Beth who had become involved with Tom but not in the way she had feared. Not in the way these people thought. She picked up the diary and slowly opened to the very last page. 'This is all I have left. This is all I have, Tom,' she said sadly.

He has gone to the Mohican to find me! I cannot wait for him to return. Perhaps I might go to meet him. But dear Beth reminds me that we might easily miss each other by taking different routes. It is a half-holiday for some reason. I will ask her now ... she says it is by decree of the department. It is a teacher's half-day! Whatever that means — but I am grateful.

She thinks it highly amusing that I write in my book. She wants to know who it is for? I am stumped. I said it was just a habit. What for? she asks. She is a provocateur! She is interrupting me even now! How vexatious she is! I threaten to toss her down the bank and she dares me!

Perhaps I have written enough. I can see she is suspicious of my intentions.

It is mid-afternoon and I have slept for hours. Beth is gone and I am anxious. I will wait no more than a half-hour and then I will go to meet him.

She flicked forward and found no further entry. This was the very last thing he wrote. What happened? He went to find the boy in the valley. Then he went to sea ...

* * *

ANDREW BARKER REGARDED the small man sitting on the deckchair with some distaste. Milligan also was clearly conscious of the smell. The object of their attention seemed oblivious to his surroundings, head inert and eyes downcast. He reminded Barker of a snail, in that huge green overcoat with only the left collar of a grimy shirt showing. A small, bald head with lank and wispy hair trailing like weeds.

'Mr Ullrich, you have something to tell us? Please do.' A slight movement was the only indication his question might have been heard.

'I don't know, Sarge.' Milligan shook his head helplessly. 'He said he had seen something.'

Barker leaned back. 'Mr Ullrich, it is very good of you to come forward with information. But we really are hard-pressed ... what do you have to tell us? Something about Pagett?'

The little man looked up slowly and blinked. Perfectly round, very small eyes rimmed with red. Miniature features with little flesh. A mean, pinched face but not nasty, Barker concluded, just plain stupid. He sighed. 'Mr Ullrich? You saw something a few days ago? Friday perhaps? Would you like to tell me what you saw?'

Milligan shifted uneasily. 'I'm sorry, Sarge, I thought ...'

'You did the right thing. Let's give him a little more time. Would you like a cup of tea, Mr Ullrich? A coffee? Something else?'

The head swayed slightly. 'Sherry.'

'I'm sorry. We don't have alchohol here. This is a police investigation. But tea? Good.' Barker gestured to Milligan, who left the awning shaking his head in disbelief.

'We've got a right moron in there, and I'm the unlucky beggar who dug him up. Barker'll have my hide.' The two constables in the kitchen laughed. 'And now I'm fetching the little bleeder a cuppa. He wanted sherry!' They laughed again.

'Dross with the gold, Paul; you've got to dredge deep to find the good stuff.'

'That may be true, but this piece of dross stinks like an old goat. He lives with them. Up the river. The little bastard lives in the willows up there somewhere. This is your genuine hermit, for godsakes.' He poured a cup of tea. 'Cheers,' he said as he returned to the awning. Barker had turned a deckchair so its back was towards his prospective witness, and was sitting thinking about other aspects of what at present was a vexatious enquiry. Apart from the rifle they had nothing. Not even prints. What he had expected to be a straight-forward process was not. They had no boy and in all likelihood they were not going to. Weak suspect number one was apparently drowned and they had no other, as yet. They couldn't even find Mary Mahler!

'Ah, here we are, Mr Ullrich. Perhaps you'll feel a bit more at home with this.' He watched Milligan offer the cup of tea and a paper sachet of sugar. The man pushed the sachet away and protruded his upper lip over the rim of the cup, like a chimpanzee, Barker thought. A slurping noise followed, and a sigh.

'Now, tell me about the river, Mr Ullrich. You live up the river, I understand? Yes?' He nodded as he spoke, encouraging, and was rewarded with a nod in return though whether that was some kind of autonomic response would remain to be seen. 'And where you live, you could see a few things? Yes?' A barely perceptible nod and another long slurp. 'So, Mr Ullrich, I would be very, very grateful if you would tell me whether or not you saw something near the river, near your home perhaps, that you think might be of interest to us. I would really be very grateful.'

Milligan stared fiercely at the back of the man's head. He struggled with the temptation to give him a quick cuff behind the ear, but forced himself to emulate Barker's air of equanimity. Ullrich turned his head to peer out the door. He's exactly like a fucking turtle, the detective thought incredulously.

'Ullrich!' Barker shouted suddenly and the head returned more quickly. The tiny eyes widened with alarm. 'I'm sorry, Mr Ullrich, but I need an answer.' Barker made a quick assessment. 'Now!' he barked. The mouth opened and stayed open, fixed. Then: 'I seen him.' And closed.

'You saw him? Who? Who's him?' The eyes closed and reopened.

'I seen him and that ... that ...' His right hand began to make small circular motions. Barker found himself mimicking the action.

'With what? What did he have?' The hand continued to prescribe small circles and Barker noticed that he couldn't see into the man's eyes. They were opaque. Cooked! He thought angrily.

'You know ...'

'What? What do I know? What is this?' Then he calmed down. The man was not trying it on. He genuinely was trying to be helpful. Take your time, Barker, he told himself, and all will be revealed. 'You saw a man?' he began again. Ullrich nodded. 'And the man was carrying something?' A nod. 'Great. Was the man carrying something nasty, perhaps?'

Ullrich blinked and said: 'Rifle.'

'A rifle. He was carrying a rifle? You are sure?' Ullrich nodded. 'And you saw this man and the rifle down by the river?'

'By the beck.'

'What? What's the beck?' He glanced at Milligan but the constable shrugged and shook his head.

'The beck.' Ullrich was insistent. 'That's where. By the beck.'

Barker took a deep breath. 'All right, he was by the beck. What did he do? What was he doing by the beck? With the rifle?' Barker leaned forward but the flat eyes prevented any communion. Instead, the man repeatedly shoved both hands towards Barker. 'He threw the rifle?' A nod. 'He threw the rifle in the river? Is that what you saw, Mr Ullrich? Did you see the man throw the rifle in the river? Yes, or no?' A nod. 'Say yes, or no!'

'Yeah.'

Barker sat back, his eyes narrowed momentarily, and he rolled his head to alleviate the ache that had arisen in the back of his neck. He caught Milligan's eye but the constable looked studiously blank.

'Mr Ullrich. I am very pleased that you have come to talk with me. I am very grateful. I am thinking we might have a little drop of something somewhere. I might be able to persuade Constable Milligan here to go have a look for that drop, if we can just get a little more information.' He was pleased to see the eyes alight for the first time. Little creep, he thought. 'Would you care to see if there might not be a drop of something a bit stronger for Mr Ullrich, Constable?'

Milligan left the awning.

Barker stood up and stretched. 'Tell me something about the man, Mr Ullrich. Anything at all. Tall? Fat? Young or old? Anything you can remember.' He smiled warmly at Ullrich. I'll screw it out of the little bastard if I have to, he thought. But he smiled again and was rewarded when the man's lower lip dropped.

'Big.'

'Ah. Big. And you know him?'

Ullrich seemed to ponder this question. Confused perhaps, Barker thought. Too many concepts at once. 'So, he's big? Bigger than me?' He glared at his witness and was rewarded with a nod. 'Bigger perhaps than Constable Milligan?' A further nod.

'He goes about.'

'He goes about? What's that? You mean you've seen him before?'

Ullrich nodded and Barker felt a surge of excitement. 'He lives here, does he? He lives in Mokau?'

Ullrich went blank.

'Does he live here? Mr Ullrich? You have seen him here before?' Blast, he thought. Now I'm confusing this half-a-lightbulb. He continued more gently, 'Do you know this man?'

A frown appeared on the small forehead. 'I don't know him, 'xactly,' he said ponderously.

Barker took a deep breath. 'But you recognise him?' He waited eagerly, hopefully, and felt relieved when the head nodded. 'You do not know him, but you see him about? Is that right?' Ullrich nodded more confidently. Barker noticed with disgust that the man had an awful rash under his arm. Milligan returned, a plastic tumbler in his hand and a question on his face. Barker nodded and took the tumbler.

'Here we are, Mr Ullrich, a nice ...'

'Draft beer, Sarge.'

'A nice beer. But before I give it to you, can we just go a little further? Now, you saw a man who you recognise, throw a rifle in the river at the ... beck. And he is a big man. Bigger than either myself or Constable Milligan here. Now then, what else can you tell us about that man?'

'What's his name?' Milligan immediately regretted opening his mouth. 'Sorry.'

'Do you know it? His name?' Ullrich slowly shook his head. 'Okay. We do not know his name but we recognise him. Is he a Pakeha?' God give me patience, Barker seethed.

Ullrich shook his head and held out his hand towards the tumbler. 'Not just yet, Mr Ullrich, if you would just bear with me a moment. The man is not a Pakeha. Is he a Maori?' Ullrich nodded. 'Ah! You recognise this Maori because he's big, and something else. His hair perhaps? His nose?'

Milligan snorted and immediately turned away, ears burning.

'Mr Ullrich?' Milligan could hear an ominous edge in his superior's voice.

Ullrich raised his hand to his right eye and covered it. He sat with one eye regarding Barker and the other covered. Barker frowned. 'He has one eye?' Ullrich shook his head but kept the hand over his eye. Barker glanced at Milligan.

'Does he mean he's got a patch, Sarge?'

Barker looked scornful. 'A patch? A patch? Milligan, what do you think this is? Treasure Island?'

'He's got a patch,' said Ullrich.

'What?' Barker could not conceal his surprise or irritation. Milligan bit his lip. 'The man's got a patch? You're sure about that? Which of my eyes would have the patch if I were him? Point at the eye.' He glared at Ullrich, who again covered his right eye. 'Find Buchanan, quickly, Constable. Get him here.' Milligan hurried out once more.

* * *

'BETH!' MARY STUMBLED in the dark hallway and burst into the tiny living room. 'Beth, the fire! The valley was on fire and the boy was there, wasn't he? That's what happened. That day when you were there.' She thrust the diary forward, open on the last page. Beth stared as though she had been struck, her head shaking. 'Here! Beth. Right here, for God's sake!' Mary felt angry as she jabbed the page. 'Can't you read?' She shouted, 'The boy was in the valley! Why didn't you say?' She looked at Beth's frightened face and recovered some equanimity. 'Sit down, Beth, sit down.' She pulled a chair up for herself.

'I haven't read it. I haven't seen ... please?' Beth reached for the diary and turned it so she might read the last page. Her head pounded as she read the final entry. 'My God! My God, they're searching for Sean, but ...'

Mary desperately connecting events. Tom drowned and the boy in the valley. What had happened? Why had he gone in the boat? When? What was he doing?

'I'll have to tell Brian. They'll have to know. They're searching. They're searching ...' Beth covered her face with her hands and began to cry.

But Mary needed to think. When the valley was set on fire, Sean had gone to the Mohican and Tom had followed. And the boy had not been found. Tom waited and saw the fire? What did he do then?

What happened to the boy? Her chest heaved at the image of a little boy running. She shook violently and closed her eyes tight. Started as she felt Beth squeeze her arm. 'I'm okay,' she said, but her voice cracked and she fought furiously to retain her composure.

'We must tell Brian.'

'I know. I know.' But they both understood that it was too late. 'Where was he going? Where was he going?' Mary shook her head. It didn't make any sense. Had he found the boy? Her hopes soared momentarily and then crashed as suddenly to nothing. He would have taken him to the village surely? Raised the alarm? Made sure Sean was safe. If he was injured ... even more so. He would take him into Mokau. But he hadn't. He had gone to sea ... The boy in the valley. Tom going after him and either finding him or not. Alive or not. If he didn't find him ... coming back to the cottage — or not? Must have, for the boat. And if he had found him, then surely he would have gone somewhere safer? But then — drowned?

'I do not know what happened,' she said simply. 'It makes no sense to me at all. It is like the most horrible dream. I simply do not know.' She shrugged helplessly. Beth mute, nodded. Then she said: 'I'll call.'

She heard Beth pick up the phone and dial, heard her speak calmly. Then her voice changed, became hesitant. 'There was a book. A diary — yes. Yes, he kept it. Yes, I have it.' There came a long pause. 'Yes, okay.' She rang off.

'They're not ... they're angry about the ...' She gestured at the diary.

'I can imagine.'

'They want to see it.'

'It doesn't matter, Beth. There's nothing in there anyone needs to be ashamed of. They've got to have it.'

Beth had gone pale. 'I took him there that morning ...' she said and slumped down, covering her face. 'I left him there.'

Mary crouched at her side and wrapped her arms around the sobbing woman.

* * *

'THE KID WAS in the valley.' Milligan was profoundly shaken. 'Beth Gilbert — the teacher — said there's a diary — Mahler's. He must have written something. She said the boy was in the burn-off.'

Barker was speechless, and as the hard face transformed Milligan understood. Barker blinked several times and walked away. He shook his head. 'Shit!' he said softly. The other men looked on silently.

When Barker turned he sounded deeply tired. 'Call the search off. No! Get Lambert on the line for me.' He strode outside and looked towards the sea. Looked at the surrounding bush-clad hills and wondered how it was the sky could be so blue.

Milligan approached with the phone. As he took it, Barker told him to fetch the diary. 'Any word on Buchanan?'

'No sir. But we'll find him.'

* * *

'CAN I SEE his boat?'

'Of course, Mrs Mahler. Now?'

'Yes, if we could, Constable.'

Neither spoke as they drove along the riverbank to the boatshed.

'I'll open up.' Priddock was business-like. 'I'll open up and you go have a look. I'll wait here.'

She nodded absently and watched him find the key. The lock came away and he pulled one door open and the other partially. Then he returned to the car.

'Take as long as you like, Mrs Mahler.' He watched her pause in the opening with one hand shielding her eyes. Making out the curve of the gunwale and the thwarts. She extended her hand to touch the wood and shivered. Both hands now, she clasped the gunwale and pressed herself against the boat.

Then seeing Tom sitting as she imagined on the centre thwart. He would have been facing away so she moved until he was side on, his back bent as he hauled on the oars. Pulling back and then pushing forward, knees bending and straightening as he rowed. She reached out in the half-light and touched his shoulder.

'There you are, Tom.' She had imagined it to have been larger. 'You silly man,' she said softly, and smiled. 'You silly man.' A 'sea going' vessel, he called it. Then a deep and abiding pain as she realised how he must have known that Sean was gone when he went to sea. He must have known. He must have known, too, that something so obviously unseaworthy as this would not keep him safe for long. She studied the sides and the floor. The peaked, half-covered bow. She studied the transom where her hands squeezed the timber. She felt the indentations in the stern. This boat was his death. She let go with a feeling of revulsion, even anger and she hurried from the shed to blink in the sunshine.

'Okay? I'll lock up.'

She nodded and returned quickly to the car. Shutting herself in, even as the squeaking iron doors on the shed protested.

'The weather's broken,' he said awkwardly as they drove. 'Longest spell of easterly I can recall but it's breaking.'

She nodded dumbly.

'Well, if there's anything else I can do, Mrs Mahler?'

There was nothing, she said, and hurried in the door. She wished to be in Beth's little room. Away from everything. Away from the wind she could now feel coming from the sea. Carrying the smell of the ironsand and seaweed that she had not detected before. She glanced at the sky and noticed the high, streaky clouds. The weather was changing at last.

12

HE LISTENED TO the wind rising in the west. He had not liked the calm. It had been too hot and the bush made sounds he did not enjoy. This is what Tom Mahler wanted too.

He returned to the fire and turned the meat on the spit. 'Soon,' he said to the boy who lay in the dead fern. He wondered what was keeping the girl. Wondered what Tito was thinking. I will ask, he thought, and he knelt and bowed his head, his hands on his knees. When he raised his head he was face to face with the old warrior.

'I am Ringatu.'

The chief studied him with disdain.

'You have failed.'

'Perhaps I was meant to fail. I am unsure. Perhaps my mission is unworthy?' The buzzing grew louder and Titokowaru smiled thinly. 'Do you think the Pakeha a noble race, Ringatu?' Ringatu was puzzled. 'Fool! The Pakeha sent the mercenary von Tempsky.' He was contemptuous. 'Sneaking to Te Ngutu o Te Manu and that is where he was snared. That is where Tito snared the Pakeha hawk. Not with talk but with this!' And he brandished his musket. 'With this, Ringatu. You who become weak will not notice until one day he moves you from your own place — your turangawaewae that you have cultivated for many centuries. Preaching his God while he puts his hand up your woman's cunt. That is the Pakeha way.'

He stepped towards Ringatu, a much smaller man but dangerous. 'It is not Titokowaru's way, Ringatu. Do not be mistaken. We were killed for taking back what was ours. The Pakeha was filled with righteous indignation that we, Ngati Ruanui, should have presumed to take our rent. Do you understand me?'

'I do, great chief, I do.' And immediately the turehu quietened and Ringatu lay back on the fern and closed his eyes. A smile spread and stayed on his thin dark lips and the smell of roast meat filled his nostrils.

* * *

THE TWO WOMEN sat at the little table in the garden. Beth refilled their glasses.

'Did it help? Not really help! I mean ...'

'It wasn't like I imagined. It was small. Much smaller than I thought it would be. He was ... silly.'

'Or brave?'

They ate in silence, mostly avoiding each other's eyes.

'What did you think of it?' Beth asked at last. 'I was so impressed.'

'With the boat? Well, I suppose ...' Mary looked doubtful, gazing down the garden, recalling the shape in the shed. 'I wasn't really looking at the boat. Well, not as a boat, if you understand me.'

'Of course not. I mean, of course you wouldn't.'

'That's true, but there were things.' She frowned, as though recollecting a distant dream. 'There were things that puzzle me. The size; Beth, it was so small. And there was something else. No, there was more than something else. It was painted!' She looked perplexed. 'And it had marks, on the back. Marks, Beth! He didn't have a motor!' Her eyes widened. 'It cannot be Tom's boat. That's not the boat. Beth, he built a dory!'

She pushed away from the table, her eyes feverish with excitement. 'I know what you're thinking but it's true. I am not deluding myself. That is not the boat. And he didn't paint the boat. He said so himself. He didn't even have a motor. He wanted to row the dory. He hated motors. He knew nothing of motors. And why wasn't it there? If he had one, why wasn't it there?'

'It could have fallen off, it ...'

'No! Beth, it didn't fall off because it was never there. Don't you see? That is not Tom's boat. Not that boat in the shed! It's not!'

'But Mary, please, Tom was seen in that boat. Many times.'

They stood, one wild with excitement, the other deeply concerned.

'I don't care what people think they saw. I know that is not the boat. I saw the picture a million times, Beth. It was on Luke's wall for half his life. It didn't even look like that.' Then a new thought flashed through her mind. 'Draw it!'

'What?'

'Draw it, Beth. Please, just draw the boat. You saw it. Draw it so I can see.'

Beth found paper and a pencil and sat at the sitting room table with Mary opposite, willing her, and Beth hesitant and afraid.

'I saw it mostly upside down. Just once the right way ...'

'Just draw what you saw, dammit!'

Beth closed her eyes and recalled. She recalled the lean-to and the grass. She recalled the dog sitting nearby with a chewed stick in its mouth. She recalled the long, sleek shape, upside down. She tried to remember what it was that was distinctive. It was something about the bow and the stern. It was what Tom said — 'Like a banana.' Yes, that was it. It was like an inverted banana. And each end was almost like the other. Narrow and pointed. That's why it was so easy to row. It divided the sea both ways.

She began to draw the boat as near as she could recall, as it had sat on the grass next to the lean-to. She sketched the simple shape quickly. She drew the lines progressively harder on the paper as her confidence increased, then stopped and turned the paper around so Mary could see it as it might have been, sitting on its keel.

'I knew it! That's a dory! Just like Luke's picture. But it's not the boat in the shed. It is not! They are so different. Let's go! Let's go. Quickly.' She pulled Beth by the arm and grabbed the drawing.

'But Mary, what difference can it make? He's gone, Mary ...'

'No, he's not! Don't say that. He's not gone. He's out there, in his dory.'

Beth followed, anxious and frightened for the other woman and terrified at this sudden grasping at the remotest, most unlikely eventuality.

Neither spoke as they approached the roadblock. 'Go straight up the track,' said the constable. 'He'll be waiting.'

The gate opened and Beth accelerated up the bumpy farm track.

'Wonder what that's about?' The policemen watched the small blue car jump and bounce up the track.

'Beats me. Good-looking women, though.'

'Mind on your work, Sargeson.'

So this is it? Mary stared at the burnt remains of the house. How strange? She saw a policeman standing outside the tent and she lunged from the car as Beth pulled up.

BARKER was irritated. At last he met this woman, but it was she who was running the interrogation. 'The boat?' He echoed. It was Buchanan he wanted and the man was out of contact. 'Mrs Mahler. Please slow down. Over here?' He gestured to a table under a small awning. The increasing wind was causing the entrance to flap and another policeman was tying the flap down.

'I have seen the boat, Detective. I have seen the boat that Tom was supposed to have been in when he disappeared. It is not the boat. *It is not the correct boat.*' He remained impassive. 'I know this sounds strange, but believe me, Tom did not go out to sea in the boat you have in the shed. He went out in this.' And she drew Beth's picture from her pocket and spread it on the table. 'This is his boat. He built this, up at the cottage. This is a dory, Detective. This is what he built. Not that little thing in the shed.' She spoke quickly, authoritatively.

'I can see that.' He nodded thoughtfully. 'Who drew this?'

'I did. I saw the boat. Mary is right. I haven't seen the boat in the shed, but I believe her.'

He frowned and took the picture in both hands. 'How long would you say this is?'

'I don't know,' said Beth. 'I don't know the length of boats. Quite long. It always seemed big to me though.'

'Dories are long. Long and narrow. Could you pace it for me? Here?' He pointed to the grass as he rose. 'This is one end,' and he dropped a book from the table onto the grass. 'Pace it out, Miss Gilbert.'

Beth rose uncertainly, looked anxiously at Mary, and then walked six paces. She stopped and looked back. Then she took one more. 'About that. Maybe a tiny bit more. It's so hard to tell.'

'That's about what I would expect. About twenty feet. The boat in the shed is a dinghy — no more than fourteen feet. Please?' He walked back to the table, sat down and waited. 'I have a problem. You say he built this boat. And I believe you. There is no boat on the property so it has certainly gone somewhere. But here's the catch, and I hate to have to say this, Mrs Mahler, but he was seen with the boat that is in the shed. We know he rows it in the river. Then the boat and he were seen together ...' He hesitated. 'By the boys ...' He frowned at the recollection of the two small brown faces and the large, imaginative eyes, the feet twisting anxiously in the grass. 'But leaving that aside for a moment, there's one other thing. We have no evidence of a trailer and the cottage is a hundred feet above the sea. There's nowhere to launch a boat up there. And no one has seen him tow this ... unusual boat through the town. And we found his car but no trailer. Believe me, someone would have noticed. Do you see what I'm saying?'

The two women listened and no one spoke.

'I understand what you are saying, Detective. I don't know the answer ... but what I do know is that the boat is wrong and Tom's boat is not there. I am certain he took it to sea, on that day.' She spoke deliberately and with certainty.

'How could you know that, Mrs Mahler?'

'Because he said so,' she lied.

'Pardon? Do you mean you spoke to him? I thought you were on a plane? Not in New Zealand?'

'His diary. I don't know how he did it, but I know that he did.'

Barker looked at the sky and the streaky cirrus clouds. He focused on the rising breeze. About ten knots, he calculated, but it would rise quickly, and with it, so would the sea. It was possible, he thought; people had survived much longer.

'He's been gone five days and no one's seen such a boat. There have been many boats at sea, in the calm weather. We've had a chopper out there. This boat would have been seen.'

'Well, it hasn't! That's possible, isn't it? The sea is huge and Tom is out there. Now! He's out there, Detective! I know he is and we cannot wait.'

Barker examined the woman's face and looked away. Shit! he thought. It's just possible, but on the other hand they needed the chopper more than ever.

'We'll do a sweep. Excuse me.' He strode away.

Mary slumped and placed her head on her arm, her eyes tightly closed. She felt Beth's hand on her shoulder. 'I'm going to find him, Beth. I will.'

Barker returned. 'The chopper's leaving now. We stopped at five k's last time. If we'd known about that boat ... and the diary.'

'Well you didn't.' Mary rose, folding her arms, and looked down the valley to the sea. Barker offered tea, then excused himself. The two women sat alone under the awning and did not speak.

She hated Barker's words, but even if they had seen him, so what? Just another fishing boat, surely? It could easily be missed. If Tom was lying down ... she caught the lump in her throat. She knew Tom would be lying down. It had been days ... and nights. She felt the wind and hated it: the westerly gusts and the clouds streaking across the sky.

The tea was delivered.

'At least you'll know,' Beth said.

They finished the tea in silence and Mary paced the lawn restlessly. Stopping and staring off into the distance and then continuing. Her chin high and her arms folded across her chest.

An hour later Barker approached and shook his head. 'No sign, I'm sorry.' Mary waited. 'I'm sorry, Mrs Mahler.'

'*Chisholm!* You can't have finished yet,' she said, her voice tight. 'You can't. How much could you have searched?'

'We've done a grid twenty kilometres off the coast and twenty long.' He shrugged. For an instant, uncertainty flickered in her eyes but he saw it ruthlessly crushed.

'Well, it's not enough! What do we have to do? Do I need to pay? I'll pay whatever it takes. Just tell me.' She breathed deeply. 'Detective, I will not give up. He is out there and we must find him.'

'I understand how you feel.'

'No you don't!' she shouted. None of you! You haven't the faintest fucking idea! I've come across the world to find Tom, to this crazy place, and I'm not leaving him here. I will find him. Are you helping or not, because if you're not, tell me where to hire someone who will!' She stepped towards him and looked him straight in the eye. 'It is not enough. Tell me what to do?'

'We could put up a fixed wing aircraft. A fixed wing can cover more area quickly. But what else ...'

'Thank you.'

He shrugged. 'I'm not confident, Mrs Chisholm. It's a rowing boat. He will have to be a long, long way out.'

She concentrated on his words. 'How far could a boat be rowed?'

'How do you mean?'

Mary stared intently at the grass. 'How far could a boat like that be rowed? Like in eight hours — or ten?'

'Twenty to thirty I guess. The question is, why would he row for that long? Why would anyone?'

Mary's head hurt but she could feel a growing certainty.

'Let's say twenty to thirty,' she said, ignoring him, 'and the wind ...'

By God, she's an angry woman, Barker thought, and smart. 'The wind has been off the land. And the sea ... assuming he rowed for that long, and with a tail breeze he could be more than ... thirty kilometres, maybe even forty. But Mrs Mahler? Why would he do that?'

She looked at him evenly and Beth knew she was right.

'He went to sea ... to be with his son, Detective.' She paused and blinked back her tears. 'He went to sea to be with Luke, our son. He built that boat for Luke. My son is dead. And Tom built it for him. And then he fell in love with a little boy who lived with a monster!' Her voice rose. 'With a monster. And this town hated Tom for loving a little boy who was being destroyed by one of their own. And Tom ... and Tom, tried to rescue, thought he was rescuing that boy from the fire and failed. Detective! That is why he rowed that dory. That is why he has done what you cannot understand! He was being destroyed, by this place. That's why!' She swung away. Beth put her arm around her shoulders and felt the grief shaking her.

'Mrs Chisholm? I'm sorry. The chopper's coming in shortly. Would you like to go?'

She looked back, wiping her eyes. 'Thank you.'

* * *

BUCHANAN TURNED OFF the engine. Calm down now, he thought, and loosened his tie. Calm down. But it was not possible the moment he retrieved the Glock from its locker. For a minute he stared into the shade beneath the tree and listened to the incessant clacking of the cicadas. He looked at the black object in his hand that seemed to grow heavier. He saw the small white face framed by the ginger hair. 'Sooty's dead,' said Paul, and a single tear had rolled down that freckled cheek.

Buchanan slipped the gun into his jacket and wiped his brow. I'll get him another, he thought and opened the door. Maybe I'll get him a dog, he thought as he strode into the trees and onto the narrow track that might have existed for centuries.

He knew roughly where it went — along the ridge and dipping down the seaward side of what had been a significant pa in pre-European days. Then rising again to the flattened top on the headland where rows of tall palisades would once have held attackers at bay. It would have been open ground in those times but now the bush had crept back to cover everything. Cover for him and Wherry.

This is my show, he thought fiercely. I tracked this bastard down and I know what he's done. It wouldn't be any better if we had a squad up here. Worse — there'd be no chance of surprise. He left the verge and plunged into the cool shade. Along the ridge for several minutes, treading softly and pausing often to listen. Easing the Glock from inside his jacket and feeling reassured by the cool metal and the weight in his hand. Creeping through the gloomy half-light under the green canopy on the neck of land that joined the pa, wiping the ferns aside, peering at the hard clay track that revealed little though occasionally he could see crumbling or a scrape. His heart thumping and his breathing deep. He felt close. This was Wherry's place. It made sense. Not so far from Pagett's block and warm, facing out to the setting sun and with some sort of ancestral significance. Probably a limestone cave, he thought, but maybe a hut. Well, we will see, Mr Sam Wherry, who is the smarter.

Buchanan jumped at the heavy beating of wings then paused to recover, his hand gripping the handle of the gun too tightly. There was an indentation in the bush a hundred metres further on. A small indentation and what might be a ledge. Right, he thought. Right! Slowly now, creeping through the scrub. Taking hold of each thin branch that blocked his way and releasing it so it wouldn't swish. Feeling the heat of the sun bursting through the manuka and cursing his pale shirt in the dark bush. Thinking about the imminent confrontation. Thinking how that bastard would react when he had him cold! Imagining how Barker would be when he brought Wherry in.

The first thing he saw was a blaze of white. The white hair on the head of a small boy whose eyes widened before he turned and fled. Buchanan was astounded.

Jesus! He's got the boy. His head flooded as he broke into a run — kidnapped! Shot the boy's father and kidnapped the boy! Jesus — have to separate them — get the boy clear before it's too late. He breasted the rise and stopped, his gun hand extended. The boy standing near Wherry. Clearly petrified. Wherry implacable — expressionless. Huge! The bastard was huge, and he held a long pole. Solid piece of manuka. A bloody dangerous weapon.

'Wherry!' Buchanan pushed his voice up, authoritative, 'Wherry! I'm placing you under arrest for kidnap and murder. Put the stick down and step away from the boy. Now!' He held the gun with both hands and centred the barrel on Wherry's chest. A bead of sweat trickled into his eye. 'Wherry — put the stick aside and step away.' Buchanan took a cautious step forward then stopped. The man was moving. 'Stop! Stop where you are! Drop the stick!' But Wherry had gone into a strange half-crouch and his tongue protruded. A war dance. The bastard was challenging! Coming towards him now and swinging the stick in his two hands. Small forward thrusts, then a circle and twirling that thing to bemuse and hypnotise.

'This is a warning — I will shoot. Stop where you are! I will shoot!' He gazed along the tiny barrel that now seemed totally inadequate as the tall man in his long brown coat and his strange eye came without pause, tongue flickering like a snake and the stick swinging and humming through the heavy air like a giant bee. Another sound now — behind him — a shout somewhere off in the scrub behind. But still Wherry coming and filling the sky. The fucker's not going to stop.

Another shout behind but can't turn. 'Stop or I'll shoot!' The stick that could take off his head, humming through the air.

Running feet in the bush? But the stick coming at him. Four paces, three — Buchanan fired, twice. At the first Wherry faltered and stared with eyes popping, but at the second he fell, not a pace from Buchanan's feet. Thumped to the ground with the stick catching the ground and turning his arm at a strange angle. Eyes open and a weird gurgling. Huge. On the ground at Buchanan's feet and the bush ringing with the concussion. Buchanan looked up sharply to see the boy running. Then turning at a new sound and seeing Manuhuia in slow motion, his mouth wide but no sound and coming across the open ground in effortless bounds.

Buchanan mystified, lowering the pistol and seeing the horrible sight of the boy clinging to the neck of the monster. Clinging to this murderer. His father's murderer — it was too much. He seized the boy and tried to pull him away but the boy clung with amazing strength. Unnatural soundlessness. Buchanan took the boy around the chest with both arms and attempted to lift him but could not. 'Jesus!' he cried. He was lifting Wherry as well and then he was struck an enormous blow and tumbled away from the man on the ground, becoming aware of Manuhuia's weight and breath on his neck. Struggling clear and both rising to stare at the strange spectacle.

Manuhuia crouching, then placing his hand on Wherry's neck and looking up expressionless. Looking at Buchanan gazing in horror at the boy, and another voice coming. A high voice crying and coming down the track. Buchanan watched old Louis stagger from the trees with his eyes wide and a look of terror on his face. Staggering towards them like a rickety ewe and seeing Wherry. His mouth working silently now, and without slowing, grabbing up the stick and swinging it into Buchanan's chest. Swinging with all his strength that stick, and hitting him again and his face resolute. Buchanan not moving but taking each blow, striking with an audible thunk, until Bill strode between them and seized the old man. Pulling him close and the stick falling and shivering and a low wail coming.

Buchanan turned away. Just noise in his head. No feeling but swirling static like a wartime radio and an apparition materialising from the darkness. Walking unsteadily with her hands held at a peculiar angle and her face frozen. Walking so lightly across the clay and yet unseeing, those large eyes, and stopping near the body, that young woman, without a sound. Just staring at the man and the boy and the fresh blood trickling as bright as a flower on the white clay.

* * *

THE PILOT TURNED to shout. 'From here on,' and he gestured seaward, 'this is the new area.' She nodded and pressed close to the window and felt afraid. Like seeing the awakening of a monster: this wild waste that was not the natural abode of human beings. It ate them up. But not this time, she breathed. Please, God, not this time and she stared with painful intensity and knew that she would have to see him. He was depending on her.

Up and down they went. Into the wind and then with it. Out into the darker blue and then back towards the turquoise waters of the coast. Criss-crossing the sea and conscious only of the thrashing of the rotor and the wind whistling through the cracks in the door. An hour passed and the other man in the cockpit turned and gently shook his head. She looked away and willed the dory to appear on the long green waves. Unable to believe he was not there. Unable to believe they had searched far enough or for long enough.

The younger man, Tim, was saying something too but she refused even to acknowledge him and allowed his words to be whipped away in the din. It cannot be, she thought, and her hope was renewed because they were still moving towards the seaward horizon. The helicopter dipped and slowed and she peered anxiously until she saw the half-submerged log and felt consumed with anger and resentment. Tim gestured helplessly.

'We have to go back, Mrs Mahler.'

How strange to hear that name. How strange when it would be the very last time. She closed her eyes and tried hard not to cry. Feeling the craft swing about and gather speed, soon to be back on land. Soon to pack her bag and to fly far, far away, never really knowing.

The radio crackled: 'North west,' she heard and the chopper wheeled and the noise increased: 'Fifteen clicks,' she heard, and clung to the grab rail and felt sick. 'ETA 10 minutes.'

With her forehead pressed against the cold sill and her eyes closed so tight. He was tapping on her shoulder. 'Found it!' he shouted. 'Five minutes!' Then his words were lost. He turned away and she jabbed him in the back. 'Is he there?' she shouted. 'Is Tom there?' He paused a fraction of a second too long. 'Is he in the boat?' He opened his hands and shrugged.

She sat back exhausted and the rotors mashed her thoughts into random things that drove her mad. Tim swung past and began unclipping equipment. Moving her aside while he worked with lifejackets and jangling harnesses. The three of them with their heads close, ignoring her.

Then the older man with the broken sunglasses turned and pointed. Prodding the air and watching her without expression. She leaned forward and stared across the sea. Stared over the streaky sea a few hundred feet below and stretching endlessly, and she saw the smoke, a thin, orange trail that started near an object in the sea that could easily be another log, disappearing in a trough. The chopper shifted violently and she lost sight of the object and even the smoke and clambered to the other side, lost her balance and cursed volubly as the aircraft swung in the opposite direction. Descending rapidly now and the horizon wheeling, then suddenly stable and she recognised it instantly — the unmistakeable lines of a dory, rising and dipping, rising and dipping.

The two men shouting: 'Hook up … go down … into the wind …' She watched the sea flatten under the rotor wash as they approached the boat that appeared sluggish and heavy though unthreatened by waves that were still low.

'Tom?' she cried. The boat tilted as though responding and she saw the figure lying motionless. The boat surged back and then they were above it, and she desperately trying to see but her view obscured.

'Where is he? Where is he?' she screamed, but she might not have been there. Tim suddenly alongside her, pushing her roughly into her seat and refastening her belt. 'Do not move!' he shouted in her ear. 'You must not take the belt off!' He glared until she nodded dumbly.

Only then did he back away, fixing his gear and sliding the side door open and she clapped her hands to her ears.

The pilot signalled and Tim fought his way out the opening, catching a buckle on the floor and wrestling to free himself before he disappeared. The chopper swinging under the steady beats of the rotors and she undismayed by the wind and vibration and longing only to know, but pinned to her wall like an insect.

The other man crouched in the opening and reaching to where she could see Tim's sandy hair, then his back, swivelling into the chopper. Tom still obscured and the door pushed closed and the noise instantly reducing. Tim looking over his shoulder with a small grin and turning his thumb up.

Alive! She cried out and was blinded by her tears. Wiping furiously, trying to see. His face strangely distorted, angular and red. Blisters on his cheek and forehead and the lips cracked and pale. Eyes still closed but she could see the movement in his throat. Alive! She grabbed the other man and pulled at her harness and he helped her unbuckle and remove the straps from about her shoulders.

He was so thin. So spare in his blue shirt, his burned arms hanging slack. She placed her head on his chest and held him, aware that someone was supporting his head with a pillow and wetting his lips. But her concern was to keep him warm.

She remained close, holding him until the chopper touched down at the Base Hospital in New Plymouth.

* * *

BARKER GAZED AT passing hedgerows and cows meandering on grass going brown in shimmering afternoon heat. Toetoe bobbing in the streaky light and a pair of pied stilts flew low towards the beach.

A police homicide at the very moment everything seemed to have fallen into place. Only minutes after they had received news that Mahler had been found and was alive, and only minutes after an eye-witness had described the killer. Buchanan had shot and killed a cattle poacher!

'Whose is that?' he asked as they pulled alongside an old flatdeck. No one knew. 'Let's go.' He led the way through the bush to a scene as strange as any he had seen. In the centre of a small clearing lay a dead man. On one side, clinging to the man, was a boy with snowy hair, and on the other an old man kneeling, head bowed with his hands on the man's chest. Standing alongside, Buchanan, apparently unconscious of the bizarre spectacle of which he was part. A few paces away sat a Maori, and with him a young woman of mixed descent he guessed. In the same instant, Barker knew them all. Afterwards he described it as being like the final scene from a school pantomime, only no one felt like laughing.

The squad moved forward quietly and surrounded the small group. No one spoke. It didn't seem necessary, Milligan said afterwards. We all knew why we were there and what had to happen next. It was like we were all actors and we all knew our parts. He took Buchanan aside and two constables went to the two people sitting and began to talk to them quietly. Barker knelt alongside the dead man and helped the old man to stand. He motioned Spencer towards the boy.

'Who is this, Louis?' Barker nodded at the dead man.

Louis blinked and his hands moved gently but he did not speak. 'Come on, Louis,' he said gently, and repeated the question.

'It's Sam.'

'Sam?' Barker focused on what he had assumed to be an injury. But it was not. It was a black crescent tattooed below the man's right eye. 'Milligan!' The constable stepped away from Buchanan.

'It's him!' he said.

'Yes. Oh yes ... Look after him.' He motioned towards Buchanan. 'Louis — this man, Sam? We have a witness who saw him throw Pagett's rifle in the river on Wednesday night, shortly after the murder.' Louis showed no surprise. 'You knew?'

'It was those words. I knew when I saw the words. He showed me the photos,' Louis gestured at Milligan, 'and when I saw those words I knew you had it wrong. It was all smeared but it never did say "Mary". It said "Money". That's what Sam said. "The love of money is the root of all evil." That's what he said.' A tear trickled down the old face. 'He was a good boy,' he said softly. 'He was always a good boy. Right from when he was little he was different, but he was good.'

THE sun was near the horizon as the procession of cars drove along the seaboard, south and away from the hills. Three squad cars and an old flatdeck coming up behind. They had left four constables to secure the site, and the forensic scientist working under a tarpaulin.

'Our job is not to deliver summary justice, Milligan. Whether or not the bastard deserved it.'

'Yes, Sarge. But what Buchanan did ... figuring it out and tackling someone he knew was as dangerous as that, out in the bush and by himself. I'm only saying you have to hand it to him.'

Barker grunted. An intensive manhunt had been averted. An aerial search probably supported by the Armed Offenders Squad was now unnecessary. It would have been a long and dangerous assignment. Instead the bastard was nailed, the kid was okay and Buchanan was stood down. But he should fare well enough. He would be put through the wringer and he would survive and people would see that Buchanan had done a pretty heroic thing. Ironic, he thought wryly. And what had looked like turning to custard for Andrew Barker was just possibly coming good.

'You want to know who's impressed me most, Milligan? Out of this whole horrible affair?' He looked towards the sea that had transformed from brilliant blue to a muddy grey. 'Mary Chisholm, that's who. Amazing woman.'

The car pulled alongside Buchanan's station house on the main road. 'I shall look forward to meeting her again.' He climbed from the car and turned to speak through the window. 'And I can't wait to see this ex-husband of hers. Five days at sea in a dory he built himself. That he launched down a bloody cliff and then rowed halfway across the Tasman.' He shook his head with bemusement. 'You wouldn't read about it!'

'No, Sarge.'

13

AN UNTOUCHED CUP of tea sat next to Merv Layton on the teakwood table.

This has been a great place, he thought moodily. A great place to build a business and have the kids grow up. Good mates and good people, mostly. This house — like nothing my old man could have dreamed of. Sitting up here and looking out over the Mokau. I built this place. I built a place for my family and it's been good.

Look at those houses down there. Bloody shanties, but they never bothered me before.

He adjusted his weight in the chair and stared up the valley into the heavy bush. All his life the bush had been there. Everywhere, with just a narrow strip of green grass along the coast, but beyond those farms the bush stretched for miles and miles. Too much of it? They reckoned they had tracks all through that stuff once, all the way to the King Country and west to Taupo even. Pulled huge canoes through that stuff, they reckoned. Bloody strange. Who could live in there now? Certainly not any of them! Bastards could hardly make ends meet down by the river in a proper house.

He tried to remember the woman but it was a long time ago and she hadn't been there long. Bit of a flirt, they said, but he'd never noticed. Pagett had always kept her away. Blonde and a lot younger, and now he remembered her eyes. That one time they had met in town and he thought what a pretty girl, though she had not spoken a word. Didn't need to ... those blue eyes said it all.

I don't know what's going on, he acknowledged. And now ... Patrick!

His wife called from the kitchen. Did he want another cup of tea? No, he didn't. Patrick didn't mean it like that, she said. He did, he had retorted with certainty. *Blacks* he called them. He'd never heard his son use that word. He didn't like that word even after what had happened to the digger. It was a cunt of a word. *Blacks.* He hadn't known what to say but he knew he was feeling very uncomfortable about things. Bill was not a black. And nor were any of the guys on the job — like Hohepa and Wetere. Good guys despite those other extremist bastards.

'That's not what this is about,' he told Patrick on the phone.

'But you showed them, Dad. I'm proud of what you did. All the guys are talking about it. You're a bit of a hero down here.'

What was happening? Merv rubbed his forehead, unsettled by the tangle of thoughts. Roading and contracting was never like this. Just put in a price and get on with it. But this was far too complicated. And now my boy ... what did that mean? How could he have even suggested that thing?

'I'm going to call him back,' he said to his wife as she appeared with a plate of sandwiches. She sat across the table and studied him. 'I don't like what Patrick said,' he continued. 'I'm going to tell him.' She nodded uncertainly.

Bulldoze the anchor stone! Merv was incredulous. How could his boy even think that? Jesus! What was happening in that school that he should think his dad would even contemplate taking the D8 and running over the anchor stone of the *Tainui*? The anchor stone of the first of the great canoes on the Mokau coast. And Merv Layton running over the thing because someone smashed the digger! What in God's name was Patrick on about? And why was he talking about 'blacks'? There wasn't a single bloody Maori in that school! He shook his large head dolefully. 'I'm going to talk to him.'

She nodded. 'Have a sandwich — it's tomato and tuna.'

He grimaced as though his favourite sandwich filling had become wet concrete.

'And that bloody Pagett? Jesus!'

'It's terrible.'

Merv shook his head in wonderment. 'I never really knew Wherry,' he said. 'Not since we were kids.' He pictured young Sam back at school. Just another Maori kid. Good at sport and a fast runner. Played a good lock in the rugby pack. Friendly he'd been, but then he kind of disappeared off the scene like so many of them did. Left the district for a long time and when he came back he was *Ringatu* and a bloody mystery. Not unfriendly, but remote like he was no longer in touch with the ordinary things in life. That seemed kind of typical too.

Some of them just seemed to lose touch with things. It was a bloody mystery, and it would be helpful all round if the bastards would only get the thing sorted out.

He recalled the evening when they last met. They had nothing to talk about. Sam hadn't played rugby for years and he dressed strange and sounded even stranger. And with that peculiar tattoo ... Still, who would have thought that the things that had happened would have? And now he was dead. Merv shook his head and couldn't figure it. Killed Pagett, they reckoned, but then look what that prick had done!

'Something's rotten,' he stated flatly. 'Something has gone rotten here and I don't like it.' He peered up into the hills and noticed dark cumulus towering. 'The tangi's tomorrow morning.'

'It might rain,' she said.

* * *

'YOU WERE IN the helicopter?'

She nodded and his hand crept across the covers. She loved feeling that squeeze and gave one in return. 'I can't believe it,' he said again, and closed his eyes.

'I decided it was time for the cavalry.' He nodded and smiled and the room was comfortably silent. She enjoyed the reassuring smell of the hospital and marvelled at how well he was looking after so short a time.

'I didn't want to ...'

'It's all right.'

He struggled to raise himself. 'No, I have to tell you. I have to tell you this. I went fishing!'

For a moment she thought he was truly demented, then they both laughed. They laughed fiercely and he tugged her hand and snorted like a horse, rolling his eyes, and suddenly they were filled with tears and his laughter turned to sobs and she took him in her arms.

'I tried to come back. I didn't know what was happening. Anywhere.'

'It's okay, you can tell me some other time.'

'I did at first. Mary, I went out there hoping the wind would take me away. Take the boat and me. I felt I had nothing left.'

'I know. And I've got something to tell you ...'

'But I got way out there and I started to think about other things. I started to think about Luke in a different way. I began to think about him as being dead, maybe for the first time. I accepted that he was dead and that I was living. But that doesn't mean I have to think he is gone from my life.'

'No!'

'But I did! And then ... I sort of reinvented him. Luke, I mean — with me, but not. I talked to him and he talked to me. And I became confused. About all sorts of things. And then ...' He pulled away and fell back on his pillow, his eyes blinked rapidly. 'And then ... I found Sean and he ...'

'It's okay.'

'No! And he got ...'

'No, he didn't.'

'He got lost in the valley ...' His eyes brimmed over again and the tears flowed. 'God! Mary, it's obscene!' And he covered his face.

'Tom. He didn't get lost. Not like that. He's safe. That's what I have to tell you. He's safe.'

He blinked. 'What? Are you mad? I was there!'

'No! You thought he was in the valley but he wasn't! Ringatu found him ...' She faltered.

'Ringatu? He found him? But he was with me. He was with me on the beach. How?' The smell was in his nostrils, the blast of heat and the sight of the wretched possum scampering. The unearthly sounds of exploding branches and the pain in his smoke-burned lungs.

'But how? I searched and searched, Mary, he went into the valley and the fire — it came so fast. So horrible. And I ran and ran. Like a mad thing I ran but there was no sign. How?'

'I don't know, but he did! The police have Sean now. They're looking after him. They have a psychologist helping.'

She stopped speaking and he stared fixedly at the end of the room. His face became calm and he dried his cheeks. Then allowed his hands to fall onto his lap. 'Good God.' A smile appeared. 'Thank God.'

'Yes,' she nodded. 'Are you okay?'

'Okay? Am I okay? I cannot remember feeling so good! I cannot remember hearing such good news, Mary. It's fantastic! I have been so ... Give me a hug!' He made humming noises and squeezed her and she stroked his hair. 'I have been such a lunatic!' he said.

She sat back and took a deep breath. 'Tom, I have some bad news too.'

'He's not ill? Don't tell me — not burned?'

'It's not Sean. It's Ringatu.' She swallowed hard and wondered whether it was too soon. 'Ringatu ...' There on the beach in the early morning he was: Ringatu. Lying on the front porch of the cottage and guarding her. 'Not very brave,' he had described those he shooed like flies.

'What is it?'

'Oh, Tom! It's all so awful. So awful! He was shot.'

'Shot.' He echoed dully. 'Pagett?'

'No, the police. They believe he killed that man and then he threatened them and they shot him. And he had Sean all the time and they thought he had kidnapped him. It's all so horrible. We must go home! Tom, we must!'

Tom levered himself up, eyes wide, 'I knew!' He fell back and stared at the ceiling and they were silent for a long time. Suddenly he said: 'Why haven't you brought him here? Why do you tell me and you haven't brought him here to me? Why not?' His voice rose sharply and she recoiled from something in his eyes she did not understand.

'Who?'

'Luke! Why haven't you brought him?'

'Don't call him that — he's not Luke! He's Sean! Stop calling him that, please.' The wild, impenetrable stare softened.

'I'm sorry. I'm so tired. So tired. I'm sorry.' He sank back into the pillow and his bandaged hands covered his face.

'It's okay. I understand. I will bring Sean to see you.'

He nodded. 'Yes. It's too soon ...'

She watched him until his breathing became slower and more regular. Waited patiently until she was sure he was asleep, and then reluctantly she left his room.

* * *

PLUGGY WISHED HE had closed as soon as he'd heard. He could sense how things were. Many, many years behind a bar taught you about that. When things were going bad. It was serious drinking with at least fifteen on one side and a dozen on the other. That was not good. The bar was divided. Them, with their hoods and bandannas, and these others with their ruddy outdoor faces, and barely a sidelong glance between. It should not have been possible to hear that old ceiling fan. He wondered whether he should warn the detective.

When the news about Wherry reached town some had cheered, for godsake! For others there was great anger.

He tried to remain cheerful. Not many got rough if you were laughing, but look at this bastard. Just taking the beer and no eye contact. With that cross on his face.

Pluggy asked one of the Maori boys about the big crowd tonight and was alarmed by the evasive answer. 'They got some stuff on their mind,' and his brown eyes slid smooth as bowling balls.

Noise rising in the corner. That young Matt Harkness — like his dad. Not particularly pleasant when he'd had a few. Pluggy moved efficiently across the bar and touched the boy's arm. He leaned towards the ominously glazed eyes and whispered in his ear, 'Prefer you kept to sport tonight. Okay?' He stared hard into the boy's eyes and was disappointed. Cleared a couple of empties and returned to the taps.

Someone talking about the bushfire now. About Pagett and Wherry. 'That murdering brown bastard.' Getting louder. 'White cunt ...' hung in the air like neon. Pluggy reached for his phone but knew he was too late. A push and anger about to erupt.

'Outside!' he ordered and fumbled the receiver. It missed the hook and clattered to the floor as he barked: 'Outside, you two. We'll have none of that. Hendriks! Take it out!' There was a movement towards the door. Remarkably quiet, but menace rising fast.

MILLIGAN listened to the tapping of the keys and thought about Faye. By the end of the week he should be clear. Dinner and a movie would be great. And after that ... he smiled.

Reports. Ringbinder files in triplicate. Kitteridge had been typing for many hours. Nearly a hundred interviews, all up. Milligan glanced around the room. Harris opposite poring over a local area map and using marker pens to colour-code the operation. Spencer reading his notebook and frowning and Wilmshurst asleep in his chair, mouth agape.

Running over events in his mind and thinking about Perry. Wiremu Tutira Perry otherwise known as 'Mercury'. Twenty-five years old, of no fixed abode, just happened to be temporarily resident in Mokau, where, he said, his grandmother lived. Two convictions for assault and two for burglary and one for possession of a Class A drug. A cross tattooed on his right cheek. Father a sickness beneficiary in Papakura and mother on the dole in Wellington. Well, it looked as if for once Mr Perry was not at the centre of anything — at least nothing that had come to light in this investigation.

He thought of something else, but then the phone rang. Wilmshurst answered: 'Right,' he said crisply and hung up. 'Fracas at the pub, sir. About fifteen involved.' He grabbed for his hat as the others rose.

'Harris — you stay here.' Milligan reached for his jacket. 'Fracas?' he thought. He shook his head and at the same time wished Barker had not chosen to be in New Plymouth this particular evening.

Three cars drove rapidly from the motel to the highway north. 'Light us up,' he told the driver, and the sharp peals of the siren caused cows to gallop from the fence and Gertie Ngahere to turn off the TV and put her hand lightly on Bill's arm.

Beer crates outside the pub were being used as weapons and blood sprayed warm and sticky as the melee banged against the wall. Beyond the oscillating lights on the squad cars lightning flashed above the dark hills and thunder rolled in the valley.

* * *

'WHEN CAN I see Sean?'

'Soon. He's a very disturbed little boy, as I am sure you understand. We're giving him some professional help.'

Tom frowned. 'Tomorrow?'

'That may be a bit too soon, Mr Mahler. I'll talk to the psychologist.'

Barker opened his notebook. 'You're a very lucky man. Your wife — I'm sorry, Mrs Chisholm — wouldn't give up.' Barker studied Tom's face. 'And with this weather turning ...' He shook his head but Mahler did not respond. 'Your dory would not have survived long in this. Anyway, we won't be long. I know you're tired.'

Tom turned slowly to return the detective's gaze. 'What?'

'I appreciate that you've been through a lot. And that was quite a feat, to get that boat down the hill from your cottage and into the sea. I would not have believed it possible. I daresay you wouldn't want to repeat it.' He smiled.

Tom looked blearily at the detective. 'I was helped.'

Barker glanced at him with new interest. 'Helped? By whom?'

'By Ringatu.'

'Sam Wherry?' Barker was sharp. 'He helped you launch your boat?'

Tom nodded slowly. 'I thought you knew.'

'Not exactly. But that was in the afternoon? Earlier on? When was that?' He pretended to write. 'When did you actually get the boat into the water — about four, wasn't it?' Barker studied the bottle drip at the head of the bed.

Tom frowned and closed his eyes. He pictured Ringatu standing alongside the dory. 'I may not let you go,' he had said, and Tom had sworn at him. He winced at the memory. He winced as he thought of the big Maori standing waist deep in the surf and waving as Tom rowed. 'Take your waka ...'

'Would that have been about four, Mr Mahler?'

'No, it was later. Five or a bit after. Five-thirty more like.' '*Take your waka ... we brought nothing into this world ...*' And then he had gone. Climbed the hill and gone to Pagett's farm and shot the man. He said he would and that's what he had done.

Barker studied the face with the blistered skin on the cheeks, and despite himself experienced an unpleasant feeling of turmoil. 'At five? How can you be sure it was five?' he said quickly.

'No, it was closer to five-thirty. I know because I saw the time at five and we were nearly to the water. Maybe about ten minutes away. So it would have been five-thirty by the time I left.' He pictured

Ringatu glaring into his eyes: '*Pagett is dead!*' Ringatu was truly mad. '*I will eat that fucker!*' It hadn't seemed real but that's what he'd done. All that time ... all those discussions and yet it had been apparent. The man was demented. Tom opened his eyes and felt the thumping in his head increase. He closed them again. 'Got a helluva headache,' he said softly. 'Does all this matter?'

'Just for the record, Mr Mahler. We need to tie up all the loose ends.'

'You certainly did that. Killing him ... that's tying up a major loose end.' The voice was strained and Barker did not answer. He looked at his note, which read: 'Mahler claims he was with Wherry at 5.30 p.m. on Wednesday.' Alongside he wrote, 'Rachel Lynch stated that she heard the shot at exactly 5 p.m.'

* * *

'THERE WAS A fight?'

'Yes, there was a fight.'

'Wish we'd seen it.'

'No, you wouldn't want to see it.'

Matty looked across the breakfast table to Jake and mouthed silently, 'Wish we'd been there.' His brother returned his nod so vigorously a berry flew from the jam on his toast and landed on his father's arm. Matty snorted with laughter as Bill absently wiped the berry onto his own plate.

'It's time for you to get off to school. And I mean school. I do not mean fishing or some other damn thing or you will be in deep trouble.' Gertie cleared the plates amd the boys frowned and slid from their chairs. 'Did anyone get killed?'

'No one got killed, praise the Lord!' said Gertie. 'Now get your raincoats and do as your father says.'

'Raincoats? It's hardly anything.'

'Come here!' She wiped the jam from around Jake's mouth and kissed him on the forehead and his face wrinkled. 'Get along and be good.' She attempted to bat his behind. 'How is Louis?' she asked as the boys rattled out the front door.

'Still in bed.'

She nodded slowly. 'This is a dreadful thing for him. A dreadful thing all round, but for him? Like one of his own boys.'

Bill nodded. 'Yep. And his own boy? Never told! The old tyke never told me. I can't believe that. Hiding away up there all that time and Louis knowing. He took him kai, did you know?'

'What's going to become of this place? That's what I'm wondering. What's going to become of this place now folks is hating each other? Roll me one,' she demanded. 'That brawl? I'm just thankful you weren't down there, that's all I'm thankful about.'

'I might have helped.'

'You? You might have helped all right — public brawler that's what! Thanks.' She lit the cigarette and drew deeply. Bill sighed and wished he had been in the pub. Those young fullas need some older heads about. That was the problem.

'We got to get on with the tangi,' Gertie continued. 'Lot of work to be done there. That's what I've got to do. I'll need to organise those layabouts to get the food done. Make sure the marae is looking right. What about you?'

'Oh, I'm going to see Louis.'

'This has been a big shock. That young Sam? I can't hardly believe what he's done. No one can hardly believe all this. That young Sam ...'

'Man, I hoped it wouldn't turn out this way. I hoped fit to bust that it would be a Pakeha that did this to Pagett. Now it's about as bad as it can get. Another bad Maori, that's what we got on our hands. And that's what's hurting Louis the most. That's what's draining him away, that old man. He knows that what Sam did comes right back on him. Comes right back on all of us. That Sam went his own way. That's what's hurting Louis the most. He wasn't there to help that boy get through and now look.'

They sat silently and smoked and listened to the gentle patter of rain on the iron roof.

BILL knocked several times then entered the gloomy little hall. He called out and on his third hail received a muted response from the bedroom, dark save the chinks of light like golden blades. Louis was lying under a blanket, fully clothed and unshaven. Bill pulled the little chair close and studied the old man who would not open his eyes. Bill asked how he was feeling and received a sniff in response. He asked whether Louis had had something to eat that morning and saw the grimace on his face. He sat for some time, silent and thinking.

He thought about the brawl and felt worried. He worried about how it would all end and he wondered what he should do. He recalled Sam Wherry lying there, dead, with that little boy hanging on for dear life and he felt bemused and saddened. He remembered Sam well and he liked that boy. He was a bit different but that was fine. Bill felt respect for how Sam was, even though he thought he was an oddball sure enough.

He thought about Merv Layton and his own job and felt a renewed sense of incredulity. Anger too. He felt angry about what Merv had done and he still found it hard to credit. How could he ignore the tapu like that? How could he trample on Louis's mana in that way? It was like a madness had come over him. He'd seen it in his eyes that day. Madness and it seemed it was everywhere now. Things were out of balance all right and the bad was coming onto the good in people. Things needed to be balanced up again, but how? That was the thing.

What was happening with those young fullas? He thought about Jimmy who was now in Base Hospital with burns. That was a sad thing. But it showed that no one was listening to the tupuna. No one was doing the right thing because they had lost their ear. They couldn't see the tupuna standing by, waiting to help. Why? It was a kind of blindness coming onto folks.

One old eye had sneaked open for a peek and then closed. To see if he was still there, Bill guessed, and was pleased.

He cleared his throat loudly and watched. 'I've been thinking,' he addressed the wall above Louis as though he were alone in the room. 'I've been thinking about what needs to be done. The tangi needs to be getting going. Gertie's going to get all that food and stuff done and get the kuia together. But the kaumatua will need to be about. Seeing things are all right. That's for sure ...' There was no movement in the bed. 'Only the kaumatua can lead the speaking. Where would we be if he were not about? Our mana would be nothing! Bad ... that would be truly bad.' He cleared his throat again. 'And he needs to be showing the young fullas. He needs to be showing the young fullas the right way. Even when a bad thing has happened that he might think it was himself that was at fault. Maybe for not being there? Maybe for not seeing that the darkness was coming and blaming himself for that thing? Even when no one could expect to see. Even when it was just a mistake and proves only that the kaumatua is needed more then ever!' He slapped his knee to give emphasis. 'And after the tangi ... that's what I'm thinking about. After the healing has begun. But it needs to go on. Afterwards, that's when only the kaumatua can show how we can restore respect. For the tribe. That's when.'

Bill sat in the darkness of the room with its blinds drawn close and not a sound to be heard but the slow breathing of the old man. At last he pushed back his chair. 'I have to go and do some things now.' He hesitated by the door but there was no movement so he let himself out.

'What's he doing?' Gertie asked when he returned.

'Oh, he's thinking.'

'Hurrumph!' she snorted.

* * *

'I AM NOT going and that's that!'

Rachel listened to Pete rinse his coffee mug in the sink and felt vexed. 'Why not?'

'Because he's a murdering bastard! That's why not.'

'You went to Trevor Pagett's funeral.'

'I didn't know then. If I'd known what that bastard had done, I wouldn't have gone.'

He poured a cup of coffee and sat at the table drumming his fingers on the wood. She continued to stitch the patch on the knee of his jeans but it was not going well.

'Pete, some things have to be ...'

'Nope! And that's final.'

'Will you just listen! I know it's terrible but you can't blame everyone for one person who didn't know right from wrong! They aren't all bad. Gertie is a friend. Bill and Louis and those boys, and the others. Plenty of good people. You can't blame them all for what he did.'

Pete frowned and sipped his coffee. 'That's not the point. I'm saying I'm not going to a tangi for a bloody murderer. I'm not saying I blame them all.'

'We'd be going for the others. Not for Sam Wherry, we'd be going to show that we don't blame everyone else.'

'Nope!'

She cast the jeans aside. 'Oh, mend these yourself!' And she stalked from the room, as Pete peered after her with surprise.

* * *

RAIN DRIZZLED LIGHTLY on the bar window.

'This place is going to the dogs! I've never seen anything like this. Hoods smashing things up. That black bastard killed Pagett. What'd they expect? A medal?' Porter banged his glass angrily on the table.

'That was bad, what happened last night.'

'Bad! Terry? Bad! It was diabolical. It makes me so pissed! And the cops just gently, gently. Don't want to upset the tangata whenua. Tongue-up-your-arse more like! If any one of us had done that we'd have been shot. At least good old Brian did the deed. And now look? Run out of town! Kills a murderer and kidnapper and he gets the brick. Can you believe that?'

The men were silent as they sipped their beer.

'Made a mess of the hardware store — and old Merle's place. Poor old girl.'

'Yeah, Derek and that's another thing! She's just about a pensioner for chrissakes! Old Merle — what's she ever done to anyone? Serves them for twenty years and gets her windows smashed in! It's gone too far. This bloody kowtowing to the natives. Too bloody far! This country's going back to the Stone Age. That's what they want!'

'That fucker Wherry was done properly. I take my hat off to Buchanan. Got some balls, that bastard. I never knew. Quiet sort of a cove. Once or twice I thought he was going to the mat — but when the chips were down he knew what had to be done.' Harkness drained his glass and swung around to the bar. 'Another one, Pluggy.' He turned back to his companions. 'We can't let Buchanan be hung out to dry — that's my view. Should get onto the politicians. Let them know they should pay attention to what's happening here. Police officer does his duty and gets sacked. That's criminal, that is.'

'It's criminal,' contributed Terry, shifting his bulk on the small top of the stool.

'Best things that have happened around here were Merv getting into those shithouse cooking stones and that nutcase Wherry getting his!'

'He's gone to the tangi.'

'It's a funeral, Terry, a funeral! You know, where people get buried? And the sooner the better.'

'Merv Layton? At the funeral? That's pretty odd.'

'Yeah.'

'Merv Layton?'

'Yeah.'

Silence descended again. Derek thought about Tom Mahler. He had quite liked Mahler. They talked one time outside the hardware. Months ago. He had seemed friendly. He had suggested they went for a drink but Derek had to go through to New Plymouth. Then they hadn't gotten round to it. Course, that was before he knew that Mahler was doing funny things with the kids — so they said.

'Strange about Mahler getting saved,' he said.

'Strange? Pity more like. This town's going to the dogs on a fast train! Murder, tangata fucking whenua and a pedo! Crazy stuff. My dad would have blown his bottle! Worked all his life, clearing bush and farming. Turning this place into something. He'll be rolling in his grave, I can tell ya. What about the races? Those horse races on the beach were part of this town. Part of the history but now look. No races because a turd might float up from the longdrop! Bloody hell!'

'That pissed me off too. That bloody Patai woman. She's the biggest shit-stirrer. You see her on the telly again? Yeah, she was on again. Spouting about the — what was it? "The lack of cultural sensitivity." Yeah, fair go!' Porter blew the top of his beer onto Derek's arm and laughed. 'Sorry, mate.'

'Harping and harping about how there's no respect for "her

heritage"! What about ours? We don't go round harping on about our heritage. Damn right — and why? Because we're getting on with it — modern technology and stuff. They wanna keep using greenstone.'

Terry giggled.

'Shit, that's a funny noise, Tel. Coming from someone as big as you! Like a fucking girl!' Terry frowned and sipped his beer. 'What about old Gert?' Porter continued. 'I dare say we won't see her around for a bit.'

'She never says much anyway. Funny old bird. I always thought she was all right. But blood's thicker than water, as they say.'

'Yeah.'

'But what's Layton doing at the funeral? That's bloody odd! I'd have thought he would be the last one. That's got me screwed.'

'Maybe he heard about Pagett,' said Derek.

'What about Pagett? What?'

'About Pagett killing that woman. You didn't hear? The cops found her bones — out the back of the farm. She was topped. They're saying it was Pagett.'

Porter stared at Derek as though he had been hit right in the nose. The beer he had been about to sip slipped from his hand onto the table and slopped across the formica. He barely noticed. 'No way?' His voice faded.

'Yeah.'

'All those years ago?' His face changed colour. 'Well, fuck me!'

* * *

MERLE TURNED THE sign in the door so it said 'Closed'. The doorbell clanged as she locked the door — just as it had since she and Herb had arrived. It was a cheerful little bell in the name of 'Dawkins'. But she did not feel cheerful today. Troubled and sad. But things had to be done. 'Life goes on, Herbie,' she said.

She put up her small mauve umbrella against the light rain and stepped back to inspect her front window. Bill Manuhuia had come and boarded it up for her. He was a good man. But what a fright she'd had. What a terrible noise in the middle of the night. That brick coming through the window. Why?

Saddened, she began to walk up the hill.

'Good morning, Frederick,' she said, and the mechanic grinned.

She walked past the post office and said hullo to the McIntyres and the Loveridges. 'Yes,' she said, 'I'm going to the tangi.' They looked at her strangely.

She walked up the hill and was passed by two cars full to overflowing. There must be a lot here, she thought. That's good. It didn't matter what the man had done, when the Lord called it was the duty of those left behind to say goodbye in the proper fashion.

There's that man Tom Mahler, she thought with a twinge of guilt and pleasure. She was pleased she had prayed for him. She still would. It appeared that people had been wrong. But that's how it was with people. Sometimes right but often enough wrong. Thank the Lord he is alive, she thought. She started as she recognised the large man in the pale grey suit. Good Heavens! That's Merv Layton. Good Lord! She made her way towards the small group of Pakeha standing some distance from a much larger group of Maori, silent — all so quiet.

HOW fitting it should rain, Mary thought. Not heavy, just a light, misty rain. Warm and not really wetting. But obscuring the tops of the hills and darkening the bush below. She squeezed Tom's hand.

Now she heard voices from somewhere beyond the gates. Wailing. High-pitched, keening voices from somewhere out of sight. It was an eerie and thrilling sound in the gloomy morning light. She nudged Tom and directed his gaze towards the elaborately carved red archway above the entrance. He smiled, then steered her by the arm.

'This is Rachel Lynch, and Pete.' Tom spoke in a warm but hushed tone.

'It's so good to see you, it really is.' Rachel gave him a hug and then Mary too. Pete solemnly shook his hand. 'I don't think we're welcome,' he said and glanced nervously at the people assembled nearer the archway, some shuffling through, others stationary and blank as stone.

'We have to be called,' Rachel said doubtfully, and glanced at Merv Layton but he would not catch her eye.

'Come on,' said Pete, with a resolution he did not feel, and he led them towards the gate. Imperceptibly at first, people moving. Pete leading the way but no way forward — their route blocked, Pete face to face with a young man who stared back with blank, expressionless eyes, arms folded across his chest.

Pete hesitated. 'Excuse me.' The man did not move. 'We'd like to come in.'

Two more shifted to a position behind the shoulder of the first. Mary felt the rising tension and took hold of Tom's arm. There was no sound at the gate — everything had stopped.

I was bloody right! Pete thought, but he had never heard of anything like this. He looked the young man in the eye and knew he wasn't a local and knew he wasn't going to let him past. Before he could speak he heard Tom Mahler.

'Ringatu was my friend.' His voice carried across the silent gathering. 'Ringatu was my friend,' he repeated, and the words hung in the mist.

Pete felt Rachel's hand creep into his and he thought about how she wanted to help. He thought about how she was with the Manuhuias and about those small boys eeling and watching rabbits down the bottom of the farm. And he felt angry.

'We've come to pay our respects ... to Ringatu's people,' he said to the young man. 'It's right. We want to pay our respects — all of us.' Pete motioned towards the knot of people behind and breathed deeply. 'We're all friends here.'

The distant sound of the surf was suddenly broken by a voice calling from the gateway. A strong voice, imperious: 'What are you doing? What are you doing? Stand aside! Stand aside!' People cleared a way and a small woman strode towards them.

Rachel smiled with relief: 'Gertie! Gertie.'

'And so! And so, it is my good friends the Lynchs and that Painter Tom! Stand aside!' she commanded sternly and the men fell back. 'These people have come to talk! That's what we do! Talking!' And she glanced once at the big man in the pale grey suit who looked so uncomfortable, but just for an instant then she took Rachel's arm and led her towards the gateway to the marae. She paused and turned to Tom, and Mary was surprised to see tears in her eyes.

'It is so good. It is so good you are back,' and she held Tom by the arms and leaned forward until their noses touched. 'Would you like to speak?'

'Thank you, Gertie,' he said. And Mary found herself held and pulled close, and realised she must touch her nose with the older woman just as Tom had. She continued to hold Mary, looking up into her face with keen, searching eyes. 'I have been praying for this traveller. Tom is a very fortunate man. Later, you must return to my house.' And she released Mary and moved to welcome Merle.

'Look, we're being called.' Mary followed Tom's gaze to the women assembled near the whare nui. Many people, mostly in black, were gathered near the entrance. They had turned towards the visitors so she could see the women who keened in that unearthly way.

'Join with these manuhiri,' Gertie directed. She stood at the front of the visitors and answered with a strong, clear call, and the larger group outside the gate began to move slowly and silently behind her.

There is some anger here, Tom thought. For Pakeha? No, not so much, he thought. It is for the big man. For Merv Layton, and he must be aware.

They had stopped just a few yards from where Ringatu lay in the open casket.

'Haere mai, haere mai, haere mai,' called across the space between them, and the man in front of Gertie responding. Louis seated in front of the whare with several of the elders. Short speeches he did not understand, but knowing they contained both sorrow and anger.

God, that you would be still alive, he thought, then realised Gertie was signalling and the silence hanging above the marae descended like the mist that cloaked the hills. He moved alongside her and she squeezed his arm. He looked across at Louis and was pleased to see his nod returned. He stared at the casket and thought about the man and remembered their meeting on the beach. He remembered their long discussions on his front porch with a beer and a fish to share.

'Tena koutou, tena koutou,' he said, and heard his greeting returned. 'Ringatu came to my place many months ago. I did not know what to make of him. He was unlike anyone I have ever met.' He heard a gull cry overhead. 'He said I was the last of the gulls to peck at the rotting carcase ... and as it so often was when we talked, I felt insulted.' A soft murmur followed his words. 'You, Ringatu. You told me many things that at first made little sense to me. When I met you I believed you were mad.' A ripple ran through the two parties and he felt the hand on his arm tighten. 'Now I know how wrong I was. I cannot say anything about what you have done. That is for you and your God. But I can say much about what you have meant to me ... I came here with preconceived notions of how the world is and you contradicted me at every turn. You are a cantankerous man, Ringatu. But I learned much. We shared much. I learned that there are other ways to think about land. About trees and birds. I learned to think about many things in a different way. Sometimes we continued to disagree but I remain grateful for everything you had to share ... Ringatu, you were there when Mary needed someone,' he continued. 'She is so grateful and so am I. You were there when the boy needed someone and I am so grateful. I do not know what to say to you about how things are now. I am certain that you will be with your ... tupuna. I hope so. Ringatu, you are my friend. You told me not to die like the tarakihi. I took your advice to heart and I am here. You are like the shark. Rest in peace, my friend.'

He stepped back into Pete and apologised. He was aware that Louis was replying but his ears were full of the noise of the bush and the coast and his last meeting with Ringatu. He knew Louis was addressing him in Maori but that he also reserved words to tell him how pleased the tangata whenua were to have such a friend who could hold the hand of Ringatu and who could guide the hands of those children who wished to paint. 'You are Painter Tom,' he said as he concluded. 'And we are grateful, Painter Tom, that you have returned from your voyage to be among us. You will always be welcome.'

They formed a file and he touched noses with each of the welcoming party. Soft touch and gentle exhalation. Hands holding arms for a moment, and a softly murmured 'Tena koe.' Thank you, he said, and he held Louis for a long time and then suddenly was looking into the casket. Looking at the proud face with the dark patch. A peaceful face now, but Tom knew. '*Never forget that I am a Maori …*' His dark eyes gleaming and the wicked smile on his lips. Standing in the surf, holding the gunwale of the dory and his face … anxious? Yes, he had been anxious. '*We could die together.*' Tom reached forward and touched the cold hand and tears fell. Striding towards him on the beach as though he was alone on the planet. Totally self-contained, and Tom's absurd feelings of having been slighted. Ringatu, pacing angrily by the cottage and proclaiming on behalf of the virtuous Titokowaru or berating the insidious Pakeha. You saw few shades of grey, my friend. And cooking a fish and sharing it on the porch. An image of murder flashed unbidden and unwelcome. This was a man of a world Tom could only partly understand.

'COME! Welcome, come.' Bill led them towards a long low building from which emanated cooking smells and surprisingly gay laughter. 'It is so good to see you, Tom. And Mary.' In moments Tom felt his mood changing, lifting. He found himself surrounded by people keen to greet him, to welcome him 'home', and who wanted to be introduced to the woman who had travelled so far to 'rescue' him. She was already legendary, he smiled to himself. The American lost in New Zealand had to be rescued by his wife! No one seemed very concerned at the lack of legal accuracy, he noticed with amusement, but he didn't care. And on the edge of the group, a painful outsider, Merv Layton wished fervently he could rip the choking red tie from his neck.

'Painter Tom!' Tom could not see the speaker though he recognised the mischievous voice instantly.

'Jake?'

'Yo, Painter Tom!' Portentous.

'Matty? Ha!' He spied the two bright faces peering at him. 'So, you boys! I am pleased to see you.' They grinned.

'There's heaps of food. You want to come?' asked Jake.

'Heaps!' echoed his brother. 'Where's Walker Boy?'

'I do want to come.' He replied even as he noticed Merv Layton hovering. 'And Sean? Well, I hope he will be back soon.'

'Where is he?'

'He's ... getting some help, Matty. He's had a tough time and some people are helping him.'

'He should come eeling. Or swimming.'

'He will. I am sure he will. But just give me a moment or two?' He extended his hand to Merv Layton.

'Good to see you back,' the big man said uncomfortably, and Tom smiled. 'This ...'

'Tangi,' Rachel helped.

'Yep.' Merv breathed deeply and glanced around. 'I'm not sure ...'

'I think they'll be pleased,' she said.

They all felt their incongruity. Except Merle, Rachel thought. That uncomplicated face with too much rouge and an accidental smear of lipstick. Merle is perfectly happy to be here. Rachel turned to Tom. 'What are your plans now, Tom? Or is that a bit blunt? Yes — I can see it is. I'm sorry, I should mind my own business.'

'Not at all. I'm sure I owe many explanations. But ...'

'We're not sure yet, Rachel. There are a few things to be worked out.'

'Of course, Mary.' How clumsy I am, she thought. I am just a dairy farmer! 'Well, do come and visit Pete and me. Regardless of what you decide. You won't just slip away?'

'You're too kind. And no, we won't just slip away.'

Looking about awkwardly. 'Over there,' Tom said with enthusiasm. 'I think Gertie wants us.'

They moved with others into the dining hall and found three long trestle tables.

'You folks sit here,' said Gertie. 'Just here. This is a good place and we'll bring you something. You just wait,' and she hurried towards the heavily laden table at the end of the dining room.

'This is amazing.' Mary looked about in wonder.

'I know. I almost feel ... You know, I almost feel like I'm home, already!'

'Tom?'

'Yes?'

'Oh, it doesn't matter.'

He put an arm around her shoulders.

MERV Layton was too hot. He didn't know what to say to Merle and the whole thing was unnerving. He had seen them all looking. Well, too bad, he thought. Too bloody bad. But then he'd been hugged by two people as though he was a long-lost son. He hadn't known what to say then, either.

There he was. Across the dining hall in the corner with that old Louis and a couple of others. In their suits too. That was a strange thing. He wondered whether he might be able to get Bill away for a minute. But then he thought — what the hell! And rose abruptly, startling the old girl with pearls in her ears.

'Sorry,' he said.

'I'm fine thank you, Mr Layton,' and she watched with shrewd interest as he made his way around the wall.

Louis extended his hand. 'I am glad you made it, Merv Layton. It is good to see you.' Merv shook the thin bony hand gently and replied that he was pleased too.

'I wouldn't not have come,' he said. 'It's important. It's important to see your folks off.' He tugged at his collar with a finger.

'It's pretty hot in here.'

'You're telling me, Bill! But my missus would scrag me if I took this off!' They laughed politely. 'This is a good do ...'

'Ah well, these things have a way.' Bill looked at Merv's sweating face and tried not to focus on the broken skin on his right cheek. Must hurt like mine. The bastard!

'There's something,' said Merv. 'There's a couple of things ...' The group listened politely. Merv took a deep breath and looked mostly at Louis, 'And this — well, to you, Mr Ropata, but to all of you actually ... I just wanted to say that what I did with the digger was wrong. I just wanted to say I was right out of line, that morning. I don't know what got into my head. There.'

Louis was nodding slowly, eyes downcast, but Bill was regarding Merv with new interest. 'So, that was it,' continued Merv. 'I want to apologise for that and I wish there was something I could do.' Merv looked Bill straight in the eye. 'And the second thing is this, Bill. I would be very pleased if you'd come back — to work. You know, like back on the job, but when you're ready,' he added hastily. 'I know you've got lots of stuff to do and that.' He nodded vigorously and his large hand lifted and fell and he stretched his neck. 'Bloody hell,' he said softly.

Bill allowed a small smile. 'Thanks for that, Merv. Thanks for both those things. But I have to tell you I'm thinking about doing some contracting — for myself.'

'Oh. Yeah, well, that's good. But you know the offer's there.' Chastened, Merv turned to Louis who lifted his gaze across the hall. Absorbing the clattering, noisy, happy melee.

'It's a pleasure to have you on the marae, Merv Layton,' he said. 'It's a pleasure to have a man who can say what you said. It is tika. I hope you will stay for a while.'

Merv breathed a sigh as he accepted Louis's hand again. 'And for me. It's a pleasure, Mr Ropata. And I will join you, thanks. Bill?' Merv thrust out his hand and the two men smiled as they shook hands.

'My Gertie said we should talk.'

'She's a smart lady.'

Louis took Merv by the arm as he showed him a chair. He stayed next to Merv for a minute or two, with his hand resting lightly on Merv's shoulder and talking about people who were there and people who couldn't make it. He gazed around the eating hall and waited until all could see him standing there, with his hand on that man's shoulder. When he was satisfied, he stepped back.

'Aren't you going to join me?'

'We will, Merv, but only after the manuhiri have eaten. Then we will have our turn.'

Merle Simes observed the events at the head of the table with great pleasure. It was good to see Mr Layton and Mr Ropata like that. And people had been so nice since she arrived. Even the younger ones — well, not all of them, but that's how young folks are. They're just awkward and they grow out of it. And didn't he look good and so dignified. She waved and Louis came around the tables.

'Good morning to you, Mrs Simes. That's a very nice dress.'

'Thank you, Mr Ropata. I don't know how long I've had it but I am fond of these colours.'

'They look well on you, if I may say so.'

She beamed. 'Will you join me?'

'Well, I could sit for a moment, but you tuck in.'

And they talked about the town and Louis said that things would settle down okay. She was relieved to hear that. She told him how hard it was, being alone, without Herbie, and he understood. He told her she was welcome to come and see him any old time. He told her not to wait for an invite — just to come. She said she couldn't possibly do that. She would feel like she was intruding. So he said he would send Jake and Matty to call on her. She said that would be fine and she was most appreciative.

When he was gone she turned to the woman next to her.

'Do you know, I only met Mr Wherry two or three times, but he seemed a good man.' She smiled.

'I heard he went strange,' the woman said.

* * *

SHE WATCHED FROM a distance. Watched the people coming and going and listened to the waiata lifting in the air. She regretted now that she had put on her smartest clothes because she knew she was not going onto the marae. She knew she was an outsider here. More even than him. She waited a long time and saw Tom Mahler and his wife. That must be who it was. His wife who had come all the way from America. It gave her another stab. America, that he had described so often. Chicago ... she would never see it. She would just remember his words and she would try to picture him there, in Chicago.

She removed her leather jacket and slung it over her shoulder.

THE old Toyota cruised along the foreshore and turned up towards the highway.

'They're all at the funeral.'

'Not my dad. He said he wasn't going to a funeral for a murderer.'

'Serves the fucker right. Police shooting him. The black bastard!'

'Yeah!'

The car stopped where they could see the edge of the marae and the cars and people milling.

'Scared me that morning — a bit.'

'Yeah! He looked like a gorilla coming over the bank.' They laughed.

'Hey! Look! Look there!' They all watched the young woman with her short skirt and high boots, coat draped over her shoulder, walking along the verge. Napper whistled softly. 'Whoa!'

'Well, well. If it's not the Melanie babe herself.' Sly put the car in gear and slowly drove until he was alongside.

'Hey ya, babe! You not going to that old funeral?'

She glanced at him without speaking and continued walking. Sly kept pace alongside.

'You want a ride somewhere? We've got plenty of room.' She did not pause. 'You think you're better than us, don't you, Melanie. Well, I've got news for you — you are!' And he laughed loudly. 'But that's okay. That's how it is.' She stopped and he jerked to a halt.

'You got any screwdriver?'

'What?'

'Vodka and orange.' Disdainful, but she stepped towards the car.

'Ah, nope, but we can get some. We can call by the bottle store.' She walked around to the other side of the car and opened the front door and stood waiting. 'Get out, Napper! Get in the back — can't you see?'

She climbed into the front seat without looking at the astonished faces.

'Well,' she said, 'are you going to get this heap moving or what?'

* * *

HE WOULDN'T BE long, the woman said. She offered them magazines and a cup of tea but they declined both.

It's been almost two weeks, Tom mused, and wondered again how it would be. Two weeks in which more had changed in his life than at any previous time. More than had changed over many years. It seemed like a year since he had been running in the forest, frantic with fear for this boy. Feeling his whole being torn to shreds when he concluded the worst had happened. Rowing in a state of dementia out into the open sea. Alone on the ocean for days and suddenly wanting to live more than he could have believed. Despite the pain of loss and confusion, knowing with startling certainty that he wanted to live and knowing that his chances were rapidly diminishing. But quelling the panic and feeding his determination with the voice of Ringatu and the new perspectives he had formed about his own boy.

'What is your tikanga, Tom Mahler?' Ringatu was right. He had been inventing things for a long time. Ever since Luke died he had invented things instead of being true to his nature. *'And what is this boy, Sean, to you? Does he have your respect or do you simply wish for him to replace what you have lost?'* It stung and he had been angry because he knew that Ringatu was right. He had not respected the memory of Luke or the boy, Sean. He had wallowed in the loss and the unfairness the world had bestowed on Tom Mahler.

'Don't talk to me about respect!' Tom had cried, *'You who kills another man's property without compunction and hides in primitive myths!'* And they hadn't talked for days.

But alone on the sea, wanting to live, he could see that in order to live properly he had to strive for something higher. It was not easy but then that was the nature of ideals. He had spent nearly twenty years striving for professional excellence and he knew he had achieved it on many occasions. But not always ... ideals are demanding. But he could now see how rarely in all that time had he challenged himself to live properly. To truly respect his family and colleagues. To truly respect and understand his own tikanga.

Now he faced a test. A small boy who had no one — who had lost his parents and Ringatu too. A small boy disadvantaged by a life distorted by so little love and an inability to communicate. What would Tom Mahler do? What could Tom Mahler do that would be tika?

The woman reappeared and called them through.

* * *

THE YOUNG MAN walked around the classroom inspecting the walls.

'There is some very good artwork here. She must have been quite talented.'

'She was a good teacher. Very enthusiastic. And I think she got people in the community involved as well.'

'I hope to do that. It's important — especially in places like this.'

'Places like this?'

'Oh, I mean in small country schools. Not because it's Mokau or anything like that. Nothing to do with the events.'

'And you're not bothered?'

'No. I've taught in five different communities now, and one of those was in an area where assaults, and worse, were commonplace.' He paused. 'This is very unusual — strange really.' He studied the running horse with its head turned, looking back with fearful eyes, he decided. And with good cause — the weird animal behind the horse was clearly intent on capturing it. It was a disturbing scene but it was also strange how the styles differed. Both done quite quickly, but there was a sophistication in the depiction of the horse that was not present in its pursuer. The eyes of the horse were too large, but then what of the eyes in the nameless animal? Not only too large but ghoulish — with that mouth agape? A kind of human mouth on an insect, it seemed. It was not a nice picture. He made a mental note to take it down later in the morning.

'Where did you say she went?'

'She's got a job in the Bay of Plenty. Te Puke. She's a good teacher. We're sorry to lose her.'

'Personal thing?'

'Mostly. She needed a change. We all do from time to time.'

'Yes.'

14

THE RIDGE WAS steeper than he recalled. Maybe the sun was hotter this time. Tom paused to catch his breath and gazed across to the red tin cottage. So small. So crude. And yet nestling there on that little grassy flat and surrounded by the bush it looked right. Home for Henry for near thirty years and himself for only a few months. But Henry had lived a life there. Happy for a time and then ... Maybe he adjusted to his loss. Maybe he accepted his lot and Georgina simply became a loving memory.

I have so much more, he thought, and allowed his eye to wander up to the skyline above the cottage and then back to the slope that ran to the beach. He examined the slope and tried to make out where the dory had passed but it was not easy to see a trace of the turbulent descent. Perhaps there was one broken mahoe and that could have been from the wind.

The sea swished the black sands almost to the bottom of the hill. Full tide, and the mussel rocks on the point were concealed under swirling white water. Green waves curled high and rolled in over hundreds of yards. Tom tried to imagine rowing the dory out through that surf and knew it would not be possible. He stared far out to sea, at the whitecaps that merged towards the horizon, and felt amazement that he should have been out there — beyond sight.

A tui flew by with its characteristic dipping and swooping. Heavy wings whipping the air. He turned up the hill and continued to climb, but head cast down now — concentrating and not wishing to look about just yet. Not until he came to the rock outcrop. Then he peered over and shivered. Trembled in the hot sun, with sweat in his eyes as he peered down the burned valley. Noticed the remnants of leaves near the top of the Mohican, on the tips of the highest branches but turning brown in slow death. Stared down the undulating, broken ground to the sea and felt a deep sadness at the black sticks like a giant's pincushion.

He found a patch of withered grass against a rock and sat, cross-legged, facing the sea. Fumbled inside his shirt and withdrew a small book and from his pocket a short pencil. He began to sketch. The giant trunk and huge limbs rapidly transposed. The tufts of old leaves and fire-shortened astelia still clinging, now growing lush and vibrant on the paper. The twigs restored and birds coming to roost and feed on bountiful berries. Shaded beneath the trunk the smaller trees that benefited from the benign presence of this monarch. A man appeared. Out of proportion this man, standing near the tree. A tall man with flowing hair and a strange blackness below his right eye — a dark crescent moon. His right arm raised. Tom studied his drawing for a long time. The tree and the man.

Then he said: 'Go home!' Louder: 'Go home!' He tore the page from the book and held it in his hand, staring at the pencil lines — staring down the hill. Felt the breeze backing over the edge and swirling up. He released the piece of paper and watched it lift in an unseen eddy. Over his head momentarily and then out towards the sea. 'Go to your home ...' Higher it wafted, settling in places, then continuing until it was lost in the bright air.

He glanced at his watch again and sat with his eyes closed against the glare of the sun on the blue sea and waited. A few minutes later, the sound of a faraway engine: an aeroplane high and far out to sea, flying north towards Auckland. He peered until he caught the glint of sun on the steel wing. That small plane that would soon be a bigger plane that flew even higher and further. Northeast towards the west coast of America. His eyes ached as the plane receded into the north. Finally the glint vanished and the sound of engines faded to nothing. Only the sound of the distant surf tumbling on the wild landscape. And an oystercatcher scudding along the line of the tide and uttering its rapid, high-pitched song. 'Chi, chi, chi, chi ...' and its mate following close behind.

There is still much to look forward to, Tom thought. There is much to look forward to. Perhaps we won't have to wait so long.

After a while he stared at the blackened ground near his feet and noticed tiny green plants. Myriads of seedlings that had come with the rain.

* * *

'NOW YOU KIDS just remember — you're not to touch a thing! You got that?'

'Yeah, Auntie. We know.' Jake grimaced at his brother, 'We'll play outside. Hey! Look at that quad. I wonder if we could ride on that?'

'Don't you even touch that bike! Not unless Mr Lynch tells you. You are not to embarrass your dad, you kids. I told your dad that. "They'll make you proud!" That's what I told your dad.'

'We're all proud of you. Ratbags! Can't use a yo-yo but we're all proud of you.' Louis patted Jake's leg as he gazed at the house. 'I came up here a few times. Before the Lynchs. Way back. There was a big old macrocarpa over there and some pines. But they've gone.' He looked about the yard. 'You should park in the shade there, Bill, or else we'll have our bums burned to a crisp.'

'Our bums!'

'Be quiet, Jake. And watch your language, Louis.' Louis and the boys exchanged conspiratorial grins. 'And don't think I don't know what you're up to back there!'

'We're being good, Auntie,' but they convulsed in silent laughter and Louis poked them.

Rachel and Pete appeared at the front door and regarded the car with pleasant apprehension. They watched the people tumbling out.

'This shirt scratches.'

'Be quiet, Bill. Oooh, look at these flowers!'

Rachel approached shyly. 'It's so good to see you. I'm so glad you've come. You remember my husband Pete?'

'Course I do. Course I do. How are you, Pete? That's a nice shirt. And here's Bill and Uncle Louis.'

'Good to see you.'

'And these are Bill's ratbags, Matty and Jake.'

'I've seen you boys before.'

'I bet you have all right! Everybody's seen these boys! But they're coming along — aren't you? Say hullo to Mr and Mrs Lynch.'

They did. They said they saw three rabbits down the bottom last week.

'Yep, I know they're there,' said Pete.

'You going to shoot them?'

'I don't know.'

'Be quiet, you boys! Shoot them! Good grief! Go and play for a while. And don't touch anything.' They sidled away. 'And I've brought you something, Rachel. I've brought you those old chrissies. Bill,' Gertie nudged him, 'open up.'

Bill opened the boot of the car and handed a bunch of flowers wrapped in newspaper to Gertie.

'Oh, that's great! That's just great. Thank you.' Rachel received the bunch and held the golden heads to her nose. 'I'll plant these this evening. That's so kind — but come on in. Do come on in. It's not very tidy.' And she led the way as first Gertie then Louis and Bill and finally Pete walked out of the sun into the dark hallway and into the front drawing room.

'This is a nice place, Pete.'

Pete nodded appreciatively and silently admired the bruise on Bill's cheek. It was hard to say whether he or Merv had come off worse. 'Yeah, well, it needs a paint but I don't seem to get around to it.'

'You wouldn't know it — would you, Uncle?'

'You would not. It looks as good as new, it surely does.' They listened to the women in the kitchen. They listened to Rachel talking about her irises and the pond she wanted to build against the wall. And Gertie saying that was a grand idea if she had ever heard one, and telling Rachel about the pond her grandmother had that was so full of frogs sometimes you could hardly talk!

'Not so many of them now.'

Pete looked enquiringly at Louis. 'Not so many frogs now,' Louis affirmed. 'Buggers seem to be dying out. I don't know.'

'That's true. Could be the sprays.'

'That could be it. Could be the sprays … you seen any, Bill?'

Bill shook his head. 'Cicadas — that's all I've been noticing. Buzz like a million chainsaws. Never seen so many of them.'

'Must be this funny season.'

'I'd say so.'

They listened to the sounds from the kitchen. Rachel was talking about Tom Mahler getting found and how wonderful it was. It surely was, said Gertie — it was the most wonderful thing in a week of fearful tragedy. 'A week of tragedy,' she repeated.

'That was something. Him getting found like that.' Bill shook his head in wonder.

'Way out. He was a long way out, they say. You'd wonder what he was doing. He was in a dory he built. I remember him mentioning it when he came up here. I've never seen one but he said it was good at sea. A fishing type of thing. Over there in America they're all over. That's what he built.'

Gertie said it was a blessing for that woman, and said maybe they should do a welcome home sort of thing — a party — and Rachel said that was a great idea. And Gertie said those scones looked delicious.

'But where did he launch that thing?' asked Louis. 'Only a cliff out there and he never brought that boat to the river that anyone knew about.' And they agreed that was a particular mystery.

'And what about those boys — said they saw Mahler in the river? Little bastards!' And they all laughed and cocked an ear to the noise at the end of the garden where they could hear the little bastards playing with the cattle dogs.

And Rachel was asking how Bill was getting on after the thing that happened with Merv Layton and Gertie said he was doing fine but had all sorts of fool ideas about what he was going to do next, when the obvious thing was to accept Merv Layton's offer of his old job. But no ...

'I'm thinking about doing some contracting,' Bill said suddenly. 'Hay and shearing and stuff. Should be plenty to keep me going. Thinking of taking that young Jimmy on. When he's okay again. Thought I'd take him on.'

'That'd be good,' agreed Pete. He thought about the situation then said: 'I've got hay down the bottom. I usually use a crowd from Te Kuiti, but you can do it if you like.'

Bill laughed. 'Ho, well, I wasn't coming around here looking for work! But that's good of you.'

'Yep! That's good, Pete,' chimed in Louis. 'I knew folks would rally round.'

'Well, that's what neighbours are for,' said Pete, and felt pleased. 'Would you guys like a beer?'

'That'd be good. It's a damn hot sort of a day again,' said Bill.

* * *

ANDREW BARKER DROVE carefully into the clearing of the red cottage. Mahler was standing on the verandah waiting.

'May I?' Barker asked after they had exchanged greetings. He seated himself on the sofa. 'Fantastic view,' he said, and declined the offer of a coffee. 'I've never spent much time in this area but I have to say on days like this, I'm impressed. It's a beautiful piece of coast.'

'It took me a while. But then I arrived in the winter. It was pretty bleak at times.'

'I imagine so. But now? This is quite something. Not much like home though?'

'Not at all like home! In every respect.'

Barker stared at the boatshed. 'That's where you built your dory? Was it difficult? Building a boat, I mean, way out here? Had you done it before?'

'This was my first, and yes, I would say it was difficult. For me certainly. I've never done much with my hands.'

Barker laughed. 'Me neither. Not my line at all and I'm all the more impressed.' He rose and walked across the grass to the edge of the hill and peered down the bank to the sands below. 'My word, that is quite a drop!' He shook his head in genuine wonder. 'It's hard to imagine.'

Tom grimaced. 'I have some difficulty myself, just thinking about it.'

Barker peered about the hills and along the coast. He stared out to sea. 'Amazing,' he said quietly, then he returned to the verandah and sat down. He stared at Tom who remained standing with his arms folded. 'I'm about to decamp, Mr Mahler. I'm heading back to town. But before I do there are a couple of things I wanted to discuss.' Tom nodded and waited. 'I understand you are thinking of fostering or adopting the boy?'

'Yes.'

Barker nodded thoughtfully. 'That's the act of a Samaritan and no mistake.' He continued to stare at Tom as though he expected to see something change. 'I mean that. That kid has been through a lot. He is one disturbed boy. But you know that too.'

'I'm not sure what you want, Detective.'

'No, I suppose not. Well, this is not official business, if that's what you mean.'

Tom said, 'I have known this boy for some time now. I do know he has had a pretty tough life. I know he has no one else and I am more than fond of him.' A wry smile. 'Though I am not sure I could say that to some, even now.'

'Yes. I understand. And I'm sure you know what you're doing. It's a big thing all the same. It's a very big thing.' Barker paused and seemed to assemble his thoughts. 'Let me get right to it. I do not believe Ringatu Wherry killed Trevor Pagett.' He watched Tom's face closely and saw only bemusement. 'Wherry was certainly there, at Pagett's, but he did not kill the man, because Pagett was already dead.'

Tom's hands dropped to his sides and he stepped forward. 'Then who? So you think ... me?'

'No! No, I don't think you committed any crime, Mr Mahler. You were too far away at the time and so was Wherry. Though I admit you featured in our thoughts. But no, it had to be someone else. Of course it begs the question why Wherry was there at all ... did he simply arrive too late?'

Tom flushed as he recalled Ringatu's words: "I will *eat* that *fucker*!"

'Possible, isn't it? Wherry helped you launch your boat and must have gone directly to Pagett's farm. In fact he drove your car. And my guess is that he then took your dinghy and rowed back up to the farm. Curious behaviour, but then he was a curious man. I can't help wondering whether Wherry said anything more about his intentions. But you've already said, you don't remember ...' Tom did not respond.

'No. Well, anyway, Wherry arrived at the farm and found Pagett dead and then he did a most peculiar thing. He went right in the house. Right into the kitchen of the dead man's house and he wrote in the dead man's blood, "For the love of money". Makes my skin crawl. You too?'

Tom frowned. 'It sounds pretty strange.'

'Oh, it's pretty strange all right. But what is even stranger is that he then took the murder weapon, wiped it of prints and took it all the way to the river. That, in my mind, is a very strange thing indeed. Wouldn't you agree?' Tom nodded but wished he didn't have to listen. 'Does that suggest anything to you, Mr Mahler? What Wherry did? I puzzle about these things but I'm always interested to hear from someone who has been much more closely involved.' He stared at Tom, pulling his right ear lobe thoughtfully.

Tom turned away and looked across the sea that had become calm again and watched two steeleyes drop in quick succession into the bay. The 'plop, plop' carried clearly. 'Not really. Ringatu was an angry man. He was angry about Pagett burning the forest. As many were. He may have gone to speak with him ...'

'Yes, he may have gone to speak with him,' replied Barker dubiously, 'But that's not what I'm referring to. I'm referring to the fact that he should hide a weapon for a murder he did not commit. I am less concerned with the fact that he wrote a message in the man's blood. That is evidence enough that he felt pretty strongly about Pagett's actions. Vengeful, you might say, but then many were ... No, it's the rifle that intrigues me and I wonder that it might not intrigue you?'

Tom shrugged. 'I'm not a policeman.'

Barker sighed. 'Look, Tom,' he said, 'I am trying to be helpful. It may not appear that way, but I am. So, this is what I would like you to consider. You went to find the boy, Sean, in the mistaken apprehension that he was in the valley and was caught by the fire. Thankfully that was not so. Clearly, he was somewhere else. Wherry helped you launch your boat and then went to Pagett's farm and was seen to throw the rifle in the river. I think we can safely assume that he did this to protect someone else. Not only was he trying to protect someone else but he left a piece of incriminating evidence in the infamous words. What happens then?' He paused and opened his hands, wonder on his face. 'He turns up with the boy and it is clearly not a kidnapping situation!'

'I'm still not sure where this is leading.'

'No? Really, Tom? I am surprised. Well, there is one other fact that I have not mentioned. The bullet that killed Pagett entered his chest from an eccentric angle. Do you follow? If you or I were to have fired that shot I think either we would have been crouching or we would have held the rifle at waist height. Unusual? Of course, we cannot be sure what led up to that particular moment, and the two could have been in different positions, but then nor can we see that there had been any struggle. The shot was fired from a distance of at least four feet and possibly more. So, what do we have? A shot from an unusually low angle that I concede could have been a hip shot. But then Wherry arrives and takes pains to conceal a weapon he did not use and then finds the boy and keeps him safe, you might say, out in the bush.'

'And?'

'And?' Barker sighed. 'Well, nothing and everything, really. I wanted to share my thoughts with you in the hope that might be ... helpful. From our perspective the case remains open, and of course I would be most appreciative if anything comes to mind. Anything Wherry may have said, for instance ...' he held Tom's eye and smiled. 'Did you know that Pagett was not the father?'

'Yes.'

'Good. Yes, the girl was pregnant before she arrived here. Pagett took her in but it was always difficult I understand. She was much younger, pretty ... Sean was three years old when she died ...' Barker rose and stepped down onto the grass. 'It may take some time, Tom — the application to adopt. You've got plenty of time to think about things.'

'Thank you for your advice.'

Barker extended his hand. 'You're welcome. And I truly wish you all the best. However it works out. Oh, and do give my best to Mrs Chisholm. Will she return?' He frowned. 'I'm sorry, that's not my business.'

Tom watched him drive up the track. He waited, listening until there was no sound, then he walked inside. From the drawer in the sideboard he withdrew a folder and from the folder he took an envelope. He opened the envelope and spread a folded piece of paper in the patch of sun.

"What do you really know about him?" Mary had asked. "His father, Tom, what about that ..."

"Pagett wasn't his father. And I can help. It's nothing that millions haven't coped with since the dawn of time. It's the right thing to do!"

"I don't know," she said. "I need some time too."

And he remembered the pencil zizzing across this piece of paper and Chinook moving on the porch. He had been thinking about how things might be even as the drawing progressed. A big man and a boy had appeared on the paper and Tom became interested. Or a little disturbed? The big man seemed to be recoiling from the boy. And then the swiftly moving hand had stopped. Thinking, Tom supposed. What thoughts in that small head? What imaginings were occurring? And he had smiled as he visualised how they would draw. How they would paint and talk and run. Eventually, they would visit art galleries, see movies, play in parks. They would build a new boat maybe. There were so many things ...

He looked again at the man's eyes which were so wide they dominated the face — larger even than the mouth that was an almost perfect circle. But the eyes filled the remainder of the face. He remembered the unease growing and even now. The small hand had ceased pushing the soft pencil over the paper. The head motionless and staring fixedly at his creation. As still as stone the small boy had been, and Tom had been about to ask him what he had drawn when suddenly it became obvious. The alarm on the man's face, with its startled eyes and gaping mouth. And the hands, reaching towards the boy, almost like talons. But pitching backwards the man — off balance, thrown backwards by a fearsome blow.

And the boy? Tom could see that the long arms held a dark stick, but not a stick at all — a rifle, clearly, from which bled an effusion of particles, almost like a shower of sparks. And Tom had experienced an icy chill as he gazed mesmerised at the drawing — at the sparks hitting the man as they poured from the rifle into his chest. The sparks were killing the man. That was the hole in the man's chest. It was a bullet hole, and the man was thrown back by the sparks.

The recollection was as vivid as if it had occurred this very moment. A possum had called from nearby in the dark bush. Chinook had shuffled and a mouse had run clear across the bare floor into the darkest corner. Tom had reached for the paper and gently removed it, folded it, and inserted it in his jacket pocket.

He remembered the blue eyes, mauve in the half-light with thin slivers of tears glistening on his cheeks, round his nose, catching the curve of his lips. A small hand extending to touch. As light as gossamer.

Tom staring, probing for something, he knew not quite what. A hammering in his head and looking at each other for many long moments. Then a little voice said: "Frightened, Tom."

Many things whirling. Fearful, wild things. He could hear Mary's voice: "What do you really know about the boy?" He could see Pagett with his bulging face pursuing him and the fear he felt as he ran from the farm. He looked into the eyes of the boy and wondered desperately if he would see the snake uncoiling, and he saw only a small boy touching the bark at the base of the Mohican, exploring and smiling at the pleasure of discovery. The small boy rolling on the ground with Chinook leaping and licking.

He had reached out and put his arms around the boy, pulling him close and held him there, like a wounded bird. Felt a faint fluttering. "Don't be frightened, Sean. Don't be. I'm here. Don't you be afraid."

And the only sound had been the beating of their hearts.

TOM took the drawing to the mantelpiece above the fireplace and found a packet of matches. He laid the drawing in the grate, lit the corner and watched the yellow flames lick across the white paper until it curled black with only the faintest of lines. Then he took the poker and gently crushed the remnant to ash.

* * *

'THERE'S CHINOOK.'

Sean nodded and grinned. He made a sign with his hand and the dog leapt the Manuhuia fence down by the river and gambolled to him, licking his hands and allowing the boy to knock him to the ground. They wrestled.

'He's our dog too,' Jake asserted.

'I know. But he's still with that Walker Boy.'

'I know.'

'We should go down to the river mouth. See if we can get a kahawai,' Matty suggested.

'Yep.'

'You want to come fishing?' Matty leaned towards Sean.

The Walker Boy looked up, solemn, while the dog searched the garden for a suitable stick. He nodded.

'I'll get that old rod.' Jake jumped the verandah and emerged soon after with the rod and lure. The dog jumped excitedly.

'Get out of the way, you dopey animal!'

They walked down the bank to the black, shelly sand and headed towards the sea.

'You going to stay with Painter Tom and stuff?' asked Matty.

'Yes,' said Sean, and at the sound the two Maori boys came close and stared at Sean's mouth as though magic had occurred and then Matty punched him in the shoulder. They grinned.

'The one who doesn't get a fish will drown for the eels.' Jake's eyes widened.

'Aw, that's all bullshit!' said Matty. 'That's just for kids!'